I0690633

Book Five:
A Story of Reighton,
Yorkshire 1727 to 1734

A Time for Reaping

Joy Stonehouse

Grosvenor House
Publishing Limited

All rights reserved
Copyright © Joy Stonehouse, 2024

The right of Joy Stonehouse to be identified as the author of this
work has been asserted in accordance with Section 78
of the Copyright, Designs and Patents Act 1988

The book cover is copyright to Joy Stonehouse

This book is published by
Grosvenor House Publishing Ltd
Link House
140 The Broadway, Tolworth, Surrey, KT6 7HT.
www.grosvenorhousepublishing.co.uk

A CIP record for this book
is available from the British Library

ISBN 978-1-80381-923-5
eBook ISBN 978-1-80381-924-2

Other titles in the series

Witch-bottles and Windlestraws
New Arrivals in Reighton
Whisper to the Bees
Bonfires and Brandy

For present and future Jordans,
an imaginary window into our past.

Acknowledgements

A huge thank you goes to Pam Williams for her first reading and editing, and for painting the book cover; without her patience, this series would never have reached publication.

Thanks also to members of the Hornsea Writers Group. They have continued to offer advice and the support needed for publishing.

Special thanks must go to Lisa Blosfelds for her transcript of the Reighton parish records—an invaluable aid. She has also been most helpful in loaning local history books and allowing access to her collection of documentary evidence and maps.

Thanks also to Pat Sewell whose research into my Jordan family history provided the essential springboard for the novels. I appreciate her continuing encouragement.

Last but not least, I would like to thank the helpful and friendly staff at the Treasure House, Beverley, and the Hull History Centre; both sites make research a pleasure.

Author's Note

The novels are inspired by the parish records and, although I have carried out extensive research into East Yorkshire in the early 18th century, I must stress that the stories in the series are works of fiction. The names of most of the characters are taken from the parish records, yet some are invented. Any omissions or deviations from these records are made for the sake of narrative interest.

The main characters, and those of higher social standing, speak in Standard English. Lesser characters and the older generation speak with a slight East Yorkshire accent.

Although Reighton is mentioned throughout as a village, the people of the time would have called it a town. I have opted to spell Bridlington as it is known today, though the town was formerly known as Burlington and was often referred to as Bollin'ton.

The Jordan Family Members

The sons of Francis and Dorothy Jordan of Uphall:

William*(see below)
Francis (living at Argam)
Thomas
Samuel
Richard

The sons of William*and Mary Jordan, living on St Helen's Lane:

Francis (married to Lizzie and living at the bottom of the village)
Young William
John
Richard
Matthew

Contents

Part One

The New Couple

Chapter 1

1727

The road from Reighton to Rudston stretched westwards into the mist. It was a still November morning, not long after dawn, as William Jordan steered his horse and cart round the worst of the holes. A thin layer of frost sparkled on the road in the low sunshine.

He shook his head and smiled, never thinking he'd be riding out to collect his son and new wife, and certainly not a wife with a child well on the way. Like father, like son. At least both knew their brides were fertile. He'd been caught out too, but there the similarity ended. Francis was nothing like him. It would be good to have a grandson, though, someone to inherit his land one day, but a granddaughter would be equally welcome; she might even resemble young Mary.

By the time he entered Rudston, the sun had melted much of the frost, and beads of water hung from the bare branches and cottage eaves. He turned the cart towards the church where the ancient monolith loomed tall and dark. It stood like an eerie sentry, as ominous as William's thoughts on his son's married life. He paused, reluctant to move on to the vicarage where Francis and Elizabeth would be waiting. The damp weather had lowered his spirits and he couldn't get Robert Storey out of his mind. That man had tainted everyone he touched in Reighton with his strict ideas of chastity; he'd ruined the happiness of one Elizabeth and now he'd be doing the same with another. Could Francis lead a happy married life, or would he be like Robert and devote himself to God, and shun earthly pleasures? William, unsure of the answer, glanced at the church and shuddered.

In Reighton, Francis's mother and his aunt, Elizabeth Storey, were busy lighting a fire in the glebe cottage, warming the

3

place in readiness for the arrival of the newlyweds. It was a narrow dwelling at the lower end of the village, partly chalkstone, the rest earthen. The thatched roof had leaked, but William had stuffed gorse into the gaps and trusted the repair would last the winter. The two women had already swept the floors and cleaned the tiny windows. There was only a kitchen and a parlour with space for storage under the roof. Elizabeth stood back from the fire and let Mary add more kindling.

'I've managed to persuade Robert not to come and visit them on their first day. Let them be, I said. They need time alone together. You'll have plenty of opportunity to see Francis.'

Mary remembered her own wedding and winked. 'I think winter's a good time to start married life—the days are short, the nights longer.'

'That never helped me with Robert.'

'Oh, it'll be different with Francis. He's much younger than Robert was.' Mary piled another heap of gorse on the fire and watched it blaze. 'You just keep Robert away from him and he'll be fine.'

William left the horse and cart at the front of the vicarage and knocked on the door. To his surprise, the vicar answered and welcomed him in.

'We heard you pull up outside. Come into the kitchen. We've been waiting. Have a drink and get warm while Francis and the lads load up.'

'Is there *much* furniture?' William was not expecting a great deal; Francis had not had time to save up.

George Gurwood passed him a mug of hot, spiced ale. 'We've managed to collect a table, chairs and a bed. And my wife and daughters have organised the bed linen. It's enough to begin with.'

'You're very generous. Thank you.' William was surrounded by smiling faces, all wanting the best for the young couple.

'I'm sorry,' cried the vicar, 'you two haven't met. This is the new Mrs Jordan.' He turned to the young woman. 'Lizzie, meet your father-in-law.'

4

She stood up and curtsied, at which point the vicar's two daughters pulled her back down into the chair and whispered, 'You're not our servant now. You're a wife.'

William realised by her figure that the young woman would be giving birth in a month or two at most. Also, he thought, her eyes were swollen as if she'd been crying. Maybe it was too much of a change to take on both marriage and motherhood at once.

'I'm very pleased to meet you at last,' he said. 'I'm sorry I couldn't be at the wedding, but everyone will make you very welcome in Reighton.' He didn't add 'apart from Robert Storey'.

Francis popped his head round the door to announce that the cart was loaded. 'Are you ready, Lizzie?'

She gave a slight nod and stood up again. The vicar's daughters hugged her in turn and wished her happiness. She put on her hooded winter cloak and curtsied to the vicar and his wife.

'Thank thee both fo' makin' these last years best o' me life. I won't forget thee. Thoo've been most kind since me trouble.' Tears flooded her eyes as she bent down to pick up her bag of personal belongings. After brushing a tear from her cheek, she moved to the door.

Francis opened it wider and followed her down the passage and outside.

William turned to the Gurwoods. 'Well, it seems we're ready to leave.'

The vicar's wife put a hand on his arm. 'We'll come out to wave goodbye. You will look after Lizzie, won't you? She's been such a hardworking servant, never any bother until... Never mind, we can't stop the young being young, can we?'

'You're most understanding, thank you. My wife and I will do our best, you can be sure.'

They reached the door to find Francis and his wife already settled on the front seat of the cart. William climbed up and, for safety, sat on the other side of Lizzie so that she was wedged between them. He took up the reins and, with final waves and shouts of good luck, set off.

5

Father and son began immediately to discuss the latest goings on in Reighton, who had been hired by the family at Uphall and how everyone was coping with the new workers.

Lizzie bit her lip and stared fixedly at a field full of sheep. She knew nothing of these people, and how could Francis forget so soon that she'd been a hired hand? Now, though, she was a wife and a Jordan, a member of a well-known family of yeomen. This was good; it was a step up in life. But it was a big change, a world away from her life as a servant at the vicarage.

As they neared Reighton and she caught sight of Filey Bay, she gasped and gripped Francis's arm. The sea was pewter grey, the cliffs a murky brown, and the rocky end of the Brigg was just a dirty smudge hardly visible in the mist. She closed her eyes against the comfortless scene and thought of how it would be to give birth among strangers. Whatever happened, she must be strong.

When the cart entered Reighton, she heard Francis mumble the name Robert Storey, but his father shut him up.

'Don't let Robert spoil things,' she heard him whisper.

As they rode down the steep main street, people came out to greet them.

'You've been expected,' William explained. 'My wife said she'd be going round the village early on to collect things for your kitchen. You can see everyone's keen to get a first peep at you.' He slowed the cart to allow gifts to be handed up.

Lizzie was overcome as she received jars of honey, whole cheeses, sausages and even candles. Her heart sank, though, when they arrived at the cottage. Despite the smoke coming from the chimney, the place was bleak, the walls dirty and damp.

Francis lifted her from the cart, oblivious to her misgivings, and opened the door for her to enter first.

The passageway was dark, but on pushing open the kitchen door, she found a warm space with a glowing fire. She hadn't really known what to expect. Having been used to the large kitchen at the vicarage with all its equipment, it was a

6

shock to realise that this small room was where she'd have to work and raise a family.

Francis strode to the fire to warm his hands. 'It's not so bad, is it? Look, there's even a pot and pan left for us. Once we've got the table and chairs in it'll feel more like home.'

Lizzie saw there were two buckets of water in one corner and a pile of gorse and brushwood in another. There was also a tub of oatmeal. She wandered into the parlour, empty except for an old chamber pot that had lost its handle. There was no fireplace and, with only two tiny windows, the room was both dismal and cold.

William walked in. 'Come on, Francis, let's get everything unloaded, then you can both settle in. We'll send over some supper later—it'll save you the trouble of cooking. You don't seem to have brought much in the way of bowls and spoons. I'll see if your grandmother has anything to spare at Uphall.'

While the men unloaded, Lizzie went out the back door to see the garden. It was a decent size, big enough to keep a pig and chickens and was enclosed by an earthen wall. She knew that Francis was happy with the cottage as it came with half an acre of land as well as rights to graze livestock on the moor and fallows. This was her new home and she'd better make the best of it. Though Francis had always insisted it was his fault that she'd become pregnant, she knew exactly how she'd felt on that May Day Eve. It was she who'd wanted him close and had no inhibitions. Now she must make their marriage a success. There was no reason why it wouldn't be. They were young and in love.

That night, after a simple supper of chunks of bacon and potato on borrowed pewter plates, washed down with beer sent from the blacksmith, Lizzie blushed and said it was time for bed.

7

Chapter 2

Lizzie went into the parlour first to undress. She carried a lit candle and, after tilting it so that the wax dripped onto the earthen floor, she set the candle down. Then she paused to gaze at the bed in the flickering light; its pillowcases were embroidered with an F and an E in a heart of green leaves. She sighed. Not once since that May Day Eve had she and Francis tried to be alone. They'd both been determined after that night to avoid drink and had aimed for a more chaste courtship. It had been such a shock to find herself with child.

With nowhere to leave her clothes, she draped them over the end of the bed. She shivered, put on her new nightdress and crept under the cold covers. Tonight was nothing like that evening at the end of April. Then, they'd both been flushed with excitement, and the barn had been warm, the straw welcoming. Now, there were icy sheets in a stark, empty chamber. Also, being seven months with child, she wasn't sure how they'd manage any intimacy or whether they should be doing anything at all. Yet the vicar's wife had said it wouldn't harm her or the unborn child, and she should know, having had nine children; she'd even told her it was possible to do it sideways. Francis would hate to think they'd been discussing such things.

Francis was taking his time putting the lid over the fire. As he stared at the dull red glow of the gorse, he was desperate, and yet also afraid, to be in bed with Lizzie. The last thing he wanted was to hurt her. His body urged him on, and he left the kitchen.

After knocking politely on the parlour door and asking if she was ready, he entered with a candle and set it by his side of the bed. He didn't possess a nightshirt. Instead, he just removed his jacket, breeches and stockings, folded them neatly and laid them on the floor. Then he climbed in, holding his shirt down for modesty's sake.

He lay on his back. Beside him, in the low candlelight, Lizzie's enlarged belly looked bigger than ever. There was no

8

way he could climb on top as he'd done that first time. Raising himself on one elbow, he peered into her face, his eyes drawn to the bare flesh below her neck. The space between her collarbone and the start of her cleavage was so smooth and white. She was beautiful and she was his.

'Francis,' she whispered, 'it'll be alright. I've 'eard I can be comfy if I turn o' me side.'

She leant towards him and, with the bump between them, kissed him on the lips. As he began to breathe heavily, she turned the other way, raised her nightdress and curled herself, spoon-like, into his stomach.

Surprised by the sudden thrust of her bare bottom, he did nothing for a moment. Then he wrapped an arm round her and pressed his face into her neck. She smelled wonderful, the dried lavender in the pillow blending with that particular aroma that Lizzie always exuded—a mixture of rose petals and newly baked bread. Unsure how to enter her, he fumbled about, jabbing the wrong places until she helped him. The overwhelming pleasure made him gasp. He fought to control the urge to push in further, hard and fast. When she kept telling him she was fine, he surrendered to his need, his forehead against her shoulder, his mind a blur. It was over in a minute.

Afterwards, he turned onto his back and coughed. Alarmed and ashamed by his animal instincts, he stared at the wall. Then, without saying a word, he reached down to the floor and snuffed out his candle.

Lizzie turned over to face him. 'Was it alright fo' thee?'

'Of course. But it's *you* we should worry about.'

'I'm fine,' she lied. Already her womb had tightened and there was a recurring ache, coming and going at regular intervals. What did she know of labour pains? Maybe the baby would come early. She leant down and snuffed out her candle. In the darkness, she lay again on her back and concentrated on taking long, slow breaths. Gradually, her body relaxed and the pains subsided. She realised that Francis was still awake, so reached for his hand.

'I love thee.' She kissed him on the cheek, surprised to find his face wet.

9

'Thank you,' he mumbled. 'Are you sure you're alright?'

'Yes, really, I am.' She squeezed his hand. 'Goodnight, husband, sleep well.'

Francis was the first to wake in the morning and see the cold dim light of the late November dawn. He was haunted by his frenzied behaviour of the night before. It was sickening to think he'd been no better than a dog humping a bitch. What a shameful start to a marriage. Robert Storey would not have approved.

He eased himself from the bed, dressed and, before leaving the parlour, stood for a while to watch Lizzie sleep. It wasn't her fault. She'd only done her duty as a wife and for that he should be grateful. He was the guilty one. Her head rested on the pillow, her face turned slightly to the F embroidered there. She looked so innocent, her dark eyebrows and eyelashes prominent against her pale face. His dark angel.

After rekindling the fire, he put water on to boil. He was about to add oatmeal when there was a knock on the door.

His mother came in with a jug of fresh milk. 'You'll need this for your breakfast.'

'Thanks. Lizzie's still asleep.'

'I suppose that's best after yesterday's journey.' She raised her eyebrows in question. 'I trust you had a good night?'

'Yes… thank you.' He took the milk and poured half of it into the water, the rest into two mugs.

His mother took the empty jug. 'Tell her I'll come later to help.'

Lizzie woke when Francis peered round the door to say breakfast was ready. She could hardly believe she'd slept so long. It was the first time in years that she hadn't been up to make breakfast and see to everything. She used the chamber pot and then dressed quickly, unused to the cold earthen floor beneath her bare feet. In the kitchen, she saw that Francis had set two bowls of porridge on the table, and the fire was burning well.

'There,' he said as he pulled out a chair, 'this won't be happening every day, you know, so enjoy it while you can.'

He smiled and kissed her cheek. 'I think there's sugar in that bag, or there are pots of honey here to choose from if you like.' He sat down and began spooning in his porridge. 'It's getting late, so as soon as I've eaten, I'll have to go. I'll have dinner at Uphall to save you the trouble.'

When she looked disappointed, he added, 'I'll be home for supper of course. I'll be home early—as soon as it's dusk. Oh, and my mother said she'd call round to help.' With that, he left the table, kissed her on the cheek again, grabbed his hat and jacket and walked out the door.

The kitchen fell silent apart from the crackling of the fire. Lizzie rested an elbow on the table, chin in hand, and let out a long sigh. In Rudston, she'd have been planning the day ahead with the vicar's wife, or doing something with the daughters.

'Alright,' she cried aloud to herself, "ere we are Mrs Jordan. Thoo'd better get used to it.'

She opened a pot of honey and, as she was alone, took a large spoonful and watched it drizzle from a height onto her porridge. There wasn't even a cat in the cottage—another change from the busy vicarage. Maybe Francis's grandparents at Uphall had a cat to spare. Now that the cottage was occupied again, mice would surely follow.

She finished her porridge and then went to the window. There wasn't much to see—an empty street, cottages along another lane and little else. Just as she was thinking how lonely life could be without company, she saw a woman cross the street, heading for her door. Two boys trailed behind. She had no idea who they were, but the woman had a determined air and wore a good quality cloak.

'Good morning,' Lizzie said shyly on opening the front door.

'Good morning,' the woman replied, removing her hood. 'I'm Francis's mother. I'm Mary.'

All of a sudden, Lizzie found herself held in a firm embrace, and then a formal kiss was planted on her cheek. She blushed on being released, and curtsied nervously before leading the way in.

1 1

'My sister's called Elizabeth, too,' Mary announced as she followed. 'We tried to make your cottage as clean as we could. Sorry if it's not what you expected. These are two of my boys—meet John and Matthew.' She pushed the boys ahead into the kitchen. 'They're going to help today.'

'I thank thee.' Lizzie curtsied again in panic. She hadn't cleaned the porridge bowls or the table. There might be a trail of honey somewhere. This was no way to meet your mother-in-law. 'I've just finished breakfast,' she mumbled in excuse.

The boys hung about by the door, reluctant to venture further. The eldest, who seemed about twelve or thirteen, had a vacant stare while the younger boy frowned and scuffed his feet in the doorway, obviously unhappy to be there.

Mary began to give orders. 'You, Matthew, you've seen me clean our pots. Here's a bag of sand. Take the porridge pot and bowls outside and give them a good scour. Then give them a swill round. Look—there's the bucket of water.'

'Do I have to?'

'Yes. John is going to fetch more water. You're not big enough to carry it, and you won't want to wait at the well with the women, will you? John doesn't mind.'

The boy called John picked up the other bucket. It was still half-full.

'Pour it into that other pot, then off you go.' Then, with the boys out of the way, Mary sat at the table.

Lizzie joined her, feeling like a guest in her new home. Her mother-in-law knew she'd only been a servant. No matter what she did, there'd always be that difference between them. And hadn't Francis once told her that his mother was a Smith—a sister of Matthew Smith who was doing so well? Lizzie gave a weak smile.

Mary smiled back. 'At least you have a good fire going. Francis can be very helpful at times.'

'Yes. He's been kind.'

'He'd better be careful when—you know, with a baby due.'

Elizabeth reddened. 'Oh, yes. I'm fine.'

'Good.'

1 2

The two women stared across the table, assessing each other. Mary saw a pretty, young girl, uneasy in her new abode; she was sure she'd have no trouble with her.

Lizzie saw the lines on Mary's brow and round her mouth. There were no corresponding laughter lines about the eyes. Feeling a tear prickling her eye, she was the first to lower her gaze. She glanced at the fire, wondering whether to add more gorse or leave it to the boys. With Mary there, she was paralysed.

Mary saw her advantage. She leant forward and took Lizzie's hand. 'May I call you Lizzie? That's what Francis calls you.'

'Yes, of course. I've allus been Lizzie.'

'Good, now there's one thing I should warn you. It's nothing to do with your condition—it's about Francis.'

Lizzie's eyes opened wide.

'He can be very strict with himself—and others.' She gave a knowing nod. 'He'll often deny himself certain pleasures. Once, he stopped eating meat; he fainted out in the field.'

'We both shun overindulgence,' Lizzie replied meekly. 'Neither of us likes strong drink.'

'Ah, right then,' Mary snorted, 'you're well-suited.' *You'll be fine*, she thought, *so long as Francis doesn't see too much of Robert Storey.*

1 3

Chapter 3

After what seemed like a long day, Francis left Uphall to return home for supper and, he hoped, an early night. As he walked down the hill, he thought of the work to be completed that week. The recent wet weather meant there was still the wheat field stubble to finish ploughing so that oats could be sown in the spring.

He couldn't say he'd enjoyed his first day back at Uphall. He'd done his best to fit in with the hired lads, but they regarded him with suspicion. No doubt they resented the preferential treatment he received as one of the Jordans. He shrugged, not caring too much, for he had a new pleasure ahead. Maybe the hired lads envied him going home to a young wife. Quickening his step, he imagined greeting Lizzie in the kitchen. He could creep up behind and wrap his arms round her. She'd turn and give him such a smile, and then they'd kiss. Perhaps after supper they could recite Bible verses they knew by heart. They'd always liked that at the vicarage.

He prised off his boots at the back door and tiptoed along the passage. There was a welcoming aroma of pork, apple and onions. He pushed the kitchen door open a fraction and peeped in. Lizzie was standing over the fire, her back to him. As he stepped inside, she turned and rushed towards him.

'Oh, Francis, come an' see.' She was excited and pulled him by the hand towards the tiny pantry. The stone shelves were neatly organised into pickles, preserves and cheeses. 'An' tha mother's sent a pot o' tha favourite—pickled red cabbage. I didn't know thoo liked it so much. Thoo can 'ave some tonight wi' pork slices she sent.'

On returning to the kitchen, Francis noted the changes. There were curtains at the windows, and hanging from the bar over the fire were ladles, tongs and even a pair of old bellows. A bright copper pan shone in the firelight.

1 4

When she turned back to the hearth, he put his arms round her from behind and pressed against her back, kissing the nape of her neck. 'I love you.'

She manoeuvred his hands further down to her swollen belly. 'Thoo knows what we really need? A warmin' pan for our bed.'

'Until we get one, I'll heat a cobblestone in the fire. You can wrap it in an old cloth and use that.' Uncomfortable at feeling her bump, and hoping to avoid any talk of childbirth, he stepped away. 'I'll go out and get a stone now if it's not too dark to see.'

As he left, she added, 'An' I'd like a toastin' fork, an' we need a chest or a chest o' drawers fo' clothes.' Although she heard the outer door close behind him, she shouted, 'An' we'll need a crib soon, don't forget.'

He came back almost straightaway with a stone taken from the rubble of a nearby broken wall. Having placed it in the fire, he sat at the table to watch his wife bend over the hearth and then serve their supper. She looked pleased with herself as she sat down, her cheeks flushed from the heat. He smiled, and after saying grace, he reached for the pickled cabbage and heaped a large spoonful onto his plate.

'I think, Lizzie, you're going to make a wonderful mother.'

She winked. 'I 'ope to be a wonderful wife first.'

Embarrassed by the turn of the conversation, he concentrated on his supper. He was hungry after a full day's work outside and soon emptied his plate. When he glanced up, he saw that Lizzie was still eating. He watched her eyes glitter in the firelight. She was so lovely and deserved to be treated well. With this in mind, he decided to be more considerate in bed. He should take his time, and show how much he loved her.

Their supper over, he gave up the idea of reciting Bible verses and used the tongs to pull the stone from the fire. She passed him a piece of flannel and he hastened to place the hot stone in the middle of the bed. He returned to find her clearing the table.

'Lizzie, leave that. Let's sit by the fire while the bed's warming up.' He moved the two chairs close to the hearth

1 5

and they sat side by side holding hands. 'It's nice, isn't it—just the two of us?' He was concerned that she missed the Gurwoods, especially the daughters.

'Mmm. It is nice. I 'ad company today though—tha mother an' brothers came to 'elp. She was kind, but...'

'But what?'

'Nothin'. She was just worried about me.'

'Hmm. Mother used to be worried about me, too. But we're fine, aren't we?' He poked the fire to settle the ashes and did not add more fuel. 'We'll wait a bit longer, then I'll cover the fire.'

They stared into the glowing embers, neither breaking the silence. The tension was palpable.

She squeezed his hand tighter and whispered, 'I think the bed should be warm now. I'll go and get ready.'

He waited only a couple of minutes before knocking on the parlour door and then entering. She looked beautiful against the pillow. He undressed quickly and joined her, snuggling up close to benefit from the warmed patch of sheet. She'd wriggled the hot stone to the bottom of the bed, so he stretched his legs until his toes could feel it. Both competed for the warmth, their feet curling about the stone and round each other's ankles.

She tried to tickle him.

'That won't work, Lizzie. I'm not moving my feet. You move yours. You've been in bed longer.'

'I'll move them for a kiss.'

'Cheat! You win.' He rested on one elbow and began with a gentle kiss on her forehead before moving to each cheek, each ear and her neck. Finally, he kissed her on the lips with such a gentle, persistent pressure that she grew breathless. When he lowered his head to her breast, he even heard her moan.

'Lizzie,' he said huskily, raising his head, 'do you mind if I try to love you like we did in the barn? I can use my arms and my knees to keep off the baby. What do you think? I want to see your face.'

'Alright,' she whispered, thinking that she'd burst if he didn't do something soon. Ever since she'd been with child,

1 6

she'd been thinking more and more about that night in the barn. For months, her body had felt more alive, a constant reminder of that newly found pleasure. She pulled him towards her lips and continued to kiss him as he positioned himself rather gingerly.

This time he entered her with ease. He was determined not to rush, and revelled in her loving kisses and the way she moved her hips beneath him. Ignoring all Robert Storey's teachings about moderation, he abandoned himself to the moment.

The young couple lay in each other's arms afterwards, content, their heartbeats slowly returning to normal. They watched the candlelight flickering in the slight draught from beneath the door, casting strange shadows against the walls.

'If married life is as good as this,' he pronounced, 'I wish we'd started earlier.'

'Me too.' She took his hand and turned it so that she could kiss the palm. 'There now, that's a fine medicine fo' blisters. We'd best blow candles out, thoo's workin' early again tomorrow.'

In the morning, Francis woke up with a desperate desire to make love again. He turned to face her, so grateful for their shared happiness.

'Lizzie,' he murmured, 'are you awake? Do you mind if I love you again?'

She responded with the widest of smiles.

Soon afterwards, she began to experience that tight ache across her womb, and thought of the unborn child.

'Francis, we must have a crib soon—just in case.'

'Yes,' he answered happily, 'don't fret. You can have anything you want. Tell me, is my mother going to bring food *every* day?'

'She said she'd 'elp out over winter, an' after our child's born.'

'That's very generous.'

'She did say that tha gran'mother ought to 'elp as well, though she led me to believe tha gran'mother was close-fisted.'

'I'll say she is. She still hoards her candles and uses rushlights. And woe betide any waste.'

1 7

'Hmm.' She decided to confess her fears. 'I'm a bit wary o' thy mother. I'm afraid she'll find me not good enough fo' thee.'

'Don't worry, she'll soon appreciate you. My grandmother probably made life difficult for *her*—can't have been an easy mother-in-law.'

'No, maybe that's it. Oh, an' thy aunt Elizabeth called to say she'd 'elp us wi' food—at least until we 'ave our own chickens i' spring. It were she who brought our apples an' onions.'

'Good, and you can plant up the garden. We should be alright eventually. Tell me, did her husband Robert come with her?'

'No.'

'Did she mention him?'

'No.'

Francis nodded. 'Good.' He knew, though, he'd have to face Robert soon—maybe later today...

Chapter 4

Robert Storey waited in the late afternoon light beside the church gate, thinking of young Francis Jordan. The falling leaves served to emphasise the fall of the couple from grace. Unable to forgive and forget the lad's moral lapse and subsequent hasty marriage, he'd vowed to return Francis to a chaste way of life. Already, he'd wasted two days; his wife had persuaded him to let them settle into the cottage first. However, he knew he'd never visit; the last thing he wanted was to sit at the table of the woman who had, without doubt, seduced Francis. No, he'd catch Francis on his own as he left work. He pulled his black coat collar higher against the northwesterly wind and stamped his boots. All the while, he kept his eyes on the comings and goings further up the hill.

Francis left Uphall with thoughts of a warm reception from Lizzie and an even warmer reception in bed. The sight of Robert Storey emerging from the gloom ahead hit him like a slap of cold water. There was no escape.

'Ah, Robert. How are you?'

'In good health, God be praised. But how are *you*?'

Francis was unsure how to answer. Robert would not understand wedded bliss; he'd certainly not condone carnal pleasure with a wife expecting a child. He prevaricated with talk of the cottage.

'We like where we live. Lizzie has already made it into a home. We do still lack furniture and various tools, but we're managing for now.'

'I'm not interested in your worldly affairs. I'm concerned for your moral well-being. I'll walk down the hill with you.'

Francis swallowed hard. He knew he'd let Robert down, had fallen a good way short of the standards Robert had set for him. The new happiness with Lizzie had turned his head.

Suddenly, Robert stopped walking. He held Francis back and looked him in the eye, his gaunt cheekbones and sharp nose almost in Francis's face.

'You must answer me this,' Robert spat. 'Do you truly regret what you've done?'

When Francis didn't answer and began walking again, Robert tried a different approach.

'It's not all your fault, Francis. I know women are to blame. You see, they have such strong appetites. Once aroused, they can't be sated.' He shuddered as he recalled the early days of his own marriage when he'd felt consumed, devoured by his wife's passion. For years he'd been appalled by her lustful advances. 'No,' he repeated, 'it's not your fault.'

Francis halted. 'You're wrong, Robert. I take the blame as well.'

'Then you're in a worse state than I thought.'

They walked on again, frowning, both deep in thought. As they reached the bottom of the hill, Robert paused by the pond, reluctant to go any nearer the cottage.

'Francis, the only way to redeem yourself is through self-denial. You must be strict and develop good habits. Restraint will make you a better Christian. You'll free yourself from the material world and allow time for spiritual improvement.'

Francis sighed. There was truth in what Robert said. Just lately, he'd hardly thought of anything but Lizzie. On the other hand, he was grateful to God. He sighed again.

'Lizzie will have supper waiting.'

'Goodbye for now then, Francis. I can see by your face that you're repentant. God will help you.' As he turned to go back up the hill, he added, 'Don't forget what I've told you about women. Be on your guard.'

Francis wiped a tear from his eye and trudged across the road to the cottage. He'd been so looking forward to greeting Lizzie and enjoying her kisses. He took his time removing his boots and then paddled quietly into the kitchen.

When Lizzie glanced over her shoulder and gave him such a welcoming smile, he knew it was going to be nigh on impossible to deny her anything.

'What's the matter?' she asked, disturbed by his downcast eyes.

'Nothing.' He lifted his head to face her. 'You're so lovely, that's all.'

'I thought summat must 'ave 'appened.'

'No.'

She approached him, expecting a hug, and was surprised when he responded with a quick kiss on her forehead and then sat down for his supper. She let this go and, as they ate, she told him of her day spent at his mother's house, combing and carding wool with his brother John while Mary did the spinning.

'Is John a bit slow?' she asked. ''E's very good at combin' wool, but 'e's not like other boys 'is age. 'As 'e 'ad some kind of accident?'

'No. He's always been like that.'

When Francis couldn't be cajoled into conversation and didn't ask questions or even mention his day's work, Lizzie grew more concerned.

'Summat's wrong. What is it? Ever since thoo walked in thoo's 'ad a face like a cold puddin'.'

'I met Robert Storey on my way home.'

Her face darkened. Francis had talked so much about the man over the years. She'd never met him, yet he had a hold on Francis, and the man's attitudes had almost blighted their courtship.

'What did 'e 'ave to say?'

'The usual. Lizzie, I'm not blaming you for anything, but we need to be more careful. Tonight, let's pray together before we go to bed.'

She was relieved if that was all they had to do.

After supper, she placed the hot stone in the bed, and then knelt by the fire with Francis to say prayers before they retired.

Once in bed, they lay rigid side by side. She stroked his arm and kissed his shoulder, yet he didn't respond. Instead, he sighed and then reached down to blow out the candle.

'Blow yours out Lizzie. We'd better get to sleep.'

She did as she was told, then turned away from him. Stemming her tears, she trusted that he would soon relent.

21

For the next few days, Francis endeavoured to restrict every appetite. When he did finally relent, it was a compromise; they would enjoy each other in bed every other night. Even so, he often found the mornings a problem. Instead of getting up and rushing off to work, it was tempting to stay with Lizzie. They were snug and warm in bed and her breasts were ample and soft by his side. He had to grit his teeth and think of other things before he could leave her.

As he worked outdoors in the early December frosts, he knew that simply avoiding Robert Storey was not going to help. Since he'd been about fourteen, Robert's teachings had been part of his being; they ran deep. If Robert was correct about women being so lascivious, then he'd have to curb Lizzie's lust as well as his own. Perhaps she'd be less demanding once the baby was born.

His mother guessed the problem when she visited with a gift. She found her daughter-in-law sitting and knitting by the fire with such a sad, faraway look in her yes.

'Are you alright? Is Francis treating you properly?'

''E's seen Robert Storey.'

'Ah…' She carried the other chair to the fire and sat beside her. 'You know I told you—Francis has often denied himself pleasures of all kinds, but he loves you, I know that much.'

Lizzie changed the subject. 'Is that a piece o' soap thoo's brought?'

'Yes, it's from Francis's grandmother. This time of year, there's so much tallow at Uphall that Dorothy makes a new batch. At other times, she thinks it wasteful to make soap—she prefers to keep the fat for candles and waterproofing the boots. This is left from last year.'

Lizzie took the soap and sniffed it. She suspected it was made from beef fat. Although it was white, it was grainy and hard as rock.

Mary saw the look of disappointment. 'It's probably not what you're used to at the vicarage, eh? It's free, though, and you'll be glad of it.'

'I thank thee, Mary.' She didn't say that the Gurwoods had Castile soap made from olive oil. It was pure white and

22

lasted for years. She'd washed clothes with it and the whole family had even used it to wash their hair.

Lizzie stroked the homemade soap with one finger and asked, 'Dost *thoo* use this soap, Mary?'

'Of course. It's all we have. Mind you, William and the boys think a wash is just a rinse of their hands and face. You'll need that soap when the baby comes—only another month or so, eh? Stand up. Let's see how you're carrying.'

Lizzie stood and slowly turned about.

Mary clapped her hands. 'You're carrying it high, and you're thick all round. It's a girl you'll be having. That's good, isn't it? You'll have help in the house. There's too many men in our family—I've a house full of them.'

Lizzie smiled weakly and sat down. 'Didn't Robert Storey ever 'ave any bairns?'

'No, and it's a sore point with Elizabeth. It's not for want of her trying. You'll find out, I'm afraid, what Robert thinks about us women.'

Lizzie bit her lip. She couldn't confide in her mother-in-law. 'Tell Elizabeth she's very welcome 'ere. I'd be glad of 'er company.'

Mary felt a pang of jealousy. It would be just like her sister to take over. Elizabeth had more time; no doubt she'd love to get her hands on a new baby. Saying nothing for now, Mary made an excuse to leave. Then, as she left the cottage, she remembered suddenly about Christmas.

'The whole family usually spends Christmas Day at Uphall. That means you and Francis too. Shall I tell Dorothy you'll come?'

'Yes, but I wonder what Francis will think. We've never joined in any drinkin' an' games before. We won't be dancin' neither.'

Mary rolled her eyes. It was the least of Lizzie's worries. As she closed the door behind her and headed home, she wondered what Dorothy Jordan would make of the new addition to the family. One thing was certain—Dorothy would speak her mind.

23

Chapter 5

In the weeks leading up to Christmas, Francis often visited Robert Storey's house on his way home in order to read the Bible. Aunt Elizabeth always welcomed him, and always delayed him in the kitchen; he knew she'd have preferred him to stay there in the warmth and chat to her over a hot drink. Instead, Robert would lead him into the cold parlour and close the door.

Late one afternoon, the two men were sitting opposite each other. Robert was about to open the Bible when Francis asked if they could talk first. He knew he wasn't coping with the recent changes in his wife.

'Sometimes, in bed at night, her breasts leak. Now, I love Lizzie, but it's disturbing to see that wet patch on her nightgown... and the smell—I can't get used to it. And then, sometimes in bed, I've felt the baby kick. It could be a warning—a timely reminder to forego my pleasure.'

'You're right,' Robert replied, 'and I know how you feel.' He was recalling the times he'd been sickened by the smell in the house during his wife's monthly bleeding. Although she'd always made sure to cover the buckets of soiled cloths put in to soak, and had scattered lavender on the floor, there remained a certain odour of iron pervading the rooms. It was a relief when she was older and all that stopped.

'You poor lad,' he continued. 'For your own peace of mind, you must reject your wife's advances.' Once, as a youth, he'd seen a couple of dogs together, the bitch squirming and encouraging the dog that frothed at the mouth, drooling while sniffing her. Whenever Elizabeth had tried to seduce him, he'd pictured that bitch on heat.

'Yes, Francis, shun your wife's approaches.'

'I don't want to upset Lizzie, though, especially when she only has a month to go.'

'When it comes to saving your soul, there can be no compromise. The body, for all you think it's strong and healthy, will fade and die, yet your soul is immortal, made in the image of God. It's your soul you must care about. Set your affections on things above, not on things of this earth.'

Francis frowned. 'But in lawful marriage, a man and wife *can* take their pleasure.'

'The purpose of marriage, it's true, is to beget children. You've already sinned, though, when your lust got the better of you. Now, don't you go thinking that marriage will subdue that lust. Moderation is the answer; otherwise, your marriage will only inflame and heighten any brutish appetites.'

Francis sighed.

'You may be downhearted, but there's no misery compared with the loss of your soul. And your worst enemies are those closest to you. Remember, Eve disobeyed God; she was tempted by the serpent and took the apple. The devil is a dangerous adversary, and women can be as subtle and as cunning.' He recalled the many ways Elizabeth had attempted to seduce him. 'Beware, Francis, there's a hook under their bait and, if you bite, you are lost.'

Francis realised anew the extent of Robert's aversions, and shivered; the parlour was cold and there was frost on the window. He noticed that Robert kept rubbing his hands to warm them and, although Robert's lips were almost blue, his eyes glittered as if on fire. Francis touched the Bible, about to open it, and then let his hand drop to his side in defeat. He loved Lizzie, and he loved God. There must be a way to live with both.

'Help me, Robert. Help me lead a good life.'

'This is a start. Be humble and beg for grace. I think you should pray both morning and evening—begin and end each day in communion with God. Remember, though, that prayer will only be useful if you are wholehearted. Don't let your mind wander.'

'Thank you, Robert. I'll go now and do as you say.'

As he opened the door, he bumped into his aunt, eavesdropping behind.

25

She stepped back in alarm. 'Oh, Francis! I was coming to see if you wanted something to eat.'

'No thank you. I'll be eating at home soon.'

'Don't tempt him,' Robert interrupted. 'He'll eat just enough to keep body and soul together, no more.'

Elizabeth glanced from her husband's determined expression to Francis's downcast face, and made her decision.

The next morning, Lizzie opened her door to receive the most welcome of visitors.

'Elizabeth! Come on in.' She gave her the widest of smiles. She'd seen the Storeys at church but had never been properly introduced; Robert always seemed to avoid her.

'Can I call you Lizzie? I know that's what Francis calls you.'

With a brief nod, Lizzie showed her into the kitchen, apologising for the lack of furniture, the lack of home comforts.

'It's a lot better than when you first came,' Elizabeth remarked as she removed her pattens and gazed round. Although there were more utensils and the fire brightened the room, the floor still felt cold under foot. She knew that, yesterday, William had dumped a load of rushes at Mary's door, a part payment towards a carrier job he'd undertaken; they gave her an idea.

'How would you like a rush mat in here? It would be warm to walk on and it would stop that draught.'

'We can't afford such a thing, and I've never made one myself.'

'Neither have I, but I saw them made at home. It was years ago, but I'm sure we could manage together. Listen, I'll go now to Mary's and bring rushes.' She fastened on her pattens and left.

Minutes later, Elizabeth returned with Mary and her son John, each carrying a bundle of rushes in their arms. The kitchen became so crowded that there was no room to move. Seeing the alarm on Lizzie's face, Elizabeth took control.

2 6

'Alright, we'd best leave the rushes outside while we make a space here. John—can you go and fetch more water? We need to dampen them. We can't work them dry.'

Lizzie pointed to a corner. 'There's a bucketful over yon to be goin' on with.'

Mary bit her lip. Already, her sister was taking over. In sulky silence, she helped Elizabeth move the rushes into the yard and then lifted the table and chairs to one side. There was still little room to work.

Elizabeth went outside and gave more orders. 'John, you spread out the bundles and wet them like this. While they're soaking, we can enjoy a drink. Once we start plaiting the rushes, we won't be able to stop.'

She returned indoors where Lizzie had hung a pan of the local ale over the fire.

'Is that Martha Wrench's brew?' Mary asked. 'It smells like it—sage, if I'm not mistaken, maybe a dash of honey.'

'I don't know what's in it. We dilute it for ourselves. We don't take strong drink.'

'No,' Mary mumbled. 'I know.'

'Well,' said Elizabeth, 'you'd better sit down, Lizzie, and rest while you can. We can do most of the work to start with.'

John returned to say he'd finished wetting the rushes. Once the ale had warmed up, Elizabeth sent him out again, this time to gather sticks for the fire. She winked at the others.

'We don't want lads listening to our conversation. Here, Mary, you and Lizzie take a chair to have your drink. I'll sit on this chest.'

While the rushes absorbed the water, the three women sat close to the hearth, each cradling a pot of spiced ale. The drink had an almost instant effect. Feeling warm by the fire, Mary relaxed and thought of her youth. She spoke first of what was in all their minds.

'It was when I was with child that I most enjoyed being with William. I used to look forward to bedtimes. Happy days—and nights, I should say. Listen, Lizzie, it's not so easy once you've babies to see to. Make hay while the sun shines.'

27

Lizzie coughed in embarrassment. What did these women know about her predicament?

Mary persevered. 'Is everything well with you and Francis? He can be very stubborn.'

'And what's more,' interrupted Elizabeth, 'he's been listening to my husband. I'm sorry, Lizzie, but I can't help thinking that Robert's gone too far this time. What he's done to me is my affair—he mustn't spoil your life too.'

Lizzie blushed and shifted on her chair. 'It's alright, thoo mustn't worry about me. Once me child is born, then I'm sure we'll be alright.'

Elizabeth shrugged and raised her eyebrows in disbelief. 'If he's anything like Robert, be careful. Don't expect too much. Some men need time. They're not used to women and they can't be rushed. Whatever you do, don't force yourself on him. I once...' She stopped herself. 'Never mind, you'll find a way, I'm sure. You have a pretty face and a comely body. Let's drink to that.'

They raised their pots. 'To you, Lizzie, and a long and blissful married life—and lots of children.'

John barged in with a sack of sticks and set it near the fire. He smiled at the women and then laughed. They looked so pleased with themselves.

'Can I work with you?' he asked.

'Of course,' his aunt replied. 'Now that the rushes will have softened, you can start to flatten them. Fetch them in and I'll show you how with this mallet.'

When he'd flattened enough rushes, Mary wondered about the empty meat hooks fastened to the ceiling above them.

'Couldn't we tie the rushes to those hooks? Then it would be easier to plait them. John—you stand on the table. You'll be able to reach, and you know a reef knot.'

Elizabeth tied nine rushes together at one end with twine and handed them to him. 'There you go, John, fasten them tight. I'll pass you two more sets. We'll each want a separate hook. *You* needn't do the plaiting; you just wet and flatten more rushes.'

2 8

Elizabeth didn't have to demonstrate how to plait, but she did remind them to keep the plaits tight and even. As the rushes were almost ten feet long, she said they'd make a narrow mat to start with. 'I think we have enough to do without weaving in more rushes, and the kitchen won't take a much bigger mat. But, listen, we *must* keep them taut. Keep yanking them—be tough with them.'

As the women began to plait their strips, John kept sniffing the dampened rushes. He looked up and smiled. 'They smell like the stream at the bottom of the meadow.'

Mary was so pleased to see him happy. She worried constantly about his future, how he'd fit in and work with the family at Uphall. He was now thirteen and, so far, he stayed mostly at home to help with his younger brothers and do the household chores. Last year, he'd taken a liking to the old shepherd and had worked on the moor with the sheep. Maybe he could learn from Greasy Jack and become a shepherd himself one day.

Lizzie interrupted her thoughts. 'Would John like a drink? 'E's been workin' all mornin'.'

'Don't give him ale! If you have some milk, that'll do. John—can you help yourself? Find the milk and pour out a mug—we can't let go of the rushes.'

He stumbled towards the pots and pans and found the milk. There wasn't a spare mug, so he drank straight from the jug, leaving a moustache of cream. He grinned and wiped his mouth on his sleeve.

Mary clicked her tongue but smiled. 'Oh, John, you muck tub.'

By midday, they each had a long, three-inch-wide strip of plaited rush. Elizabeth was satisfied with their progress.

'When we have enough strips, we'll be able to stitch them together.'

Mary butted in with an idea. 'Dorothy has flax twine at Uphall. I'm sure she'll let us have some. And I bet she has big needles as well.'

Lizzie sighed. The plaiting was a strain even though she sat down to the work. She was relieved when her strip was complete.

29

'I don't think I can do any more,' she mumbled, rubbing a hand across her brow.

Elizabeth saw how tired the young woman looked. Lizzie's eyes had bags beneath them and she was so pale.

'Leave it to us now. We'll tidy up, we'll get your dinner and let you rest. You go and have a lie down.'

Lizzie thanked them and went into the parlour. She stepped over a bundle of rushes by the bed and snuggled under the top cover, fully clothed. It was soothing to hear the low murmur of the women as they talked in the kitchen. She listened to the companionable noises of the fire being poked and the table being laid, before falling asleep to dream of a child playing on a bright, new rush mat.

Chapter 6

By Christmas Eve, the rush mat was complete, a pleasing array of pale greens and browns with tinges of blue. The edges were bound with linen, and the women had woven in lavender so that the kitchen had a homely herbal aroma. Lizzie was pleased with the result, and remembered the instructions to freshen it up by sprinkling it with water at regular intervals.

She took Elizabeth's advice and did not force herself on Francis. Each night, she endeavoured to provide him with a different supper, made sure the bed was warmed and joined him in prayer. Rather than lovers, they were good friends, and she could manage—for the time being.

On Christmas morning, they made their way to church. A great disadvantage of living at the bottom of the village was the long trudge up the steep hill. Heavily pregnant, Lizzie hung onto Francis's arm. Snow was falling and settling already, making the church bells sound closer in an otherwise silent landscape. Lizzie pulled her cloak hood tighter.

Throughout the short service, she remained anxious about the imminent dinner at Uphall. The vicar was in a hurry to get back to Filey, so few carols were sung to distract her thoughts. The cold pew offered no comfort either as she recalled meeting Francis's grandparents on her first Sunday at church. That introduction had been brief, her 'reception' as chilly as the November fog. Mary had told her that Dorothy's bark was worse than her bite, but Lizzie still had to face the woman. How would Dorothy Jordan greet her and where would she make her sit?

After the communion, Lizzie and Francis followed the rest of the Jordans the short distance to Uphall. She watched Francis's uncle Thomas cross the street and lead the way with a large sprig of holly and a bit of mistletoe sticking out of his pocket. It was intimidating to see the whole family together with their children and the hired hands. She dug her fingers into Francis's arm and clung on for reassurance.

'Don't worry,' he repeated, 'Grandmother will be far too busy seeing to the food to bother you. And Grandfather's getting soft in his old age. Look, we're here now. Stamp your feet and leave your pattens there inside the door with the others.'

As she struggled to unfasten them, Mary came to help.

'Don't you bend down. I'll do it. And,' she whispered, 'I'll have you sit near me at the table.'

Lizzie smiled with relief. 'Thank you.'

Having removed her cloak and allowed a servant girl to hang it up, she stepped into the kitchen where the blast of hot air smelled of roast meat, oranges, nutmeg and cinnamon. A goose was on the spit over the huge fireplace, fat dripping constantly into a tin beneath; another servant girl with a sweaty and shiny face was standing at the side turning it slowly.

Francis noted the direction of Lizzie's gaze, afraid she'd want to assist. 'It's not your job now,' he hissed, with a firm hand on her arm. 'Remember you're my wife—you're a Jordan.'

There was such a racket. Everyone talking at once, and the children shrieking with excitement until pushed to a corner to sit at a separate table. Lizzie and Francis were ushered to one side of the main table to sit towards the bottom end near William and Mary. William's brother, Thomas, the last one still living at Uphall, sat on the other side.

'Here's Dickon,' whispered Francis as their old foreman sat down with a grunt next to him. 'He's too crippled up in his joints to work much, but he knows a lot and he's harmless.'

Two of the hired lads were allowed to join the table, squashed in opposite them next to Francis's other aunt and her husband, John Dawson. Lizzie saw that the lads had trenchers whereas everyone else had pewter plates. She smiled at them but they seemed surprised, frowned, and then avoided her eye.

32

There was a bowl of oranges on the table, a rare treat, and the hot punch now being served smelled of lemons.

'Don't give me much,' Francis insisted. 'Nor Lizzie, thank you.'

The serving girl passed on to other more appreciative guests.

Lizzie felt old Dorothy Jordan's eyes boring into her. She risked a glance to the top of the table only to be met with a cold, scrutinising stare. Immediately, she looked back down into her lap.

Dorothy saw a young woman swollen with child, her abundant hair denoting health and energy. The woman should be good breeding stock, and Francis could have done worse. Yet, when she spoke, she was harsh.

'Aye, thoo's right to look down. Lift thy 'ead, lass. God will be thy final judge, not me.'

Everyone at the table fell silent.

Lizzie gulped, determined not to cry though she had no control over her neck and face, which grew hot and red. She felt Francis grip her hand so tightly it hurt.

'She doesn't mean it,' Mary whispered.

The serving girl had finished filling everyone's glasses and stood to one side waiting on her mistress. She saw Lizzie's discomfort and coughed.

Distracted, Dorothy Jordan acknowledged the girl with a nod. She was satisfied with her effect on Lizzie and stood with her glass raised. She nudged her husband who then rose slowly to his feet to join her in the toast.

'To our absent loved ones,' Dorothy said, 'an' 'ealth an' 'appiness to ev'ryone.'

As they drank, the family remembered the two daughters who'd died young, and John, who'd left home over ten years ago and not been seen since.

Dorothy raised her glass again. 'An' a toast to our son Samuel an' 'is family, an' to Richard an' 'is wife. I'm sure both sons are 'ere i' spirit.'

Thomas nudged his sister. 'I bet Richard hasn't any children yet. He's not like the rest of us, eh?'

33

'Shush, Mother will hear. It's just rumour, and it's not fitting today of all days.' She pointed to Dickon. 'Look—he has the right idea.'

Dickon was holding up his glass for a refill as the serving girl passed by. After she'd poured him a hefty measure, he took a sip and licked his lips, keeping an eye on the goose.

'Save some o' that fat fo' me. I can rub it o' me legs of a cold mornin'.'

'Aye, nowt'll be wasted.'

William kept the conversation going. To avoid further outbursts from his mother, he shouted down the table. 'Dickon—have you given the cattle their sheaf of corn for Christmas?'

'Aye,' he grumbled, 'an' i' mornin' we're bloodlettin' our oxen an 'osses.' He glanced at Thomas opposite him. 'Thoo'll 'elp, won't thee?'

'If I've sobered up from today. If I can move after I've eaten pudding and that goose.'

Lizzie didn't know what they were talking about, and Francis only hinted that it was an old rite.

'I don't reckon to it,' he explained, 'but Dickon sticks to old customs. I hope I don't end up helping him. I can't see Thomas being fit.'

At that moment, two plum puddings, as big as footballs, were carried to the table and plonked in the middle. Amid cheers, Francis's grandfather stood up again, called for hush and pulled a bit of paper from his pocket.

'Instead o' sayin' grace, I'll read out this verse. It's one I cut out an' saved from an almanac.' He held the paper in a trembling hand, focussed his eyes and began.

> *Now that time 'as come wherein*
> *Our Saviour Christ was born.*
> *Our larder's full o' beef an' pork,*
> *Our garner's filled wi' corn;*
> *As God 'ath plenty to us sent,*
> *Take comfort o' thy labours,*
> *An' let it never thee repent*
> *To feast thy needy neighbours.*

34

'Hear, hear!' was the general cry, despite the year's poor harvest.

'Aye,' old Francis continued, 'it's fine for us Jordans with our own land, but we remember those less well off.' He closed his eyes. 'We pray, Lord, that thoo 'elps them i' need, an' make us grateful for our food today. Amen.'

After a moment for due reflection, mayhem erupted as everyone except Francis and Lizzie held up their plates.

'Come on, Francis,' Mary urged, 'or are you going to leave more room for the goose?'

'Mother, we'll have a *bit* of pudding. We're not pigs. We can wait to be served.'

'Alright, but you won't be disappointed. There's suet in there to keep you warm. There's plenty of dried fruit, and I know your grandmother used mutton *and* beef broth.'

As the couple received their portions and began to eat, Lizzie's eyes were drawn to Thomas on the other side of the table. He had such a confident air and she often caught him glancing in her direction. After he winked, though, she kept her head down.

Mary noticed. 'Don't worry about him. He's all bluster and swagger, not like William's other brother Richard. You'd like *him*—he's quiet and gentle. You might meet him one day. He often comes to stay here and help out, though he's supposed to live with his wife in Carnaby.'

When she saw Lizzie's puzzled expression, she added, 'It's a long story. It can wait.' Perhaps it was best Lizzie didn't know too much. Francis would get to know and then Robert Storey, and then who knew what would happen.

Francis saw his wife was holding her spoon in mid-air. He nudged her gently.

'Eat a little pudding. Make an effort—I know it's very rich.'

She took a spoonful of the heavy mixture and found it so full of flavour that she soon emptied her plate.

'Well,' Francis declared in surprise, 'it must be your condition.' He was still only halfway through his small portion.

Thomas leant forward to address everyone. 'I bet Robert Storey won't be enjoying much food today. He'll be fasting.' He turned to Mary at the end of the table. 'Sorry, Mary, but your sister's suffered every Christmas since she was wed.'

Francis felt obliged to defend his uncle. 'Robert will be tending his soul—and his wife's. There *is* something to be said for moderation.'

Thomas grinned and helped himself to more pudding. 'Is it true, Francis, that he won't even say Christmas? Says it sounds popish, so he calls it Christ-tide?'

Francis nodded.

Dickon, sitting beside him, rubbed the bristles on his chin. 'Oh Lord, I've allus called it Kesmas. I never thought owt wrong wi' that.'

Thomas continued to goad Francis. 'I hear Robert won't abide any decorations, especially holly—says it's pagan. Nor mistletoe,' he added as he spooned in more pudding. 'A pity,' he spluttered with his mouth full, 'since it makes women fertile.' He stared pointedly at Lizzie.

Everyone was now looking her way. She coughed in embarrassment and bowed her head.

Mary changed the subject. 'That goose smells delicious. It must be cooked by now.' She made a big show of popping her last crumb of pudding into her mouth. 'I'm ready now, anyway.'

The others smiled and, as they followed Mary's example and cleared their plates, Dorothy Jordan had little choice but to bring the goose to the table. She bade the serving girls put out the roast potatoes, the mashed peas, the gravy and the jug of orange sauce.

'An' then thoo can start servin' ale.'

Lizzie cheered up and deemed it as good a dinner as she'd ever served at the vicarage. Instantly, she felt Francis grab her hand under the table, and he gave her a warning glance. No, her eyes replied, there's no need to worry. I'll show moderation.

Francis spoke on her behalf as his grandfather carved the goose breast. 'Just one slice for us, thank you.' He also dished out a small potato for her, as if she couldn't serve herself.

36

While he turned his head to speak to Dickon, Mary took the chance to offload one of her own potatoes to Lizzie.

'Remember, you're eating for two,' she whispered. 'You must build up your strength. And I've yet to see Francis stint when there's pickled cabbage to be had.'

Halfway through the dinner, Thomas began to sing 'God Rest Ye Merry, Gentlemen'. Others joined in, depending on how much ale they'd quaffed, and the children sang the chorus.

Lizzie turned to see Mary's boys. So far, she'd only had dealings with John and Matthew. She didn't know the eldest one, William, but knew he was fifteen. He looked too big and out of place amongst his younger brothers and his girl cousins. Maybe he should have been allowed to sit at the main table. John seemed happy enough, though, but then he was so easy to please. As for the two youngest boys, they looked like trouble, teasing the girls by pinching food from their plates.

Suddenly the three girls joined ranks; they put their tongues out and then yelled across to their parents.

'Can we play Hoodman Blind?'

Lizzie guessed the reason—the girls could get their own back.

Thomas stood up with a grin. 'What a good idea now we've all eaten enough. Shall I go first?'

'No,' shrieked the girls in unison.

'Pick Richard here, or Matthew,' the eldest suggested.

'Alright, let's choose Richard. Matthew's too young yet.'

The main table was carried to one side, and the benches and chairs moved to the walls. Richard, aged ten, was half-dragged from his seat and stood in the space in the middle of the kitchen. Thomas put a sack over the boy's head, twirled him round five times and then danced out of the way.

Richard staggered as if drunk, his arms outstretched for balance. He hoped to catch someone and guess the name. Thomas patted him on the right shoulder and then dodged to the left.

37

Meanwhile, the girls had taken down their cloaks and tied each into a bundle with a heavy knot, ready to clout him.

Richard hardly knew what hit him. He was walloped on his behind and, before he could respond, he was battered from the front. Whichever way he turned, he was hit by one of the three girls. The spectators were helpless with laughter and, whenever he stumbled blindly towards them, Thomas yanked him back to the middle.

When Richard could not catch, let alone identify, anyone, Thomas rescued him. He pulled off the sack hood and announced he'd go next.

'I'm more experienced *and* I can take the hits.'

He should have guessed that the hired lads would take this unexpected opportunity to punish their master's son. They used their belts as well as their jackets to whip him round the room. Their sport was only curtailed when Thomas made a sudden dive to his left and fell on top of one of the hired lads.

'I think it's John Dawson.'

'No!' everyone yelled. 'It's Sammy Owt.'

Thomas leapt off and tore the sack from his head.

'I've had enough of this game,' he announced, blushing and smoothing down his shirt. He didn't want to be likened to his brother Richard who preferred lads to lasses. In a foul temper, he threw the sack into a corner.

'Get up, Sam, for God's sake. We all need better sport than this.'

His father held up his hand. 'Whoa there, Thomas, I know what sort o' games thoo'll want. If thoo's intent o' rough an' dangerous games, we should let bairns an' their mothers leave.'

'Lizzie,' Francis murmured, 'let's go as well. Stand up.'

On seeing her struggle to her feet, Mary stepped in. 'He's right. This is no place for a woman in your state. Get yourselves home.'

Lizzie was handed her cloak. She fought off the impulse to curtsy as she thanked them and bid goodnight to the Jordans. As she headed to the door with Francis guiding her by the elbow, Dickon called them back.

38

'Wait on,' he cried, 'can thoo 'elp me i' mornin'? I'll be bloodlettin' like I said.' He glanced at Thomas. "*E'll* not be up i' time an' neither will yon lads. I know thoo's sober, Francis, I can trust thee.'

Lizzie felt Francis's hand tighten on her arm. She knew he didn't want to be part of the ritual. When he hesitated, his father butted in.

'Just do it. It's time you learnt more about caring for livestock. That time in Rudston's spoilt you.'

It wasn't the time to argue. On the doorstep, Francis accepted the offer of a lantern. He soon found it wasn't needed for the snow had settled a couple of inches deep, and the white ground showed up clearly in the moonlight.

Lizzie held on to Francis and trod carefully through the yard to the main street. Tonight, there'd be hardly any fire left in their hearth and there'd be no hot stone to warm their bed.

Chapter 7

Early next morning, as Francis was coaxing the fire into life, he heard a rap on the back door. He opened it to find his brother William knocking the snow from his boots.

'Is anything the matter?'

'Father's sent me. I'm to help you and Dickon—you know... the bloodletting.'

Francis had forgotten for the moment and his heart sank. 'Wait here a minute while I tell Lizzie. She'll have to see to the fire, and *we'd* better have breakfast at Uphall.'

More snow had fallen during the night and William, with his lopsided walk, had a difficult tread through the deeper drifts at the bottom of the village. As they reached the church higher up the hill, they found that the northeast wind had blown much of the snow to one side. Already, the hired lads were shovelling it from the Uphall yard, resting every so often to get their breath back.

'Serves them right,' muttered Francis as he strode past them to the outbuildings. 'They're not up to it. They ate and drank far too much yesterday.'

They found Dickon waiting for them, standing beside one of the oxen, its coat steaming in the frosty air. He held a sack in one hand and a wooden-handled blade in the other.

'Now then, Francis, go an' ask thy gran'mother for a pan of 'ot ashes fro' fire.'

While waiting for his brother, William picked up the wooden club by Dickon's foot. 'Can I have a go? I think I know what to do.'

'Nay, lad. Thoo can catch blood i' yon pail. It's a shame thy uncles aren't up yet for I've 'eard, if thoo drinks it fresh, it clears thy 'ead. I've 'eard it tastes sweet—never tried it meself.'

As soon as Francis returned with the ashes, Dickon put the sack over the ox's head. 'I've tied 'im up, but if I do it right, 'e won't know owt about it. Francis—'old 'im just i' case.'

40

William stood by the ox's neck, ready with the pail.

Dickon held the small triangular blade above the jugular vein, and William passed him the club.

'Watch an' learn. I'm goin' to drive this blade in with a quick sudden jab fro' this club.' He did it as he spoke.

Francis flinched, yet the ox hardly moved as blood spurted out.

When the pail was half-full, Dickon called for the ashes. He smeared the warm ash onto the wound and staunched the flow of blood.

'Thoo *can* use mud, but I prefer ashes.'

William peered into the dark, thick liquid. Already a film was growing over the surface.

'Go on Will, take it to kitchen. They'll be waitin' for it. Thy gran'mother's goin' to make black puddin'. Maids 'ave been busy choppin' onions an' siftin' oatmeal.'

Francis stared into the distance, feeling superfluous. He could have been at home having a leisurely breakfast with Lizzie. As he waited for William's return, he watched Dickon examine the other oxen, stroking their hides to assess their condition. He decided to speak up, to challenge Dickon on his old ways.

'You know, in Rudston, they used leeches. A woman would come round and bleed the animals for us.'

'Aye, I've 'eard o' cow-leeches. Why pay a lass to do it, though, when thoo can do it thassen?'

'In Rudston, they have a shed for the oxen. They're kept in stalls in winter. They're kept warm and dry.'

'Aye,' Dickon pondered, chafing the stubble on his face, 'that's all very well, but if they're inside all time, their 'ides grow thin. An' if we keep 'em indoors over much, they'll feel cold when we let 'em out i' spring. Nay, it's best if they can go out, then they'll 'ave thicker skins.'

Francis hadn't finished. 'Do you feed them nettles? In Rudston, the cattle are given a handful to stop their skin flaking off—and it makes their coats glossy.'

Dickon cocked his head to one side. 'Oh, aye?' he said with more interest. 'I'll try owt.'

41

When William returned with the emptied pail, Dickon continued with the bloodletting.

Francis hated the business; it brought back memories of the bull baiting in Bridlington. Always squeamish at the sight of blood, the sight still haunted him as did the time when he'd witnessed men fighting in the street, knocking each other's teeth out. He declined Dickon's offer to bleed the last beast, and was disgusted to see his brother jump at the opportunity. William almost drooled at the prospect.

William saw the task as a useful skill for the future; with any luck, one day, he'd be in charge of the oxen. Keen to promote his chances, he ordered Francis to hold the pail while he took the blade and club from Dickon. With a great show of confidence, he tapped in the blade. As the blood shot out, he showed off his knowledge, 'It's true, isn't it, Dickon, that cattle put on weight if we bleed them?'

'Aye, it does 'em good. Francis! Watch what tha's doin' wi' that pail. Don't spill it.'

William winked at Dickon. 'Perhaps Francis would prefer looking after the sheep.' He smirked as he added, 'He's always liked knitting.'

Francis did not rise to the bait. He gripped the pail tightly and clenched his teeth. *I'm older now,* he told himself. *I'm married and will soon be a father. My brother shouldn't still be able to provoke me like this.*

As Dickon staunched the flow of blood, so the tension between the brothers subsided. The job finished, they went to the house, took off their boots and padded into the kitchen with the last pail of blood.

Dorothy Jordan was by the hearth giving orders to the maids. She gestured with her head towards the table where slices of cold goose lay heaped on a platter. There was also a dish of leftover stuffing and a large pot of pickled cabbage.

''Elp thassens. Lasses'll bring ale, an' there's a bit o' plum puddin' left if tha wants.'

William was the first to sit down and begin, stretching across the table with his knife to stab a thick slice of goose. 'Where's Grandfather?' he asked as he reached for the stuffing.

4 2

''E'll be down soon. This cold weather, 'e takes longer to get goin'.'

'Is Uncle Thomas still in bed?'

'Aye, 'e's not settin' a good example. Just as well Christmas is only once a year.'

They all turned as the door opened. They watched old Francis Jordan shuffle in, make straight for the fire to warm his hands and then stand with his back to the heat.

'That's better,' he said as he massaged his behind. 'I trust thoo's finished out there?'

With a stiff back and knees, he eased himself into his chair, and then asked the maid to stick a hot poker in his ale. As he cupped his drink in two hands, the bracket clock on the wall struck eight o'clock. He pulled a long face and surveyed the food on the table.

'Time's passin',' he moaned. 'Another Christmas, another year nearly gone. I won't be 'ere forever.' He stared at Francis and William. 'It'll be up to likes o' thee one day to see to Up'all.'

Dickon echoed his sentiments. 'Aye, we're not gettin' any younger.'

Dorothy Jordan butted in. 'Enough o' such talk. Why, thoo can still show these lads a thing or two.'

The older men settled down to their breakfasts, hoping Dorothy was right. They still had a few good years left, God willing.

Afterwards, when Dorothy was alone in the kitchen with her husband, she finally voiced what she'd bottled up for weeks.

'That Francis of ours should never 'ave wed so fast. They that wed before they're wise, it's said they'll die before they thrive.'

'Oh, Dorothy, don't be so miserable. Francis 'as been a good lad, an' these things do 'appen.'

'It never 'appened with us. Why, we 'ad bundlin' in our day, an' it worked fine. It's what we all did when courtin'. Many a time we laid i' bed, two of us, me wi' me feet tied together, an' thoo wrapped up in a separate blanket.'

4 3

He chuckled at the memory. 'Aye, it makes me feel young again to think back. Come 'ere, lass, leave what tha's doin' an' 'ave a kiss.'

'Get away—thoo's an old fool an' thoo needs a shave.' Nevertheless, she leant down and they kissed on the lips. 'We don't need mistletoe, do we?'

Chapter 8

1728

As Lizzie's time drew near, both she and Francis were content to just kiss and cuddle each night before sleeping. She suffered from indigestion and sometimes her ankles were swollen. Towards the end of January, she had a sudden surge of energy and began an early spring clean.

When Mary visited and saw her washing the windows and then sweeping the yard, she nodded wisely and said it wouldn't be long.

Two days later, straight after breakfast, Lizzie had her first labour pains. Francis, instead of leaving for work, ran through the lightly falling snow to his mother's, his heart beating so fast he felt sick.

As soon as he'd blurted out the news, his mother smiled and shook her head. She'd never seen her son so jittery.

'Calm down, Francis, you've plenty of time to get the midwife. Take a horse from Uphall and, when you get to Hunmanby, ask at the grocer's—the woman lives nearby. And don't worry—it'll be hours yet before there's a child. I'll go now and stay with Lizzie.'

As soon as he'd gone, Mary loaded a basket with candles, linen, sugar and spices. She chose her son John to accompany her, and they set off. Once at the house, she sent John to bring his aunt Elizabeth and the blacksmith's wife.

'Oh and tell Martha to bring her ale—tell her what it's for.'

He ran off, excited at the prospect of seeing a baby born; he wondered if it was like having piglets.

While waiting for John's return, Mary did her best to reassure Lizzie.

'I know it can be frightening your first time, but you'll have plenty of help.' How she wished, though, that Sarah Ezard was still alive to see to the deliveries. When Mary had first given birth, she'd also relied on the vicar's wife who'd had nine of her own. Poor Lizzie had to make do with the midwife from Hunmanby. Mary remembered the last time she'd seen that woman attend. The midwife had told such outlandish tales of the births of beasts and half-human monsters that Mary shivered at the recall. She tried to forget such images and concentrate on the here and now.

'I'll make some raspberry tea, Lizzie. It helps ease the pain.'

Lizzie shook her head and paced round the table once more, and then up and down the kitchen.

'Alright then, I could rub your back instead.'

Lizzie nodded and smiled. The pains came about every fifteen minutes and were more of an ache, easily borne.

As soon as Elizabeth Storey and Martha Wrench arrived, John was sent out to fetch water.

'Fill every bucket you can find, and any empty pans and jugs. Off you go. And,' Mary held him back with a warning, 'when you've finished, stay in the kitchen, do you hear?'

He nodded his head numerous times and ran out. It was exciting. The sheep often had twins, and the sow at Uphall sometimes had nine piglets.

Martha Wrench had brought a small cask of ale. She poured it into a pot and added Mary's sugar and spices, stirring well. Then she hung it over the fire to warm up.

'It's me golden tansy brew.' She winked at Lizzie. 'Thoo'll need it, believe me.'

'No—Francis wouldn't like me drinkin'. I don't think I should 'ave any.'

Martha tossed her head back in disgust. ''E's not givin' birth!'

Mary stopped rubbing Lizzie's back. 'Listen, it will help. Take whatever's offered.'

As if on cue, a sudden cramp seized Lizzie's womb. She gasped and clutched the edge of the table.

'Breathe out slowly, Lizzie, that's what I used to do. Does it feel like you've a belt round you, tightening up? It always felt like that with me.'

46

Elizabeth looked on, wringing her hands. She had no idea what labour pains were like, but had been present at enough births to know they could be severe.

Martha tested the ale with a finger and lifted the pot from the fire. 'Do try an' drink it,' she urged. 'We're goin' to 'ave some—it's custom.'

Lizzie shook her head and, as the pains increased, her eyes welled with tears and she bit her lip. Still, she didn't cry out.

The three women watched, helpless.

Mary poured out a mug for herself and one for Lizzie. 'There—you can take a sip or two. Just try it.'

'Aye,' Martha echoed, rolling her eyes, 'get it down thee.'

Lizzie began to sip the drink and, as time passed, she took larger mouthfuls. The warmth and sweetness were a welcome comfort and distraction.

John came and went delivering water, and they waited patiently for the midwife. It took them all by surprise when Lizzie's waters broke. Elizabeth was the first to cry out in alarm.

'Quick, get her off the mat!'

Mary glared at her sister, and then spoke quietly to Lizzie. 'Never mind the mat. Come on Lizzie—it's time you were in bed. I'll change your mattress and put the straw one on.' She went into the parlour with a lighted candle and closed the curtains.

Lizzie followed meekly with Elizabeth while Martha stayed in the kitchen with John. She reminded him on no account whatsoever was he to enter the parlour.

'But will I see them afterwards?' he asked.

'Of course, silly—tha mother an' aunt won't be i' there forever.'

'Perhaps there'll be two or more.'

Martha blinked. She didn't know what he was talking about.

At that moment, Francis arrived with the midwife. His mother put her head out of the parlour door and told him to go to Uphall and stay there.

'Lizzie's doing fine. We'll send a message later.'

4 7

The midwife waddled into the kitchen and, without a word, dumped her bag on the table. She removed her thick cloak and mittens, shook the snow off them and then warmed her hands by the fire.

'I'll 'ave a mug o' that ale,' she said to Martha. 'It's freezin' out yonder.'

Only when she'd finished her drink did she grab her bag and venture into the parlour. She stood proudly in the doorway.

'There's not much furniture in 'ere,' she announced with a sniff. 'Where's bairn goin' to be put? I can't see any drawers or owt else.'

Mary put her right. 'The crib's at my house. We'll fetch it after.' She remembered the loss of her own first two children, and didn't want to tempt fate by bringing the crib too soon. Her own marriage had been blighted by the deaths; she didn't want the same for Francis and Lizzie.

The midwife saw Lizzie lying in bed, pale and trying not to cry. She took a bottle of belladonna from her bag.

''Ere lass, take a drop or two o' this. It'll 'elp tha pain.'

Lizzie turned her head away as the midwife offered a spoonful. 'I won't take it. Me pain is what us women must bear. It's our lot i' life. Take it away.'

Mary shook her head, a tear in her eye. 'Oh, Lizzie.'

'Right then,' snorted the midwife, 'I'll see 'ow far thoo's got.' She lifted Lizzie's skirt and examined her. 'Won't be long. Thoo's young an' broad about beam. Thoo'll do fine.' She put her head round the door and ordered Martha to make sure the water was ready.

Lizzie began to cry out in pain. When there was hardly time to recover between spasms, the midwife told her to kneel and face the bedhead.

'Grab onto end o' bed. Not long now. Bairn's strugglin' to be out.'

Mary stood by Lizzie's head. 'You can hold my hand if it helps.'

Lizzie declined the offer and clung tight to the bedhead. 'I want to push. Shall I push? Oh, God!' She took a huge breath and pushed.

4 8

The midwife saw Lizzie's bloodshot eyes. 'Steady, lass!' Don't force so 'ard.' But already she could see the tip of a dark head appear between Lizzie's thighs.

'It's coming,' whispered Elizabeth, enthralled as ever by the prospect of a new member of the family. She leant forward for a better view as a baby girl emerged, covered in downy black hair that looked soft as a kitten.

Mary wiped her eyes on her apron. 'I'm a grandmother.'

'Fetch water then, someone,' the midwife snapped. As Elizabeth went to the kitchen, the midwife smacked the little girl to make her cry. Then she told Mary to hold the baby while she helped Lizzie turn and lie on her back.

Mary gulped and wanted to cry, overwhelmed by the birth of a granddaughter. It would have been so special if young Mary had lived to be a mother.

When Elizabeth returned with a large basin of warm water, the baby was washed and the cord cut. As soon as the baby was swaddled up tight, she was passed to Lizzie.

Mary, still in a daze, watched as the child was put to the breast. 'Don't worry, Lizzie, it'll help your milk to come through, as well as the afterbirth. I had trouble once, so do what we say.' When she saw that Lizzie's breast began to ooze a clear liquid, she relaxed. 'I'll tell John to fetch that crib. No, I'll go with him. It's heavy and awkward. He can't carry it by himself.'

Mary needed to be alone and in the fresh air. She hoped that William would be equally delighted, though a granddaughter was no substitute for their Mary.

John padded home with her in silence, holding her hand and responding to her feelings much like a pet dog. As they approached the house, he stopped.

'Are you sure there was just one baby? Dickon says if you wait a bit, more come out.'

'No, John, I'm sorry—just the one, but you'll love her.'

When they returned with the old family crib, she told John to run to Uphall and tell Francis the good news. She entered the parlour to find Lizzie had already been washed. The soiled mattress had been taken out, the mess cleaned up, and lavender had been strewn on the floor. The parlour no longer smelled of blood, and the baby was fast asleep in the crook of Lizzie's arm. All was peaceful and quiet. Even the midwife looked satisfied.

Mary took the baby and laid her in the crib. She nudged it gently with her toe and set it rocking so that the dark oak panels, almost black with age, shone in the candlelight. It was years since last used. So many Jordans had started life in that very crib. Now, there was another generation. She smiled at Lizzie.

'You rest now. We'll let you sleep. I'll make you some porridge later.'

The women left the parlour and stood about the kitchen. There were only two chairs so the midwife took one, and Mary bade Elizabeth take the other. Martha poured out more of her special ale, and the women drank in silence for a while.

All of a sudden, the midwife tilted her mug to get the last drops. Then she wiped her mouth on her sleeve.

'There, that's better.' She belched and held out her mug to be refilled. 'Good job it were a lass delivered an' not a rabbit.'

'Don't start,' Mary muttered under her breath. 'I remember you telling me all sorts the last time you were in Reighton—women giving birth to bits of rabbits… and eels.'

'Well,' the midwife huffed, 'I bet thoo doesn't know about that woman who 'ad as many as *nine* rabbits.' She paused while they took this in. 'Aye, nine, an' all delivered by a man-midwife i' space of a week. It were somewhere down south… Every one of 'em died, though.'

Elizabeth pursed her lips. 'I don't believe it.'

'It's true—was written i' papers. An' one woman gave birth to three legs of a cat. I'm told it were a tabby. Aye, an' a rabbit's leg an' all.' She leant across the table and lowered her voice as if confiding a secret. 'Thoo knows it's dangerous to fondle a pet while thoo's wi' child—or dream of a beast. Bairn can change an'—'

Mary had had enough. She slammed down her mug. 'What drivel! William told me that rabbit woman was a cheat.

50

She'd pushed bits up inside her. I think she even went to trial. She's probably in prison.'

The midwife shrugged. 'Believe what tha likes.' She tapped her nose. 'I've seen an' 'eard stranger stuff.'

'No,' Mary interrupted. 'I thank you for your help today.' She put a hand into her pocket. 'There's a shilling for your trouble. Francis will give you more after the baptism. When he comes, he'll have someone ride you back to Hunmanby.'

The midwife took the money and stood up. 'I know when I'm not welcome. It's cold, but I can walk to Up'all an' be on me way.' With that, she finished her ale and left.

Elizabeth cheered. 'Good riddance! Do you know, Mary, while you were fetching the crib, she tried to rid Lizzie of the afterbirth. She told me she was going to go up inside her "an' scrape it out"—that's what she said—"scrape it out." I told her to stop and wait. Thank God it all came away after a few minutes.'

'To be fair,' Martha said, 'she did rub 'er 'ands with oil first.'

Chapter 9

Francis arrived at the cottage with John, his heart thumping. He found his mother and Aunt Elizabeth sitting at the kitchen table, and the place stank of ale. He stood, hat in hand, his feet frozen to the spot.

John stared at him. 'Don't you want to see the baby?'

'Go on, Francis,' his mother urged, 'you're a father now. Get yourself into that parlour and congratulate Lizzie. She did a fine job.' Seeing John about to follow, she called him back. 'Sorry, not you, John. Leave Francis and Lizzie on their own.'

Francis tiptoed into the curtained parlour, lit by the one candle. Both Lizzie and the baby were asleep. Taking the candle, he peered into the crib to see a miniature face, a perfect yet tiny nose and pink lips, the rest of her swaddled tightly and out of view. His daughter was beautiful, and the room was so peaceful. God had shown mercy on his failings. He brushed away a tear and swallowed with difficulty. Full of humility, he knelt to pray.

Lizzie woke to hear the end of his prayer, a vow to honour the teachings of the Bible and to praise God in both his work and leisure.

'Amen, Francis.'

'Oh, Lizzie, I've woken you. I'm sorry.'

'Don't be. Come 'ere.'

He got up and approached the bed, took her proffered hand and kissed the palm.

'What does tha think o' tha daughter?'

'She's lovely—like you.'

'I don't feel lovely. I've been well looked after, though, an' our bairn's already taken me milk.'

Francis frowned. This was good news, yet he wasn't prepared to know details. 'I'll let you get more sleep. You know I'll be spending the next month with my family, but I'll

52

visit as often as I can.' Suddenly, reflecting on the baby's size, he realised the importance of an early baptism; his daughter's soul might be in jeopardy.

'Listen, Lizzie, I'll arrange for her to be christened as soon as possible. It's Sunday tomorrow, so I'll see the vicar.'

He kissed her hand once more, bade goodbye and took another peek inside the crib on his way out. He could scarcely believe he was a father.

'You haven't stayed long,' his mother complained.

'I'll visit again tomorrow to let her know about the baptism.'

'I'll stay the night here,' offered Elizabeth. 'Mary, you go home now with John. I'm happy to stay all week.'

Mary frowned, bit her lip yet said nothing.

Francis turned to his aunt. 'What about Uncle Robert? What will *he* say about that?'

Elizabeth sighed. 'I'll tell him my plans later. It's not often I get the chance to nurse a newborn.'

Mary picked up her things and pointed John towards the door. 'Come on, we're leaving.'

'But I haven't—'

'Shush—we must let your aunt Elizabeth get on, mustn't we?'

The baptism was on Tuesday. There was a brief lull in the weather; the snow flurries had died away and the sky was clear though the ground remained frozen. Francis hurried to the church with his aunt, she carrying the baby muffled up like a precious parcel. They met Robert at the gate who gave them a rare smile, obviously delighted to be chosen as a godparent. The only ones expected to be present were the vicar, the churchwardens and family members.

Francis's mother met him with other Jordans at the church door. They'd missed out certain old customs at the birth, and she feared for the child. She held Francis back as William and the boys filed past into the church.

'Sarah Ezard,' she chuntered, her breath steaming in the cold air, 'she used to mark the corners of my cottage with a

5 3

cross, and she said a special prayer. *And* there was a witch-bottle under the hearth.'

'Yes, Mother,' he replied politely, 'but they didn't prevent the deaths of your first two children, did they?'

'No... but then I made your father carve a witch-mark on the kitchen beam. That made all the difference.'

'I prefer to place my trust in the Lord, but I thought you always said *I* survived because of some lucky coin you were given.'

'That's right. Yes, I got it from the Scottish pedlar. And here, look at you now—a father.'

He shook his head. There was no point arguing; she'd always cling to her superstitions. He led her to the family pew and, as he turned back to walk to the font, he overheard her reprimanding his brother William.

'And stop that scowling before you start,' she hissed at him. 'You've only had Francis at home with us for three nights. There's another twenty or more, so get used to it.'

Young William hadn't replied. It was true, though, Francis realised; he'd be at his old home for the whole of February.

Just then, his grandparents entered late, each carrying a cushion.

'We're too old to be sittin' o' cold pews,' his grandmother explained. 'We don't want to end up wi' piles. I 'ope thoo's fastened a witch-brooch to bairn's christenin' sheet.'

'No, I haven't, and neither has Elizabeth. Please, keep your voice down or Robert will hear.'

The baptism began as soon as the vicar arrived from Filey and changed into his surplice. John Sumpton stood by the font with the godparents, and read the service.

Robert Storey, stiff as a statue, focussed his eyes proudly on a distant beam in the roof. A smug smile broke out on his face; the words of the baptism could have been his own.

'Grant that all carnal affections may die in her,' the vicar chanted as he gazed towards the baby, 'and that all things belonging to the spirit may live and grow in her.'

'Amen,' said Robert and the churchwardens.

'Amen,' echoed the rest.

54

'Grant that she may have power and strength to have victory, and to triumph against the Devil, the world, and the flesh.'

'Amen,' said Robert with loud conviction.

The vicar asked for the child's name.

'Dorothy,' Francis murmured, and the baby was handed over.

The vicar was about to dip his hand into the font when he noticed a film of ice on the surface. Undeterred, he tapped it with his knuckle and proceeded to sprinkle water on the girl's forehead.

The baby wailed as the sign of the cross was made, and she was duly welcomed into the Christian faith.

Robert had not been a godparent before. He seemed to grow in height as he pledged to teach the little girl the Creed, the Lord's Prayer and the Ten Commandments. He gave a slight nod in Francis's direction as if to say, *You can trust me. I'll do my best for the good of her soul.*

It being a Tuesday, work took precedence over any celebrations. There were just brief glimpses at the baby girl before the Jordans went their separate ways and Elizabeth took her back home to Lizzie.

Mary noticed the disappointment on John's face. 'Never mind,' she whispered, taking his hand, 'there'll be plenty of time to see more of her.'

Late in the afternoon, Lizzie had a visit from Francis. She was sitting up in bed, and told him she'd soon be allowed to get up and sit in a chair.

'Elizabeth's been wonderful. She does ev'rythin' fo' me— ev'rythin'. An' she says she'll stay as long as I want.'

Francis felt superfluous. Although he talked about the baptism, the child didn't need him, and Lizzie seemed perfectly content without him, happier even, with her female company. He rocked the crib while Lizzie spoke of Elizabeth's plans for the spring, all the jobs they could do together.

Suddenly, the baby woke and began to cry.

'Don't be frightened, Francis. She's only wantin' me milk.'

55

'I'd better leave now,' he said, excusing himself. 'It's getting dark and my father wants me to help teach my brothers.'

He kissed her gently on the cheek and then lingered, thinking about a longer kiss on the lips, but Elizabeth popped her head round the door.

'Come on, Lizzie, you'd best feed her again.'

He left them to it, and trudged out of the house and up the lane, his hands thrust deep into his coat pockets. Even at his old home, he didn't feel too welcome. His brother William barely spoke to him after giving up his bed and having to share a truckle bed with John.

As soon as Francis opened the door, John flew towards him and pulled him to the kitchen table. The boys had already begun their evening lesson, sitting on the benches at each side with their father at the head.

'Francis,' his father ordered, 'take John and Matthew. Sit by the fire with the sand tray and get them to practise their letters. I'm struggling enough here with these two.'

Young William and Richard glowered. They'd rather be writing letters in the sand as it was much harder to use pen and ink.

'What's the matter?' their father demanded. 'It was you, Will, who wanted to learn. Come on, look what you're doing. I bet Ann Smith's tutor doesn't have this trouble.'

Young William sulked. He knew that Ann's other possible suitors could write. Stephen Jefferson, for one, was ten years older, so was well ahead; worse still, the man had an ailing father and would soon be a yeoman in his own right. With a deep sigh, he gripped his pen and copied the words his father had written, all to do with the names of fields and various crops.

'I bet Ann Smith writes better things,' he grumbled with his head down. 'I bet she's allowed to write letters to people, or copy out songs.'

'When you can write well enough to be a yeoman, then you can choose what to write—not before. Now get on with it.'

Francis wondered why his brother should be so concerned about Ann Smith; surely, William wasn't thinking to woo his

56

cousin. He smoothed out the dampened sand in the tray and gave each of his brothers a stick to practise writing their names. The kitchen was quiet apart from the scratching of pens and the rapid click of their mother's knitting needles.

After another half an hour, when the boys began to fidget and make careless mistakes, their mother announced it was bedtime.

Francis stayed up while his brothers retired. Instead of lighting a pipe, he asked his mother for wool and needles.

'I'd like to knit something for little Dorothy.'

'Alright, but it's late—leave it for tonight. And don't worry, Francis, I've already been busy knitting caps and another shawl.' She added with a grimace, 'So has your aunt Elizabeth.'

Deflated, he stared into the fire, the embers low like his mood.

His father had an idea. 'Why don't you carve a toy for her?'

'Maybe.' He recalled his previous attempt at a carving for Milcah and sighed. 'I think I'll go to bed.'

'Most men are pleased to be a father. I don't know what's wrong with you.'

'I am pleased.'

'You don't look it.'

Mary put down her knitting. 'Leave him alone, we're all tired. As I remember, you found your gander months hard, William. We women have the best of it. It can't be easy for him to be apart from Lizzie.'

Francis couldn't explain his mixed feelings, didn't understand them himself. When he climbed into bed, he offered up a silent prayer for guidance.

Chapter 10

Francis visited Lizzie each day, though he never stayed long for Elizabeth was caring for his wife more than adequately. Once Lizzie was out of bed and doing light chores in the kitchen, he visited even less. On the days when he did call in, he felt an intruder. As he scraped his boots outside, he could hear the women chatting and laughing, yet the moment he stepped into the kitchen, they were quiet.

He began to spend more time with Robert instead. His uncle, rather than regret Elizabeth's absence, was enjoying a hermit-like existence, eating small, simple meals and spending each evening in reading and meditation.

On the first day of March, the gander month was over. Francis returned that evening to a home overtaken by the needs of the child. There were buckets full of dirty cloths, soaking and smelling rank and, when he kissed his wife, he caught a whiff of sour milk.

'How often do you change her wraps?' he enquired.

'Twice a day.'

'What—only twice?'

'I was told if thoo washes bairns over much, it robs 'em o' their nourishin' juices.'

He kissed her on the cheek and then sat at the table, pushing away the pile of sewing. Wherever he looked, there were signs of women's work, baskets of knitting, balls of yarn and ribbons.

Lizzie stirred the contents of the frying pan and dished up their supper. It was his favourite—salted pork with onions and fried potato. She placed the jar of pickled red cabbage by his hand.

'Thank you.'

Humbled by her thoughtfulness, he raised his head and saw her deep brown eyes, so soft and shining with happiness. He looked forward to feeling her body close to his,

58

but as soon as she'd eaten her supper, she left the table and went to the crib. She took out the baby and sat by the fire to feed her.

A chill came over him. Why, he couldn't fathom. To see a mother put her child to breast was the most natural thing in the world, yet he averted his eyes, confused. He wanted to escape, and hated himself for being so cold-hearted. Was he jealous of the baby? Did he want Lizzie to be just a wife and not a mother? He didn't know, but something was upsetting him and making him anxious about going to bed.

When it was time to retire, Lizzie asked Francis to move the crib into the parlour, to place it at her side of the bed so she could reach Dorothy during the night. After another brief feed, she placed the baby in the crib and began to undress. She'd been told that a man's seed could sour her milk, yet Mary had said it was an old tale and had certainly not been true for her. Now, after more than a month of abstinence, and little affection from Francis, she was eager to be loved.

She climbed into bed, warmed by the heated stone, and waited for him.

He walked in carrying a candle, and placed it carefully on the floor before undressing. Then he eased himself into the bed and lay on his back.

She turned to him, her heart thudding. 'Francis, I'm so glad you're back home.' She put one arm across him and laid her head on his chest.

He didn't respond.

She raised her head. 'What is it?'

'Nothing.'

She'd been so looking forward to being held tight, enjoying his kisses and feeling him inside her once again. 'Don't you want me?'

He turned his head away.

'Please kiss me.'

'I have done.'

'That was o' me cheek.'

'Listen, if we start kissing, it'll only lead to one thing and I don't think we should do it yet.'

59

'But I feel alright. We can be careful. I'm ready.'

'Well I'm not. Leave it a while longer. Let's just be thankful for what we have and praise God for his mercy.' He gave her a peck on the cheek. 'Now, turn over and let's get some sleep. I've ploughing to do tomorrow.'

She returned his brief kiss. 'I'm sorry, Francis, maybe thoo's right. We can wait.' She turned over and cried in silence, her tears wetting the embroidered pillow.

In the middle of March, the signs of spring affected even Francis. The blackthorn was in flower, and the very air he breathed made him want to assert his youth and good health. Finally, he succumbed to Lizzie's charms. The experience was so good after the long abstinence that he lay awake afterwards and worried for the state of his soul. Like his uncle Robert, he saw danger in such wild pleasure; perhaps he should curb his appetite. He'd explain his predicament to Robert.

One afternoon, as Francis and the other workers left the top field, he caught up with Robert. He didn't waste any time telling him of his temptations.

'I feel I could drown in Lizzie's brown eyes. They're so soft and welcoming. I've tried blowing the candles out, but she likes to leave one burning to see to the child.' Exasperated, he added, 'God knows I've *tried* to be temperate… and prayer doesn't always help either.'

After a long silence, Robert answered. 'I do have some sympathy. I was lucky, though. I was much older than you when I married. I've not had the same temptation.'

'Lizzie's desire seems to have no bounds.'

Robert stopped and held Francis by the arm. 'So now's the time to take control, before you're lost too.'

'How?'

'Pray for the strength to resist. Put your soul first.'

Francis walked on, not at all convinced. 'Alright, I'll try to pray harder.'

When prayer failed again, Francis compromised. It had worked before the child was born. He maintained the physical side of his marriage, but only enjoyed his wife on alternate

60

nights. To avoid temptation, he tried not to be drawn into too much kissing and cuddling as Lizzie never seemed to get enough. He made love to her in a workmanlike manner, never taking longer than necessary, never lingering. He also avoided gazing into her eyes. Before long, their time in bed assumed certain routines that never altered.

Lizzie acquiesced. What she received from Francis was better than nothing. There were many times, though, especially in the evenings, that she hoped for more attention, more kisses. She'd loved that look in his eyes when they were first married, how he'd adored her and been so grateful for their life together. Now, whether they'd made love at night or not, she found herself distracted the next day by thoughts of what might have been.

Elizabeth, ever available to help, often noticed Lizzie staring blankly through the window.

'Cheer up, lass. What you need is to be out in the garden. We'll dig over that patch of soil and then we can sow seeds for herbs.'

'Sorry, Elizabeth, thoo's right. It's just... I don't think Francis loves me as much as before.'

Elizabeth coughed in embarrassment. She felt for Lizzie, but she was hardly the person to help with such matters.

'Well, it's early days,' she said, and then talked again of the garden. 'We'll get shallots from Uphall and seeds for cabbages and carrots. And listen, we can sow half the carrots now and the rest in May. That way, you'll have young carrots to eat in summer, and I'll show you how to store the later ones over winter.' She winked. 'And I believe eating them helps you in bed—you might get Francis to give you another child next year.'

Lizzie winced. If Elizabeth had tried carrots with Robert, they hadn't worked.

On March 25th, Mary stood by the pond, arms folded, to watch the annual move of the sheep from the common moor. She stared at her son's cottage opposite. Sure enough, Lizzie soon emerged, accompanied as usual by Elizabeth. The pair

6 1

crossed the road to join her, Lizzie with the baby swaddled and strapped to her chest.

'Mind!' warned Mary. 'There's a cold breeze. You must keep her warm.' Eager to show her experience, she reached over and pulled the blanket higher. She was determined that the child survive infancy, that Lizzie wouldn't suffer as she had done. 'And make sure you keep her eyes covered when she's outside. Even indoors, you must keep her away from the windows.'

Elizabeth shrugged. She'd spent more time with Lizzie, and she was confident of the new mother's ability and common sense.

'Lizzie's quite capable. Look at her, Mary—she's born to be a mother. And she has enough milk for two children.'

Mary didn't argue and, as the last sheep trotted past, she saw her son John bringing up the rear.

He waved as he approached, a huge grin on his face, obviously delighted to help the shepherd.

'Mother, Jack says I can help with lambing this year.'

'Good. That's nice.'

'Can I see Dottie before I go?' He stopped, put his face close to the baby and then began to sing softly.

> *Lavender's blue, dilly, dilly,*
> *Lavender's green,*
> *When I am King, dilly, dilly,*
> *You shall be Queen.*

Then, all of a sudden, he kissed her cheek and ran off to follow the sheep.

Mary sighed and turned to Elizabeth. 'Poor lad, I think it's best if he takes up shepherding. It might be the making of him. He's never going to be able to run a farm himself.'

'I thought you were teaching him to read and write?'

'Yes, but even the youngest two outshine him. No, it's best he helps with the sheep.'

As it was such a sunny day, Elizabeth suggested they take a basket each and walk to Speeton Ravine to collect violets. When Mary frowned at the idea, Elizabeth gave a good reason.

62

'Listen, Lizzie hasn't been outside the village yet, and we all need a change from our usual chores. Come on.'

They strolled up Oxtrope Lane to the cliffs, Lizzie taking time to listen to the meadow pipits warbling high over the field. Once on the cliff top, they faced a fresh breeze. Immediately, Mary shielded the baby.

Lizzie ignored the gesture and stood still to watch the cobles sailing in the distance. As they scudded through the long raking waves, she gulped in huge breaths of the salty air. It was a long time since she'd seen the sea.

They carried on walking southwards and, once they reached Speeton Ravine, they were sheltered from the wind. Many different birds flitted in the undergrowth seeking dried grasses and moss for their nests.

'It's beautiful 'ere,' Lizzie murmured, enjoying the dappled sunlight. 'I'd no idea there'd be a place like this.'

As a pair of yellow wagtails darted across the stream, she reflected on her married life. But for Francis's strange reluctance in bed, she'd have been in heaven. She sat on the mossy trunk of a fallen tree and fed her baby while Mary and Elizabeth searched for violets, well away from each other. She'd have liked to stay longer in the ravine, but there was linen to wash and dry, and a man would be coming round to collect the rent on the cottage. At least now she'd have violets to strew on the floor for any visitors.

On their way home, Mary sidled up to Lizzie. 'Didn't you say you wanted some chickens? William's going to Kilham market next week. There's a man breeds and sells them. He can get you half a dozen and a cock. You've room for them, and they can roam free and forage for themselves. Francis could build a hen house.'

Lizzie clapped her hands in delight. 'Oh, that would be perfect. Thank you, Mary. I've looked after 'em before.'

Elizabeth had reservations. 'It would depend on the breed though. You don't want any game fowl—they're used to breed cocks for cockfights. They're noisy and aggressive, and they need a lot of space.'

63

Mary stopped walking. It was annoying the way her older sister sought faults in her suggestions. 'Well,' she mumbled, 'I don't know what breed they are, but I think William would ask for the same sort I have, and the same as those at Uphall. Red Dorkings I think they call them.'

Lizzie grew excited. 'Do they 'ave dark, reddish-brown feathers? Oh, an' do they 'ave five toes?'

'Yes.'

'Then that's what we 'ad i' Rudston.'

Mary narrowed her eyes as she smiled in triumph at her sister. 'And if you're lucky, Lizzie, they'll lay over a hundred eggs.'

'I know, an' they 'ave plenty o' meat on 'em too. Oh, I can't wait.'

The pullets and a cock arrived soon after Easter. Francis, relieved to do something practical to please Lizzie, had collected driftwood and bits and pieces from the carpenter to make a substantial henhouse that stood off the ground. He tarred it to make it waterproof, and lined each box with straw. A wooden ramp led up to the doorway. He stood in the back garden with Lizzie and watched the fowl settle into their new surroundings.

'Father said they should lay two eggs a day by the end of spring. And I remember Mother making us gather shepherd's purse to feed them. It was supposed to make the yolks darker.'

'I don't know about that, but I'm goin' to dry some nettles an' then crush 'em up. I did it i' Rudston an' we were never short of eggs. I'll get Elizabeth to 'elp me.'

'She's still round here a lot, then?'

'Well, it's no surprise. She's never 'ad any children of 'er own.'

Francis sighed. He knew how often his mother visited. Were the two competing? Whatever they were up to, he was outnumbered.

64

Part Two

Youth and Old Age

Chapter 11

1728

It was dawn on a perfect spring morning in the first week of April. John's two younger brothers were to go to the newly sown fields as bird scarers while his brother William, now sixteen, was to scour the ditches with their father. John, impatient to leave the house and join the shepherd, choked down his porridge, yet he knew he must first feed the chickens and collect wood for the fire. At last, he dumped the sticks in the corner of the kitchen and leapt towards the door.

'I've finished, mother. I'm off.'

'Wait—aren't you going to tie them into faggots?'

His bright smile vanished. He stood with one hand on the door latch, the other hanging loose by his side. Torn between the lure of the shepherd and the desire to please his mother, he hopped from one foot to the other.

She hadn't the heart to keep him in. 'Oh, go on then, off you go.'

He opened the door and was halfway out before she added, 'Listen to what he tells you, and do as you're told.' As he disappeared into the passage, she shouted as an afterthought, 'And don't spend too much time visiting Dottie afterwards.'

At the back door, he rammed his feet into his boots and then sprinted to the pasture. There was a light breeze off the sea and the sky was blue. Apart from the bleating of the sheep, he heard voices in the distance, men calling out as they worked together. He grinned as he squinted into the sunshine. Today he might get to deliver a lamb.

The shepherd had already penned the ewes in groups of ten. John arrived in time to see the sheepdog leap out of the last pen.

'About time, John, I thought thoo was never comin'.'

'Sorry, Jack.'

'Never mind. All yon ewes are i' lamb. I checked their udders last week an' it's real clarty stuff came out. They'll be ready soon enough. Now, we must keep a close eye on 'em an', when any start fidgetin' an' scrapin' ground wi' their feet, then we'll move 'em into main sheepfold.'

'How long does it take for a lamb to be born? Lizzie took ages.'

Jack rubbed the bristles on his cheek. 'Ah, well, that depends. Once their bag 'as burst, it takes about 'alf an hour.'

John pulled a face. He didn't like the idea of a bursting bag.

'It's only water i' bag,' Jack explained. 'It's what lamb lives in, but if thoo sees it comin' out, thoo must tell me.'

'What—the lamb or the water?'

Jack took a deep breath, exasperated. 'Water, lad, the water. But if thoo does 'appen to see a lamb comin' out, then let me know that too.'

Jack left the boy frowning and staring hard at the ewes' bottoms. He went to set up smaller pens in the sheepfold. Just as he was adding the straw, John's uncle Thomas arrived with food for the sheep—coarse hay and a load from the pea stack. Soon, all three of them were standing by the pens, leaning idly over the hurdles, the sun now warm on their backs.

Thomas eyed up the ewes, and thought to suggest a wager. He pointed to a ewe in the far corner with a split left ear. 'I bet that one'll be first.' It was one of the Uphall flock. 'Six pence she'll be first.'

'Nay, I'm not bettin'. Thoo never stops, Tom. Why not come tonight, though, an' keep watch wi' me? They often lamb i' late evenin' or early mornin'.'

Thomas shook his head. 'It's not a job for me. I'm no shepherd. John here looks ready, though. You'll help at night, won't you, if your mother'll let you?'

John treated them to the widest of smiles, his eyes glittering at the prospect of spending the night with Jack in the sheepfold.

That evening, after supper, John was given permission to go and help the shepherd. Though it was still light, his

68

father offered him a horn lantern and suggested his brother Will go too.

'I remember, Will, you used to like working with the shepherd. You certainly took a liking to his dog.'

Young William was appalled and shook his head. 'I am *not* spending the night in a stinking sheepfold. Why, it's nothing but piss and shit, and that's even *before* the lambs are born.'

'Don't listen to him, John, you'll enjoy it. Come on, take the lantern and off you go.'

As soon as the door had closed, young William grumbled, 'And the shepherd stinks as bad as the sheep.'

Though the sheepfold was in the open air, it was sheltered from the wind, with thatch acting as a temporary roof along one side. As soon as John entered, he felt safe. The place was warm and dry, and already there were three ewes penned with their lambs. He found Jack in another pen on his knees in the straw, pulling a ewe onto her side.

'Thoo's come just i' time, John. Normally, they 'ave no trouble, don't need me at all.'

Jack pressed his knees close against the ewe's belly.

'Watch—if thoo doesn't use tha knees, she'll kick thee i' stomach, or somewhere more precious.'

John set his lantern down and let himself into the pen. He knelt beside Jack, intrigued to see him stick his hand and arm right up the ewe's bottom.

Jack soon retracted his hand. 'John—thoo 'as little 'ands. I want thee to go inside, see what *thoo* can feel.'

John took off his jacket and rolled up his shirtsleeve. Concerned only for the unborn lamb, he copied Jack and thrust in his fingers, his hand and then his forearm. It was as if his arm was trapped between tight, hot and wet walls.

'Close thy eyes, John, so thoo can attend more. Can tha feel lamb's nose an' front feet?'

After a few moments, John opened his eyes. 'Yes, they're to one side.'

'Can thoo twist 'em so they come out properly?'

69

'I'll try.' He struggled to get a grip, and managed to move the feet a little.

'Can thoo pull?'

John began to cry. 'I don't think I can do it.'

'Yes thoo can. Pull!'

'But the ewe's in pain. She's trying to get up.'

'Pull, lad, or we'll lose both of 'em.'

John gritted his teeth, closed his eyes and tugged the legs. 'I can't,' he wailed. 'I'm not strong enough.'

'Be patient then. Wait for ewe to do 'er part. She'll suddenly stiffen an' push.'

Soon, John felt the ewe tense. She strained and, with her help, he was able to draw down the lamb's front legs.

'That's it, John. I can see 'em comin'. I'll 'elp now.'

They both pulled and, all at once, the lamb fell into John's lap in a flurry of blood and mucus. He gasped at the lifeless thing.

'Is it dead?'

'It's alright, John. Watch.'

The ewe scrambled to her feet and sniffed at the lamb as Jack tore the remains of the bag from the lamb's head and cleared its nostrils. Then he pinched the lamb's ear really hard and chafed it with a clump of straw.

'See, it's breathin'. It's alive. Now, John, 'ave a tug o' one of ewe's udders—see if there's milk. Mind, though, it soon squirts out.'

John squeezed an udder and, straightaway, the milk spurted a full yard past him, missing him by inches.

Jack laughed and then put the lamb on its feet to wobble under the ewe and search for a teat. When John tried to manoeuvre the lamb nearer, Jack warned him.

'Don't 'elp lamb over much or it'll rely o' thee. Best if it suckles on its own.'

John watched the lamb stagger, but it stayed upright and managed to drink, its tail waggling furiously. 'Is that it?' he asked, wiping his bloodied hands on the straw.

'Nay, lad, we must check if there's any more lambs inside. Does thoo want to do it, or shall I?'

'Can I?'

'Well, thoo knows what to feel for. Go on then, go deeper this time, but let me 'old 'er still.' He forced the ewe up against the hurdle and held her with his knees.

She wasn't happy. She bleated and strained her neck to keep an eye on her lamb that was now tottering further away.

John worked quickly as if born for the job. When he felt nothing more inside, he smiled and pulled out his arm.

'Fetch that bucket, lad. Thoo can wash all that blood an' muck off 'er backside, an' then clean up thassen.'

'What are *you* going to do?'

'Me? I'm goin' to watch an' see she's settled, then I'll check rest o' sheep.' He noticed John eyeing the lamb's navel cord that was dangling in the straw. 'Don't fret about that— it'll dry up an' drop off after a few days.'

John stayed in the sheepfold as more lambs were born, all safely and without needing help. He sat on the clean straw in a corner with the sheepdog, keeping her quiet by stroking her ears, occasionally resting his head against her back and dozing.

At dawn, he strolled home, calling in briefly on his way to see Dottie. He popped his head through the door to check if everyone was up. When he saw that Lizzie was walking about the kitchen, holding Dottie over her shoulder, he marched in. He went straight up to the baby and whispered in her ear.

'Dottie, I've helped bring out a lamb.' He kissed her cheek. 'You're as soft as a lamb. One day I'll bring one to show you.' With that, he said goodbye, tired yet immensely pleased with himself, and rushed home for breakfast.

'Mother,' he shouted as soon as he entered the kitchen, 'I went up the sheep's bottom and saved a lamb.'

While Richard and Matthew giggled, young William slammed down his mug in protest.

'Don't you *dare* say any more. We don't want such details over breakfast.' His beer had slopped over the table. 'Now look what you've made me do. And you stink to high heaven!'

His father raised a hand to clip William round the ear. He glared at him as he spoke.

'Leave John alone. He's still learning, and he shows more interest and application in his work than some I know.'

'His breeches are filthy,' Richard commented. 'Mother'll never get them clean.'

'Yes, I will,' she declared. 'And if *you* come home once more with grass stains all down your breeches, I'll make you wash them yourself.'

No more was said, though John's brothers edged themselves further away when he sat on their side of the bench.

That evening, John returned to the sheepfold. Everything went well until one of the older ewes died while giving birth. It was one of the Uphall flock, and John watched in fear for the tiny orphan as Jack held the lamb and kept pressing its ribs. Then Jack blew into its mouth, his breath steaming in the night air. John passed him a handful of straw to dry its coat and warm it up. It seemed a miracle when the lamb shuddered and began to breathe.

'I don't think it'll live long,' Jack decided. 'Even if I get another ewe to take it on, it's over small.' He put the lamb down to see if it could stand. It waddled forwards and then collapsed.

'Can I take it home? I looked after a piglet once.'

'I don't know. Let's see if it can suckle first.' He put his finger near its mouth, and it made a weak attempt to latch on. 'Alright then, thoo can 'ave it.'

John reached up and kissed the shepherd.

'Don't be soft, lad. Thoo might regret 'avin' a pet lamb. Pass me yon bowl. I'll still be able to get some milk out o' this ewe.' He knelt by the dead ewe and pulled on her udders. 'There's a bottle an' a teat be'ind thee. Thoo can try an' get lamb to drink.'

Jack held the lamb upright on its feet while John approached with the teat. Gently, John put the teat in its mouth. At the same time, Jack massaged the lamb's jaws, moving them up and down so that the teat was squeezed. The lamb soon got the idea.

72

'Carry it 'ome under tha jacket an' keep it warm by tha fire. Give it more o' this milk ev'ry four hours an', if it lives, thoo'll 'ave to get more ewes' milk. Don't go thinkin' thoo can feed it cows' milk or it'll get squitty. Tha mother won't want runny shit all over 'er kitchen.'

John wanted to show Dottie his lamb, but it was too late in the evening and quite dark. Instead, he went home to find his brothers already in bed and his parents about to retire. The sight of the lamb ended such plans.

'Oh no, John,' his mother cried, 'don't you remember the upset over your piglet? I'm not going through that again.'

John sat in front of the fire and eased off his jacket before wrapping the lamb in it. 'Mother, it's shivering, poor thing. Feel its nose—it's soft like the inside of a bean pod.'

His father had a serious question. 'Is it a ram or a ewe? If it's a ram, it'll have to be gelded.'

John winced. He knew it was a ram and recalled the day his piglet was castrated. 'But it won't live if I don't feed it. Let me try.'

'Alright, but heed your mother. It'll lead to upset, and you'll not get much sleep. You'll have to feed it twice during the night at least.'

John gave them a smile that altered his whole face. 'Thank you. I know the lamb will survive. The Lord is my shepherd.'

'Oh, John,' his mother sighed. She foresaw only trouble ahead.

Chapter 12

In the morning, young William was the first out of bed. He noticed, while dressing, that John had not been to bed at all. Thinking that his brother was still at the sheepfold, he was shocked to find him curled up by the hearth, a bundle of something at his side. To wake him, he nudged him hard with a foot.

John stirred and rubbed his eyes. 'William, look here—I've got a lamb.' He opened his jacket to reveal what was inside.

William leant over to see. 'It's a bit small.'

'That's why I'm feeding it. Its mother died last night.'

'And our mother won't let you keep it. She won't you know. You'll have to give it up.'

John held the lamb to his chest and, as he rocked it gently, he had an idea.

'I could give it to our cousin, Ann; she's kind, and her sisters'll love it, and I bet she'll let me go and see it whenever I want.'

At the mention of Ann Smith, William knelt beside John and fondled the lamb's ears, deep in thought. A plan was taking shape.

'Listen, John,' he said after a moment, 'I could save you a lot of trouble. Let me talk to mother first and explain your idea.'

While John was outside having a wash, William sat by the lamb. He wrinkled his nose at the smell of John's jacket, wet with urine. He'd have to wash the animal and find a clean rag to carry it in and hand it over. As he rehearsed what he'd say to Ann, his mother walked in to prepare breakfast.

'Ah, so John's won you over, has he?'

'No, it stinks, but I have an idea. You don't want a pet lamb in the kitchen, do you? I think Ann and her family would love it though. I've heard you can train them,' he rambled on. 'Even her tutor would probably help. What do you think?'

She pursed her lips, convinced he was up to no good. 'Have you mentioned this to John?'

'Not yet.' He leapt up from the hearth. 'He's outside. I'll tell him straightaway.'

He found John still washing his hands, holding them to his nose every now and then before giving them another scrub.

'John, Mother says I've to take the lamb to Ann now, before breakfast. Wait here while I fetch it. You can say goodbye, and then Mother says you're to come in and have breakfast.'

John waited by the door, tears in his eyes at the thought of giving up the lamb so soon. When William emerged with it wrapped in a clean cloth, John kissed its head.

'I wanted to be its shepherd,' he sniffed, 'to lead it to green pastures and lie down by still waters.'

'Don't be daft. Say goodbye.'

John kissed its tiny nose. 'Goodbye,' he whispered, and then lifted his head. 'Ask Ann when I can visit. I'll take her the milk.'

'I will. Now get inside. Mother's waiting.'

As soon as John had gone indoors, William held the lamb by its front legs and splashed cold water over its behind. Satisfied it was a bit cleaner, he wrapped it up again and set off for the Smiths' place.

He practised aloud what to say when he arrived. He wouldn't mention John; there was no need. And he didn't feel too guilty either; their mother would never have allowed the lamb to stay. No, this was for the best. He smiled at the prospect of presenting the lamb to Ann; she'd be so pleased, so grateful. And when she nursed it, she'd think of him.

The morning mist was lifting as he entered the Smiths' yard. Suddenly, the geese spotted the intruder and hurtled towards him, honking loudly. He held the lamb above his head, away from their snapping beaks, and strode bravely through them to the back door where he knocked and waited.

Ann's mother appeared. 'Why, William, is owt wrong?'

He tried not to smile. Aunt Ellen, caught off guard, was talking like a servant. His uncle would have been ashamed.

75

'I've brought a present for Ann. Can I come in?'

She led him towards the kitchen, but asked him to wait in the passage. 'I'll see if Ann'll come out.'

After waiting a few minutes, he began to regret his impulsive decision. Perhaps it would have been better if John were there too. Everyone loved John, and Ann was always kind to him, never teasing.

Suddenly, the door opened and there she was, looking as fresh as spring. Her clean white cap, trimmed with lace, contrasted sharply with the black curls escaping beneath. His eyes were drawn to her bosom. She was almost sixteen, like him, and her breasts were beginning to push out her bodice. He thought her cheeks reddened on seeing him stare.

She arched her eyebrows. 'Well, William, what on earth have you got there?'

He cleared his throat. 'I've saved this lamb for you especially.' He lifted the cloth to show its face. 'It's an orphan. I thought it might make a good pet if you look after it.'

'Oh, poor thing, it's so small! Can I hold it?'

'Of course. It's yours now, if you want.' He handed her the bundle. 'You *will* be able to keep it?'

She winked. 'I know how to get round Father. I'll tell him the Osbaldestons used to have a pet lamb.'

'Did they?'

She pulled a face and shrugged. 'I don't know, probably not.'

'Could John come to visit? He'll bring the sheep's milk it needs. You know how he loves sheep.'

'Certainly. He's welcome any day.'

What about me? thought William. *Am I not welcome too?*

He stepped back a little, uncertain what to say next. 'I believe it'll want feeding every few hours,' he mumbled.

'You should have a pet too. Why not get yourself another dog?'

'No. It won't be the same. It won't be like Stina.'

'No… sorry.'

'Perhaps I'll come again in a few days—see how it's doing.'

She hesitated. 'Alright, but make sure my father's not around.'

76

William smiled to himself on his way out. He had the perfect excuse to visit her now as often as he wanted, with or without John.

Ann Smith, as she fully expected, was allowed to keep the lamb. Soon though, her powers of persuasion were tested again. This time, in a discussion about docking the lamb's tail, her father was adamant.

'It has to be done, Ann. Don't look at me like that—it's for its own good. A long tail will collect dirt. Worse still, the dirt attracts blowflies and then your lamb will have maggots.' When she glowered, he added, 'It might even die.'

She pouted, and then nodded in sullen agreement.

'Good,' he said, 'I'll get one of the men to do it today. It doesn't take long.'

'He won't just chop it off with a knife?'

'No, not exactly. He'll use a docking iron, I should think. The lamb won't even know what's happened, and the heat will seal the wound.'

'No, Father!' she cried as she stamped her foot. 'It's cruel. I beg you,' she pleaded, grabbing his arm, 'please don't do it. There must be another way.'

He sighed as he pulled her away. She was just like her mother, her dark eyebrows set in a determined frown, her nostrils flaring.

'Well, I suppose we could tie the tail tight—see if it drops off by itself.'

'Oh, Father, thank you.' She reached up and kissed him on the cheek before rushing back to the lamb in its basket of straw.

He didn't mention castration.

John and William visited the lamb daily, always with an excuse, either to bring more milk or to offer advice. One morning, as soon as they knew Ann's father was out, they entered by the back door and went straight to the kitchen. As usual, Ann's brothers and sisters were crowding round the basket, each vying to feed the lamb. Their mother batted them away with her hands as if shooing off flies.

77

'Thank God thoo's come,' she said to John and William. She turned to her children. 'Listen, all rest o' thee—leave lamb alone. Let John 'ave a turn now.'

When the Smith children made way, John sat cross-legged by the basket and took the lamb into his lap. A silence and calm descended. They all held their breath as John put the teat to its mouth. Gently, he rubbed the lamb's muzzle and, as it began to suck, everyone breathed out again.

While the others focussed on the lamb, William could gaze at Ann, unnoticed. Her head was tilted and her face, as she watched the lamb, was almost divine. If only she'd look at him that way. The spell lasted until the bottle emptied and the lamb struggled to stand.

'Have you given him a name yet?' John asked, still sitting by the basket and scratching the lamb's ear.

Everyone turned to Ann.

'No, I haven't. Do you have something in mind?'

John smiled and stared deep into the lamb's eyes. 'David,' he pronounced. 'David—you know, after the shepherd boy who loved his sheep.'

John continued to visit each day with milk from the ewes. As he held David in his lap, he had time to admire the white eyelashes, the soft black nose and the shiny black hooves. After each feed, he lingered, crooning to the lamb.

No one seemed to mind John's presence in the kitchen although Ann's father warned her about young William.

'I don't like John's brother coming in here getting over friendly. I don't trust him. I've seen the way he looks at you.'

When the lamb was a few weeks old, the shepherd went out of his way to speak to Matthew Smith. 'Yon lamb needs geldin' if thoo's keepin' it as a pet; it'll make it easier to manage.'

Matthew frowned. He knew his daughter would object. 'Can you do it soon then, and before anyone knows?'

'Well...' Jack scratched his unshaven chin. It sounded like a knife scraped over grit. 'Usually, we geld i' mid-June on a wanin' moon. A man comes to 'elp an' 'olds lambs down fo' me.'

'I could hold the lamb. That's not a problem.'

'An' it's best done either before or after fly season.'

'So now would be a good time, yes?'

Jack rasped his fingernails across his chin again. 'Aye, I suppose so.'

At dawn, as arranged, Jack tapped quietly on the Smiths' kitchen door. Ellen appeared and handed Jack a pewter plate; on it was a ball of butter mixed with chopped tansy leaves as per Jack's instructions.

Matthew carried the lamb, and the two men walked far away from the house in case the children heard any bleating. In a corner of the pasture, Jack put down the plate, while Matthew held the lamb tight, its legs splayed ready.

The castration was done in a moment. Jack took his sharp penknife from its sheath and, with the smallest of cuts, slit open the bottom of the scrotum. Then he used his teeth to draw out the tiny testicles. He dropped them onto the plate. As the lamb bleated more and struggled to be free, Jack smeared the butter and tansy over the wound, leaving hardly a mark to show the deed.

'There, that stuff'll keep off any flies, an' it'll soothe an' 'elp mend.'

That morning, Matthew's wife cooked him a special breakfast before the children awoke; she fried the testicles with parsley. When she dished them up, he peeled off the outer film and then popped them into his mouth. They almost melted on his tongue.

'No wonder they're such a delicacy,' he murmured in appreciation. 'Anchitricoes we used to call them. Don't tell the children.'

As young William was not welcome in the Smiths' kitchen, he had to wait until the lamb was bigger and spent more time outside. By then, the lamb had bonded so well with Ann and John that they could call David by name and he would trot towards them. William strolled into the Smiths' yard late one afternoon to find the lamb standing quite still while John poured water over its back and Ann scrubbed its fleece. The lamb's short tail was waggling with pleasure like a dog.

Ann barely acknowledged him. 'David loves this,' she explained. 'We'll take him for a walk later, won't we, John?'

John nodded and put down the empty bucket. He began stroking the lamb's face, talking to it all the while.

'There, you like this, don't you? We'll walk you down Oxtrope Lane if you like, then onto the cliffs. Then we'll find you some clover. You'll like that, won't you?'

Young William felt sick. Ann and John were ignoring him, totally absorbed by the animal. When he saw them fasten on a halter, he made an excuse to leave; the last thing he wanted was to be seen walking out with a pet sheep. He might want to be with Ann, but there were limits.

Chapter 13

The lamb survived the spring. Ann's father put up with it in the kitchen, but ran out of patience when it grew bigger and wandered about leaving puddles of urine.

'Ann, I thought you were going to train it,' he complained over the breakfast table.

'It's a 'he' and he's called David.'

'Then either wrap *his* behind in something, or *he* lives outside.'

Ann turned to her mother for support. 'You don't mind, do you?'

Her mother was torn between her children's happiness and her husband's displeasure.

'Well,' she replied, concentrating on her enunciation, 'he is making the kitchen smell, and there's more to clear up now. I don't mind picking up the dry tods, it's the other mess on the floor...'

'So,' he pronounced, 'out it—*he*—goes. You can keep him in the yard, and fence off a corner. Sheep need company. They're flock animals. What you're doing isn't natural.' He leant back in his chair and pushed away his empty plate. 'Besides, I'm thinking of having a better house built—one that certainly won't have animals in the kitchen.' He looked at his five children. 'I'm not paying your tutor for nothing. One day, you'll be gentlemen and ladies.'

Once David had been weaned, he spent the whole day outdoors either fenced within the yard or in the pasture. William had less time to visit as he was busy at Uphall or was in the fields sowing barley. Ann still ignored him whenever John was present, and he was sure she did it on purpose. The two of them would call David by name and the lamb would trot towards them for a treat, usually a bunch of clover. They'd discuss the lamb's progress, leaving him out of the conversation.

8 1

He decided she was nothing but a tease. There were five other girls in the village about his age. He'd show her.

There were three Marys, two of them a year younger, and one a year older than him. There were also two older girls—a Jane and another Ann. The only one he thought remotely pretty was Mary Huskisson.

As the family left church one Sunday, his father noticed him gazing at the girl.

'Don't bother with that one,' he advised. 'Her uncle's a wife beater. Her father, for all we know, might be as bad behind his own door.'

His mother agreed. 'You don't need to look for trouble. There are plenty more girls.'

Each Sunday, as he left church, young William chose a different girl. He hoped that at least one of them would respond to his smiles and, preferably, when Ann Smith would see. After the last failed attempt, he trailed behind his family as they strolled back down the hill. He knew he walked lopsided, and he didn't have a good reputation; he'd been known to avoid work and slope off with his uncle Thomas. He was even responsible for the death of his own dog. In despair, he kicked at the dandelions by the roadside. He knew some of the other farmers laughed at him— especially Stephen Jefferson and his yeoman friend, the big and brutish William Mainprize. Maybe he should resign himself to the fact—no one would want him. And why should they?

By the time he reached St Helen's Lane, he'd lifted his head in defiance. After all, in spite of his odd walk, he was already doing a man's work and, now that it was spring, it was a good time to start afresh. He'd work harder and show Ann and her father that he *was* a worthy suitor. Yes, he'd show her.

In May, Francis's baby girl found her arms free of the swaddling, though the rest of her body remained encased. Even Francis relaxed more in the spring sunshine as he repaired the old sty in the yard. He brought a piglet and stood with Lizzie for a while, both leaning on the wall to admire the clean, pink pig as it made itself at home. It snuffled through the fresh straw, grunting to show its pleasure.

'I love it,' Lizzie exclaimed. 'Just look at its long eyelashes an' its floppy ears.'

'Don't get too attached,' he warned. 'It's for fattening up. When the time comes, I'll take it to Uphall and *they* can deal with it. I remember facing the killings at home every November.'

'Let's not think o' that. Let's enjoy spring. Can thoo smell bluebells?'

He could. He inhaled deeply and caught the scent of hawthorn blossom too. When she put her arm round his waist, he didn't object. Instead, he turned with a smile and kissed her forehead.

During the lighter and warmer evenings, Francis responded more to Lizzie's tempting kisses. Although he continued to pray and fast, he was happy to go along with his wife's view of life. 'We were brought together by God i' marriage,' she often told him. 'Now we're 'avin' children an' carryin' out God's will.'

The beautiful spring weather didn't last. Like a fickle partner, it altered with little warning; at times it was sunny and warm, and then the skies clouded over, bringing storms. The cloudless days gave a false sense of security for the predominating weather was rain. After last year's dry summer, the soil had plenty of goodness in it, and the grass now sprang up long and lush. Jack, the shepherd, was pleased to see the new lambs thriving on the pasture.

Dickon, the old foreman at Uphall, ambled down the hill with his master to inspect the meadow. They stood there in the grass, now knee-high.

'Here's a sight,' Dickon cried. 'I've never seen it so tall.'

Neither man smiled though. They foresaw the problem of finding a dry spell of weather to make hay. Dickon pulled on his ear, deep in thought.

'We could watch oxen,' he said at last. 'When they sleep o' their left sides, it means better weather's comin'.' When Francis gave no response, he added, 'Or we could watch out fo' spiders.

83

I' wet weather they leave their nests an' roam far away. Aye, an' moles'll send up more earth.'

Francis shook his head. Such 'forecasts' were nonsense.

Everyone waited. When there was no dry period, the consensus was to mow the grass anyway, even if it rained. The rest of the village agreed. There was no choice.

On a damp July morning, the men gathered at the meadow with sharpened scythes. Dickon and his master were there to supervise, both too arthritic to help.

Thomas was complaining before they'd even started. He surveyed the meadow, shaking his head at seeing the grass lie almost horizontal in places. The wind and rain had done their worst.

'It's going to be difficult,' he grumbled. 'Look—there's not much left standing upright. And even if we manage, who's to say it won't rain and it'll be spoilt?'

It wasn't what they wanted to hear. Without hay for the winter, the animals would have to be slaughtered. The workers set to their task regardless, hoping for sunshine.

Once most of the meadow had been mown and the grass spread to dry, it did begin to rain. Despite the next few days spent forking it over and moving any dry hay under cover, a large proportion of it was ruined.

Thomas didn't help matters as he stood with his father by a puddle in the yard. 'I told you so,' he muttered. 'Things are getting worse. Have you heard about the sheep stolen from Hunmanby? It's a sign of how bad things are. *Five*! And one had even been clipped before they found it.'

His father looked on, a defeated man. With a stooped back, he stumbled towards the house, chuntering to himself about the shortage of hay.

When the main harvest began in August, there was more disappointment; the stormy summer meant the crops had been flattened. The absent vicar, still choosing to reside in Filey, sent a man to collect his tithes. Robert Storey, standing in the drizzling rain with the two churchwardens, met the man outside the church. They steered round the worst puddles as they walked to the barn. Even Robert, much as he was

84

against harvest celebrations and tithe suppers, could see how miserable an event the tithe collection had become.

'Is there any chance of the vicar ever coming to live here?' he asked.

The man smirked. 'I doubt that very much. It's just been made official this month—John Sumpton's the curate of Filey.'

At Uphall, the mood was sombre. There was little to look forward to though they'd toiled as hard as ever throughout the harvest. Thomas stood gloomily in the cart shed with the workers, sheltering from the latest heavy shower. Young William, his brother Francis and their father joined them. Thomas was the first to speak.

'I remember the last tithe supper we had. Our old vicar understood when times were bad. He didn't demand his full rights. He was one of us and he shared what he had.'

'Aye,' they agreed.

Young William nudged his father. 'Didn't you have roast beef and a bottle of claret? I remember you telling me about it.'

'And plenty more as well... a barrel of ale and food out in the street for the tenants. Tell me, Francis, does George Gurwood still give tithe suppers in Rudston?'

'He does. Lizzie was always kept busy making pies and such.'

They sighed. How they'd love to go back to those days when the Gurwoods were in Reighton.

Dickon summed it up. 'Aye...we're abandoned 'ere.'

As the rain eased, everyone drifted away, and Francis went home early. On his way down the hill, he looked back on the time when the Gurwoods had left the vicarage. He'd really missed them once they'd gone to Rudston. He'd never fitted in with the hired lads at Uphall, and his father and uncles had more time for his brother William. Uncle Thomas had spent hours with William, snaring birds and training Stina to chase ducks. He knew he could never take part; such sport repulsed him. He'd felt left out, but Robert Storey had befriended him. Only Robert understood.

8 5

He was approaching his cottage, still feeling dejected, when he heard laughter from inside. As soon as he entered the kitchen, the women stopped.

His aunt Elizabeth and Lizzie were sitting on the rush mat with the baby who was stark naked.

Lizzie wiped her eyes on her apron. 'Oh, Francis, I wasn't expecting you. We were just playing.'

'Shouldn't Dottie be swaddled?'

Elizabeth stood up and smoothed down her crumpled skirt. 'Babies need to be free sometimes. Look at her—she loves to kick. Anyway, she's been indoors so much this summer, and it's time she was out of swaddling.'

Francis stared at his aunt. 'I'm surprised Robert lets you spend so much time here. Don't you have your own duties at home?'

Elizabeth ignored the question and spoke to Lizzie instead. 'I'm sorry, I'd better go.' She glanced down at the baby. 'Bye bye, Dottie, bye bye.' She waved her hand about, and the baby kicked out both legs and gurgled in response.

'Thoo'll come tomorrow, though?' asked Lizzie.

Elizabeth nodded. On her way to the door, she whispered to Francis. 'Don't tell Robert I was here again.' As she left, she turned to add, 'We were only playing.'

Lizzie hastened to tie a cloth round Dottie's bottom, and wrapped her up ready for a feed.

Always disturbed by the sight of breastfeeding, Francis went out and stood in the back doorway to watch the poultry. He wished he didn't feel so trapped. The rain had stopped and the chickens were out again pecking in the dirt. Instead of feeling grateful for the sight, all he saw was a bunch of filthy hens and a ridiculous strutting cock.

In the autumn, Elizabeth found more excuses to be at Lizzie's cottage. The pig had been slaughtered at Uphall, and the meat sent back. As well as the salting and pickling, they had to store the apples and potatoes. She arrived one afternoon with a large wooden box.

86

'I said I'd show you how to store carrots. You've pulled them up, but you haven't washed them, have you?'

'No, thoo told me not to.'

'That's right, so just cut off the leaves and the little end.'

While Lizzie did this, Elizabeth knelt by the crib to talk to the baby. Now nine months old, Dottie could haul herself up to stand and she was holding onto the hood for balance. Elizabeth kept ducking out of sight behind the hood and popping up again to make the girl giggle.

'Come on,' Lizzie urged, waving the last carrot in the air. 'Leave 'er an' tell me what to do next.'

Elizabeth got to her feet. 'Did you get the sand we need? And is it dry?'

'Aye, it's i' yon sack.'

'Watch then. You should only do this on a dry day.'

Elizabeth heaped handfuls of sand into the box and smoothed out a layer at the bottom. Then she laid the carrots separately on the sand, making sure they didn't touch. Another layer of sand went on top.

'There now, *you* carry on like this while I see to Dottie.'

As soon as Elizabeth returned to the crib, the girl held up her arms to be lifted out.

'Come on then, you little rascal.' She held her up high and swung her about before setting her down on the mat.

Dottie's eyes sparkled in the firelight as she anticipated more fun.

'Are you ready? Jack be nimble...' Elizabeth paused to heighten the excitement. 'Jack be nimble, Jack be quick...' She paused again. 'Jack jump over the candlestick!' she cried as she grabbed Dottie round the waist and swung her across the mat.

The girl giggled, helpless. And so it went on as her mother filled the box with layers of sand and carrots.

'I've finished,' said Lizzie. 'Thoo'd best go now, Elizabeth... before Francis comes home.'

That autumn, there was an outbreak of fever in the village. Stephen Jefferson's father, being frail, was the first to succumb and soon died, making Stephen a yeoman and therefore a much better prospect for Ann Smith. Most blamed the illness on the wet weather. Dickon blamed the lack of Sarah Ezard's remedies, and he was one of the first to take precautions. At breakfast, he advised the hired lads.

'Thoo wants to do same as me an' thy master. Drink a large spoonful o' lime water with a bit o' milk ev'ry morn.'

'Oh, aye?' Sammy Owt retorted, rolling his eyes. 'An' strap a dock root to our legs an' all?'

'Thoo may laugh, but it doesn't 'urt to try it.'

They shook their heads. Dickon was also known to scratch his legs with a holly branch.

Dickon's efforts to avoid illness were in vain. The next morning, he awoke with a dry mouth and, when he tried to get out of bed, was dizzy and fell back. The lads who shared the chamber under the roof had already gone down for breakfast.

'Where's Dickon?' Dorothy asked.

''E's still i' bed.'

'Is 'e alright? It's not like 'im to miss breakfast.' When the lads shrugged and carried on eating, she sent Thomas up to see him.

Dickon was almost hidden under a thick blanket, sweating yet shivering with cold. There was no doubt—he'd caught the fever.

Chapter 14

Dickon's master and mistress were appalled to hear of his illness. Dorothy, already fearful for herself and her husband, did not want to tend the man herself.

'I'm too old to be runnin' up an' down,' she chuntered in the kitchen. She eyed her husband with a frown. 'An' *we* don't want to catch it. Thoo especially!' This past year she'd noticed a change in him. '*We're* in our sixties; God knows 'ow old Dickon is.'

Thomas, still loitering after breakfast, couldn't understand the fuss. 'Why can't the kitchen maid look after him?'

His mother put a finger to her lips to shush him. She gave a slight shake of her head, and whispered out of the maid's hearing. 'She's not up to it. Not enough up 'ere.' She tapped her forehead. 'Thoo can go an' ask Mary. If she 'as time to be out fussin' over 'er grandbairn, she can find time to tend Dickon. 'E's done enough for 'er bairns i' past.'

Thomas arrived at Mary's house as the family was still finishing breakfast. When he asked for help with Dickon, neither Mary nor William minded the imposition.

Mary was even pleased. At last, someone needed her. 'My lads are big enough to fend for themselves for a few days,' she explained, 'and it'll make a change.'

The boys glanced furtively from one to the other, wondering who would do the cooking, who would fetch water. Their father slammed a hand onto the table.

'You can all do your share—every one of you will help. Dickon was a good friend to your sister, and he's been more than kind to you, John. It's time to repay him.'

When Mary had left the house, William spent a few minutes organising the boys' household duties. Only young William was exempt; in accordance with his vow to show Ann he could work hard, he'd offered to help his father with the muckspreading.

As Mary walked up the hill to Uphall, she tried to remember what Sarah Ezard prescribed for fevers. Apart from making sure Dickon drank plenty and kept warm, she had little to offer. One thing she did recall was the precaution of washing out her own mouth with vinegar.

When she entered the chamber, she found Dickon's bed in isolation. Already, the lads had moved their beds to the other side, as far away as possible.

'Now then, Dickon,' she said, helping him to sit up. 'Dorothy's sent up this warm milk.'

''As it got lime water in it?' he croaked. When she nodded, he asked if she'd mind dusting the chamber. 'Thoo must get rid o' spider webs. If even one's left, then fever'll linger there.'

She fetched a brush and, knowing he was watching, took her time going into the corners. For the rest of the day, she kept him company, telling him about her granddaughter, and reminding him of young Mary's antics.

'She used to come home after being with you in the stable. Then we'd all have to hear about the best way to clean leather straps. She never shut up.'

'Aye, I remember. She were a good lass, so keen to learn.'

When he slept, Mary took out her knitting. It was peaceful at the top of the house. The hired lads were out working, and the noises coming from the yard and kitchen sounded distant. Later, once she'd settled him for the night, she went downstairs and rinsed her mouth and nostrils with vinegar. She also scrubbed her hands before going home.

After a few days, when Dickon was no better, John brought home a fleece he'd borrowed from the shepherd. He unrolled it and passed it to his mother.

'See—this will make Dickon warm, won't it. He can keep it till he's out of bed.'

'Thank you, John, and I'll ask your father to bring a bottle of ague water from Hunmanby.'

The next day, Mary visited Dickon with the fleece, the bottled cure and the apothecary's advice to try bloodletting or blistering.

90

'Over my dead body!' was Dickon's answer. 'I'll never be bled.'

Mary was surprised. 'But you do it to animals.'

'That's diff'rent.'

Mary shrugged. 'Won't you try a blistering plaster then? You say your back and your shoulders ache. I could get one and put it on for you.'

Dickon's back was aching so much he felt sick. After a moment of indecision, he agreed to the treatment, though with reservations. 'I'd much rather 'ave 'ad Sarah Ezard's embrocation.'

'Sorry, we haven't got any.' Mary was equally frustrated by the loss of their local remedies. 'Look, I've brought you a fleece. It was John's idea. Let me put it over you.'

Dickon's eyes welled up. 'John's a good lad, always 'appy to 'elp out. That shepherd must be glad of 'im. It's a pity...' His voice failed him and he didn't finish the sentence.

Mary turned away while he wiped his eyes. She didn't know if he was going to say it was a pity her other sons were not more helpful, or it was a pity John was a simpleton. Maybe Dickon was sorry that he was too old and too incapable to work with John anymore.

When she went home in the evening, she told William how Dickon's eyes often filled up, especially when he met any kindness or spoke of old friends.

'It's the same with my father,' he replied. 'He never used to be like that. The older he is, the softer he gets. Now my mother... she's just the opposite. She gets tougher—hard as flint.'

'Speaking of being tough, I want you to buy a blistering plaster. Dickon said he'd try it.'

The next day, William showed Mary the plaster in its paper wrapping. 'Don't tell him what's in it, or he might balk at it.'

'Tell *me* then. I'd like to know.'

'Spanish Fly.'

'What?'

'That's the powder. It's ground blister beetles. I asked the apothecary and he explained. Apparently, it's very potent.

9 1

You must only leave the plaster on for a few hours. Then, when the blister is full, you'll need to snip it and drain out the badness. Put a bit of clean linen on it afterwards and let it heal. You still have some healing salve, haven't you?'

She nodded.

'Oh, and I almost forgot—don't let him drink too much while the plaster's on or it won't work so well. The apothecary also said that men can have a hard time passing water afterwards.'

She now wished he'd never gone to the apothecary.

In the afternoon, she rolled Dickon onto his stomach, pulled up his old shirt and covered his bare bottom with the blanket. After tearing off the wrapping, she placed the plaster over his lower back where he seemed to have the most pain. She wasn't sure, but thought it smelled of pepper and mustard.

Instantly, Dickon felt it sting. 'What i' God's name 'as thoo put on?' he shouted. 'It smarts like very devil.'

She tried to sound assured. 'Don't worry. Bear it for just an hour or so, then the blister should be ready.' She stayed by his side and chatted about the livestock to distract him.

The pain of the plaster soon got rid of the backache, one pain cancelling out the other. He often spoke tearfully about the old days when Ben and Sarah Ezard had been alive.

Neither he nor Mary mentioned his wife, though Mary knew Isabel was often in their thoughts.

When the sun began to go down and the room darkened, Mary lit a candle. She saw that the plaster had risen, and it was time to remove it—a task she was dreading.

Gingerly, she lifted the plaster at one corner, and then another, just enough to see if it had done its job. There was quite a large red blister underneath.

He flinched as she eased off the rest of the plaster.

She picked up her knife. 'I'm going to cut the blister now, so keep still. We want the badness to drain out. Then you'll start to feel better.'

She lanced the blister right down the middle. A pale, bloody fluid ran out and trickled onto the bed. After mopping up the mess as best she could with a cloth, she smeared a bit of salve onto a clean piece of linen.

'There now,' she said in triumph, 'I'll put on this dressing. Stay on your belly for tonight, and tomorrow we'll see how it is, and then you can sit up or lie on your back again.'

He wondered if it was worth the effort.

Over the next few days, he grew worse. He was sick if he ate anything and, when he couldn't keep his drink down, he became delirious. Once, he mistook Mary for Isabel; he lay stroking her hand, telling her how much he loved her.

It was another week before he began to get better and, finally, the kitchen maid was allowed to deal with him.

Mary still visited him each day. She was worried about his weight loss, for winter was almost upon them, and he was frail. In December, she heard of another illness sweeping through the towns and villages. This time, people thought they'd just caught a cough and a bad cold, but soon they were in bed with a fever, hardly able to move, and ached all over.

In Hunmanby, only a few miles away, old Sir Richard Osbaldeston contracted the illness. He was buried on Christmas Eve, leaving his eldest son, William, to inherit the estate.

Dickon, still feeling low after his illness, forecast hard times ahead. He'd noted already the abundance of rose hips and hawthorn berries. Now, as he stood peering at the snow falling in the yard, he predicted a harsh winter.

Chapter 15

1729

In January, Reighton lay trapped in a valley of ice. Church Hill was so frozen that Robert Storey forbade his wife to visit Lizzie. As a result, Mary looked forward to Dottie's first birthday without the presence of her sister.

'I do feel a bit mean,' she confided to William. 'It's just that Elizabeth's *always* there—and I get left out.'

He didn't support her, didn't grasp the depth of her resentment. 'Well, Elizabeth was bound to spend more time there; she's no children of her own.'

'But they spend so much time together that everyone calls them the two Lizzies.' She could tell William was losing interest, and didn't add that Dottie always turned to Elizabeth first. That really stung, and she hated being jealous. Yet I *am* the child's grandmother, she kept telling herself. Sighing, she realised how hard it was to be a mother-in-law. She should have made more effort to befriend Lizzie at the start.

Mary and her family arrived for Dottie's birthday, bringing a fruitcake and a small homemade present from John. They toasted the little girl's health with Francis's diluted beer and then John approached Dottie in her mother's arms. He'd carved a sleeping sheep out of a piece of driftwood, and had stuck clumps of wool all over it.

Young William looked away in embarrassment; the toy was such a clumsy attempt. Dottie grinned though, and reached out to take the sheep. As John let her hold it, he gave her a gentle kiss on the cheek.

There was silence for a moment as everyone watched the girl fondle her new toy. Then, suddenly, a noise from outside took her attention and she craned her head towards the door.

'She'll be 'oping it's Elizabeth,' Lizzie explained.

Mary's initial cheer evaporated and her lips were tight. It made no difference that Elizabeth would not be there.

Unusually for him, William noticed the change in atmosphere. He coughed and filled the next silence with talk of the weather.

'All the tracks are frozen. We can't get supplies in or out. I did try the sledge, but soon gave up.' He'd used one years ago. He was older now, though, and it seemed far too cold to be out for any length of time on the exposed roads beyond the village.

'Can't tha brother Thomas 'elp?' Lizzie asked.

William pulled a face. '*He* won't volunteer, and I don't suppose you, Francis, would like a trip out.'

Francis shook his head.

There was no more conversation; it was chilly in the kitchen and not just because of the poor fire. When there was no more fruitcake, the guests bade farewell and stepped back out into a flurry of snow.

The Jordans, like everyone else, huddled in their kitchens to keep warm, reluctant to put a foot outside. They slept in their clothes, and their bed covers and clothes were full of bugs. William's sons were covered in blotchy red bites and, due to their reluctance to remove any garments for a wash, the boys had also begun to smell sour.

One evening, William and Mary sat by the fire with their boys, fidgeting and scratching because of the lice. He took one of the lit candles and ran it slowly along the seams of his breeches.

'Watch carefully, lads, this is how you kill them.'

They heard the sharp crack as the lice popped under the heat. 'It's tricky,' he warned, 'only drip the hot wax on the seam where the cloth's thickest. Otherwise, you'll burn your legs.'

Young William had the first go and, leaning over his breeches, his face soon grew freckled with spots of blood as the candle wax hit some extra-large lice.

John watched in awe, trying to recall a rhyme that old Ben used to say; it was about getting rid of fevers, yet it might

95

work on bugs. It had to be spoken by the eldest in the family, so he whispered into his father's ear, asking him to say the rhyme aloud, and say it up the chimney.

It was a childish notion, but William put his head near the chimney and began to recite.

Tremble and go!
First day shiver and burn,
Tremble and quack!
Second day shiver and burn,
Tremble and die,
Third day never return.

John smiled, satisfied. 'That should do it.'

Whether the rhyme or the candles worked, the lice were less bothersome, though the house still smelled stale. Mary was relieved when the snow stopped at the end of the month. As soon as there was a warmer spell, she made them strip off all their clothes so they could wash and put on clean ones. In disgust, she burnt the worst of the bedding.

The snow melted, leaving the meadows standing in water and the roads still impassable. At the end of each day, William stood at the top of the village, staring at the expanse of fields. He had no eyes for the glorious sunsets of early February, for the bands of dark pink and mauve that striped the sky, or for the distant hills, bright yellow with gorse. What mattered was the drainage on those top fields. Now, approaching the age of fifty, he feared the long, weary days of ploughing in clarty soil. His younger brother would have to do more, but Thomas was increasingly morose; if he wasn't complaining about working on the land and having to see to the stock, he was complaining of toothache.

One morning, while William was in the Uphall kitchen discussing jobs for the day, he heard Thomas asking his mother to have another look at his teeth. She stood his brother in the light by the window, made a brief inspection with her eyes and then poked her finger to the back of his mouth. She had a good feel all round.

'I bet it's a tooth o' wisdom. I can't see owt else wrong. Listen, thoo can't keep askin' me fo' poultices. There's nowt for it, Tom. If thoo keeps gettin' pain, thoo'll need to 'ave it pulled.'

Thomas grimaced. 'I'll wait and see. It might sort itself out.'

He bore the discomfort for a few more weeks, putting off a visit to Hunmanby where there was a sign advertising *Shaving, Bleeding and Teeth and Stumps Drawn*.

His mother had an idea. 'Tha brother Samuel's often in 'Unmanby when 'e works there for 'is father-i'-law. Ask 'im to go wi' thee—'e'll give thee courage.'

A day was arranged and, before Thomas left for Hunmanby, he rubbed his teeth clean with salt, and rinsed his mouth. In defiance of his mother, who urged him to eat a good breakfast, he left the house with an empty stomach. He was too nervous to eat and dreaded the coming ordeal. He'd heard terrible stories of someone's uncle or cousin who'd had a bad time at the hands of the barber-surgeon. He'd never actually met anyone who'd had the experience firsthand.

On arrival outside the shop, he waited for Samuel. Now, he had second thoughts. Hung in the window was a grotesque necklace of rotten teeth, presumably to show off the man's expertise. Suddenly, he felt a push from behind. He spun round, angry.

'Samuel! You blockhead!' Then he gave a weak smile. 'Thank you for coming.'

'Let's get it over with, then. Come on, Tom. You can do it.'

Thomas took a deep breath and opened the door. He heard a bell jangle.

The barber-surgeon emerged from the back room. He was wearing a bloodstained apron that reached down to his ankles.

Thomas stared at the apron; if the stains were from shaving, it didn't bode well for the man's competence.

Ignoring Thomas's alarm, the man made an affectatious bow. 'Zachary Clarkson, at your service.' Then he noticed Thomas's swollen cheek. 'Ah, I can guess what's wrong. A rotten tooth is it? I can soon see to that—have it out before you know it.'

97

'No, no,' interrupted Thomas. 'My teeth are good. I think it's a tooth of wisdom that's the problem. I think there's no room for it to come through.'

'How old are you?'

Thomas hesitated. It was an impudent question.

'It matters you know,' the barber-surgeon urged. 'It's not easy pulling such teeth and, the older you are, the more difficult it'll be. If you're over twenty, the roots are fully formed, you see, and the surrounding bone is harder.'

'I'm thirty-one.'

The man sighed and shook his head.

Thomas blinked, anxious. 'Can you do it then... or not?'

'Yes, yes, I can manage.' Then, thinking he should give Thomas some inkling of the job ahead, he added, 'It's easier, like I said, to extract teeth in the younger, but... if you're prepared for the extra pulling and tugging, then I'll proceed.'

Thomas glanced at the low seat fixed to the floor, then gulped and turned to Samuel. He raised his eyebrows in question.

Samuel shrugged. 'Why not?'

'Alright then,' Thomas decided. 'What do you want me to do?'

'Sit down there and tilt your head right back. And you, young man'—he gestured at Samuel—'I want you to stand behind him and hold him still. Be firm, and hold on tight. Can you do that?'

Samuel bit his lip and nodded.

'Right then, I'll tell you when I'm going to pull. Understood?'

Samuel, his eyes wide with fear, nodded again but with less conviction.

Zachary Clarkson leant over to inspect Thomas's teeth. He saw there could be a problem on both sides of the mouth. One of the unwanted teeth would certainly need to come out, maybe more. He decided to pull the one from the lower right side as it had erupted a little; any others were still under the gum.

Thomas grew more alarmed when Clarkson rolled up his sleeves and took an implement from a drawer—a strange, long, steel tool, shaped like a claw at the end. His eyes widened in horror as the man stood in front of him and wedged his body between his thighs.

'Open your mouth again, there's a good man. Open it wide.'

Unable to move, Thomas did as he was told. He felt the steel cold in his mouth. The claw scrabbled to gain purchase while the other end pressed painfully against his gum and nearby teeth.

Clarkson tried in vain to get hold of the tooth. 'It's no good—the pelican can't get a grip. I'll use a knife. Hold him still now,' he warned Samuel, 'I'm going to have to cut the gum first.'

Thomas flinched and gripped the arms of the chair as the knife did its work. He almost choked as blood trickled down his throat.

Clarkson went in again with the pelican. He lifted the flap of skin off the tooth and attached the claw.

'Are you ready?' he asked Samuel. 'I'm going to lever it and pull.'

Thomas yelled out in pain; it felt as if his gum was being crushed. He wanted to wriggle free and tell the man to stop, but he was pinned to the chair.

The tooth didn't budge, so Clarkson rocked back and forth to try to loosen it from the bone. When this didn't work, he rammed his foot against Thomas's chest, ignored any cries and pulled harder.

Samuel had a difficult job holding Thomas down, for the barber-surgeon had the strength of a blacksmith. Just when he thought he couldn't hold on anymore, and Thomas looked about to faint, the tooth came free. Blood spurted out, and Clarkson stuffed a wad of cloth into the hole. It stank of oil of cloves.

'Bite down on this for a while. That'll stop the bleeding and ease the pain.' He wiped his hands on his apron and turned to Samuel. 'Well done, young man.'

Samuel realised he still held Thomas in a tight grip. When he let go, his arms and legs were trembling. He didn't want to go through that again and neither, he suspected, did Thomas.

When Clarkson offered to extract another tooth, Thomas raised a hand and shook his head slowly. He closed his eyes for a moment. Never had he felt so weak and shaky, and his gums, what was left of them, were so sore.

'Not to worry,' said Clarkson, pleased with his work, 'you can come back any time. If you like, stay here a while, just till the bleeding stops, then you must leave it to heal. Whatever you do, don't prod it with your finger or feel it with your tongue. It'll take a week to heal over, then a month or two for the hole to really fill in. When you get home, rest for a couple of days. Don't do anything too strenuous.'

Thomas remembered he'd missed breakfast. 'Can I eat?' he asked, his voice muffled by the wadding.

'Take only soft foods for a week. You can start by rinsing your mouth with hot, salty water—as hot as you can stand. Oh, and don't smoke your pipe for a week—it'll delay the healing.'

When Thomas finally left the barber-surgeon, he was tired and miserable and a shilling lighter in his pocket. He was also hungry and very thirsty, yet dreaded having anything in his mouth. Samuel tried to cheer him up, but Thomas, who had never suffered the least illness in his life, was inconsolable. As he trudged after Samuel down the main street, he fought off the tears. He mumbled, holding a cloth to his mouth.

'Won't be able to work much... Father won't be happy.'

Samuel stopped and turned. 'How is Father?'

'Slowing up. Dickon's even worse. God—my mouth hurts!'

'Does Father need help? I could come over. We have a good foreman here, so I could find the time.'

Thomas shrugged. At that moment, he didn't give a damn.

Chapter 16

Thomas's face was bruised, swollen and stiff, and his chest had an ugly mark where the barber-surgeon had anchored his foot. Over the next two weeks, the hired lads took more interest in him as the bruises changed colour, ranging from black to dark blue and purple, then to violet before turning a sickly yellowy green. Eventually, his face was just a dirty brown.

'I'm sure that man has damaged my good teeth,' Thomas fretted. 'I'm sure he's loosened them.'

When Samuel arrived to help at Uphall, as promised, he regaled everyone with details of the tooth extraction. While Thomas grimaced at the memory, still in some discomfort, the lads revelled in the description; they could sympathise, though, with his refusal to repeat the experience.

The cold weather did not help Thomas's recovery and, by Easter Sunday in the middle of April, spring seemed as far away as ever. Dickon chuntered and glowered at the ground frost on the way to church. The brief service by their vicar, who had other services to conduct elsewhere, did nothing to improve Dickon's mood. As he left, he voiced the old prediction.

If dry be buck's 'orn o' Holy Rood morn,
'Tis worth a kist o' gold.
But if wet be seen 'ere Holy Rood e'en,
Bad 'arvest is foretold.

Old Francis Jordan and his wife nodded wisely, and no one gainsaid Dickon.

It rained in the afternoon, and the cold, pinching east wind threatened the sprouting winter wheat. Though Dickon had recovered strength following his winter illness, he now plodded miserably about Uphall and the top fields.

101

He complained about the sea rokes that lasted for days, chilling the air and dampening the chalk walls.

'Once an east wind, allus an east wind,' he kept repeating to the hired lads.

Only one thing did please him—the return of Samuel. He welcomed the Jordan like a long-lost son and, though Samuel never stayed for more than three days at a time, the extra help was a great relief.

Now in his late twenties, and with a healthy son and daughter to his name, Samuel was approaching his prime. He was no longer the spotty and lanky youth, but had grown tall and muscular and was full of ideas to improve the Jordans' land. He slipped into the work routine as if he'd never been away and, each day that he spent at Uphall, the more he became the acting foreman. Instead of Dickon, Samuel decided with his father on when to sow the spring wheat, the oats and the peas; the rest of the village trusted his advice and followed suit.

William, though he was the eldest and the expected heir, felt pushed out. He and his sons worked a piece of land that his father had bought with a loan years ago; not only were they farming that piece with the expectation of inheriting it in future, they were also helping out in the top fields. Now, if his suspicions about Samuel's motives were correct, then he was working in vain. Almost twenty years younger, would Samuel really use his youth and energy to usurp his brother's rightful place?

Early one morning, Thomas stood with his father outside the kitchen door, watching Samuel give instructions to the lads in the yard. The sky was overcast, and another day of drizzle expected.

'It's good Samuel's 'ere,'his father confided, 'but it's a worry.' He put his unlit pipe in his mouth, a new habit whenever anxious. 'I fear fo' future... when I'm gone. William's not as fit as 'e used to be, an' *thoo*...' He removed his pipe and spat on the ground. 'Thoo's never taken a proper interest. Thoo's allus avoided 'ard work—looked for easier ways to earn money.'

1 0 2

Thomas turned his head and stared into the distance. He couldn't deny his love of sport and gambling.

'Aye,' his father concluded, 'we could do wi' Samuel 'ere all time.'

Thomas sighed and made an excuse to leave. 'Dickon says one of the horses needs shoeing. I'll take it to the blacksmith.'

As he left, he heard his father spit again. No doubt his father would be grumbling about the time wasted drinking and gossiping at the forge. It was true, he did enjoy being at the forge, especially in bad weather, and there were always tools to take for repair or sharpening. Today, with it looking like rain, he took the opportunity to loiter.

As often happened, the blacksmith had an avid audience. A few other farmers with unexpected time on their hands were sitting on upturned logs and buckets. They lit their pipes and waited to hear news of the rest of England.

Phineas Wrench rolled up his sleeves and raked the fire in preparation for his next bout of work. 'Think thassens lucky,' he told them. 'There's been a tornado down south somewhere.'

'Nay,' a couple of men disagreed. 'We 'eard at market it were a waterspout that became an 'urricane.'

Phineas rolled up his sleeves even higher. 'Well, whatever it were, it wrecked ev'rythin' in its path fo' twelve mile. Aye, an' uprooted 'undreds of oak trees an' orchards.' He'd heard details from the various pedlars that passed through the village, and now he was keen to show off his knowledge. 'Folk lost their roofs, an' their windows an' doors were blown in. I've been told a cheese press were carried two 'undred yards, an' even an 'ouse were shifted two inches north'ards. Think o' that!'

'Thank God *we* didn't have to face it,' Thomas remarked, and the others mumbled in agreement.

Phineas hadn't finished. 'I were told there were so much gravel an' dirt an' broken glass carried by wind that it drove into walls like gunshot. Aye... think on.'

It did give them pause for thought. Thomas smiled and rubbed his hands together; no one would mind his time spent at the forge if he returned with such fascinating tales. As he listened, he heard local news of even more interest—to him at least.

Scarborough had become quite the place in the summer for the rich to stay and sample the air. He learnt that coaches arrived regularly from York bringing gentry from the West Riding as doctors approved of bathing in the sea and drinking the mineral waters. Even ladies were bathing, venturing from wooden huts on wheels towed into the sea. Better still, Thomas heard, there was a bowling green and places for gaming. There were foot races and horse races, ample scope for placing bets. Thomas's eyes shone as he also thought of the rich widows who might be there. He left the forge wondering why he was stuck in Reighton.

Lizzie found the cold April a challenge; the hens were late in laying, and the frosts had delayed the garden planting. Her daughter, now able to walk on her own, was confined indoors most days and was proving more difficult to control. Though desperate to take the girl outside, Mary had warned her, 'Whatever you do, *never* take Dottie out in an east wind.'

Lizzie obeyed, having heard from Elizabeth how young Mary had died. Her mother-in-law's constant warnings, though understandable, were disheartening and undermined her confidence. Elizabeth, on the other hand, was a joy, and came one morning with exciting news.

'There's kittens at Uphall. They were born at Easter so you'll be able to choose one in the summer. You did say you wanted a cat?'

'Oh, I did. I can't wait to see them.'

'They're quite wild, though, so we'd better leave them alone for a while. They're free to roam the barns, and no one bothers with them much, but I'm sure you'll be able to tame one.' She picked Dottie up for a cuddle. 'And *you'll* love it. You can grow up together.'

The news about the kitten rankled Mary. Indignant that Elizabeth would interfere so much, she took her frustration out on William. No sooner had he returned for supper than

1 0 4

she laid into him. She banged down the ladle she was about to use and folded her arms.

'You'll never guess what that sister of mine has done now! She's only gone and told Lizzie she can have an Uphall cat. She must be mad. I've been trying to get Lizzie to train Dottie on the chamber pot. How's she going to do that when there's a kitten playing around? Elizabeth has no sense.' She retrieved the ladle and turned to the broth warming over the fire.

William kept quiet. The mood Mary was in, it was best to say nothing, leave her to cool off. The boys seated at the table also kept their heads down.

Mary spun round. 'Well, William? What do *you* think?'

Unable to escape, he mumbled, 'I don't know… Elizabeth can help… can't she?' his reply petered out as he realised he'd said the wrong thing.

Mary almost threw the broth pot onto the table, making the boys jump.

'Oh, fine! Do you know how often she's over there helping? No, you don't. Anyone would think *she* was Dottie's grandmother. Fine… Elizabeth can help, Elizabeth can train Dottie, *she* can take her for walks, *she* can show her how to garden and collect eggs. Elizabeth can do everything.'

Carelessly, Mary ladled out the broth, disregarding the spills. The boys ate quickly and in silence. Even John did not try to calm his mother.

The summer did bring warmer temperatures although the prevailing weather was poor, with rain most days. William was sick of the struggle, sick of complying with Samuel's ideas and sick of his wife's grumblings about Lizzie and Elizabeth. The kitten was now in its new home and was an ongoing bone of contention. During the long summer evenings, he took refuge in the Bible. At first, he read alone and quoted verses to his sons, verses that only made them miserable. When they complained, he made them read with him.

'But Father,' young William protested one evening, 'we've been working all day. Can't we go out and do as we please?' He thought of the others his age, congregating in the warm

1 0 5

evening. There were new families living in Reighton, some with daughters, and he wanted a closer look at them. He knew Stephen Jefferson would be out there eyeing the girls; it would be insurance against not winning Ann Smith.

His father was adamant, though. 'Let me remind you, *you* were the one who asked to learn to read.'

'Yes,' Mary echoed as she sat mending a shirt. 'Do as your father says.'

The boys sat at the table, obedient but resentful as their father opened the Bible at Ecclesiastes and found the place he wanted.

'You start, Will.'

'I have seen all the works that are done under the sun,' he read slowly. 'And behold, all is vanity and vex... vexation of spirit.'

'You're too slow,' his father moaned. 'Here, let me finish it.'

Young William sighed with relief.

'If a man live many years, and rejoice in them all,' his father read aloud, 'yet let him remember the days of darkness; for they shall be many. All that cometh is vanity. Rejoice, O young man, in thy youth; and let thy heart cheer thee in the days of thy youth... but...' He paused to glare at his son. 'Know thou, that for all these things God will bring thee into judgement... childhood and youth are vanity.'

He lifted his eyes again and noticed the boys glance despondently at each other. At the same time, Mary gave him a half smile and winked.

'Alright,' he relented, 'off you go. Have a bit of time to yourselves.'

After the rush to the door, John remained, still sitting quietly at the table. Mary could see that he was upset. His eyes were wide, brimming with unshed tears. Maybe he was confused by words he didn't understand.

'Go on,' she urged, 'go and join the others outside. Your father can read to me.'

'No, it's alright.'

He didn't want to be out with the others. They made fun of him because his voice was beginning to break, and his brother William had scolded him. 'You can't go on stroking girls' hair anymore,' he'd said. 'You just can't. And don't stare at them. You'll frighten them. They won't like it.'

He wiped a tear from his cheek at the memory.

'What's the matter?' his mother asked, leaving her mending to sit by him on the bench.

'I don't have any friends.'

'There's Ann Smith.'

'She's not allowed out in the evenings.'

'Then why don't you go and see Dickon, or spend time with the shepherd?'

John's face was transformed by a smile. In his hurry to leave, he fell off the bench and then stumbled to the door.

When the door closed behind him, Mary shook her head sadly. *Poor lad*, she thought. *Jack and Dickon won't go on forever. What would he do without them?*

Chapter 17

John noticed how often Dickon stopped work to catch his breath, and how he sometimes bent over in pain. Late one afternoon, they were hanging up the leather traces after a day of harvesting, when Dickon fell back suddenly against the stable wall. John watched in horror as he slid down, and then lay slumped on the straw, clutching his chest.

'Can't breathe,' he gasped.

John ran to the Uphall kitchen for help, where his grandmother, without fuss, wiped the flour from her hands and then followed him to the stable.

'Now then, Dickon, what ails thee?'

He'd already recovered from the worst of the spasm and was breathing normally, though his face was grey and his eyes wide with fear. He shook his head, hating to admit his failing health.

'I'll be fine, it's just me old 'eart tellin' me to steady up.'

John helped him to his feet and then held onto his arm, reluctant to leave until he was sure Dickon wouldn't collapse again.

'Have you any medicine?' he asked.

When Dickon shook his head, Dorothy had an idea. 'I remember Sarah Ezard used to keep a jar of 'awthorn berries i' brandy, but it smashed when 'er place caught fire. She used to make a drink wi' foxglove leaves as well. John—thoo can 'elp. Go an' gather plenty o' leaves an' I'll try that cure.'

John left immediately to scour the ravines. It was now August and most of the flowers had gone to seed; he didn't know if that made any difference. His grandmother made the drink anyway, and Dickon drank it in good faith.

Dickon's heart wasn't the only problem; the hired lads noticed he was getting more forgetful. Often, he'd slip into

108

the past and shout for Tom to come and help, though Tom had left years ago.

John loved Dickon and hated to hear people laughing at his expense. As he went home, he wondered why Dickon kept calling for Tom, or Tommy Owt.

'Who's Tommy Owt?' he asked his father.

'Oh, he means Tom, not your uncle Thomas. You won't remember him—you'd be about five when he left. Dickon used to work with him all the time, treated him like a son. They were good together. And the reason he called him Tommy Owt,' he explained patiently, 'was because Tom, when he was younger, would have to do owt—you know, any extra little jobs at Uphall.'

'I saw Dickon behind the cow shed with his breeches down. He was whipping his legs with a bunch of nettles. Why did he do that? The lads laughed at him.'

William smiled. 'Oh, I reckon that was one of his rheumatism cures. He and old Ben got up to all sorts.'

'Will Dickon get better?'

'He's getting old, like the rest of us. You'll have to help him more.'

William kept a close eye on Dickon during the rest of the harvest, making sure he just supervised the work. He asked John to keep him abreast of the work in the stable. He heard that Dickon would feed the horses and water them, and then try to do it all over again.

November proved to be the warmest in living memory, and Dickon was too hot in his winter clothes. He sweated and suffered, too stubborn to remove a single item. Even John couldn't talk him into taking off his coat. Everyone saw that Dickon wasn't looking after himself. He wasn't washing or shaving, wasn't cutting his hair or nails. He'd been the same after the death of his wife. The hired lads complained that Dickon stank like the dung heap and, at mealtimes, they rushed to sit the furthest away.

One day, Dorothy Jordan was so fed up that she told William to have a word with Dickon. When he offered to give him a shave, though, Dickon took umbrage.

'I'm not useless. I can fend fo' meself.' He glowered at him and raised a fist. 'Thoo's like rest on 'em. Thoo can go jump off cliff!'

From then on, William approached him with caution, gauging his mood before speaking. He found that Dickon was kind and even patient with John, but with those who'd known him longest, he could turn angry and be violent. He knew that Dickon was desperate to remain independent, yet his hands were arthritic and clumsy. John was now doing even Dickon's menial jobs.

Dickon cursed his unreliable hands, and hated to be pitied. His only respite from a black, despairing mood was when his mind slipped into the past. Then he could have conversations with Ben, Tom or Sarah Ezard and, best of all, his wife Isabel.

John listened to Dickon's stories of the past and repeated them to his mother when he went home. He liked to see her smile at her recollections of Ben's strange waterproof hats, and how Ben had slept with the mule that no one else could handle. Suddenly, he had a thought.

'Can Dickon come and live here?'

'No, John, I don't think that's a good idea.' It was one thing to tend Dickon at Uphall, quite another to have him live with them. Besides, their house was cramped already.

'I don't think he'd ever leave Uphall,' she explained. 'He's too proud to admit defeat. But, look, I've mended this old shirt for him. When I take it, I'll see how he is and find out what your grandmother thinks.'

Late the next day, Mary went to talk with Dorothy about the state of Dickon's health, of both his body and his mind. William's mother made it very clear that she couldn't deal with him anymore. She'd had enough. Though Mary wanted to repay Dickon's kindness to her family, she didn't offer to take him on.

Dorothy gestured with her head towards the yard. 'Thoo'll find 'im i' barn. That's where 'e goes. Thoo'll soon see 'ow 'e fares.'

On pulling open the great barn door, Mary saw him sitting alone on a bench. He was muttering away to himself in the gloom. When he raised his head and saw she was handing him a shirt, he batted her away.

'I don't need thy charity,' he grumbled, and the shirt fell to the floor.

Mary picked it up, shook off the dust and sat down next to him with the shirt in her lap. Very quietly, she began to talk, telling him in detail everything she'd done that day. She used the same tone that Dickon had taught John to use with the horses—gentle, calm and repetitive, making no demands. After a while, she was able to hold and massage his hand.

Dickon became confused. He thought Mary was his wife and, for a few moments, he was happy. He was in the prime of life once more, in charge of the hired lads and full of plans for the top fields. Here he was in the barn, and Isabel had come to fetch him for supper. Soon, they'd be walking home together to their cottage.

'Let's be goin', lass,' he said.

'Where do you want to go?'

'Why, 'ome o' course. Thoo's got supper ready an' I'm starvin'.'

Mary realised his mistake and was in two minds whether to go along with his daydream, or end it and risk the upset. She decided to walk him past his old cottage and then take him to her house for supper. Maybe he'd like to stay there, and they could all look after him. John, she knew, loved him especially.

'Come on then, Dickon.'

He walked slowly, holding onto her arm. They went through the yard and turned to go down the hill. As they reached his old cottage, which he hadn't lived in for years, he stopped in alarm. There was a different door, and the roses that Isabel had planted were no longer growing at the sides. He threw a wild glance at Mary.

'What 'as thoo done? Why 'as tha changed it?'

'I haven't,' Mary explained gently. 'This *was* your cottage, but that was a long time ago. Someone else lives there now.'

'I'm goin' to knock o' door an' see fo' meself.'

'No, you can't do that. Listen, there's a young family there now—it's Dorothy and John Dawson's cottage now. See the

1 1 1

smoke coming out the chimney? They're going to have their supper, then get their daughters to bed.' She waited while he absorbed the information.

'Aye,' he murmured, 'poor bairns, they'll want their supper.'

'Yes, we'll leave them to get on with it. And we'll go and have *our* supper. Come on.'

There was a tear on his cheek as she led him away. He walked like a lost lamb, trusting anyone to lead him to shelter.

Once inside Mary's house, he cheered up at the sight of the boys seated up to the table waiting to be fed. Mary explained that Dickon would be living with them for a while—having time off from work.

Young William blinked. Now seventeen, he certainly wouldn't share his bed with a smelly old man.

His mother ignored his alarm. 'That's right, isn't it, Dickon? You're needed here more than at Uphall.'

He didn't know what she was talking about, but these days this was nothing new. He nodded and smiled, so confused he'd have agreed to anything.

Mary elbowed young William. 'You can move out of your bed and sleep with one of the others. Dickon needs a bed to himself.'

He wasn't happy with this arrangement either. He'd enjoyed having Francis's bed to himself and hadn't ever expected to share with his brothers again.

John reached across the table and took his hand. 'You can share with me—top to toe.'

Young William scowled. 'Thanks, but I'd rather share with Matthew—he's a good bit smaller. *And* he doesn't snuffle and snore. You can share with Richard.'

John shrugged. He didn't really mind although Richard was known to fidget at night.

Matthew glanced from one to the other and accepted his fate; as the youngest, he had no choice.

Dickon ate his supper, ate whatever was put in front of him. He didn't even balk when William offered to trim his hair in the morning.

After a few days in the family's company, Mary was pleased to see Dickon looking much better. He was shaven and clean and wore fresh clothes, yet his mental state remained the same. She realised anew the challenge ahead. Dickon had no proper tasks to do. He sat miserably in the kitchen all day just waiting for the boys to return home. Maybe she'd made a big mistake.

Chapter 18

Mary was finding it hard having Dickon watching her, shadowing her every move. When it told on her nerves, she thought up chores they could share. As the weather was still fine, she decided to wash more clothes; the unseasonal warm winds would soon dry them. Two days before the washday, she told him they were going to make the lye.

He watched her take out a wooden box with holes in the bottom. Then she asked him to help her put in a layer of straw and twigs. It was a novel experience for him. He'd never seen his wife do the washing as he'd always been out at work.

Mary spread a piece of muslin over the top of the box, and balanced the box over a large tub. She fetched a bucket of what appeared to be ash, and began piling handfuls onto the muslin.

'It's gorse ash, saved from the fire,' she explained. 'I'm going to pour water over it—steadily, like this, as much as it'll hold.'

Dickon peered over her shoulder to see the water begin to seep ever so slowly into the tub beneath.

'When it's all dripped through, I'll put the washing in to soak. Pass me those shirts, Dickon. I'll see which ones are worst.' On seeing the grass and grease stains on one of them, she clicked her tongue in disgust. 'I'll bet this is Richard's shirt. I don't know how he does it.'

Dickon shrugged. 'Isabel told me she used stale piss o' washday… kept a small trough of it.'

'Yes, I've heard it's good for soaking.' She didn't fancy the idea, though, of her boys filling a trough, and changed the subject. 'Anyway, we can leave this to drip through now. You go and feed the chickens. See if there are any eggs, while I make oatcakes.'

Mary knew that, when left alone and unoccupied, Dickon became morose. At times, even with her company, he fretted about being a burden. Towards William, he was often surly and looked for arguments.

For the next two days, until the lye was ready, she tried to keep Dickon busy. First, they gathered apples together and he passed them up to her to place carefully on straw in the loft. Then she sent him with John to fetch more flour and meal from the miller. This was a good idea for she could guarantee that John would look after him; they'd be gone some time and she could relax again in her own house.

The evening before washday, Mary checked the strength of the lye. Finding that it could float an egg, she put the shirts in it to soak.

'There you go, Dickon. If you can, swish the shirts around with this stick. Tomorrow, we'll boil them.'

The next day, Mary was up before dawn. She went outside and lit the fire under the set pot. When Dickon and the boys got up, she sent John to fetch plenty of water from the well. Straight after breakfast, she'd just begun to take the shirts from the soak when there was a knock on the door.

'You see who it is, Dickon.'

He found Lizzie standing there with Dottie, the little girl trying to hide under her mother's petticoat.

'Get off, Dottie, stop it!' Lizzie cried.

'Aye, lass, don't twist about so, thoo'll spoil tha mother's clothes.'

'Can Mary look after 'er today? I can't get on with 'er under me feet all time.'

Mary came to the door, drying her wet hands on her apron.

Dickon smiled. 'We're 'avin' little lass today.' He bent over to speak to Dottie. 'We can manage, can't we?'

Mary frowned. Washday was not the time to have a child toddling about.

'Please,' Lizzie pleaded, 'just fo' today.'

Mary wondered why Elizabeth could not have Dottie; her sister was always at the cottage. It was too much to hope that the 'two Lizzies' had fallen out.

'Alright,' she agreed. 'Dickon can help.'

With that, Lizzie gave Dottie a quick kiss, untwisted the child's fingers from her petticoat, and was gone.

The girl began to cry immediately.

Dickon bent down to her. 'Come wi' me,' he whispered. 'Come an' see chickens. There might be an egg fo' thee.'

Mary sighed as she watched Dottie take his hand and toddle into the garden. She pushed the stray greying hairs back under her cap and resumed taking the wet shirts from the soak. Then she carried them outside in a basket, laid them over a bench and began to rub the stains with a soap as hard as stone.

When Dickon heard Mary bashing the shirts with a bat, he brought Dottie over to see. He pretended to wallop Dottie's bottom, and she had a fit of giggles when he timed the 'hits' with the noise of the bat. Their fun ended when Mary stopped and put the shirts in the pot to boil.

'Come on, you two, let's go inside for a drink, and Dottie can have a treat.'

She strapped the girl onto a chair so she didn't slip off, and gave her a carrot dipped in honey. While Dottie was occupied sucking and chewing, Mary and Dickon sat opposite each other at the table, cradling mugs of beer.

He noticed her rough, red hands and shook his head. 'I used to rub goose grease into me chapped 'ands.' Then, reckoning she wouldn't think much of that remedy, he added, 'I've 'eard thoo can wash thy 'ands i' bran an' milk—to soothe an' soften 'em. Or thoo could try tatie water.'

As they were having potatoes for supper, she decided to try the latter remedy. Dickon was proving to be quite useful, and he certainly had a way with children.

She grasped his hand. 'I don't know what I'd do without you.'

He gazed at Dottie at peace with her bit of carrot. This set him reminiscing about the past, recalling the times he'd spent with young Mary.

'Thy lass, you know, she took ev'rythin' so serious, like. I'll never forget 'er big eyes starin' round Up'all kitchen when she thought 'er new puppy were bewitched. An' she were so

116

disappointed that time cattle wouldn't kneel o' Kesmas Eve. I could tell she were close to tears, an' I did try me best.' He scratched his bristly cheek. 'Cattle just would not go down.' He took a swig of his beer, and then wiped his mouth, smiling at another memory.

'Thy Mary thought she were a queen that day we collected stuff fo' bonfire. There she sat o' top o' cart wi' roses in 'er curls.' He shook his head. 'By, she were a fine lass.' He laughed as he remembered the way she imitated her grandmother, and copied the striding gait of Robert Storey. 'An' she were so patient i' stable, 'elpin' me oil leather straps.'

Mary interrupted. 'I think you're confusing her with John. *He's* the one with patience, and you have *him* to help you now. Come on,' she added briskly, wiping away a tear, 'finish your drink. We'd best get the clothes rinsed and wrung out or they'll never get dry.' She took one glance at his swollen, trembling hands. 'Listen, *I'll* see to the shirts, and you look after Dottie while I lay them on the hedge.'

The day stayed warm, a westerly breeze taking most of the moisture from the shirts. In the afternoon, Mary left Dickon and Dottie to have a nap together on the double bed, while she sat spinning wool for a very pleasant hour. While she spun, she thought about the two Lizzies, smiling to think they'd had a disagreement.

As soon as Dottie had been woken up, put on the chamber pot and given a drink of sweetened milk, Mary carried her home. She put her down to walk before they reached the cottage, and then went to the back door. In the yard, she stopped short.

Lizzie and Elizabeth were sitting on stools, laughing together like old friends.

Dottie pulled free of Mary's hand and tottered towards them.

Elizabeth leapt up to catch the girl; she swung her round and asked if she'd had a nice day.

Dottie nodded as she was put down, and then snuggled her face into her mother's lap.

1 1 7

It was obvious to Mary what they'd been up to. There was a stink of tallow and the remains of an outdoor fire. She glanced at the large pot and the wooden mould—signs of soap making, a hazardous task that took all day. No wonder the two women were so smug, and no wonder Lizzie wanted rid of Dottie. Then she caught a whiff of spearmint. Infuriated, Mary put her hands on her hips.

'So—doesn't our Uphall soap smell good enough for you?'

Lizzie hesitated. 'It's alright, but... we wanted to 'ave a go at makin' our own. Dorothy told us what to do.'

'Yes,' added Elizabeth, 'she gave us nearly a gallon of her lye—and the tallow.'

Mary sniffed. 'That's unusually generous of her.'

'Well, she did say she'd have a block of soap in return.'

Lizzie's eyes shone as she turned to Elizabeth. 'It were a good idea o' thine to use spearmint in our soap. I'll smell nice fo' Francis. Oh, I can't wait to make some more. Maybe we could try lavender... or dried rose leaves.'

Mary recalled how, as a young wife, she'd liked to experiment too. She'd put all kinds of herbs into her pastry and puddings, yet had never found the time to make soap; there'd been too many children in the way. Now she was assigned to baby minding while her sister was with Lizzie, and doing the things *she'd* have loved to do.

Lizzie offered to give Mary a piece of soap when it was ready.

'No, thank you, I'll make do with what I've got. I certainly don't need to smell of spearmint.' She turned to leave. '*I* can't stay chatting all day. I have supper to cook.' As she left the yard, she heard Lizzie shout a belated thank you for having Dottie. She was sure she heard them giggle afterwards.

In bed that night, Mary couldn't settle. She hated herself for envying her sister, and knew she was being ungenerous. She kept telling herself that Elizabeth had never had children, had only Robert, while she had the boys as well as William. And now she had Dickon too, and he was proving to be good company. She made herself think of Dickon and the boys and, at last, she fell asleep.

In the morning, Mary was more content with her lot. She doled out the breakfast and, once the family had left, gave Dickon the job of heating the flat irons by the fire.

'Pass them to me while I iron the shirts. And here you go...' She handed him a piece of waxed paper. 'Dab off any soot with this. And spit on the iron to check it's hot enough.'

He enjoyed helping and, each time the iron hissed under his spit, he passed it to her with a smile. He saved her a lot of time, and his presence took her mind off her sister and Lizzie.

Later, when the boys came home with their father for supper, the first thing they wanted to know was what Dickon had been doing.

Dickon didn't remember. As everyone sat at the table, he gave a garbled version of events of the distant past mixed with chores he used to do at Uphall.

William winked at his sons, for Dickon looked so happy.

As they spooned in their diced pork and apple, John was dying to ask Dickon a few questions. Eventually, he could wait no longer and asked, 'Who's the baldest in Reighton?'

Young William rolled his eyes. 'For God's sake, John, we've heard this before.'

Dickon took the question seriously. 'Now then,' he answered, 'that's a difficult one. I reckon it's Bart 'Uskisson. 'E's a real bladder o' lard. I've seen better 'air o' bacon.'

John giggled. 'And who's the tallest?'

'Ah, well, that might be Robert Storey. 'E's a long streak o' pump water.'

Matthew, the youngest, leapt from the table to stand proudly in front of Dickon. 'And who's the thinnest in Reighton?'

'Why, it must be thoo, Matthew.' Dickon felt the boy's ribs. 'Thoo's nowt but a bag o' bones.'

The boys' parents smiled and, instead of reading the Bible after supper or making the boys practise their writing,

William chose to smoke a pipe or two with Dickon by the fire. When the boys went to bed, all was quiet. Mary, content, sat opposite the two men as she knitted. Just lately, Dickon's presence had been a godsend. How long his good spirits would last was another matter. The coming winter would be the test.

Chapter 19

1729-30

When the weather turned wintry, Dickon had pains in his joints as well as his chest. Mary did as he asked, with reluctance, and poured melted pig fat onto his knees, as hot as he could bear. This remedy didn't convince her, so she sent William to Hunmanby for a tonic.

He came back with a bottle labelled Peruvian Bark. He'd been told that, if given in non-toxic doses, it could control fevers and, if added to red port, it would be a good general tonic. He wasn't warned that, if you drank too much, it was a laxative.

Mary had to deal with the ensuing mess; it was worse than having a cow in the house and she didn't know where to put Dickon, it being too cold in the garden. In the end, she stripped off his clothes in the kitchen and stood him in the washtub.

Dickon was relieved the boys were not at home; he was spared that shame. Afterwards, though, he began to weep.

'It's come to this,' he kept repeating. 'I'm goin' fast, Mary. I think I've almost gotten to far end.'

'Don't be daft. You'll be on the mend soon.'

As she dried him and sat him in a blanket by the fire, she did wonder how much more either of them could bear.

That night, he had to sit up in bed so he could breathe more easily. The boys, squashed together in their shared beds, could hear him wheezing. They also heard him praying.

''Ave mercy upon me, Lord, for I'm weak. O Lord 'elp me, fo' me bones are sore vexed.'

John was frightened, thinking Dickon might die. He crawled out of bed to kneel beside him and fumbled under the covers for Dickon's hand.

121

'Please get better,' he murmured. 'I'll pray for you. I'll pray every day, and twice on Sundays.'

For a few days, John thought the prayers had helped. Then, one morning, as they got up for breakfast, they found Dickon curled up on the floor.

Mary and William were shocked to feel him so cold; he'd obviously been dead for some time. When John began to cry, his younger brothers shuffled off to the kitchen, unsure how to react. Their father followed them, equally lost for the moment.

John sat cross-legged by Dickon's head and stroked smooth the thinning hair. He couldn't believe that Dickon was gone.

Young William tried to pull him away.

'Leave him,' said his mother. 'Let him be. He's doing no harm.' She rested a hand on John's shoulder. 'He was old and in pain, John. At least he was happy here for a while. Be glad that you were a good friend to him.'

She gestured with her head to young William. 'You go in the kitchen and help your father with breakfast. I'll be there soon.'

As she straightened out the stiffening body, her eyes filled with tears at the thought of Dickon dying alone. She didn't know if he'd died suddenly or if he'd been trying to get help. Perhaps it had been apoplexy. In that case, Dickon couldn't have suffered too much. She hoped it had been over very quickly, and clung to that thought. As soon as the family had gone out to work, she'd lay out the body.

There was heavy rain on the day of the funeral. Dorothy Jordan stood sheltering in the church porch with her husband, and pronounced what Dickon would have said on such a day.

'Blest is bride that sun shines on, an' blest is dead that rain rains on.'

She watched the procession arrive, three hired lads carrying the coffin with William, Thomas and Samuel. With bowed heads, she and her husband Francis joined the rest of the mourners.

Dorothy and Francis hoped for an uplifting service, full of praise and thanks for Dickon's life. They were disappointed. The vicar adhered strictly to the Book of Common Prayer. The words were familiar and should have given comfort, but even the talk of resurrection did not relieve their melancholy.

Francis shot a glance at Dorothy; she was faring better than he was. He didn't reckon he could hold out many more years. Dickon had worked on longer than he should, and little good had it done him. Later, as Francis stood by the grave, he assessed the rest of his family. He wondered if William was the right son to inherit Uphall; his eldest son had grey hair now, and his back had developed a stoop. Thomas looked well; he was strong and healthy, though not to be trusted. Samuel didn't even live in Reighton. It was a dilemma.

Dorothy noted her husband's distraction and nudged him. 'Thoo'll feel better when we're back 'ome. A feast is best way to say goodbye to Dickon, an' our maids 'ave got all food an' drink ready.'

After the funeral, wet hats and coats were draped about the Uphall kitchen, and room was made on the settle for the vicar to sit close to the fire. Everyone else clustered about the fireplace to dry out and get warm. The maid brought the vicar a glass of rum punch, and then served others. The hired lads made do with warmed ale; the children had it diluted.

Francis Jordan raised his glass. 'Aye, plenty o' drink is best when we're both grievin' an' thankful. 'Ere's to Dickon— finest foreman anyone could 'ave.'

After the toast, Dorothy invited the mourners to help themselves to slices of pork pie and boiled beef. Her efforts helped to assuage her guilt; she knew she could have helped Dickon more during his last years. She pointed out the rich currant cake.

'Come on, take a piece. Me an' maids spent ages makin' that. We didn't stint—it's full o' best butter. Nowt's too good fo' Dickon.'

'Aye,' her husband interrupted, 'they've even brushed it wi' rosewater an' sprinkled sugar on it before bakin'.'

In spite of the feast before them, the older generation was in a sombre mood. They'd known Dickon in his prime and had missed his presence in the village and the fields. Only the vicar, the new hired lads and the youngest children made the most of the food. John, with no appetite, picked at his chunk of pork pie. He hadn't smiled for days.

As soon as the rain eased a little, the vicar bade his farewell, and William and Mary took the opportunity to walk home with their family. While quiet on the way back, the boys were even more subdued when they entered the house. The place seemed so empty without Dickon.

John was listless and paced round the kitchen.

'Why don't you go out and gather more gorse for the fire?' Mary suggested, hating to see him so lost. 'See—there's Dickon's old leather hedging mitten—use that.'

As John left, he held the mitten to his nose. It still smelled of the salve Dickon used for his chapped hands.

That night, young William was unusually obedient. He feared his father would become distant and miserable again, and his mother, who'd been happier while Dickon was there, might revert to being irritable and short-tempered. The future looked bleak.

Throughout December and January, the prevailing weather was cold and damp, with thick mist often cloaking the village. Bored, young William began to frequent the blacksmith's with his uncle Thomas. They heard that the fog had been so thick in London that ships had collided in the Thames. Still bored, he hung about the Smiths' place in the hope of catching a glimpse of Ann. When that failed, he sought out his brother Francis; stirring him up had always been good sport. To his disappointment, Francis did not rise to any bait but stayed remarkably calm.

'What's up with Francis?' he asked his father as they trudged home on a drizzly February afternoon. 'All he wants to do is work and pray. He won't even talk to me.'

'Don't you know he's going to be a churchwarden with me this year?'

Young William blinked in disbelief. He stuffed his hands in his pockets, and scuffed the ground with his boot. 'I suppose Robert Storey had a hand in it.'

'Yes, and Robert's preparing him for the role.'

Young William grinned cheekily. '*You* don't need preparing then?'

His father smiled. 'No, but Francis and that Robert Storey never do things by halves, do they?'

In early spring, Lizzie and Elizabeth shared a washday, and used their new soap. Lizzie was about to take Dottie to Mary's for the day, yet Elizabeth had another idea.

'We don't need to bother Mary. We can keep Dottie here with us. I'll make a pen.'

With Dottie penned in one corner of the yard, the two women could get on without interruption. Lizzie chatted as they rubbed soap onto the linen.

'I'm proud o' Francis becomin' a churchwarden. It makes up for all time 'e's spent i' winter readin' wi' Robert. Thy 'usband's been good to 'im.' She now understood why Elizabeth had married Robert; both he and Francis had strong principles and were to be admired for their fortitude. Unfortunately, though, these principles resulted in a lack of warmth and affection. The winter evenings had been dismal.

'Tell me,' she asked, looking up from the washing, 'does Robert kiss thee much?' She blushed suddenly. 'I'm sorry— forget I asked.'

'No, it's alright. He did…when we were first married, but he's never been comfortable with that sort of thing. I've grown used to his ways. I can't change him—never will.'

Lizzie frowned and rubbed harder at a stubborn stain. She didn't want Francis to give up kissing altogether and, of late, he'd been quite cold towards her, presumably distracted by church matters. At this rate, they'd never have another child.

By May, Francis had settled into his new role in the church. He believed that the gentle rain of that month was due to his steadfast prayers and forbearance of pleasure. He recalled one of

Dickon's sayings. 'A wet May makes a big load of hay; a cold May is kindly and fills the barn finely.' If so, there'd be a bumper crop this year.

On a blazing hot day in July, Francis took his sharpened scythe and joined the haymakers in the lower meadow. His brother William was to mow alongside their uncle Thomas. Keen to avoid them, Francis moved as far away as possible; it was bad enough being teased about the church without having your leg sliced by an ill-wielded scythe. As he worked, he overheard Stephen Jefferson and William Mainprize making fun of William's limp. He didn't intervene to defend his brother. No one in his right mind would challenge Mainprize; the man was almost twice his size.

When everyone stopped for a drink, Francis hoped to avoid his brother again, but William sauntered towards him with Thomas.

'Now then, Francis,' William shouted as he approached, 'don't wear yourself out—you'll have churchyard to scythe later.'

Thomas joined in. 'And church silver to clean.'

Francis ignored them. He almost wished Mainprize would take William down a peg or two. He took his drink and sat down next to his father. They watched Thomas and William stroll about, full of banter with the other workers.

'Uncle Thomas is a bad influence,' Francis pronounced.

His father nodded. 'I've heard Thomas speak of leaving, though—of going to live in Scarborough.' He winked. 'Maybe you won't have to put up with him much longer.'

The next day, the women went down to the meadow to help turn the hay. It was another fine morning, the mist clearing to allow bright sunshine. The southwesterly breeze made it perfect for drying. Even Lizzie joined in the work while Elizabeth kept an eye on Dottie. It was the first time she'd helped with haymaking; in Rudston, she'd always been too busy in the vicarage.

She stood in line next to Mary and tried to emulate the deft manner in which Mary flipped over the hay. It was impossible to match her pace and, by the time they stopped for a drink, she was exhausted. She noted that Mary had a smug look on her face.

Thomas swaggered towards the women, the sun high behind his head. 'Make the most of me, you lasses, this is my last haymaking.'

They shielded their eyes from the sun, the better to check if he was joking.

'Aye, I'm off to Scarborough—to make my fortune.'

The younger women glanced at each other and giggled.

'You don't believe me? Scarborough's the place to be. There's horseracing on the sands. People travel there from all over.'

They continued to giggle.

'There's even a theatre and a library.'

Elizabeth heard him as she walked over to join them with Dottie. 'Since when have *you* been interested in a library?'

The women laughed at his expense.

'You'll see. *If* I ever come back, I'll return a rich man.'

Mary rolled her eyes. Thomas always had plans to make an easy shilling. She had no time for him.

'You're so full of yourself, Thomas Jordan. *You'll* be back, *if* you even go.'

Two weeks later, with the hay dried and stored away, Thomas finally broached the subject of Scarborough with his parents. It was late in the evening, still light in the Uphall kitchen, and his parents had just risen from their chairs to retire to bed. As his father pulled the cord to wind up the old clock, Thomas coughed to get his attention.

'I've been thinking, Father, now that Samuel will be helping with the harvest this year, and young William can do a man's work, I might take my chance elsewhere.'

'Not another farm, surely?' his father asked.

'No, I was thinking of something else entirely.' He paused for a moment. 'Scarborough.'

'Scarborough!?' both parents cried at once.

'Yes, people are spending weeks there now—for their health and entertainment.'

127

His mother snorted. 'Thoo's not ill.'

'I know.'

'What on earth do folk do there?' his father grumbled. 'They can't spend weeks doin' nowt.'

'They walk, they take the waters. There's a special well, or a spring—the water can cure people. They bathe in the sea too.'

'Now I've 'eard ev'rythin'! Whatever next!'

Thomas didn't mention the gambling, the wealthy widows or the fact that even women bathed—in their petticoats.

'I'll soon find work there. Anyway, it's a good time for me to leave—you've a barn full of hay. Do you remember what Dickon always said? "Mist i' May, heat i' June, makes thy 'arvest come right soon." You'll have a great crop this year, and Uphall can manage without me.'

His parents stood dumbfounded.

He took his father's hand and shook it formally. 'Wish me luck. I'll be gone tomorrow.'

Part Three

Inheritance

Chapter 20

1730-31

Dorothy Jordan and her husband soon realised they were better off without Thomas. The hired lads responded well to Samuel's orders and didn't try short cuts as they'd done under Thomas's supervision. As for Thomas's brothers, they were content; there'd be one less son to share the inheritance.

When the harvest began, Samuel organised the reaping of the Jordans' main holding in the wheat field, while William dealt with the extra parcel of land that his father had bought ten years ago. William had always understood that if he worked that land, he'd inherit it one day.

Young William chose to help his father instead of working with Uncle Samuel; Uphall had become boring without Uncle Thomas.

The harvest was the best in years. There was ample dry hay of good quality, and the barns were soon full of sheaves waiting to be threshed. Perhaps due to this providence, there were seven marriages that autumn, an unusually high number.

Young William, with money in his pocket, went to Hunmanby market and bought himself a white muslin scarf. He intended to wear it as a cravat. Ann Smith would take note when he tied it loosely in the latest fashion. Already, she was aping the Osbaldestons by wearing a very large hoop beneath her gown. He heard gossip that the Smiths drank tea regularly now, as only the best houses did, and that her father often brought luxuries back from Bridlington. He feared she was spoilt, and reckoned there'd be little chance of ever courting her successfully.

In despair, he thought of Stephen Jefferson; the man still had his eyes on Ann and was a landowner. Though Jefferson was small, and looked like 'a bit dropped off' when he stood beside Mainprize, he was lean and strong and in his prime.

131

William had to admit that his rival might be the most eligible bachelor in Reighton.

He despaired again when his mother and father discussed the Smiths' plans for a new house. It was suppertime and, as soon as he heard his father mention the Smiths, he told his brothers to hush.

'Enough, Richard, I want to hear Father.'

'Don't you want to hear about John at the sheep fair?'

'Not now, no.'

'It'll make you laugh.'

'Shut up, and listen to Father.'

Their parents paused in their conversation as the boys suddenly went quiet.

'Go on then,' urged young William. 'Where are the Smiths going to build?'

'Up past the church, on the track to Speeton.'

His mother pushed away her dirty plate. 'The fine harvest's gone to Matthew's head,' she pronounced as she left the table to fetch the cheese.

Young William was puzzled. 'Whereabouts up there? There isn't room for another house.'

'There will be when he knocks down the crofts and clears the garths.'

Mary cut pieces of cheese and passed them round. 'I can't see it happening myself. Matthew has too many grand ideas—like Thomas.'

William didn't agree. He recalled his and Matthew's fascination with the new houses in Beverley, their pantile roofs and fancy red brickwork. He knew Matthew was serious.

'I think he's already had plans drawn up. He was telling me how impressed he was by houses in Bridlington, on Westgate. He's definitely aiming at two storeys with six bays.'

Mary sniffed. 'I suppose he'll want a stable block as well.'

Young William had visions of Ann Smith riding out on a beautiful horse, her hair as black as her mount.

His mother cut short his daydream. She nudged him and changed the subject.

132

'You've just been to Hunmanby market—is it still worthwhile going?'

'Not really. More people are taking their stuff to Bridlington instead. There's still a big trade, though, in rabbits.'

Mary clicked her tongue. 'That'll be Osbaldeston's warren. I bet if it wasn't for the rabbits and the smuggled goods, the market would close altogether.' She thought again of Matthew's ambitious plans. What with those and the changes in Hunmanby, the future was disturbing. She gazed at her sons, now growing up so fast it was hard to keep them in food and clothes. Even the simple and gentle John would be a man soon.

'Everything's happening too fast,' she concluded. 'There's Thomas gone to Scarborough, the Smith girls all in hoops... and now the Hunmanby market's not what it was. I'm getting old.'

Young William suddenly remembered something. 'Guess who I saw in Hunmanby. Uncle Richard. He avoided me, but he knew I'd seen him. He looked very smart. He sneaked off with a man—don't know who it was.'

His father coughed and brought the conversation back to the Hunmanby warren. 'I bet that rabbit trade must bring in more money now than sheep and cattle. No wonder Osbaldeston can afford to keep a warrener and pay him seven pounds a year.'

Young William had an idea. He grinned at his mother, full of bravado. 'If you like, I can soon get you a 'stray' coney.'

'No you don't,' warned his father. 'That warrener's keen. He guards the flock as if the rabbits were his. Don't smirk, I mean it. Only the other week he caught a man poaching. Remember, Osbaldeston's a Justice, and the man won't escape a fine... or worse.'

Already, though, young William was thinking of giving Ann Smith a rabbit fur to trim her gloves and hood.

At Christmas, due to the plentiful harvest, the Jordans planned a great feast at Uphall. On Christmas Eve, Dorothy

133

was busier than ever in the kitchen. She was so distracted by the preparations that she didn't pay attention when her husband retired early. She did notice him winding the clock as usual, though didn't see the way he leant on the wall to keep his balance, or how he staggered before climbing the stairs.

She found him an hour later, sitting with a vacant stare on the floor by the bed, his arms hanging limply at his sides.

'Oh, Francis, whatever's 'appened?'

He tried to speak, but made no sense. Not wanting to alarm anyone at Christmas, she struggled by herself to heave him into bed. Then she held a glass of brandy to his lips.

In spite of dribbling most of it, he seemed to revive.

'I'm alright,' he mumbled. 'I think I tripped over yon mat. I'll be fine i' mornin'.'

She joined him in bed, and they both tried to forget the incident. As she lay awake, she regretted there'd be no 'shooting in' the Christmas this year; it was the first time Francis had missed it since they'd been married.

On Christmas Day, Francis looked pale and shaken. He didn't attend church, and everyone knew he must be ill when he let Dorothy say grace and carve the goose. He didn't move from his chair, and no one could cajole him into conversation.

Everyone ate the food, but with little comment. Without Thomas to lift people's spirits and instigate various games, the day passed quietly. William, Mary and the boys joined in the subdued carol singing, and then sauntered home.

Dorothy could no longer ignore the change in her husband. He even relinquished the daily ritual of winding the clock, though he watched her do it with ill-concealed distrust. For the next few days of the holiday, she made sure he was warm and didn't overdo anything.

William came to help the hired lads clean out the sheds and feed the stock. He was led to believe his father just suffered from stiffness in the joints. When he found a bottle of neatsfoot oil frozen solid in the stable, he brought it indoors and told his mother to thaw it and rub it into his father's knees and shoulders.

He found his father sitting slouched in the big chair by the fire, a blanket over his legs. He leant over to reassure him.

'You leave all the work and worry to me and Samuel. You stay by the fire and keep warm.'

'Aye,' his mother agreed. 'Don't fret over owt. An' remember,' she said, ignoring his filthy looks, 'thoo can go to bed anytime thoo wants.'

Francis did fret though. Before the twelve days of Christmas were over, he'd settled his will. He told his wife the gist of it and had it written up a week later by the attorney and steward of the manor, John Grimston. When it came to signing the will, he couldn't grip the pen. After making a few spidery and unconnected lines, he gave up. He turned his head in shame when he saw the word 'mark' placed beneath his scrawl.

Dorothy thought that William, at least, should be apprised of the contents, but Francis ignored her concern.

'Nay,' he grumbled, 'I'm still master 'ere. I may be aged an' infirm but I'm perfect i' mind an' memory. William can wait like ev'ryone else. I'm not dead yet.'

Chapter 21

1731

A period of frost and snow began in mid-January, and the temperature stayed below freezing for two months. This year, no one was too worried for there was plenty of hay for the livestock and enough food to go round.

William and Mary's two youngest sons, with fewer chores to do, wrapped themselves up, pushed straw and wool into their boots, and then padded through the snow to the pond. Once there, they prised stones from the frozen ground and tossed them onto the ice, watching them skid to the other side. The black ice held firm, didn't even crack.

Richard braved it first. He stepped onto the ice, stamped on it with his heels, and finally jumped up and down. No matter how hard he tried, the ice wouldn't break. Matthew joined in and, after they'd both slid about for a while, Richard had an idea.

'I know, let's get mother's milking stool. We can tie a rope to it. You can sit on it, and I'll give you a ride over the ice.'

When this worked well enough, Richard had another idea. He stood in the centre of the pond.

'If I can make a hole through the ice right here and ram a pole in, we can fasten the rope to it. We'll have a merry-go-round like at the fair.'

Using a metal spike borrowed from the blacksmith, Richard drove a neat hole. He then fetched a broomstick from home, wedged it in tight and tied the rope to it.

'I'll have a go first—see how it works.'

He sat on the stool, and pushed off so hard that he flew off and banged his head on the ice. Undeterred, he found a way of grasping the stool's legs to hold on. With a steadier push off, he rode in a wide and scary circle about the pond.

Yet, as the rope entwined round the broomstick, this circle became ever smaller until he hit his nose on the stick.

Matthew winced in sympathy. 'Why don't you wind the rope round first? Try that.'

This time, with a push off from Matthew, Richard spun on the ice in tight, speedy circles that grew ever wider as the rope unwound. Just when he thought he'd spin off, the rope began to wind the other way back round the stick.

'Good God!' he cried. 'This goes on forever!'

When he did come to a halt, he fell off the stool and could hardly stand. He staggered across the pond as if drunk, before slipping and landing flat on his back.

'Hell's fires!' he muttered under his breath, eager for another go.

The cold air whipping past, the rumble and hiss of the stool on the ice, and the ever-present fear of falling off, made it the perfect ride. It wasn't long before every child allowed out to play in Reighton begged for a turn.

Matthew always warned newcomers to hold tight to the stool. 'If you don't, you'll spin off.'

Throughout the day, the children flew round in circles, and only went home when it grew too cold and dark. Richard and Matthew were exhausted, their hands and feet frozen. Their mother had little sympathy as they sat barefoot by the fire, holding their red, aching toes as close to the flames as they dare.

'If you must spend all day outside, I can soon find you something to do.'

Richard groaned. 'We don't want any boring jobs.'

'How about going out with Will? Your brother's offered to walk you to Hunmanby tomorrow—to see if the market's open.'

They were both lost for words. It was most unusual for William to suggest doing *anything* with them.

'So—do you want to go?'

'What—all of us?' asked Richard. 'Even John?'

'Why not? He'll have you and William to look out for him.'

137

What their mother didn't know was that William had found the rabbit traps at Uphall. He intended to sneak up to Osbaldeston's warren and set the traps there.

The next day, Mary gave each boy a hot potato. 'There, put these in your pockets. They'll keep you warm, and you can eat them later.'

They donned an extra layer of clothes before setting off into the winter sunshine.

William collected the traps from their hiding place and tied them to his back. On the way out of the lane, he explained the real reason for their walk.

'Mother's tired of cooking pork and mutton, so we're going to catch her a rabbit or two. If the warrener's about, you're to distract him.'

Richard frowned. 'What if he chases us?'

'He won't be able to run far, not in this snow.'

'Neither will we.' Richard stopped walking, less confident of William's plan.

John also stopped, and pulled on William's arm. 'Aren't we going to the market?'

'No, and you'd better keep up.'

The snow was so bright it was blinding but, with the sun low to their left, they made their way through the deep snow towards the moor. They hadn't gone far from the village when they realised John was trailing too far behind.

William groaned; John was an added risk to the venture. 'Perhaps you should go back home,' he suggested.

John blinked against the sun. 'No, I like the snow.' He spread his arms to encompass the white world. For him, the snow cast a magic spell; everything sparkled and even the air rang with a tinkling sound.

William sighed. 'Alright, but don't wander about so. Walk in our footprints—it's easier.'

One behind the other, they approached the moor at last and stood still, their lungs aching from the cold air. Powdered snow blew into their faces, smarting and making their cheeks red. Their noses dripped, and the beginnings of a moustache had frozen above William's lips. With the warren now in sight, he signalled to his brothers to kneel. There was no sign of the warrener, so he took the pack of traps from his back and blew onto his hands. Once he could feel his fingers again, he was ready.

'John—you and Matthew keep watch. I'll lay the traps with Richard.'

Looking about him, he made a mental note of his surroundings; he'd need to locate the traps when they returned tomorrow. He counted the mounds of snow denoting hidden burrows, and chose to lay the traps at the edge of the warren.

On their way back home, snow began to fall again and cover their footprints. William smiled to himself. The warrener would never suspect a thing.

'Listen John,' William warned, with one of his hard stares, 'don't you dare tell Mother any of this. We'll just say we got tired and never made it to Hunmanby. With any luck, she'll let us out again tomorrow.'

The next day, the boys set off once more. Although Matthew had painful chilblains, he didn't want to be left out. This time, William took a bag for the rabbits.

A freezing wind blew from the northeast, and the sky began to turn the colour of lead. The low sun appeared only now and then, as if emerging from smoke. When they gazed across to Filey, the clouds were a dingy yellow, full of snow.

William led his brothers in single file. They found the going easier because the snow had frozen overnight, but it made their tread noisy. The snow crunched and cracked, and the slightest sounds carried so much further across the frozen landscape. When they neared the warren, they slowed, and trod more carefully.

All of a sudden, William held up his hand.

They stopped.

Then he put a finger to his lips for quiet. He went down on his knees and signalled to them to do the same. Flurries of snow blew across the moor as he squinted and searched for the places he'd left the traps. While his brothers stayed there, he crawled forward and then lay on his belly to check the first

139

trap. When it was empty, he set it off with a stick. The sudden noise was startling, so he waited a while before crawling to the next trap. Both the other traps had caught a rabbit. Without a second thought, he pulled and twisted their necks. Then he released their legs and pushed the rabbits into his bag. He crawled back to the others, grinning.

'Mother should be pleased,' he whispered.

'Have you seen the sky?' Richard asked, pointing to the east. The snowstorm was almost upon them.

Chapter 22

Young William turned to face the oncoming storm. At least their tracks would be covered, but it would be a struggle to get home. Already, the biting wind was stronger and, within minutes, the snow came. The boys bent almost double, keeping their heads down as they leant into the blizzard. William reckoned that, if they kept the wind to their left, they'd reach Reighton. To prevent losing anyone, he made John walk right behind him.

'Hold onto me,' he yelled, and then instructed the others to walk in single file and hang onto each other's coats. This meant that in one line, they could only go as fast as Matthew, the youngest and smallest.

William trudged on, blinking as he tried to see a way through the driving snow. He was numb with cold, and the flurries danced about in such a mazy way that he began to lose all sense of purpose and direction. To stay alert, he recited bits of the Bible. He thought of his sister Mary; she used to imagine distant lands full of heroes. With her in mind, he pretended to be Moses leading his people to the Promised Land.

'Be strong and of good courage,' he shouted into the whirling snow. 'Fear not for the Lord thy God doth go with thee. He will not fail thee, nor forsake thee.'

He paused to check that his brothers were behind him, still in line, their eyes to the ground and following blindly. 'God is my salvation,' he cried. 'I will trust and not be afraid. The Lord Jehovah is my strength and my song.' He fought on, repeating every few steps, 'God is my salvation.'

Mary panicked when she saw the sky darken and the snow descend. Her daughter had died after being lost in bad weather. The dog had made the girl's rescue possible, but there was no Stina this time, and all her sons, bar Francis, were out there somewhere. It was her fault. She should have

141

kept them indoors. Unable to go and look for them herself, she paced the kitchen and kept peering out of the window. Then she tried to sit and knit. As soon as William came home, she told him to go and search for them.

He couldn't believe his sons had gone to Hunmanby. 'Good God, didn't you see the clouds building up?' He rubbed his neck in exasperation. 'And who's in charge—Will?'

She gulped, and nodded.

He wasted no more time. He rammed on his boots again, rushed outside and headed up the lane towards Hunmanby. No one else was about, and there were no footprints to follow. He strode as fast as he could over the high ground, the wind mostly behind him. Once he reached the brow of the hill, he strained his eyes to see into the distance. There, through the haze of swirling snow, he could pick out a dark line of figures coming slowly up the hill in his direction. He cupped his hands to his mouth and called their names. When there was no response, he carried on.

Young William walked right into his father without seeing him. He stopped so suddenly that John crashed into his back, the rest following likewise. At first, in a snow-induced trance, they didn't realise they were safe. The old warrener might have stopped them, or even the devil himself might be barring their way. When William saw it was his father holding him tight, he sobbed with relief. He tried to speak, though his teeth were chattering.

'I g-got two r-rabbits,' he stammered.

'Never mind the rabbits, let's get you home. Your mother's at her wit's end with worriting.'

Mary ran to the door as soon as she heard footsteps outside. She opened it wide, ignoring the blast of snow, and hauled the boys into the house.

'It's all my fault, I'm so sorry. I should have paid more heed to the weather. I should have stopped you.' She clicked her tongue. 'Just look at you…'

William pulled off their boots and coats and put them to steam by the fire while Mary brought bowls of warm water

142

for hands and feet. She sat the boys close to the fire and, once they had some feeling back, she chafed their hands dry and rubbed raw onion on Matthew's chilblained toes. Then she noticed their chapped and cracked lips.

'I'll heat up that mutton fat and candle wax. You can smooth it on your lips.'

Young William was very subdued. He leant towards the fire, his head down. 'Sorry, Mother, I'm to blame.' He lifted his head. 'I do have a couple of rabbits for us, though.'

'Yes,' his father interrupted, 'and you won't be going out on your own again, not for some time.' He faced his wife. 'They've been setting traps by the warren.'

Mary put a hand to her mouth. Not only had she almost lost her sons in a blizzard, the boys could have been caught poaching. It didn't bear thinking about. Matthew was still a child at ten years old, and John would have been so upset if he was accused of anything. She turned on young William.

'How could you! How could you lead your brothers to do such a thing? Have you no sense whatsoever?'

He suppressed a smile, knowing how much his mother would appreciate a rabbit stew. 'I thought you'd like to cook rabbit for a change.'

'Hmm.' She remained tight-lipped, but it was the end of the reprimand.

That night, it was so cold that, even sitting almost on top of the fire, no one felt warm. After supper, they went to bed with cold noses and still wearing most of their clothes. The youngest boys didn't sleep top to toe as usual. Instead, they snuggled up next to each other like spoons, their legs tucked up beneath them. Richard was relieved; at least he didn't have Matthew's feet, stinking of raw onion, in his face. Their knees ached after a while, yet they didn't dare stretch out their limbs in the icy bed. They shivered together and, at last, as their bodies warmed, they fell asleep.

In the morning, the windows were frosted over; they were pretty with patterns like fern leaves, but Mary had no time for such things. She'd seen that even the kettle of water left by the hearth was frozen. On her hands and knees, she struggled to muster up enough heat from the gorse and twigs that she kept piling onto the fire. She scraped the window with her nails and peeped out. It was going to be a dark and dismal day, one to sap your strength and make you feel older than your years.

She put on her cloak and shuffled out with a lantern to milk the cow. As she knocked the snow off her boots and entered the small byre, the cow lowed in recognition. It was close and muggy inside, the stench of urine and damp straw such a contrast to the crisp and cold air of the garden. She wiped her nose with the back of her hand as she fed the cow a scoop of meal. Then she picked up the stool and pail and sat with her cold forehead pressed against the cow's warm belly. It was so cosy sitting there, and her pull on the teats was so rhythmical that she began to doze. All at once, hailstones thrashed against the door. She sighed on becoming fully awake, finished the milking and carried the pail into the kitchen.

William had his sons in a line before him. He pointed to the two eldest.

'You're coming with me. As a punishment, before breakfast, you're going to clear snow from the yard at Uphall.'

It was a thankless task. Under the snow, the yard was rock-hard with mud and dung. No sooner had the ways been cleared than the snow came down again.

The two younger boys went about their daily job of gathering sticks for the fire. It wasn't easy ripping twigs from the frozen ground, and Matthew tore his fingernails. When they went home for breakfast, chilled to the bone, Matthew laid the twigs near the fire to dry. He gazed at his mother with tears in his eyes.

She felt so sorry for him. 'I'll get you both an apple.'

'They're too cold to eat,' Richard complained. 'They set my teeth on edge.'

'Alright then, I'll roast them.'

144

Young William, John and their father returned for breakfast to find the rest of the family huddled patiently over the grate, watching a couple of apples hiss and spit as they cooked.

The newcomers squeezed nearer to warm their hands.

'I think it must be almost too cold for snow,' Mary pronounced. 'The milk's already freezing in the pail. I'm so glad now that Dickon isn't here to suffer. It was a blessing he went when he did.'

John then thought of Jack the shepherd, out in all weathers; he'd have to scrabble about for the sheep hidden beneath the snowdrifts, while here he was about to have breakfast and looking forward to rabbit stew.

Young William was more concerned about the real reason for catching rabbits. 'Father, when you skin them, can you save the fur for me?'

'What do you want it for?'

Young William blushed. 'I was thinking to give it to cousin Ann... to trim a coat or something.'

'Give up, lad, don't waste your time. When her father has their new house built... well, she won't be short of suitors then.'

After breakfast, their father went back to Uphall to help cut slices of hay for the animals. He also loaded a sledge with hay to distribute to those farmers less fortunate. When he returned the sledge, his face was red and swollen from the cold and his eyebrows were coated in rime. His knees were seizing up so that, when he entered the Uphall kitchen, he limped in pain to the settle.

His father was sitting opposite by the fire, his face dark and glowering. He noticed William wince as he sat down.

'Aye, thoo's feelin' thy age like me. I don't know 'ow many more winters I'll see.' He gestured to the bracket clock on the wall. 'Me time's measured by them chimes.'

William didn't take his father seriously. 'Oh, you'll be fine again by the time spring comes.' His father always liked to moan in cold weather.

145

His mother, though, was paying more heed. She fussed over him, tucking the blanket tighter under his legs. Then she turned to William.

'Thoo'd best get on 'ome. By looks o' thee, thoo'd be better off i' bed. I'll get Samuel to sort lads out fo' rest o' day.'

As soon as William had gone, his father asked to see Samuel. Together, they'd finalise an inventory of the property.

Chapter 23

William was intrigued when invited by his father to a formal meeting with their local clerk. It was early February, and his brother Samuel would attend along with their brother Francis from Argam. On the appointed day, he stepped into the Uphall kitchen and approached the fire to warm his hands. He noted that only his parents were present, seated at each end of the table.

'I've told lads an' maids to keep out,' his mother explained, 'just till we've finished.'

William was full of suspicion. Of late, he'd seen his parents discussing things with Samuel more often than was necessary for the winter work. He turned to face his father.

'So what's this all about?'

'Samuel's been good enough to make a list of our goods an' chattels.'

'I could have done that.'

'Well, it's done now. An' when Samuel arrives wi' Francis, thoo can check it. I've arranged fo' two appraisers to come. It's just a formality.'

'What about Richard? Isn't he invited?'

His parents coughed, and glanced warily at each other.

His father mumbled an excuse. ''E's too far away i' Carnaby.'

'Aye,' his mother added. 'Best not bring 'im all this way fo' nowt. As tha father said, it's just a formality.'

William suspected there might be other reasons. Maybe his parents had heard rumours about Richard. If so, Richard might be written out of the will. He began to think that Samuel had seen the will already, and could have done the inventory because he was the main beneficiary.

'And what about your will?' he dared to ask. 'Do *I* get to know about it, or is it something only Samuel knows about?'

'Thoo'll get what thoo deserves, like ev'ryone else. An' don't think thoo can change owt—me will was registered i' Beverley last Wednesday—an' I'm not changin' it. There's just this inventory to see to.'

William saw that the table had been scrubbed clean. He slouched towards it and sat down heavily on the bench. He was about to ask more questions when there was a knock on the door.

His mother got up and welcomed in two fellow yeomen of the village to act as appraisers.

William wasn't a bit surprised to see William Hesslewood limp into the kitchen. The old man was a lifelong friend of his father, and had often been a fellow churchwarden; he was an obvious choice. John Palmer, the younger man, was new to the village and, though he didn't know Uphall, he was a well-respected local farmer.

William stood to acknowledge their presence. He was about to sit down again when Samuel and Francis entered with the clerk. After brief introductions, everyone sat at the table and waited while the clerk pulled a sheet of paper from his satchel.

William leant forward to see. The writing reminded him of letters he'd received in the past, those that had requested him to attend the quarter sessions. The list of items was brief, though set out clearly with the values in a neat column. Whether it was 'a true full and perfect' inventory was another question for he saw that the total came to a mere sixteen pounds and ten shillings.

He listened, bemused, as the clerk read out the details. The house contents—the beds, dresser and table and the vague reference to 'several other things thereunto belonging' were worth very little. There was no mention of the clock, just 'other implements'. He frowned when he heard of the livestock listed, but then he knew that February was always a time when the numbers were low; most of the animals had been sold or slaughtered in the autumn and wouldn't appear in an inventory. Likewise, the value of the wheat sown seemed accurate, as was the amount for the corn and hay in the barn.

1 4 8

With no hesitation, Hesslewood nodded his agreement, and Palmer, predictably, followed suit. None of the brothers raised any objection.

The clerk took out his pen and inkpot. He wrote the date beneath the inventory, and the names of the appraisers present.

'That's that then,' declared Dorothy. 'Thoo'll all stay for a drink o' warmed ale?'

The clerk and William's brother Francis declined. Both wanted to leave before the weather changed. To William's surprise, Samuel sat in the chair vacated by his mother, lit his pipe and then stretched out his legs; he looked as if he was master. William and the two yeomen moved onto the settle by the fire. They also lit their pipes and stretched out their legs, waiting for the ale to heat.

When Dorothy added the aromatic spices, she turned to them. 'It smells like Christmas, eh? If tha likes, I can serve up currant cake.'

'Aye, do that,' urged Francis. 'I'm glad this business is over. We can forget it fo' now.'

William decided that was probably for the best. His father had arranged his affairs for whatever reason and, no doubt, he'd perk up again and live for years. One anxiety remained; Samuel might have designs on the farm and lands. Here was his brother chatting away happily with their father about the cows in calf while he, the eldest son, felt left out. Maybe Samuel was in such good spirits because he really had seen the will.

His mother was full of smiles as she handed round the tankards. 'An 'ot drink's best way to conclude business. Good 'ealth to all.'

Within minutes, even William was at peace with the world. As his belly warmed, he grew more resigned. The will had been registered, and his father was too stubborn to change it. Whatever happened, he was sure his parents would be fair to each of their sons.

As William predicted, by spring, his father had regained much of his former strength. The weather was favourable for the growing crops, and the future harvest looked promising. Uphall became a cheery place once more.

The Smith family took advantage of the dry, sunny spells to pull down the crofts on the proposed site for the new house. Although the labourers were told to keep quiet about the plans, news leaked out. The blacksmith was the first to hear of the large walled space revealed underneath one of the demolished crofts. Another similar space was discovered beneath an outhouse. Word soon spread.

Young William returned home one evening with his brothers, full of the latest gossip. 'I always thought Uncle Matthew knew more about the smuggling,' he blurted out before he'd even sat up to the table. 'Now we know—he's chosen to build his house there because of those huge holes underneath. It's obvious—he'll store tea or brandy there. You'll see.'

His mother and father knew part of the story, yet didn't want their son to spread incriminating rumours.

'From what I hear,' his father explained, 'there's too much water under there to store tea or anything else. The men have probably just dug up an old well or a drain.'

Young William was not giving in. 'Alright, but what's to stop the Smiths making the holes bigger, making them into tunnels even?'

His father shrugged. 'It's none of our business. Anyway, they'll be laying the foundations soon and if the fine weather holds, the walls will be up before long. Any so-called tunnels will be filled in.'

Young William found the Smiths' new house the most exciting thing that had ever happened in Reighton.

'Will he build it in chalk?' he asked as his mother set out the cold mutton, pickles and cheese. 'I've heard he's ordered loads of it, but then I heard he's going to buy bricks as well.'

His father blew out his cheeks and sighed. 'If you're so interested, why don't you ask him? Or ask your precious Ann?'

Young William's face reddened.

Richard grinned. 'Yes, why don't you?'

A clout from his brother shut him up.

'I'll ask her,' offered John. 'I'll see her when she visits David.'

Young William bristled. 'David? What David?' He didn't know of this particular suitor.

'You know—our pet lamb.'

Young William felt stupid. 'Oh, yes, I'd forgotten. Yes, you ask her. Find out everything you can.'

The next day, John was on the northern pasture as usual with the shepherd. The air throbbed with the sound of bleating as the new lambs strayed too far from their mothers. David, the pet lamb, was now a large sheep. As he'd been castrated, he was accepted as another ewe and behaved like a grandmother. He spent his days strolling round the flock, proud of the new offspring.

Late in the afternoon, Ann Smith sauntered up to the pasture with a handful of best grass for David. John waved and walked over to greet her with David following behind, butting his legs. They stood stroking the pet sheep in silence while it chewed its gift of lush grass.

When the sheep had finished, Ann sighed. 'It's a pity he can't father any lambs. He's so good—so docile and tame.'

John smiled. 'David the shepherd boy was good too.'

'Speaking of being good... how's your brother William? Is he behaving himself? I haven't seen him properly since he left a rabbit skin for me. Even then, he didn't stay long.'

'He's alright.'

'Are you sure? Sometimes I think he avoids me.'

'He wants to know about your new house.'

'So does everyone. Tell him we're having red bricks on top of the chalk. And I'll have a bedroom to myself. Imagine that! Tell him we'll build a stable, and father's thinking of having a fancy dovecote too. Mother's a little worried by it all, but it's going to be wonderful.' As she bent over to kiss the sheep goodbye, she had an afterthought.

'I'll be here again soon. Tell William, if he wants to know more, he's to ask me himself.'

John remembered the bits about Ann's bedroom and the stable. After further questioning, he mumbled about bricks and a dovecote, and then gave one of his widest smiles.

'She said it's going to be wonderful!'

Young William wasn't satisfied. He became far too busy that summer, though, to think about the Smiths. Although Reighton, as elsewhere that year, had only half the normal rainfall, there was so much to do. He helped mow the hay, dry it and store it. Then, when the warm, dry weather continued well into August and beyond, he had no time for anything except the harvest.

Even October was warm as young William worked with his father and Samuel, ploughing and preparing the fields for sowing. Towards the end of the month, as work slackened, his father asked him if he'd like to go to Hunmanby Fair.

'You've done us proud this year and deserve a day off. You can go with John. He's wanting to help take the sheep, but you know what he's like. If he's given any money, he'll lose it or spend it on something daft.'

'Can't the shepherd look after him?'

'No, he'll be too busy.'

'Alright then.'

Now that autumn was here and there was more leisure time, young William's thoughts turned once more to Ann Smith. There wouldn't be just sheep and cattle at the fair, there'd be stalls selling all sorts. He could buy a new hat or choose a present for Ann. There'd be lots he could do. He wouldn't need to be with John the whole time. John could look after himself.

Chapter 24

On the morning of the Hunmanby Fair, young William heard John leap out of bed and fall clumsily against the other beds as he pulled on his breeches. It was chilly and still dark. He yawned and decided to wait until his brother had left the house before getting up himself. Although he'd have liked to walk with the sheepdog, he didn't want to get too involved. More to the point, he didn't want to help with the preparations. John wouldn't mind smartening up the sheep, trimming off any shaggy wool so the fleece appeared smooth and thick. No, he didn't want to get to the fair stinking of sheep. And, surely, his mother didn't expect him to wait round the sales ring either. He could keep an eye on John later. He yawned again, ducked his head under the blanket, snuggled down… and thought of Ann Smith.

While John and the shepherd were herding the sheep towards Hunmanby, young William was dressing as if for a Sunday. He didn't really need to shave yet, but used his father's razor out in the garden. With a small mirror propped in the crook of the apple tree, he shaved the fluff above his top lip. Then, after a quick breakfast, he grabbed his hat and coat and left with a promise to look out for John.

'And, yes, Mother, I'll see about a pot of treacle.'

As he strode up and out of St Helen's Lane, he found that the mist lay only on the lower ground. Once he was on the hill between Reighton and Hunmanby, the sun broke through. There, he stopped to admire the view across Filey Bay. The sea had long, smooth waves rolling in at an angle, like the furrows in the fields. He tipped back his hat to feel the breeze on his forehead, and then carried on striding down towards the fair.

Way before he reached Cross Hill, he heard the noise of the sheep and cattle being steered into pens. He also got a whiff of them. That distinctive odour of sheep was so sour

1 5 3

and pungent in the damp morning air. As he neared the market place, the cries of stallholders vied with the cacophony from the livestock, and he caught the more appetising smells of gingerbread and roast chestnuts.

He ignored the animals and their keepers, and wandered along each side of the row of traders to check their wares. Amid the usual fare of fruit, cheeses and rabbits were stalls selling brightly coloured sweets, gingerbread moulds, leather goods and knives. At the table selling walnuts, he looked about vaguely for items like treacle. Of more interest was a man selling toothpowders, and a stall set out with samples of snuff.

Just then, a woman wandered by with a baby strapped to her back. The basket she carried, laden with toys and trinkets, brought John to mind so instead of wondering what to buy, William thought he'd better show his face at the sales ring.

The bellman was already on the steps of the market cross to announce the start. Pushing through the crowd, William searched for John and the shepherd. He found them, not at the ringside, but by one of the nearby pens. They were staring in awe at a huge ram with a long bushy tail.

'Found you at last!' he said. 'Why aren't you at the ring?'

Jack spat on the ground in contempt. 'Why, there's nowt there yet—nowt worth seein'.'

John nodded in agreement, eager to speak. 'Jack says the sheep can't hold a candle to ours. They're just tag, rag an' bobtail.'

'So you've chosen to gawp at rams instead?'

'Aye,' Jack murmured, not taking his eyes from the ram. 'I want a closer look at this un. See 'is balls 'angin' level? That's a sign 'e 'as two i' good order. An' see 'is steep fore'ead an' 'is face—'e's one to reckon with. 'E's ready to be at ewes alright, an' I bet 'e could sire 'undreds.'

The ram's owner saw their interest. He tied the ram's front legs together ready for inspection, and beckoned Jack into the pen.

William sensed this was going to take some time. Not a bit interested in the ram himself, he knelt by the sheepdog.

She was lying patiently on her stomach by their side, her head between her front paws. He began stroking her ears.

'There, there, Meg, there's a good dog.'

She still had the red collar he'd given her, though it was worn now and faded. She lifted her head and wagged her tail.

The way she gazed into his eyes made him want to cry. Though it was five years since he'd lost Stina, he thought of her every single day. No dog could replace her. He carried on fondling Meg as he watched Jack sink his hands into the ram's fleece, then feel along its broad back to test the haunches.

Jack stood back in admiration and then called to John. 'Get thassen in 'ere an' learn summat.'

He explained that the choice of ram depended on whether you wanted to breed for wool or for meat. He prised open the ram's mouth.

'See its teeth, John? They should lie nicely against top gum. Aye, an' gums should be dark blue.' He turned to the owner. 'Ow old is this ram?'

''E's three.'

'Hmm.' Jack judged this age was correct, yet still he didn't commit himself, didn't want to show too much interest. He reckoned it would fetch a high price.

John tugged at his sleeve. 'Do you want it for our flock? We already have a ram.'

The owner chuckled. 'Thoo can't keep same ram fo' long. Thoo can't 'ave tha sheep inbreedin'.'

'Aye,' Jack concurred. He moved away with a last, sad, backwards glance at the ram.

John followed him with a puzzled frown. He hadn't a clue about inbreeding.

William stood up, having already seen and heard enough of sheep. He said he'd come back later when the sales were over, said he had things to buy.

He meandered back to the toothpowder stall and listened to the man propounding the benefits.

'No more yellow teeth, no more foul breath.'

'What's in it then?' asked a potential customer.

155

'Finest chalk and cuttlefish bone—to whiten and clean at the same time. I've also Peruvian bark. And if you really want to please the ladies, there's a powder scented with oil of cinnamon.' He added in a quiet voice, 'It's more expensive of course.'

William had always relied on chewing a bit of parsley, especially if he'd eaten onions or been given garlic as a medicine. There was no need to waste money on special powders. He moved on to a stall arrayed with bottles of perfumed water. Perhaps Ann Smith would appreciate such a gift.

The stallholder sensed a sale. 'Now, young man, these waters not only smell delightful, they're good for your health. This one here...' He removed the cork from a bottle for him to inhale. 'This one's rosewater. It's good for the eyes, and eases inflammation.'

William was impressed; the scent was delicate and pleasant. He was sure Ann would like it, but there were so many different bottles to choose from. After sniffing orange water and then lavender water, he was no nearer a decision.

The man insisted on the benefits of lavender. 'You can use it as a mouthwash. Dilute a small spoonful in either warm or cold water and then rinse your mouth.'

William didn't fancy anyone would want their mouths tasting of lavender. 'Thank you, I'll think about it... I'll maybe come back later.'

He glanced about. He could buy so many things. Another knife was always a temptation. He passed the snuff stall once more, and then returned to take a better look when the customers there began to disperse. As they left, one of the men squeezed another's bottom. It was an intimate gesture and, to William's horror, he realised it was his uncle Richard. Worse still, his uncle had seen him.

'Why, if it isn't young William!'

William blushed as he was introduced.

'Stephen, this is my nephew.'

Stephen held out his hand. 'Pleased to make your acquaintance.'

William kept his hand rigid at his side.

'Well,' mumbled Richard to cover the awkwardness, 'if you're wanting snuff, there's a wide choice here. Stephen bought a box of lily of the valley.'

William excused himself. 'I have to get back to the ring. John's there with the shepherd.'

'Yes, we saw them a while ago. Goodbye then. We might bump into each other later.'

Not if I can help it, thought William. He stood transfixed as the two men sauntered away from the fair. He watched them make their way down the main street, and then he followed—at a discreet distance.

Further along, the place was deserted. Everyone was at the fair. William kept dodging down the side alleys in case Richard or his 'friend' happened to turn round. He had to peer round corners to check he hadn't lost sight of them. Eventually, he saw them enter a chalk cottage, the last one at the far end of town.

He approached with caution, and saw that there was a gate leading to a garden at the back. If he were caught, he'd just say he wanted to hear about the harvest in Carnaby—a lame excuse, but he couldn't think of anything else.

He opened the gate, scurried at a stoop up the pathway, and then pressed his back against the cottage wall. There was a tiny window, not far from his head. As fast as a bird peck, he shot a glance through the glass. He was so quick he saw nothing. Now, leaning against the wall, with sweating hands and a dry mouth, he wished he hadn't followed them. What did he hope to achieve by spying? What good would it do if he saw something? He licked his lips and took a longer look through the window.

The silhouettes of two figures stood in the middle of the room, and they seemed to be kissing.

William sank to the ground, his heart pounding. He couldn't tell anyone what he'd seen. His knees were trembling when he stumbled from the garden. Then he ran as fast as he could, back up the street to the fair.

When he arrived, the sales were almost over and there was no sign of John or Jack. He asked a few people if they'd seen the shepherd and his lad from Reighton.

'Aye,' a man answered. ''E left wi' that ram 'e was after. There was no lad with 'im though.'

In mounting panic, William rushed up and down, searching for John. Finally, a man pointed out a jingling ring. There, behind the Swan Inn, was a roped circle; ten people were inside it, wearing blindfolds, trying to catch the man with bells on his legs. One of those blindfolded was John.

William blew out his cheeks with relief. He'd keep a close eye on his brother from now on. After a few minutes, someone caught the jingler and received a small prize. The others removed their blindfolds.

'John!' William shouted. 'I'm over here.'

John hurried towards him, still out of breath from the game. 'I have pennies left for another go.'

'Wait a minute, how many goes have you had?'

'Lots, but I've won prizes.' John emptied his pockets. There was nothing except cheap fairings: a tiny comb, a set of buttons, a bag of boiled sweets.

'John, we should go home.' He knew their mother would be cross. He hadn't looked out for his brother, and now John had nothing but rubbish to show for his day out.

'Let me have one last go. Please!'

William sighed. 'Go on then.' He resigned himself to wait for the inevitable and, sure enough, John didn't catch the jingler.

'What have *you* bought?' John asked after he'd handed in his blindfold.

'Nothing. I've been wasting my time searching for you. And now we'd best go home.'

'I saw Uncle Richard.'

'Oh?'

'Yes. Did you see him?'

William crossed his fingers behind his back. 'No—I didn't.'

Chapter 25

All the way back to Reighton, John rattled on about the sheep sales. He paused only to explain how hard it was to catch the jingler. As soon as he entered the house, he tipped out his pockets.

'There, Mother,' he said proudly. 'See what I've won.'

She raised her eyebrows at young William skulking behind.

'Sorry, Mother, I couldn't stop him.'

'Did you get the treacle?'

'Oh... sorry, I forgot.'

She pressed her lips together. How she'd love to crack him over the head, but it wouldn't be fair to John to spoil the day. Instead of reprimanding him, she bustled back to the fire to stir the broth.

'Your father and brothers will be home soon. Make sure you both wash your hands well—especially you John—you'll have been touching all sorts at the fair.'

At the supper table, John rambled on again about the fair, about the sheep and the jingling matches. They'd finished their broth and had moved on to the cheese and the apple pie before John reported something else.

'I saw Uncle Richard at Hunmanby.'

Young William choked on his piecrust.

'He looked like he was at a wedding. He was very happy... and pretty.'

His mother interrupted. 'I've told you before—you're to say men are handsome.'

'But he *was* pretty. His coat was blue and his breeches—'

Young William kicked him under the table.

Their father grew more interested. 'William, did *you* see your uncle?'

Not wishing to lie, he kept his head down and mumbled, 'not sure', yet his red face gave him away.

159

When John carried on, and mentioned Uncle Richard's friend, both parents were eager to change the subject. The rest of the evening's conversation kept strictly to the sale of sheep and the ram chosen by Jack.

When the boys retired to bed, young William was detained in the kitchen.

'*You* can sit up for a while,' his father insisted. 'Stay with me and smoke a pipe.'

Young William's heart sank. He watched his mother take up her knitting with a frown, and sit across the fire facing him.

'So,' his father began as he drew on his pipe, 'I'm assuming you *did* see your uncle.'

He nodded in misery, his mouth filling with saliva at the prospect of further questions.

'Who was he with?'

'He introduced the man as Stephen,' he answered, avoiding his father's eye. 'I've no idea who he is.' He busied himself in lighting his pipe.

His father waited a moment. 'Was he "pretty" as well?'

'I don't know.'

His mother joined in. 'Oh, come on, Will, you know what we mean.'

He took his pipe from his mouth and, reluctantly, admitted that both men were dressed better than most, and that Stephen wore a smart white wig.

'Where did you see them?'

'At the snuff stall.'

'Hmm. Was your uncle embarrassed to see you?'

Young William shook his head and then blurted out that he'd followed them. He heard himself admit to everything, and didn't stint on the kiss. His hand shook as he put the pipe back in his mouth.

'Never mind,' said his mother, 'your father will sort it out, don't you worry. You get to bed soon and think no more about it.'

His father coughed. 'Yes... your mother's right. I'll deal with it. Best keep this to ourselves though. Don't go blabbing this to anyone else.'

160

A week later, persuaded by Mary, William rode out to Carnaby. It was early in the morning and, the moment he set foot outside, he was struck by the chill of the November dawn. St Helen's Lane was shrouded in thick mist, but as he joined the top road south towards Bridlington, the mist cleared. He could now see the sky lightening in the east. A swathe of dark pink cloud lay over the horizon, giving him hope that his mission would not be in vain.

He had ample opportunity on the long ride to reflect on his brother's behaviour. In the past, he'd supported Richard, had rescued him from awkward situations. He'd suggested marriage, and had assumed, wrongly, as it turned out, that a wife would make all the difference. Now, it appeared, Richard was back to his old ways of being tempted by men. A gentle approach to the problem hadn't worked, yet William could hardly be heavy handed. He wasn't Richard's father, or the vicar, or the local constable. Although what Richard did was against the law, it did no harm to anyone. There were much worse crimes. Still, it didn't seem fair on the wife, and William had no idea if she suspected Richard's preference for men. Sighing, he patted the horse's neck.

'What would *you* do?' he asked. When the horse shook its mane to acknowledge the attention, he carried on talking. 'Gently does it, eh? I won't rush at this. I'll see how the land lies.'

He planned to call at the house to see both Richard and his wife together first, hoping to get an idea of their relationship. As luck would have it, though, he found Richard alone in the north field, spreading manure with a shovel from a cart. He hailed him.

Richard stopped work straight away and strode towards him. 'Is anything wrong?' he asked with a worried frown. 'Everyone alright at Uphall?'

'Yes, yes, we're all fine. I had business this way,' he lied, 'so I thought I might call on you. How are you—and Hannah?'

'We're both in good health, and we've had a good year harvest-wise.'

'You look well.'

161

'I am well—never been happier.'

William was silent for a moment, trying to think of a way to steer the conversation. 'It won't be long until the November hirings, eh? I hope you won't be doing anything foolish with the new hired lads?'

'What, me?' He grinned. 'No, I'm a changed man.'

William was not going to be fobbed off by any drivel about marriage saving a man.

'My sons saw you in Hunmanby.'

Richard didn't flinch. 'Yes, your William's grown into a fine young man.'

'Apart from his limp,' William added.

'Oh, he'll still have plenty of lasses after him.'

'He followed you—and Stephen.'

'Really? Why would he do that?'

'You tell me.' He watched his brother's face redden.

Richard took off his hat and scratched the back of his head. He stared into the distance, towards the far end of the field.

William persisted. 'Who is this Stephen?'

Richard lowered his head and murmured, 'It's none of your business.'

'It will be if word gets out. I've told Will to keep quiet, but he saw you two together. He was most upset.'

'I'm sorry for that. We'll be more careful in future.'

'And what about when you see another man you fancy?'

'Listen, it's different with Stephen. You told me once to find someone and settle down. Well, I've done just that.'

'I meant with a woman.'

'So I have a wife as you suggested, but Stephen is the one I love.'

It was William's turn to stare into the distance. 'How long has this been going on?'

'Long enough. He feels the same. Neither of us is looking for anyone else. Can't you be happy for us?'

'What about your wife?'

'She doesn't know. I think she suspects I have a woman somewhere. We don't talk about it.'

William shook his head as Richard confided further.

'Stephen is very discreet, and he's such a lovely man. The time we spend in his cottage is heaven. I feel so much at home with him. The other day we made pastries.'

'Doesn't he have any family?'

'He's a widower. It's good that he has no children either. Listen, we suit each other. He knows, without me saying, whether I want to play rough or act the pampered wife.'

William held up both hands in defence. 'Stop there. I don't need to know the details.'

'I'm just saying that what we have is perfect, and I won't risk losing it by hankering after others. And I won't give Stephen up for you or anybody else.'

William sighed. There was little he could do except warn his brother to be cautious. 'You should know—I can't vouch to help you once it becomes general knowledge.'

Mary accosted William the minute he stepped into the kitchen. Instead of questioning him about his day, she confronted him with one of her own long-standing grievances. She was in the middle of peeling apples, but stopped and waved her knife at him.

'Do you know my sister's now taking Dottie to her house—nearly every day—so the girl can spend time with Robert? She says it's a godparent's duty, though I reckon it's just another excuse to take charge of the girl. Do *you* think I made such a bad job of being a mother? I did my best to bring up our Mary, didn't I?'

William wasn't prepared to be drawn into an argument. He was tired after his ride to Carnaby and, at the age of fifty, he expected more peace and quiet at home.

'I don't know,' he answered wearily. 'I mean, our Mary could be very difficult. Everyone knew that.' He sank onto the bench by the table and put his head in his hands.

Mary hadn't finished. 'William, *you* think I did my best—don't you?'

'Yes,' he groaned, rubbing his eyes. Mary seemed to have forgotten where he'd been that day.

163

She picked up an apple and then put it down again. 'And you know Elizabeth—she'll let Robert do what he likes. If he takes it into his head to see the girl grows up like a nun, then Elizabeth won't stop him. Poor Dottie! Between Francis and Robert, what chance does she have?' When he didn't respond, she added, as if it was the worst thing of all, 'And Elizabeth has been teaching Dottie a different way to make oatcakes!'

He groaned again. 'How do you know?'

'John told me. You know how he likes to visit them. He tells me what goes on. Apparently, Elizabeth's not content with using eggs. Oh, no—she has to use ale-yeast. And she mixes wheat flour with best oatmeal. John said she makes little balls, then rolls them out really thin.'

'I don't suppose they turned out much different from yours.'

'Well, they were obviously smaller. What annoyed me was, when I called round, Dottie shoved one in my face.' Mary imitated the girl. 'She said, "I made it with Lisbeth." Hmm.'

There was silence for a while as she began peeling the apple.

'Remember where I've been today?' he asked.

'Oh, yes... Richard... How did you get on?'

'Let's just say I wish oatcakes were our only problem.'

Chapter 26

No one mentioned Uncle Richard for a while, and young William put the incident to the back of his mind. The Jordans, like everyone else, prepared for the winter; they slaughtered their pigs, brought their cows and lambing ewes into shelter, and finished ploughing for the year. Once the hedging and ditching work had been completed and enough corn threshed, people could look forward to Christmas. Young William was full of hope; he'd see more of Ann Smith.

During the Christmas holiday, everyone was invited one afternoon to sing carols and to dance in the Uphall barn. Young William hoped to dance with Ann and, if not with her, then at least dance with other girls. He'd show her what she was missing. When his family arrived at the barn, the place was already full of people helping themselves to ale. Notable absentees were Robert and Elizabeth Storey, also Francis and Lizzie.

John was most disappointed. 'Dottie's not here.'

'I know, it's a shame,' his mother said. 'Instead of having fun with us here, she'll have to celebrate at home—very quietly, no doubt.'

Young William searched the crowd for the Smiths. As soon as he saw them at the far end, though, he lost his nerve. Needing some help, he pulled on John's arm.

'You come with me,' he coaxed. 'We'll go together and say hello. You can talk about your pet sheep.'

They marched up to Ann. Although William gave a slight bow, she ignored him and smiled at John.

'Will you be dancing?' she asked.

John nodded.

William rolled his eyes. His brother would just caper round with the other lads. He nudged John and whispered a reminder about the sheep.

John grinned. 'Have you seen David today?'

1 6 5

'Yes, and I noticed you or Jack had given him his own pile of the best hay. His fleece is lovely and thick now, isn't it?'

'Like your hair,' John replied, about to stroke it, until his brother stopped him in time.

William blushed as he mumbled, 'We'll leave you for now, but...' He swallowed before going on. 'Could I dance with you later?'

To his great surprise, she stared him full in the face and said, 'That would be nice.'

He couldn't believe his luck. He wandered back to his family in a daze, and sat on a bench to wait for the music to start.

Throughout the carol singing, William sneaked glances at the Smiths, hoping he'd catch Ann's eye and she'd return a smile. She avoided him, though, and as the afternoon wore on, he grew as gloomy as the barn. His spirits lifted when lanterns were brought in, for then Ann looked even more attractive; her dark hair glistened like an expensive, well-groomed carriage horse, and her cheeks were flushed. He couldn't wait for the dancing to start, but after the carols, he heard the lads calling for the song 'The Old Tup'.

John rose to his feet and cheered. The song was an old favourite about an enormous ram; it had an easy chorus, and the descriptions grew more fantastic with each verse. As soon as John Gurwood struck up the tune on his fiddle, the women clapped in time while the men stamped their feet.

Samuel Jordan, staying at Uphall for the day, stood up and began to sing.

As I was going to Beverley all on a market day,
I met the biggest ram, me boys, that ever was fed on hay.

Everyone sang out the chorus.

And indeed, me lads, it's true, me lads, I never was
known to lie,
And if you'd been in Beverley, you'd seen him
same as I.

John's eyes glittered with excitement. He couldn't wait to hear more as Samuel, the centre of attention, strode round the barn singing loudly and flinging both arms about.

He had four feet to walk upon; he had four feet to stand,
And every foot that he set down, it filled an acre of land.

This ram he had two horns, me lads, that reached up to the moon.
A boy climbed up in January and he didn't get back till June.

Now all the men in Beverley lined up to see his eyes,
For they were perfectly round, and of a football's size.

When the song ended, everyone cheered, Samuel was handed a quart of ale and, finally, the dancing began.

Young William watched the women and girls make a large circle. They twirled, holding hands, their skirts billowing as they flew past. He tapped his foot, impatient for the mixed dances, the sort that his brother Francis would call 'sinful mirth'. He shook his head to think what Francis and Robert Storey were doing right now—probably, they were sitting round a candle eating unbuttered oatcakes and thinking of the life hereafter. All of a sudden, the music stopped. The dance had ended, and he could make his move on Ann. There she was, standing with her two sisters, catching her breath. He wiped his clammy hands down his breeches and made his way across the floor.

'Can I have the next dance?'

She teased him, cocking her head to one side as if unsure. Then she smiled with twinkling eyes and took his hand.

The next moment, the music resumed, and the two cousins were in the middle of the barn spinning round together, then losing each other as they exchanged partners briefly before reuniting for another spin.

Young William's grandparents looked on, feeling their age.

'There they go,' Dorothy declared, 'as if they 'adn't a care i' world. We're gettin' too old fo' this lark.'

Francis stared vacantly as the bodies whirled past. 'Aye,' he sighed and massaged his aching knees.

The sight of the two cousins dancing disturbed both sets of parents, for the pair were so similar, almost like brother and sister. Aged nineteen, and of comparable height, both had dark hair and brown eyes; even their smiles were alike, shy yet knowing. Mary noted that her son's usual lopsided gait was not so apparent when he danced. Although he cut a fine figure and glowed with health and happiness, she sensed trouble ahead. She whispered in her husband's ear.

'I can't see any good coming of this. Someone's going to get hurt.'

At the same time, Matthew Smith was whispering into his wife's ear. 'Keep a close eye on them. We don't want things getting out of hand.'

Oblivious to their parents' concerns, the two dancers stayed together. They parted only when the dances ended. William returned to his family, but not before giving Ann a quick goodbye kiss on the cheek. He'd never been so happy.

At home, he was in such a good mood that he entered into the evening's games with gusto. First, his father suggested that the two have a smoking contest—to see who could smoke a full pipe of tobacco the quickest.

Mary frowned at the idea, yet let them carry on. Within minutes, the kitchen was full of smoke, and young William looked about to be sick. Despite his protests, she called a halt.

'Whoa, you two! Let's say it's a draw. Why don't you see who can make their pipe last the longest instead?'

She opened the door to waft out the smoke, and then settled down with her knitting. Peace descended as her three younger sons sat about her on the floor, warming their hands at the fire. The two smokers sat on stools either side of the hearth, not speaking and concentrating on sucking their next pipe as gently as possible.

Eventually, as John and his brothers began to yawn, young William leant back against the wall, smug in victory as his father's pipe went out.

1 6 8

'Well done, lad,' his father conceded, 'here's a plug of tobacco as your winnings.'

On seeing John yawn yet again, Mary had an idea. 'Let's have a yawning match before we go to bed. Remember, you mustn't yawn at all unless it's your go. I'll give a sweet dumpling to the one who resists the most.'

Young William knew from experience that the trick was not to look at anyone's face, but to concentrate hard on something else—anything except the yawn.

When the contest began, the youngest boys and then John had their turns first. Young William was pleased to see that his brothers were hopeless. None of them could stop yawning, and they soon complained that their jaws ached. Even his mother and father were not much better. Soon, another victory was his and, when he drizzled honey over his dumpling, he ate it with the satisfaction that today was, without doubt, one of the best days of his life.

In bed that night, he reflected on his change of fortune. The mention of a football in 'The Old Tup' song gave him the idea of playing a match before the new year. Usually, they played at Shrovetide, yet the top fallow field was relatively dry. He imagined his beloved Ann watching in admiration as he helped Reighton win. Yes, he'd ask the lads for a match tomorrow. He fell asleep believing his good fortune would last.

Chapter 27

The next day, young William went round the village to see if enough men and boys were keen to play football. Then he walked to Speeton to announce the challenge, saying the contest would take place the following morning. His brothers were not allowed to play, which he thought just as well; John was big enough, but was more likely to hinder than help, and his mother said that the others were too young—they'd be trampled.

Matthew Smith did not want his eldest son to play. 'It's one thing to allow you to dance,' he explained at breakfast, 'yet it's quite another to join in such a rough sport. And think on, you'll be mixing with hired hands and other labourers.'

'But I'm eighteen,' Thomas complained. 'I'm old enough.'

His father was adamant. 'It's not your age—it's because of who you are. Remember, we'll soon be living in the new house. Your future isn't with the riff-raff. You'll be a gentleman one day.'

Thomas bided his time. He waited for his father to leave the house to inspect the horses, and then approached his mother and his eldest sister Ann for support.

Both understood his desire to take part. As soon as his father came back into the kitchen, his mother started. She enunciated every word, as required by her husband, and didn't drop a single aitch.

'Oh, Matthew, you must let Thomas play. He deserves the chance after all his studies. And my brother will be there,' she insisted. 'He'll look out for Thomas, keep him safe. Let him play… please.'

Ann did an even better job. She grabbed her father's hand and let a tear run down her cheek.

'Oh, please,' she sniffed, 'it's so unfair on Thomas. He's worked so hard this year, and he should enjoy the holiday like everyone else.'

When the other two daughters and son also joined the attack, their father gave in.

'I still don't approve, though, and I'll hold you all responsible.'

With great reluctance the next morning, Matthew led his family to the top field to watch the sport. He feared for Thomas, and was wary of the glimmer of excitement in his wife's eyes. His children were no better; they couldn't wait to get to the field and jumped up and down in anticipation.

Francis and Lizzie did not attend. The previous evening, Francis had been to Robert's house to discuss the event. Robert had denounced it as 'a devilish pleasure'.

'It's never a sport,' he'd argued. 'It's an excuse for a fight. It's bloody and it's murderous. Don't have anything to do with it. Come to my house tomorrow and bring Lizzie and Dottie. We'll read the Bible instead.'

Young William waited by the field for Francis and, when his older brother didn't turn up, he was ashamed. He couldn't understand why Francis would not want to support his own family and village. Now, he was more determined than ever to prove his strength and courage in the battle—and impress Ann.

He joined the rest of the men and youths from Reighton massing at one end of the field. Big William Mainprize was there with Stephen Jefferson. For once, he was glad see them and have them on his side; they were strong and they'd be too busy to poke fun at him today. He glared at the Speeton contingent waiting in the low sunshine at the other end. There were roughly the same numbers on each side though no one was counting.

The spectators kept to the headlands and the side balks of the field where they expected to be safe.

Young William stood beside his uncle Samuel who was giving last minute instructions.

'I'm our fastest runner,' Samuel told the men. 'So, when I grab the ball, I'll turn to face you and you just push as hard as you can. William, you and the Uphall lads are to deal with the Speeton lads... knock 'em out of the way.'

'But,' asked William, 'what happens if Speeton get there first?'

'Then let all hell break loose. Just clobber 'em till they let go.'

Despite the cold weather, the participants removed their coats and hats and rolled up their shirtsleeves. Most of them wore heavy boots. Young William hoped his lopsided gait would prove an advantage; he might be better able to hold his ground, lean in with one shoulder. His heart pounded faster as he saw Samuel spit on his hands to get a good grip.

A neutral from Hunmanby brought the old leather-bound pig's bladder to the middle of the field. He threw the ball very high into the air, and then ran for his life to the edge of the field.

The teams charged at each other, the spectators roaring in support. Samuel sprinted ahead and, as planned, reached the ball first. He picked it up and turned his back as the force of the Speeton charge knocked the wind from him. His feet were lifted from the ground, and he found himself wedged between the two sides.

Young William helped to thrust him forwards while also kicking the shins of any Speeton lad he could reach. His uncle was in the eye of a storm. Men kicked out, punched and tried to push Samuel one way or the other. Yet still, his uncle kept the ball tucked tight into his stomach with both his arms wrapped round it; he was not going to release it without a fight. Now, the question was whether the Reighton men had enough strength and guile to force him and the ball to the other end of the field, and win the match.

After half an hour, the ruck in the middle of the field had hardly moved. If it did sway one way, it soon swung back again or edged sideways. The watching families screamed at the men to push harder. Matthew's wife yelled encouragement to her brother, forgetting her future status in the heat of the moment.

'Knee 'im i' belly, Will! Put 'is eyes out!'

Once, when the heaving mass came too close, she and Matthew had to scramble to safety with their children. Ellen was the first to return and resume shouting.

Despite his embarrassment, Matthew was more concerned for his son. As time went by, he saw grown men leave the game and limp away. Those more sensible never rejoined the fray. He watched his children hand out food and drink to those taking a rest while Ellen helped to put fingers back in their joints and stop nosebleeds. He regretted allowing Thomas to be part of such a melee where there were no rules. While deemed unsporting, a strategy was used that was both unfair and dangerous; men would gang up in twos or threes on one person. Matthew caught sight of two men heading for Thomas, and shouted a warning.

Young William heard the cry and threw himself in the way only to be butted hard in the stomach. He'd saved Thomas but, bent double, he staggered away from the pack of bodies. At the side of the field, he retched.

Ann had seen it all. She left her family and rushed to him.

'Here,' she said, offering him a drink of water, 'you did a brave deed.' She also wiped his forehead with her handkerchief. 'Take a few minutes to rest. You need to recover.'

'No, I'll get back. I don't want to lose sight of Samuel or your brother. If I can, I'll work Thomas closer to the middle. It's safer there—less room to swing a punch.' With a smile, he handed back the empty mug and held her gaze. 'Thank you. I needed that.'

He turned from her, lowered his head like a bull and careered back into the men, back into the grunts and the sound of ripping shirts.

It was mid-afternoon by the time Reighton, with the help of the hefty William Mainprize, began to move the Speeton pack backwards, and it was almost dark before the game was won. Most players shook hands with the opposition or stood exhausted like Mainprize and Jefferson, their arms round each other. For others, there were scores to settle after such a battle, and one or two began a fight and had to be separated.

Young William escaped serious injury. His nose felt broken, and he thought he might have a cracked rib. Like the rest, though, he carried his injuries with pride. His bloody shirt would wash and his hurts would mend. He stood arm in arm with the Uphall lads, noting that some of their hair had been pulled out, and their ears were torn and bleeding. They should have stayed on the inside. He looked for Ann's brother, having lost sight of him a while ago. On leaving the field, he found Thomas on his knees beside his family, and holding his arm awkwardly. He could see Ann had tears in her eyes.

'I'm sorry, Ann,' he mumbled. 'I couldn't always keep with him. I did try.'

'It's not your fault, it's mine,' she sobbed and then faced her father. 'I shouldn't have begged you to let him join in. Now his arm's broken.'

'I don't mind,' Thomas protested, 'well, not really. We won, didn't we? Tell me Will, if *we're* injured, how are the Speeton lot?'

'There wasn't a single man not limping.'

'Good, but you're hurt too. Your nose doesn't look right.'

'It's fine.' William gave Ann a wink, and then smiled as he waved goodbye.

He strolled home with his family, reflecting on the day's struggle. Despite the pain in his nose and the bruises on his shins, he was euphoric. The match may have been confused and violent, yet it was wonderful to fight alongside his uncle and the other villagers. Best of all was the expression on Ann's face when she wiped his forehead. That was worth two broken noses.

Chapter 28

1732

On New Year's morning, young William rose at dawn to go first-footing. When he tried to wake his brothers, he found John the only one to respond without complaint. He watched John pull a tiny doll from under his pillow—a present he'd made for Dottie from a suitably shaped bit of driftwood and clothed in a rag of red cloth. Already, the wad of sheep's wool stuck on its head was coming loose.

He kicked the other truckle bed where Richard and Matthew were curled up, still half asleep. 'Come on, you two,' he snarled. 'If you're not up soon, we're going without you.'

'Leave them,' their father mumbled from beneath his fleece and blankets. 'They can go another year. You two get off—and be quiet about it.'

Since neither of their parents looked ready to get up, William and John went into the kitchen and cut themselves a slice of cheese. After helping themselves to a mug of beer, they wiped their hands and faces with a cold, damp cloth. William also wiped his neck, his ears and his hair in the hope of seeing Ann and wishing her a Happy New Year.

John held up his doll. 'Do you think Dottie will like it?'

'Of course she will.' He wished now that he had a new year's gift for Ann. 'Come on, then, if you're ready. We'll go to Francis and Lizzie first. I bet they'll be up.'

He collected two bundles of kindling from the corner of the kitchen, and headed for the door. 'We make a good pair, don't we, with our dark hair?'

'And your limp,' John suggested.

'It's not a limp, it's my back. Anyway, you're wrong about first-footers needing a limp; they only bring more luck if they're flat-footed—which I'm not either.' He held open the door and shoved John out.

175

It was still quite dark as they shuffled along St Helen's Lane, their breath steaming in the frosty air. When they reached Francis's cottage, there was a welcoming light in the window. To William's surprise, John rushed forward and opened the door without knocking; he then strode into the kitchen as if he lived there.

'Good mornin', John,' Lizzie said brightly. 'Oh... an' William,' she added as she saw him emerge from behind.

'Happy New Year!' the boys cried.

William thrust one of the bundles of sticks into her hands. 'There, I wish you good luck. I'll just empty your ashes, throw the old year out and then we're done.'

As William went out, John peered under the table. 'Where's Dottie?'

'She's wi' Francis i' parlour. 'E's gettin' 'er dressed. Look— 'ere they come.'

On seeing John, the little girl, now almost four, hurtled towards him with open arms.

He knelt down to meet her embrace, one hand behind his back hiding the doll. When she'd finished squeezing him and finally let go, he showed her the present.

She was speechless.

'Yes, it's for you. I made it myself. You can give her a name.'

She took it from his hand as if it might bite, and then clasped it to her chest.

'There,' prompted her father, 'what do you say, Dottie?'

'Thank you.' She kissed John on the cheek, and held up the doll to show her father. 'Feel it—her hair is soft—like wool.'

Her father laughed. 'It *is* wool.'

At that moment, William returned with the empty ash pan. He acknowledged Francis with the slightest tip of his head and, as neither brother spoke, Lizzie explained that the boys had brought in the new year.

'Now we'll 'ave good luck.'

'With God's blessing you mean,' Francis answered with a scowl. 'It's still in the balance what kind of harvest we'll get.'

'I'm sure all will be well,' she said to cheer them up. 'I thank thee both fo' comin' an' it was kind o' thee, John. Dottie's so pleased with 'er doll.'

William sensed he'd outstayed his welcome. 'We'll be going then.' He pointed John towards the door.

'No, wait,' cried Lizzie, 'I 'ave a gift fo' thee. Me an' thy aunt Elizabeth made a shavin' soap.' She took a small wooden tub from the shelf. 'We grated our best soap, then beat it up real fine. We even sieved it.' She took off the lid to show him. 'There, feel it an' smell it. We scented it wi' mint.'

'Will doesn't shave yet,' John announced.

William felt his face redden. 'Yes, I do. You don't know everything.' He smelled the soap and nodded in approval. 'It's perfect, thank you.' He looked forward to using it. If he were ever close up to Ann, she'd think his face was as fresh as mint.

As they left the house, William gave John a hefty push in the back. 'You'd better not embarrass me again, not in front of Ann.'

John stuck out his bottom lip, and they made their way to the Smiths' house in silence.

William's heart beat faster as he knocked on the door. When a maid opened it, he thrust forward the bundle of sticks.

'We wish you a Happy New Year.'

John stepped up beside him with a wide smile. 'Now you won't be short of sticks all year.'

William sighed and shook his head. 'Don't be daft. They're just a good omen—she knows that.'

'Wait 'ere,' she said, 'I'll fetch our ash pan.'

The boys stood by the doorstep, wondering if they'd see any of the Smiths and receive something for their trouble.

Soon, she reappeared carrying the pan full of ash. She handed it to William.

'Tip it out over yon, see where I mean?'

'Is Ann up yet?' he dared to ask.

'Aye, she's up—an' 'er mother. I've told 'em thoo's 'ere.' She waited for him to return the emptied ash pan, and then beckoned them into the house.

The instant William and John entered the kitchen they shouted, 'Happy New Year!'

Ann blushed as she caught William's unwavering gaze.

The boys stood still, unsure what to do next, until the maid plonked a heavy gingerbread loaf on the table. Ann's mother stepped forward and cut two thick slabs for them. They thought they might eat them there and then, but the maid wrapped them up to take home. Now, William regretted even more that he hadn't a gift for Ann; there was no reason to prolong their stay.

'Thank you for the gingerbread,' he mumbled. 'Come on, John, we'd better go home.' He followed the maid through the door without a backward glance. He'd ruined the visit with his lack of forethought, missed the chance of building on the friendship begun over Christmas. It did not augur well for the coming year.

Almost as soon as ploughing work recommenced on January 6th, the hired lads at Uphall became ill. The symptoms spread rapidly round the house until Francis and Dorothy were also affected. Samuel, helping there as usual, was the first Jordan to succumb; he blamed the 'sweating sickness' on the Speeton footballers.

The first signs of illness were a headache, a sore throat, coughing and sneezing. These symptoms were soon followed by a fever that lasted a couple of days. The young workers were fed a diet of beef tea, raw eggs and milk. They recovered enough to resume work after a week, yet still complained of aching muscles, and collapsed into bed straight after their suppers.

Old Francis and Dorothy Jordan were not so lucky. At first, the couple suffered the same symptoms and fever as everyone else. They took to their bed and sweated and shivered, tended by the maids who'd already been ill and had recovered. Francis rasped out instructions about winding the clock, and told them to put vinegar and brown paper on his head.

'Aye, an' tie an old stocking round me throat.'

When his cough grew worse, he asked them to drip candle wax onto brown paper and wrap that round his chest.

Dorothy, lying motionless beside him, had no energy to contradict his orders. She sighed, fearing they'd been in bed too long and were getting sores. Her hip was painful, so were her ankles. It was one thing after another.

'Could thoo fetch us some ivy leaves?' she asked one of the maids.

When the girl returned, she helped Dorothy and her husband roll onto their stomachs so that she could lay the leaves on their chafed and reddened skin.

Dorothy raised her head. 'Make sure to put 'em on right way up. Underside'll draw out any badness.' She then let her face drop into the pillow, too weary to say anymore.

William and Mary's family caught the winter illness but soon recovered. Once he was fit enough again for work, William visited his parents. He took them a remedy for bad lungs he'd heard used in Filey—a jelly made from boiled seaweed. When he fed it to his parents they gagged, but once he'd sweetened it with sugar, they managed to force it down.

'We miss Sarah Ezard,' his mother grumbled. 'She'd 'ave known what to give us.'

William thought his parents were being most ungrateful. He could see that everyone was rushing about, obeying his parents' orders blindly.

His father complained that he was light-headed, and gave the maid new orders. 'Crush a bit o' garlic fo' me, then rub it onto soles o' me feet.'

The girl obeyed, though it was a foul and unpleasant task; his feet were smelly, sweaty and looked as if they hadn't been washed for weeks.

William, ashamed, excused himself and was relieved to get out of the chamber into the cold fresh air.

Dorothy, usually cantankerous with reluctant servants, was quiet for a change. The one thing she asked for was a special drink to give her strength, and she was very specific in her instructions.

'Beat an egg with a fork till it froths, then put in a bit o' sugar an' two tablespoons o' water—only two, mind.' She leant back against her pillow to catch her breath before going on. 'Mix it well an' then pour in a cup o' me damson wine. An' I want it brought still frothy—understood?'

The maid did as instructed, and Dorothy drank it daily; the potency of the wine helping her relax and sleep while Francis coughed and grumbled feebly beside her. As she began to show signs of improvement, she persuaded him to try the special mixture.

The drink didn't help, and Francis grew worse. He complained of a stabbing chest pain when he took a deep breath and, when he coughed, there was blood in his phlegm.

He became so hot that Dorothy couldn't bear to be next to him and so slept on the old truckle bed instead. There she lay and listened to his shallow, rapid breathing, now very concerned that he might not recover. She wondered if his collapse and illness the previous year had weakened him, made him more prone to infections. When Francis worried about the farm and was anxious about his will, she got out of her bed and sat beside him.

'It's all sorted, remember? Thoo made out tha will last year, an' it's been signed.'

He grabbed her hand and begged her not to let Thomas squander Uphall on gambling at cockfights.

'But Thomas 'as gone to Scarborough. 'E's not even in tha will.'

Suddenly, he remembered something else. 'Who's windin' me clock up? I can't 'ear its chimes.'

'It's still goin', don't fret. They put a cloth over it at night to 'elp us sleep.'

'I want to 'ear ev'ry chime. Tell 'em to take cover off. Make sure they pull down its weights ev'ry night. I'll not rest if I can't 'ear chimes ev'ry hour.'

The effort of talking brought on a coughing spasm. Now, whenever he inhaled, Dorothy could hear a distinct ruttling noise. In a panic, she recalled an old remedy—horse dung in wine. She set a maid to the task immediately.

180

'It'll give thee strength,' she told him. 'I've 'eard it's a good tonic. I bet Sarah Ezard would've' drunk it.'

The mention of Sarah Ezard gave him confidence, yet when the glass was brought to his mouth, he gagged at the smell.

'Come on,' urged Dorothy, 'I'll nip tha nose.' This didn't work as he began to choke. 'Never mind then. We'll try again i' mornin'.'

The next day, Dorothy was well enough to return to the kitchen, but stayed by her husband's side and gave orders for the running of the house from there. She didn't try the tonic again; whenever she uncorked the bottle, he looked daggers.

Samuel, staying at Uphall for the duration of the illness, took turns the next day to sit by his father's bed so that his mother could see to the kitchen. That evening, though, when his father struggled to breathe, he sent for William and Mary.

More chairs were brought into the chamber. William was alarmed at the change in his father though his mother remained the same. Never one to ask for sympathy or display any grief, she was snuffing out the extra candles set up by the maid.

'Waste not, want not.'

The bedchamber was now gloomy with only two candles left alight. William saw his father fidget weakly and stare at the door as if expecting someone. He took hold of his father's gnarled hand; it was cold, and yet sweat glistened on his forehead.

Ill at ease, his father used his free hand to try to brush him away.

'He doesn't mean it,' Mary whispered. 'He doesn't know who you are.'

They began a silent vigil. The only sounds were Francis's laboured breaths and the hourly chimes of the old clock. William thought his father was so frail now; propped up by the pillows, his thin, wispy hair was stuck to his scalp, and his once-steely grey eyes, which had terrorised the farm lads many a time, were sunken and pale. His jaw remained square

181

and full of authority, but his once-prominent nose was now thin and pinched.

Just after one o'clock in the morning, Francis began struggling to breathe, as if he were drowning. William and Samuel raised him higher but it was no good. There was panic in his eyes and no one could help him.

'Have you any laudanum?' Mary asked.

Dorothy nodded. ''E wouldn't 'ave it before. 'E can't object now.' She went to get it from the locked cupboard in the kitchen. She dripped twenty-five drops into a glass of water. With Samuel holding his father's jaw, she tipped in the liquid. Most of it came straight back out and dribbled onto his chest.

'Maybe try soaking a bit of flannel,' Mary suggested. 'Squeeze it in.'

Dorothy tried this with more success and, after a short while, he was calmer. He closed his eyes and even slept for a time while they watched the blanket rise and fall, wondering which movement would be the last.

When the end came, they sighed with relief. His suffering was over.

Mary turned to Dorothy to offer comfort.

Samuel and William also turned to their mother.

'What's thoo gawpin' at?' came the cold reply. 'Thoo can all go an' leave me to do what's necessary. I can see to 'im. Go on, go 'ome, whole lot on ye.'

They knew better than to argue. Dorothy would accept no sympathy, not even from her sons. When Mary offered to help with the laying out and the funeral feast, Dorothy did acknowledge her with a nod, and a whispered thank you.

Samuel walked with William and Mary as far as the kitchen door, and then handed them their lantern. 'I'm afraid Mother's still sharp as a thistle.'

'She'll do her crying in private,' Mary answered. 'A lot of us do that.'

Dorothy sat by the bedside, holding her husband's hand. They'd been married for over fifty years, a lifetime of births and deaths, of good and bad harvests, of so many hired lads and maids coming and going.

Samuel re-entered the chamber as the kitchen clock struck three. The chimes echoed through the house. It was a Friday morning in the middle of January.

'Mother, I reckon the funeral could be on Monday. Maybe someone would let the vicar stay over in Reighton for the Sunday night—save him coming twice from Filey.'

She ignored him. ''E loved that clock... didn't trust anyone else to wind it.' She sniffed and fought against the tightness in her throat. 'Thoo do it later, Samuel. Thoo wind it... I can't.'

Chapter 29

Dorothy Jordan, with Mary's help, laid out her husband in the parlour. She knew his body almost as well as her own and, though still weak from her illness, she didn't want anyone else to deal intimately with him. Later, as people came to pay their last respects, she was civil and made sure they had plenty to drink. Not wanting to talk at length to anyone, she made excuses to leave and go back to the kitchen where she could be busy giving orders. There, away from the visitors, she could keep her eye on the huge rib of beef roasting on its spit and see that the maid seasoned the mutton stew enough. As she bustled about, seeing to the hams, she caught snatches of the hired lads' conversations, mutterings about the will as they worried over their futures. It was bad enough overhearing speculation in the parlour without hearing it in the kitchen too.

'Stop that right now!' she scolded. 'Thoo'll all be treated same as before. Nowt's changed 'ere. I'm i' charge, an' Samuel's overseein' thy work… so get on… don't go botherin' me wi' thy chunterin'.'

When Mary returned in the afternoon, Dorothy set her on to grate the horseradish.

'An' when thoo's done that, thoo can see yon maid makes sauces properly.'

'Would you like me to bring some of my pickled cabbage for the funeral?'

'Aye, an' anything else thoo can think of. There'll be many mouths to feed afterwards.'

The next day, a Saturday, Mary planned to make savoury pastries and sweet dumplings with raisins. She needed a hot fire all day and so kept John busy supplying her with sticks. She asked William to keep the other boys out of the house for the day so she'd have no interruptions, no squabbles or fights.

184

'Anyway,' she argued, 'your mother'll want Uphall in perfect order for the funeral. I'm sure she'll find plenty of jobs for you in the yard and outbuildings—muck heaps to clear away—lots to tidy up. She might even want you to polish the carts.'

As soon as they'd left, Mary began to dice the chicken and bacon and, as she'd done in the past, she added parsley in a white sauce to the meat before spooning the mixture into the pastry cases. Since the dumplings were easy to make, she decided to make a large apple pie as well.

'You can peel the apples, can't you John? We'll take a cheese and the rest of the food early in the morning.'

'But it's Sunday! We stay in bed longer.'

'I know, but your grandmother will worry if the food's not there in good time. She can't see to everything on the day of the funeral.'

There had been sleet showers during the night, and there was still ice on the grass when Mary and her family walked to Uphall with the food. A bitter north wind blew through the yard as they scraped the mud off their boots before entering the kitchen. They added their food to the enormous amount already set out.

The long table was laid with huge chargers of cold beef and ham, and there was a large stew pot at one end. Dorothy told Mary to put her pastries, pie and dumplings alongside the loaves of bread and the pots of butter and honey.

Mary had only just squeezed the cheese into a space on the table when she heard a scuffle at the door. She turned to see the maid come in with a large jar of brandied cherries.

'It's a gift fro' Cockerill fam'ly,' she cried in surprise. 'Who'd 'a' thought it! Servant who brung it said it were a mark o' respect fo' passin' of a great yeoman. That's what 'e said.'

Though Dorothy was moved, she bit her lip. There was still the funeral to endure and then all the entertaining. After that, she could grieve in peace.

The next day, when it was time for the funeral service, William's boys carried the coffin from Uphall. He and Samuel followed, escorting their mother to the church, one at each side. Their brother Francis at Argam was unable to attend as he had the fever, but Richard arrived just in time. He caught up with them on the churchyard path.

'I'm so sorry I wasn't here sooner. I wasn't at home when the news came.' He didn't say he'd been otherwise engaged with his friend in Hunmanby.

His mother patted his arm. 'I'm glad thoo's come.'

When she saw the vicar standing in the porch to welcome them, his nose blue with cold, she smiled to herself. Francis, who'd never taken to the vicar, would have appreciated his discomfort.

As she walked up the aisle, she felt her knees give way.

Immediately, William and Samuel supported her.

'It's me arthritis,' she lied. 'Don't make a fuss.'

It was the first time she'd been in the pew without her husband. Her son Thomas was also absent. No one knew where he lived in Scarborough, or even if he was still there. She held Richard's hand as the vicar began the service in his usual annoying nasal twang.

'And I heard a voice from heaven saying unto me, Write, Blessed are the dead which die in the Lord from henceforth: Yea, saith the Spirit, that they may rest from their labours; and their works do follow them.'

William glanced across the aisle at his mother. Her mouth was shut, clamped tight as any limpet to a rock. She'd never liked the vicar, a man who'd never bothered to get to know anyone at Uphall.

When John Sumpton began a speech about Francis Jordan, singing his praises, Dorothy snorted. The vicar had no idea about her husband, a man who could be stubborn and unforgiving as well as having the best interests of his family and Reighton at heart. She got no comfort whatsoever from the vicar's words, and wished he would shut up.

Like Dorothy, most of the mourners were only half listening. They had their own memories of Francis, of his crazy ideas to dig out a cistern or to plough up old pasture for arable, of his lengthy discussions with Dickon about the weather and the right time to harvest. He'd always been a leading figure in the

186

village. They recalled how he used to oversee the haymaking, a proud, dark figure standing above them on the hill with the sun behind him.

Samuel and Richard remembered the day after they'd lost their wages at a cockfight. Their father had ignored their mother's pleas and exiled them, not giving them a second chance. Instead, he'd kept Thomas at Uphall, Thomas who'd even instigated the gambling. There was no budging their father once he'd made up his mind.

When Dorothy followed the coffin outside for the burial, there was another sleet shower. Her sons crowded round to shield her from the worst of the weather, but she seemed to welcome the cold and wet.

'I'm fine,' she muttered. 'We won't be 'ere long. See— vicar's gettin' wet—'e'll make it brief.'

John Sumpton stood with his back to the wind, his vestments billowing in front like a sail.

'I am the resurrection and the life,' he declared above the hiss of the driving sleet. 'He that believeth in me, though he were dead, yet shall he live: And whosoever liveth and believeth in me shall never die.'

As Francis was lowered into the sodden grave, Dorothy gripped Richard's hand. Then, as the vicar concluded the committal, she turned from the grave.

'Come on, let's go. Let's get this feast over an' done.'

The Jordans followed close behind, and then came the vicar with the rest of the congregation. The maid who'd stayed at Uphall opened the door and curtsied as everyone filed past. The guests knew their places; the Smith family and other yeomen settled in the parlour while the tenant farmers and labourers with their own spoons and bowls stood ready at the kitchen table, eager to get started.

The vicar stood in the parlour doorway and held up his hand to say grace.

Dorothy, standing close behind him, whispered in his ear, 'Make it quick.'

He nodded. 'He that eateth, eateth to the Lord, for he giveth God thanks—'

'Amen,' she said to cut him short. 'Ev'ryone—'elp thassens.'

The maids and hired lads were on their best behaviour. It was vital that the Jordan sons saw them as respectful and hardworking for they didn't know who would be their next master. They went round filling pots of ale and made sure no one went without.

William wandered between the groups of people, accepting condolences. He chatted to the guests, yet was uneasy, not knowing the details of his father's will.

Matthew Smith made a point of catching William on his own.

'You'll be in charge soon, eh?'

'God knows. I don't.'

'Well, you'll always have that extra bit of land your father bought years ago. We all assumed it would be yours so long as you farmed it.'

'That's true.'

William did not want to get too involved in a conversation about inheritance. His father's purchases were often complicated, and William was never sure how much money his father had borrowed. As the eldest son, he should inherit the lot, but the Jordan land might be split up so that each son inherited. Then again, everything might be left to his mother while she lived. It was very unsettling. Certainly, now was not the time to question her.

'There's nothing I can do about it, Matthew. My mother needs some peace. I'll wait another week before I ask.'

Chapter 30

Four days after the funeral, news came from Argam that, although Francis had recovered from his illness, his wife had died. This meant he would have to bring up his children alone. Speculation was rife at Uphall. Would Francis want to move back to Reighton, or would he remarry and stay at Argam? William in particular was concerned; Francis might expect to inherit land in Reighton. As William had five sons of his own to think of, his father's will was crucial.

William and Mary rode to Argam immediately so that Mary could help to wash and lay out the body and take care of the children. It was agreed that she would stay there for the weekend and return for the funeral in Reighton on Monday. After that, Francis would have to manage by himself.

On the day of the funeral, it was too icy to take the cart to Argam, so William hitched a sledge behind the horse. The coffin would be secure, but his brother and family would have to walk to Reighton. Mary could sit behind him on the horse.

By the time he reached Argam, the sun had risen just enough to shine through the low mist, though the weak light gave little warmth and did nothing to brighten Francis's bleak, damp cottage. The family were subdued as he walked in. He spoke briefly with Mary to gauge Francis's ability to cope, before helping Francis transfer the body into the village coffin. They then loaded it onto the sledge.

The children stood watching from the doorway, bundled into so many clothes and covers that they were as wide as they were tall. They had nothing to say. The youngest, only four years old, sniffed and wiped her nose and eyes on her coat sleeve.

Francis lifted her up and kissed her. 'I'll carry you and keep you warm.'

189

'No,' Mary insisted. 'Let her sit on the horse with William. I'll walk.'

The other, older children held hands and stood behind the sledge with their father to begin the three-mile walk.

As they climbed the long gentle slope eastwards, the sky over the horizon was still pink and purple with layers of cloud in different shades of blue, ending in the palest of greys. Mary saw the beauty of the scene, yet her throat ached to see the children shuffling alongside.

William led the way to Uphall where a warm breakfast awaited. He encouraged the children to huddle near the great fire, though he could see they were overawed by the size of the kitchen, so different from their own squalid cottage.

Dorothy made a fuss, relieved to be active and useful, though another funeral just one week after her husband's was the last thing she expected. When Francis removed his coat, she noticed how thin he'd become. His children were no better—scraggy and hollow-cheeked.

'I'll soon 'ave thee fattened up.'

The youngest girl grabbed her father's hand and gazed at him in horror.

'Don't worry,' he reassured her, 'your grandmother's not fattening you up like a pig. She won't eat you. She just wants you to be well.'

'That's right, poor lass. Come on an' sit up to table.'

Dorothy had the maid serve them all steaming bowls of porridge. 'There now,' she said as she put a large pot of honey on the table and waved a wooden spoon, 'shall I dribble some o' this over tha porridge?'

The children stared wide-eyed. They only had honey at breakfast on rare occasions.

Dorothy watched them hunched over their bowls, spooning in the milky, sticky mess as if they'd never been fed. She nudged William.

'Poor bairns! Just look at 'em! At least I can give 'em another good meal before they go back to Argam... after funeral.'

190

The service was to be at ten, so Dorothy kept her eye on the clock. On time, and still mistress of the household, she organised the procession to the church.

William saw his mother take hold of the youngest girl's hand. 'Mother's getting soft, and not before time,' he whispered to Mary.

'Oh, William, it's understandable. She'll be missing your father.'

Throughout the funeral, Dorothy's thoughts were on the future. Only she knew the exact contents of her husband's will, and knew there'd be repercussions. She couldn't put it off much longer—she'd have to face her sons.

As soon as the funeral was over, she grew impatient to have Francis and his children fed and taken back to Argam. Then, she wasted no more time. She asked the vicar to return the next day in the afternoon to read the will. Though she didn't like the man, she reckoned her sons would behave better in his presence. Her plan was to get her two sons to sit with her in the parlour as soon as they'd finished work for the day. This way, she thought, they'd be tired and less likely to come to blows. With a warm, spiced ale in their hands and maybe an apple tart to sweeten their mood, they'd get through it.

The next day, the vicar was the first to arrive. He settled down at the table in the parlour where yet another fire had been lit, the third one in as many weeks.

Dorothy waited until the maid had served him a hot brandy and had left the room. She made sure the door was closed properly before handing him the document.

John Sumpton put down his drink and smoothed out the paper copy of the last will and testament of Francis Jordan. He read it to himself and, when he'd finished, he raised his glass.

'Here's to the future of Uphall. I don't know your sons too well, but I pray to God they'll accept their father's wishes without trouble.'

As if on cue, William and Samuel entered the parlour. They acknowledged the vicar with a short bow of their heads.

Their mother waited once more until the maid had brought in the ale and apple tarts. When the maid had closed the door behind her, Dorothy cleared her throat to get the vicar's attention, and turned to him with a nod.

'Yes,' he said, taking the hint, 'let's get on. I have here a copy of your late father's last will and testament.' He proceeded to read aloud.

William relaxed as his name was the first mentioned, and yet, as he listened further, he realised that the land mentioned referred to just two specific oxgangs—the piece of land his father had bought with that borrowed money years ago, the land that William had farmed on the understanding that he paid the interest on the loan. As the assumed heir, he expected to inherit that land anyway. Now he found that, if he didn't pay the £70 still outstanding plus any interest within six months, then Samuel would get the land instead.

William had hardly grasped the consequences of this when he heard that his mother was to get everything—not just the lands and grounds, but also the cottages, closes and tenements. Worse was to follow. After her death, his father didn't want him to inherit; he'd chosen Samuel. There was the added wish that, within six months of their mother's death, Samuel would give William and Francis at Argam £80 each. William realised that this would compensate him for the £70 he'd have paid for his two oxgangs, yet it only left him with £10, the same amount given to the youngest, Richard, and their sister Dorothy.

William lost focus as he tried to come to terms with the will so far. The vicar carried on, explaining what would happen if Samuel didn't follow his father's wishes, but William wasn't listening anymore. He was numb with shock. He came to his senses in time to hear that his mother had been bequeathed all the goods, chattels and personal estate, and that she was the sole executrix.

'When was this dated?' he heard himself ask, his voice sounding distant and hollow as if it came from the bottom of a well.

'I've just read that,' the vicar retorted. 'The twelfth of January—last year.'

192

William stared at his hands; they were trembling. He moved them onto his knees out of sight beneath the table. He'd no idea why he'd been treated so badly. When he raised his head, neither his mother nor Samuel could meet his eye.

'Good,' concluded the vicar, 'there's an end to it.' He finished his brandy and stood up. 'Your father was well-respected round here, and I'm sure he's done what he thought was for the best. I'll leave you now to sort things out. God be with you.'

As soon as the vicar had gone, William rose unsteadily from the table. He was desperate to ask why Samuel had been preferred, but his tongue felt like leather.

His mother saw his discomfort. 'I'm sorry, William. Thoo knows what tha father's like.'

He stared at her, not sure that she and Samuel hadn't colluded over the will. He moved towards the door, his eyes blurred by tears. They didn't call him back.

Dorothy lowered her head when the door had closed. 'Oh dear... an 'e's left 'is apple tart.'

Mary knew the news was bad the moment William walked in for his supper. He hadn't removed his boots and he didn't even take off his hat or coat. The boys looked at the dirt brought into the kitchen and wondered why their mother didn't complain.

'You boys, let your father sit down and I'll dish up.'

Although young William knew there'd been an important meeting at Uphall, he didn't dare ask questions. Whenever John attempted a conversation, he stopped him with a kick under the table.

After the silent supper, the boys were sent to bed early. They whispered in the dark about what might have upset their father. They strained to overhear any talk from the kitchen, but it was too cold to keep their heads out of the blankets and they soon fell asleep.

William and Mary sat at opposite sides of the hearth, the smouldering fire unable to dispel the gloom of the kitchen. William, without prompting, began to explain the will.

193

'Don't interrupt me,' he begged, holding up a tired arm. 'Let me tell you as I heard it.'

Mary frowned in concentration as he proceeded, biting her lip whenever she wanted to ask a question. When he'd finished, she blew out her cheeks. She didn't know what to say. After all, he was the rightful heir by law. Everyone knew that. She had her suspicions about Samuel, yet it did make some sense to have him inherit instead of William; he was almost twenty years younger and in his prime. Also, William *had* been involved in one too many court cases. Perhaps his father couldn't entrust Uphall to him; there'd always be temptations, if not of drink, then of the risky profits from smuggling.

'I'm sorry,' she said at last. She got up and knelt at his feet. Looking up into his face, she took both his hands, held them to her lips and kissed them.

'We'll get through this, William.' She remembered their lives after their Mary had died. 'We've been through worse.'

Neither spoke for a while, both thinking how they'd find the £70 by the end of July. Mary was the first to mention it.

'About that money you have to pay...' Suddenly, she caught a certain expression in his face. 'Please don't go back to smuggling. There must be other ways to raise it.'

William didn't answer. He stared into the fire, his eyes glazed. 'I don't know,' he murmured at last in a monotone. 'I just don't know anymore. I'm finished.'

Chapter 31

William and Mary had a fitful sleep that night, both thinking in circles about the inheritance and the problem of finding £70. By morning, William was in no state to discuss matters. Mary sensed this by the slow way he dressed and stood peering through the window, though there was nothing to see but darkness. She bided her time.

Breakfast was a quiet affair, the boys steering clear of their father. They watched him put on his coat and hat and leave the kitchen without a word about their work for the day. When young William leapt up from the table to go after him, his mother held him back.

'There's something you need to know... you all do... before the rest of the village finds out. Sit down again and listen.'

Young William took the news the worst. He understood at once the impact it would have on his chances with Ann Smith. 'Two oxgangs? *Just two oxgangs?*'

'Yes,' she replied wearily, knowing of the extra problem. 'I'm afraid even that land is in doubt... your father has to find seventy pounds to repay the loan.'

John and his younger brothers were less concerned. 'I can still carry on and work with the shepherd, can't I?'

'Of course you can, and the rest of you must work as usual. We mustn't turn our backs on Uphall. You never know, your grandmother might change things in our favour one day.'

Young William rose from the table. 'That's all very well, but you know she's tight as a nutshell, and I don't think Samuel likes me that much.'

When the boys left the house, Mary walked to the Smiths' farm. She thought to approach her brother and ask for a loan. William would have too much pride to do it himself, and pride was a luxury they could ill afford.

As she expected, Matthew was more than willing to lend the money, though he doubted William would accept it.

'I can't begin to imagine how he feels. It can't be easy. Somehow, he has to find a way to hold his head up—even when he knows the whole village will be talking.'

'Thank you, Matthew. I'll leave him a few days—let him calm down and get used to a different way of seeing things.'

Mary waited for two more days. In bed, where she could whisper and trust William not to shout, she mentioned the possibility of a loan from the Smiths.

He turned immediately to face her. 'You haven't been and grovelled, have you?'

'No,' she lied, 'of course not. I'm sure Matthew would help though.'

'Over my dead body!'

'Well then, you'll just have to carry on as before, but concentrate more on the two oxgangs. Listen, you mustn't give up. Your mother knows the will wasn't fair, and she might make it up to you. She'll have to make one of her own before too long.'

He groaned and lay on his back. 'You don't know what it's like. Already, the hired lads ignore me. It's all Samuel these days... bloody Samuel. You tell me to carry on, but it's so hard. Even with that strip of land, I feel as if I have to ask permission to take a plough or use the horse and cart. Every tool, every ladder and barrow belongs to Uphall and, one day, they'll belong to Samuel.'

She held his hand and gripped it tight. 'Then accept it for now, but you *must* secure those two oxgangs.'

He yanked his hand free and turned over, away from her. 'I've no choice, have I?'

Throughout the rest of the winter, William struggled to come to terms with his changed status. Each time he thought of his father's choice of heir, his eyes pricked with tears of anger and shame. On Sundays, when he walked up the aisle to his family pew, he kept his eyes deliberately on the floor so as not to catch people staring.

He continued to work at Uphall, though with an ill grace. The long walk uphill to the fields with his sons was a miserable trudge. He avoided Samuel, and took little interest in the Jordan holdings, concentrating instead on the two oxgangs that might be his in six months. He still hadn't worked out a plan to raise the £70.

Young William was appalled when he heard of his mother's idea of a loan from the Smiths; the last thing he needed was to be indebted to Ann's father. Already he was working harder than ever in an attempt to prove his worth at Uphall and have a stake in its future.

The next month, during Shrovetide, he thought to improve his standing in Ann's eyes by taking part in the seasonal singlestick duels. He'd have preferred to duel with Francis and give him a good beating. Francis, not surprisingly, declined.

'No,' his brother had said in horror. 'You know I don't approve of violence and, anyway, I vowed to God, years ago, that I'd never fight... or lose control.'

It was no good expecting John to be a decent antagonist. Though his brother would be eighteen this year and was strong enough, he was inept and uncoordinated. It wouldn't look good either if he beat John in front of Ann. Instead, he chose one of the hired lads.

The boy, Sammy Owt, though younger, was the same height as William and was up for the challenge. He bragged that he'd won such fights at his last place. The other lads didn't believe him.

Since Sammy often made idle boasts, most put their money on William.

In the Uphall yard, surrounded by the hired lads, the two young men took up their ash-stick cudgels and faced each other three feet apart. They both took a firm grip, finding comfort in the basketwork hilt that would protect their hands.

Samuel reminded them of the rules, few that there were.

'Use your left arm to parry blows. Strike anywhere you like, but don't thrust. Understood? And the first one, of course, to draw blood an inch above the brow is the winner.'

197

The combatants gave the traditional reply, 'God spare our eyes!' And they were ready.

News of the fight had spread through the village. Big William Mainprize arrived with Stephen Jefferson, both keen to lay a bet and make jokes at others' expense.

Young William's heart sank, but when he saw Ann Smith come to watch with her brothers, he cheered up and was even more determined to perform well. He knew where to aim, knew which parts of the forehead would bleed easily; it was just a matter of avoiding being hit on his nose, still not right after the Christmas football game. He reckoned Sammy wouldn't hit his nose on purpose, and yet, in the heat of the exchanges, anything could happen.

For a while, the two danced about to little effect, matching each other's strikes.

'Give up faffin' about!' yelled Mainprize. 'Young Will—thoo's as much use as a straw nail.'

'Aye, get stuck in, Sammy,' cried Jefferson. 'Clatter 'im over 'ead.'

William's other brothers were watching, expecting William to win. The way things were going, a draw would have been acceptable, but there was no such thing. The fight would end only when blood was drawn.

John frowned and turned to his brother Richard. 'I heard no one prospers if they're hit with an ash-stick. Jack told me. He said the kiss of an ash plant brings bad luck.'

Richard rolled his eyes. 'That's a daft thing to say. Why, half the men here would be doomed. Come on, cheer up, and let's see who wins.'

John was not reassured. He was anxious that William would fare badly, if not today, then in the future. He gawped as his brother aimed a few good blows at Sammy's shins, hoping to catch him off guard and then have a crack at his head. Sam anticipated the moves, though, and was quick enough to parry the blows and defend himself; he even managed to strike a hit on William's ear. The two exchanged rapid hits. John thought it sounded like when he ran a stick across the fence. Suddenly, William cracked Sammy hard on the top of his head.

'Hold!' Sammy cried out, and the match halted.

'Are you bleeding?' asked William. 'Uncle Samuel—check if he's bleeding.'

After parting Sammy's hair and finding no blood drawn, the boy was given a minute's rest.

William swaggered over to Ann and her brother.

She smiled. 'You seem to be doing alright. Father won't allow Thomas to take part, not after what happened at the football match. He doesn't know we're here.'

'It's true,' said Thomas. 'I would have liked a go though. You'll win soon, I expect—Sammy's looking a bit white about the gills. He won't last long. Another few hits like that and he won't know where he is. Then you can whip him across his forehead. The slightest cut there'll do the trick.'

William agreed with a wink. When he returned to the fight, he felt more confident than ever.

Ten minutes later, the fight was over. William was practising a well-rehearsed sequence of hits and parries, feinting and striking in perfect rhythm and then, all of a sudden, he felt Sammy's stick catch the side of his forehead. It was the slightest of hits, but the graze had opened a tiny cut above his eyebrow. He couldn't believe it.

As the blood trickled down, Mainprize and Jefferson cheered.

Everyone else went quiet. Most had lost wagers on the fight. Ann put her hand to her mouth and lowered her eyes to avoid William's gaze as Sammy's arm was held aloft in a victory salute. Only then did the spectators give a brief round of applause.

John stepped forward towards his brother. 'Are you alright?'

'Course I'm alright. Don't make a fuss. It's just a scratch.'

William could see Stephen Jefferson gloating. Now, he was so ashamed, he couldn't face Ann. Instead, he barged straight past her and went home, followed by John. To add to his displeasure, he found Francis at home and, worse still, there was also Robert Storey. That was all he needed.

Francis noted William's cut and his black looks. 'You lost then, did you?'

199

William didn't answer. He glowered at them and disappeared into the garden to wash his face.

His mother went after him and smeared grease on the cut.

He winced as he growled, 'What's Robert Storey doing here?'

'Don't you know? He's going to take over from your father this year as churchwarden.'

'Oh, God help us then. It's going to be a long, miserable year. Francis'll love it.'

His mother had a different concern; having Robert Storey as a churchwarden might have unexpected consequences for the boy's uncle Richard. Robert would attend meetings at the mother church in Hunmanby. There was every possibility that he'd find out about Richard and his friend Stephen or, worse still, bump into them.

Part Four

Robert and Elizabeth

Chapter 32

Robert Storey had waited eighteen years to become a churchwarden again. Now that he was given the responsibility once more, he determined to make a difference. His first act was to walk to Hunmanby and meet with his fellow churchwardens.

The men gathered in the dark vestry, the strong whiff of furniture polish offsetting the smell of damp. After exchanging greetings, they sat round the table to discuss outstanding repairs and any monies to be paid to labourers and craftsmen. They concluded the financial business and then talked of the weather and the sowing of crops.

Robert was keen to know of any innovations for his own land as well as that belonging to the church. 'Are the Stutvilles still sowing rape? I hear it's good fodder for sheep.'

'Aye,' John Cowling replied, 'they only grow it on their enclosed plots though. You can sell the oil over in Holland. It makes a good profit.' He winked at the other warden. 'It's always handy trading with Holland, eh?'

Richard Crozier didn't want to talk of smuggling in front of a Reighton man. 'I think the oil is sold to our tanners here. They use it when they're treating leather. You know we have a glover here now as well as a skinner.'

The mention of the glover led Cowling to talk of two men he'd seen outside the shop. 'Dressed up fancy, they were. A couple of mollies, I reckon.'

Robert frowned. He'd heard of such things. 'Not in Hunmanby, surely?'

Cowling prevaricated. 'They didn't know I was watching.'

'Do you know who they were?'

'No.'

'*I* do,' the other warden butted in, 'one of them goes by the name of Stephen Helmsley. He lives at the end of town.' He nudged Robert. 'You'll know the other one—he's one of the Jordans from Reighton.'

203

Robert shook his head. 'No, you've got that wrong. They're all married. There's only Francis at Argam who's a widower now, and it won't be him.'

The wardens exchanged glances, shrugged and then changed the subject.

'There's a new kind of fodder that Osbaldeston's sowing this year,' Cowling offered. 'Sainfoin it's called. I've heard it's as good as the best hay or corn—perfect for feeding draft animals.'

'Aye,' Crozier joined in, 'that's if it's given time to grow. I heard it takes a while to set down deep enough roots. Osbaldeston's men say they can't mow or even pasture it for two years.'

Robert wasn't listening. He was still pondering over which one of the Jordans was unnatural. It couldn't be William or Samuel; both were well known in Hunmanby, and Thomas was in Scarborough.

As he strode back to Reighton, Robert tried to recall the Jordan men as they were growing up. A picture hovered at the back of his mind; it was of Richard at Samuel's wedding. He could not rid himself of the image—like a fly round his face on a hot day. At the time, he'd been shocked by Richard's attire, the matching blue waistcoat and breeches, not to mention the white shirt with such wide sleeves. Robert had not been impressed when everyone said that Richard was wasted in Reighton—that he should be strutting along the streets of London. No, the only waste was the waste of money and the cost of vanity to Richard's soul. Men should dress in a sober fashion and not prance about like peacocks.

When he got home, he told his wife he'd lost his appetite and would read the Bible instead of having dinner.

'But what about Dottie? You promised you'd read to her this afternoon.'

'Not today.'

Elizabeth raised her eyebrows and opened her mouth to question him.

He felt hemmed in, harassed enough by his concerns over Richard. 'Look... maybe tomorrow. I don't know. Just give me time to think, can't you!' He marched into the parlour without a second glance.

He knew the Old Testament well, knew that, in Leviticus, men were forbidden to lie with other men. He sat down to read the verses. What Richard did, if it was true, was an abomination in the eyes of the Lord. He then turned to the New Testament, to Paul's letters, knowing that Paul denounced any lustful behaviour. He decided, as a responsible churchwarden, to act at once.

The next morning, Robert was in Hunmanby again. This time, he walked slowly as he entered the town from the east, pausing often as he wondered which of those homes belonged to Stephen Helmsley. When he reached the town proper, he strolled up and down the main street, loitering near the glover's shop before heading back towards the end of town. Just as he reached the last buildings at the end of the main street, he saw Richard and another man leaving one of the houses. And Richard had seen him. Robert swallowed hard, a bitter taste in his mouth as he carried on walking towards the two men.

'Why, Robert,' Richard hailed him, 'what brings *you* here?' He didn't wait for an answer and began the introductions. 'Robert, this is my good friend Stephen—Stephen Helmsley. And Stephen, this is Robert Storey of Reighton.'

Robert touched his hat by way of greeting, but to his horror, the man held out a hand. Robert did not proffer his hand in return. To cover the embarrassment, he mumbled something to the effect that he was in a hurry and was needed in Reighton.

'I'm sorry, I'm already late,' he added and rushed past.

As he strode further away, he breathed more easily. He'd been so close to touching that man's hand. At least, he thought with relief, I've not been tainted by the man's filth. Who knows in what dark corners such men perpetrated their odious dealings. That man might even be part of a secret and evil group.

When Robert reached the highest part of the road to Reighton, he stopped. Despite his mind being full of loathing and disgust, he could not fail to admire the beauty of the scene below him to the left. It was a clear day, the varicoloured cliffs of Filey shining in the morning sun, and the rocky Brigg jutting out into a calm and bright blue sea. He took a few deep breaths of the clean air. Yes, he decided, he must rid this place of its unclean passions, its vile affections. Richard had a wife and he should honour her. 'As God's my witness,' he vowed aloud, 'I'll set Richard aright.'

Chapter 33

The next morning, as soon as Robert had left the house, Elizabeth slumped onto her chair, breathed in deeply and let out a long sigh. She would have an easy day, not rush about fetching water, then cooking and gardening. Even though it was spring, the many jobs would have to wait; she wouldn't even visit Lizzie and Dottie. No, she was too tired to do anything, and was worried to lose blood when well past childbearing age. If she thought about it, she hadn't had much energy for a long time although she wouldn't admit this to anyone, least of all Robert. He hated anything to do with women's ailments, always had. Luckily, she'd managed to rinse out her rags and soiled skirts whenever he was out. She leant over the table and rested her head on her arms. It was so peaceful in the kitchen that she fell asleep.

She awoke an hour later to find her skirt soaked through with blood and, when she stood up, there was a stain on the chair. Unsure how long she'd slept, she hurried into the parlour to change her clothes. With luck, Robert would never know.

Robert came home earlier than expected from Hunmanby, and caught her in the garden tipping out a bucket of water, pink with blood. He didn't think anything of it until she blushed and looked guilty.

'I had a nosebleed,' she lied.

'Oh.' He had no reason to doubt her. 'Are you alright now?'

'Yes, I'm fine, but you're back soon—is anything wrong?'

'Yes, there is. There's something *very* wrong, yet I'm going to put it right.'

She didn't ask straightaway. They went indoors where she poured them both a beaker of milk, and then they sat opposite each other at the table.

'Elizabeth, there's something I have to tell you about Richard Jordan. It won't just affect his family, it could affect us all.'

She could guess what the trouble might be. The women at the well often made coarse jokes at Richard's expense, but they liked him. He was handsome, and they'd have welcomed the chance to change his preferences. She braced herself for the worst, and kept her eyes fixed on the milk in her beaker.

'You know as well as I,' he began, 'it says in the Bible, "Thou shalt not lie with mankind as with womankind; it is abomination." It says "they shall surely be put to death; their blood shall be upon them." So there you are.'

She raised her head in alarm.

'Yes, Elizabeth, believe me when I say that Richard's soul is in danger. He's been tempted into unlawful behaviour with a man in Hunmanby.'

She didn't know what to say. It was as she'd feared and, once Robert had deliberated, she knew there was no stopping him.

'I blame lust,' he continued, spitting out his words with venom. 'Richard's dishonoured his body through vile temptation. Saint Paul wrote to the Romans of such things... "Likewise also the men, leaving the natural use of the women, burned in their lust one toward another; men with men working that which is unseemly." Richard *must* return to his wife.'

After a pause, Elizabeth ventured to speak in Richard's defence. 'He was always a good son to his mother. It's true he was led astray at times by his brother Thomas, but he was ever kind and thoughtful—a good Christian. He's never done anyone harm.'

Robert paid no heed. He pointed his finger at Elizabeth. 'It says in the Bible, "For whosoever shall keep the whole law, and yet offend in *one* point, he is guilty of all." Now you see what I must do. The Bible is God's word, and I'm going to carry out God's will.'

He began pacing round the kitchen, muttering to himself, and then stopped abruptly.

'Right!' he announced. 'I'm going back to see Richard tomorrow. I'll have him on his own and I'm not having that—that Stephen prevent me.'

The next day, Robert left home armed with more Bible quotations. At Helmsley's house, he rapped loudly on the front door.

Stephen expressed surprise on seeing Robert Storey. Before he could welcome him in, Robert stated the reason for his visit.

'I've come to speak with Richard... alone. It's a private matter.'

'I see... well, come in then.'

Richard was equally surprised to see Robert in the kitchen doorway, and Stephen standing behind, pulling a face.

'Robert needs to speak with you alone,' Stephen explained, 'so I'll wander into town, and see you later.'

Robert waited until he heard the front door close. Then he faced Richard, still seated at the table, and began what he'd planned to say.

'Don't think you can hide what's going on here. You are living in sin.'

Richard was about to object, but Robert held up a hand.

'Hear me out! You have a wife in Carnaby, yet you choose to spend time here with a man.' He pointed his finger. 'You made your marriage vows, so you now have a duty to your wife and to God.'

'Don't come here telling me about duties to my wife. What about *your* wife? What about poor Elizabeth? Isn't a marriage supposed to be for procreation? Ha! A fine husband *you* turned out to be.'

Robert didn't even flinch. He pointed his finger again. 'You, Richard, for your fornication, for your lusting over men, you'll suffer the vengeance of eternal fire, even as Sodom and Gomorrah.'

'How dare you preach at me? Look to yourself before you criticise me. At least I have love in my life. What did Elizabeth ever do to deserve a husband like you? You're a... a cold, meagre dish that pleases no one.'

Robert, still undaunted, sat at the table. He raised his eyes to the ceiling as if praying for strength, and then took a firm hold of Richard's hand.

'I'm trying to save your soul,' he whispered. There were tears in his eyes.

As Richard didn't pull his hand away, Robert took this as a promising sign and continued.

'Saint Paul wrote to the Corinthians, "Know ye not that the unrighteous shall not inherit the kingdom of God? Be not deceived; neither fornicators, nor idolaters, nor adulterers, nor effeminate, nor abusers of themselves with mankind shall inherit the kingdom of God." Please, Richard,' he begged, 'take heed!'

Richard knew that Robert had spent his whole life caring for his soul rather than his body. Understanding this, he answered quietly and with conviction.

'And doesn't Jesus preach love? Listen, Robert, I only spend a couple of days here at a time with Stephen. I always return to my wife. But you must understand that I've found love here with Stephen, a love that I never found with my wife—or any woman. And I feel the love of God too—now more than ever. Don't sour my life with your own bitterness.'

Robert shook his head in disbelief. He couldn't begin to see how Richard could love another man. He felt defeated, let go of Richard's hand and stood to leave.

'I'll pray for God's mercy for you.'

As Robert walked home, taking the longest route possible, he resolved to pray harder, pray for understanding. Maybe he should talk it over with Elizabeth for she knew the Bible almost as well as he did. Though she was a mere woman, she might help.

Robert arrived home as his wife was making dinner. He noted she moved slowly as if exhausted. Then he saw a bucket full of rags left to soak by the back door.

'Have you had another nosebleed?'

'What? Oh... yes.'

'If they continue, you'll have to see the apothecary.'

'I will, don't worry. Let's have our soup—potato and onion. I did add a few herbs, but not many, I promise.'

'Thank you.' He said a brief prayer before lifting his spoon and starting.

Elizabeth took her bowl and sat down gingerly opposite him, afraid of further bleeding. She could see he was upset; he looked like a reprimanded child. Somehow, he always aroused her motherly instincts.

'How did it go with Richard?' she dared to ask.

'Not well.' He lay down his spoon. With fresh tears in his eyes, he confided his worst fear. 'I don't think I can save him. His soul is lost to sin and lust. I tell you, it's passion that's distorted Richard's reason. I pray God will forgive him.'

'Can *you* forgive him?'

Robert was so startled by the question that he was lost for words.

'Can you?' she repeated gently.

'Richard says he can't love women, says he loves the man... says he feels God's love more than before... I don't know.'

'The Bible says we must love and be fruit—faithful.'

'Not a man with a man, though!'

'There's nothing in the Ten Commandments about it. I don't think there's anything in the gospels either. Jesus doesn't mention it. I'm not excusing it, I'm just saying...'

He blinked and stared at her as if seeing her for the first time. She had dark rings under her eyes, and her cheeks were pale. She must be sickening for something. Certainly, she didn't usually argue with him.

Elizabeth hadn't finished. 'Robert, I've been thinking about the Old Testament. *We* don't abide by every single law. We eat foods that the Bible says are unclean, and we don't circumcise our children, yet we believe we can still be saved. We believe we're saved through the grace of our Lord Jesus Christ.'

He reflected on this and searched for an answer as he pushed his soup round the bowl with his spoon. He couldn't deny the truth of what she said.

She sensed victory. 'Also, I know from the Bible there was even one eunuch who was converted. You know, they're usually banned by the Jews, so that means they're banned from heaven. Yet he was baptised and welcomed. So long as he believed in Jesus as the son of God, he was saved.'

Robert didn't like the direction the argument was taking. Eunuchs didn't marry and neither could they procreate. He himself had not fulfilled that aspect of his marital duty, though Elizabeth had never blamed him to his face. He finished his soup in silence.

For the rest of the day, Robert strode about the hills trying to reconcile his wife's arguments with his instinctive distrust of physical love.

In bed that night, he couldn't help resuming the discussion. He was on his back with his arms crossed over his chest, keeping his usual distance from Elizabeth.

'It is all about lust, you know, this thing with Richard. He shows no self-control. It's his insatiable appetite that's led him astray.'

'No, Robert. If it were that, then he'd have found a mistress or young men somewhere. Richard's different. He loves this man. We can't choose who we love—it just happens.' She was about to touch his arm, yet drew back her hand.

As he didn't reply, she took the chance to drop a hint about her illness.

'Robert, I didn't want to alarm you before but, those nosebleeds I've been having, they're making me weak.'

She sensed his body grow tense. He was anxious.

'I've been thinking,' she added, 'I want you to forgive Richard, just as you've forgiven me for not having children.'

He was about to interrupt, but she raised herself on one elbow to face him. 'You've loved me in your own way, I know, and been faithful. If Richard is also faithful to Stephen, isn't he reflecting God's love? And doesn't he merit grace?'

Robert remembered Richard's words about 'poor Elizabeth'. Torn between his wife's argument, bred of a loving nature, and his own loathing of the body and its temptations, he clutched his head with both hands. What was he to do?

212

Chapter 34

Elizabeth's bleeding worsened. She found it difficult to keep clean and was forever rinsing out her petticoats. One morning, she dripped blood onto the parlour floor, and had to rub it out with her foot before Robert noticed. She was glad that Lizzie alone knew of the problem and glad that she'd been sworn to secrecy.

Robert now slept apart from his wife, on a straw mattress on the floor. Though this had been Elizabeth's idea, he was relieved to be spared the details of what he now suspected was a woman's complaint. The only help he offered was to pray and then fast at mealtimes; when that didn't work, he believed it must be God's will. Yet he could not accept that she deserved her suffering unless, of course, it was all to do with her stance on Richard Jordan. Certainly, she was adopting a loose interpretation of the Bible as regards the man's sins, and he knew she still resorted to superstitious remedies. He didn't approve when she took off her shoes and stockings and placed them in the shape of a cross.

'But it's to take away my cramps,' she explained.

'And I suppose that's why there's a basin of cold water under the bed.' When she nodded, unrepentant, he grumbled on. 'And you've made the parlour stink of turpentine. Why?'

'Lizzie brought it to ease my backache. You sprinkle a hot, wet flannel with it.'

'You should see the apothecary.'

'Yes. I wish Sarah Ezard was here though. She'd have known what to do.'

'Hmm, no doubt she'd have prescribed even worse things. I still say you should see the apothecary.'

'I will.' But she knew she wouldn't. Nor would she confide in her sister. Mary still resented her friendship with Lizzie, and was obviously jealous of Dottie's regular visits. No, there'd be no comfort from that quarter.

What upset Elizabeth the most was the fact that, of all the ailments she could have had, she should be suffering from one connected to her womb. There was a saying about women's monthly bleeding—no flowers, no fruit. Well, she was bleeding enough now but it was too late; it would be too cruel to die of a fruitless womb.

Mary had noticed her sister's pallor and thought it was merely a sign of ageing or the result of the winter indoors. She had something else on her mind—how William was to find £70. It was insulting to hear her brother's ambitions for his new house and his lavish spending. The house, up the lane to Speeton, was taking shape now and, with the weather more favourable for transport, cartloads of bricks and chalk were arriving daily. This gave her an idea and, without telling William, she visited the site.

When she found Matthew standing beside a couple of workers, she waved to get his attention. As soon as he approached, she began.

'You remember that money we need by the end of July? We still don't want to borrow it, yet I was wondering... seeing these carts coming and going, do you think you could employ William as a carrier? He's done that before, remember, off and on... you know, when he gave up his job with the customs.'

Matthew surveyed the busy scene before him. It was a beautiful, fresh spring morning and the builders were singing or whistling as they worked. The new house was meeting all his expectations. He put an arm round his sister, and squeezed her shoulder.

'You know I'll help any way I can. If that's what he wants, I'll see to it. He can start tomorrow.'

She thanked him. 'Only don't let on to him that I came to ask.'

That evening in bed, she told William she'd heard that extra carriers were wanted for Matthew's house. 'I'm told they're paid well. You see, Matthew's in a hurry—he wants the house finished this year.'

William turned onto his back and wondered. It would be easy taking trips to Hunmanby and back, maybe the odd ride to Bridlington. To compensate for his loss of time in the fields, his two youngest could do more work. It didn't take him long to make up his mind. He stretched and put his hands behind his head.

'You know, I think I'll speak with Matthew tomorrow. I'll work as his carrier, and I'll get that seventy pounds with less effort than I thought.'

William used the Uphall cart and loaded bricks from the enormous stacks piled up just outside Hunmanby. He ferried them, sometimes twice a day, and hoped to stop work before the summer. Once the weather was warmer, there'd be new clamps of bricks burning steadily and filling the whole area with thick smoke; he didn't relish returning home each day with his hair and clothes reeking worse than a bonfire.

One afternoon, he was leaving Hunmanby with another load of bricks when he saw his brother, Richard, walking ahead. He slowed as he passed, and leant down to speak.

'Hey, Richard—how are you?'

'Oh, William, I wasn't expecting to see *you* here, and not on a cart.'

'It's only till summer. Then I'll be working the fields again.'

'I'm on my way back to Stephen's. Would you like to meet him?'

'No, not really.' William stopped the cart. 'Listen, Richard, you know what I think about this. It's going to end badly. People will talk.'

'No they won't. Look, his cottage is over there, right on the edge of town, and I can walk into his garden without being seen.'

'Don't ever believe that. Even the trees have eyes around here.'

Richard frowned. 'I suppose you know about Robert Storey's visit?'

'No, I don't.' This was alarming news. 'What's he been saying?'

'Nothing good. He hates my life here with Stephen.'

'I did warn you—if it becomes common knowledge I can't help you.'

'He says I disgust him. That man sullies everything. He turns love into lust, makes my life seem filthy, unnatural—like something you'd throw in the gutter.'

'Well, I have to say you've brought this on yourselves. You are what you are, but there's no need to flaunt it. Most people are tolerant, but you can't go giving them reason to complain—especially Robert Storey. You wouldn't poke a hornets' nest, would you? No, it's best if you lie low for a while. Stay indoors and don't give people excuses to abuse you.'

Richard nodded. 'Mm, you may be right. I'll do as you say.'

William sighed; he couldn't trust Richard. As a parting shot, he added, 'Remember, there's never any sense in offending people.'

'I know. When you see Robert, though, you might put in a good word for me.'

'Ha! I don't think that'll happen. Even Mary and Elizabeth are hardly on speaking terms.' He flicked the reins to move on and gave a final reminder.

'Lie low!'

Robert Storey had other worries besides Richard's sinful life. He received a message that the vicar was moving from Filey to Reighton. There'd been rumours before of such an event, but this time it was official and, as a churchwarden, he had the responsibility of ensuring the vicarage was habitable. The news could not have come at a worse time. For years, Elizabeth had kept the vicarage clean and had kept it aired in readiness, but the arrival of Lizzie and then Dottie had taken up her time. Now, just when he needed her, Elizabeth was ill. He paced the kitchen as he thought of the enormity of the task before him.

Elizabeth put a hand out to him as he passed by the table a fourth time. 'It'll be alright. Lizzie can see to the vicarage. She's young and full of energy, and she can get others to help her.'

'Yes, but what about the roof? I'll have to patch it up.'

'You see to the roof, and scythe down the garden. And you're not alone, remember. The other churchwarden will help. You and Richard Maltby can leave your work in the fields for a day or two.'

As soon as he'd gone out to organise the work, Elizabeth sighed and smiled to herself. Robert would be fully distracted for a while and wouldn't be harping on to her about the abomination of Richard Jordan. It was a relief that, in deference to her wishes, he'd kept the matter between themselves. She'd keep an eye on him though; he was simmering like a pot of broth over the fire, and she mustn't let him boil over.

John Sumpton left Filey in mid-April when the roads were easier for travel. The coach he'd hired also carried his wife Mary, his son Henry and Henry's new wife. A cartload of furniture and belongings preceded them. It was a warm, sunny afternoon when the coach rattled down into Reighton and then moved slowly up Church Hill. Spring cleaning paused as women went into the street to gawp.

At Uphall, Dorothy Jordan waited upstairs to see the vicar's arrival. She stood on an upturned chamber pot and craned her neck to get a better view through the window. She saw the two churchwardens waiting by the vicarage door to give a welcome. When the vicar had stepped down from the coach, he helped the women alight.

The first woman was small and almost as wide as she was tall, dressed in dark clothes as if for a winter funeral. Dorothy guessed it was the vicar's wife for the woman stood by the gate with her arms folded. She stared at the chalk house and seemed reluctant to move any further.

The next woman to emerge was taller and wore a pretty gown more in tune with the season. Also, she was heavy with

217

child. Her husband stepped out last of all. He almost leapt from the coach, and then stood with his feet wide apart, surveying his new surroundings. He wore a short white wig, and looked as if he belonged there already.

Dorothy gave a rueful smile. Her husband would have liked to see the vicarage inhabited again. The vicar's son, though, might ruffle a few feathers, might want to make changes. She guessed Robert Storey must be of the same mind for he was frowning and, if her eyes weren't deceiving her, chewing the inside of his cheek.

Chapter 35

Later that day, Robert was pacing his kitchen again. At last, he sat down heavily at the table to talk to his wife, something he was doing quite often now.

'Elizabeth, don't misunderstand me. Of course I welcome the vicar. I'm glad he's here, but it's his son Henry who worries me. Apparently, he's to live here with a view to oversee the glebe. What am *I* supposed to do? I've seen to it as well as my own land, looked after it all the time of the Gurwoods. George never found fault. And John Sumpton knows full well I've been looking after his interests for years now. He's had all his tithes on time.'

'Perhaps he'll want you to help Henry. You know, share the glebe work, show him how to manage the different soils.'

He sprang to his feet and began pacing the room once more. 'And Dorothy Jordan's telling everyone that Henry Sumpton's fit as a butcher's dog. How can I keep up with such a man?'

'Then, for peace of mind, you'll have to go to the vicarage and have it out with him.'

The next morning, Robert knocked on the vicarage door.

The younger of the women opened it. 'We're very busy,' she announced. 'Whatever you want, it'll have to wait.'

Robert took a step backwards. He was not used to such cursory treatment. 'I need to speak with the vicar and his son. Tell them it's Robert Storey waiting to discuss the maintenance of the glebe.'

She left him waiting at the door.

The vicar soon appeared. 'Come in, Robert. Go into the parlour. Henry's in there. He's studying an old map of the glebe.'

Robert's heart sank as he saw the vicar's son poring over a large piece of paper. Dorothy Jordan was right. Henry

Sumpton exuded health and energy and, without his wig, his shaved head made him look leaner and more primed for action. Robert, now in his mid-fifties, felt like an old man.

Henry smiled and moved round the table to shake Robert's hand. 'It's good you've come today. I've had a good look at this map and I'd like you to make a tour of the fields with me. If you've time, we can do it now. No time like the present.'

'Yes, about the glebe land…' Robert coughed, embarrassed to ask about his future. 'You see, I've worked those lands for years. I know them like the back of my hand. My question is—will I still be needed?'

They were interrupted by the young wife entering with drinks.

'Ah, thank you, Ann. Robert, please take a glass of Oporto wine.'

Robert never drank anything stronger than small beer, yet could hardly refuse.

Henry raised his glass. 'Here's to improved husbandry.' He swallowed his in one gulp.

Robert lifted the glass to his mouth and then balked at the strong, cloying smell. He let the drink just wet his lips and tried his question again. 'You see, I'd like to know the role I'll be playing.'

'Never mind that for now. Come on, drink up, and we'll go.'

Robert, frustrated, took a tiny sip and put down his glass. 'I'm ready then.'

Henry reached out for his wig, pressed it firmly on his head and strode to the door. He hesitated on seeing Robert wearing a coat. 'Hmm, I think the weather is set to be fine. I'll go out as I am.'

Robert followed him out of the house and couldn't keep pace as Henry marched down the hill, the rolled-up map tucked under his arm. It shamed him to walk a step behind; he felt like an old retainer tottering after his squire. The young pup even looked the part in his clean white shirt, his well-fitting breeches and black boots.

'According to the map,' Henry said over his shoulder, 'I need to be at the north end of St Helen's Lane somewhere.

Whelpdales—it borders a field called Wandales to the south. Come on, keep up.'

Turning left to go along St Helen's Lane, they passed the pond. Robert pointed out the lane opposite where the cattle were taken to pasture. Henry showed no interest, but did pause as he reached the well. When he waved to the women drawing water, they stood open-mouthed.

'Good morning one and all,' he shouted. 'It's a fine day we have. I hope the water is clean and tastes sweet.'

Robert, standing behind Henry, turned away in embarrassment while the women stood, still, dumbfounded.

'It's the vicar's son,' one of them whispered.

'Yes, sir, the water's good,' another girl cried, and then began to giggle.

Robert dreaded the women's banter. 'The field's this way,' he prompted before the women could say any more.

When they reached the field in question, Robert pointed out the land that comprised the church's eight acres. 'Matthew Smith has the land next to it on your right. He keeps it as extra pasture. He doesn't always trust his cattle to mix with the others, doesn't want them to catch diseases.'

Henry surveyed the whole field. 'Is it always left just for grazing?'

'Yes, it's excellent pasture for sheep. As you can see, the shepherd keeps the ewes here at lambing time. That's why there's a fence.'

'Hmm, it seems a waste to me. It might be better cultivated. We can let the sheep manure it and then I think we should plough it afterwards.'

'You'd best speak to Matthew Smith first.'

'As I understand, it's the Smiths and Jordans who have the most land.'

'And there are others, like Maltby and Mainprize. They're to be considered *if* you want to change the way we work.'

Henry ignored this and unrolled the map. 'I know the church owns two cottages here. I can see by the map there's one back there at the bottom of the hill, the other one near the top. I'd like to see if they're in good repair. Come on, let's not waste time.' He set off back down the lane.

'But,' Robert argued, 'no one might be at home this time of day.'

'I can still go inside and inspect. They don't have locks on their doors do they?'

'No.'

'Well then, on the vicar's behalf, I'm entitled to enter their house and garth.'

Robert thought this an unnecessary intrusion. It wasn't as if Henry was collecting tithes, and the Easter ones had already been paid.

'Listen,' Robert countered, 'this is your first walk round Reighton. Perhaps it's best to take things more slowly. You can see the outside of the cottages as we walk back. Then we could go and see your other land in Long Dike. You've about ten acres there, *and* it's all arable.'

Henry carried on his brisk walk. 'True,' he conceded, 'I am keen to see the main fields.'

Nevertheless, Henry stopped to see the state of the thatch on the cottages and he noted the poor earthen walls used as fences. Unimpressed, he strode on past the church and onwards to the top main fields.

When they reached Long Dike, they could see men and boys busy spreading manure. Henry stood still to watch, shielding his eyes from the bright sunshine.

'They're very long fields,' he remarked. 'I can barely see to the end. Over there—is that winter wheat showing through?'

Robert nodded. 'Yes, we plant wheat, then barley or peas, sometimes beans, and then leave it fallow. We can graze livestock on the stubble—let the manure feed the soil and then leave it as grass for a year.'

'I'm wondering if all this fallowing is really necessary. You could be growing so much more grain. I've heard of husbandmen cultivating a field for six years in a row.'

'But the yield would get less each year.'

'It says in the Bible, "And six years thou shalt sow thy land, and shalt gather in the fruits thereof. But the seventh year thou shalt let it rest and lie still." Now, you're a man of God—you wouldn't disobey.'

Robert sighed. 'And the Bible also says, "The thoughts of the diligent tend only to plenteousness; but of everyone that is hasty only to want." So perhaps it's best not to rush at things.'

Henry was not giving in. 'It's worth thinking about though.'

Robert knew such changes would not be welcome. It was a good job Henry Sumpton was outnumbered; the church land was minimal compared to the size of the other strips.

They turned and began to walk back to the village.

'Sometimes,' Robert ventured, 'we do plant peas on the fallow. They restore goodness to the soil, and peas are good for improving pastures too. You could plough a pasture in January and sow peas later on. When they're in full bloom, you flatten them into the ground and plough them in twice. Then you can sow clover and rye grass.'

Henry had stopped listening. It was the time of year for St Mark's flies to swarm and, from the hawthorn hedges round people's garths, clouds of the sluggish, black insects drifted towards them. They seemed attracted to Henry's white shirt and wig. They hovered over his head, their long legs dangling down. Though he knew they wouldn't bite, he kept batting them away.

'I've seen enough,' he announced all of a sudden. 'Thank you, Robert, for your time.'

'So, shall I carry on as normal?'

'Yes, yes,' Henry retorted, flicking a pathway through the flies.

Robert smiled. God certainly moved in mysterious ways.

Chapter 36

Mary suspected something was wrong. She never saw her sister anymore at Lizzie's house, never saw Elizabeth out at all except in church on Sundays. At first, she thought it might be Robert's doing; the man was obsessed with his reputation as a churchwarden and made more demands on Elizabeth's time. Then she thought that perhaps the two Lizzies were no longer such bosom friends. She determined to get to the bottom of it.

Taking a fresh block of her newly made butter, Mary knocked lightly on Lizzie's door and then walked straight in.

Dottie swivelled round, hoping to see Elizabeth and receive a treat. Her face fell.

'I've brought butter for your mother,' Mary explained, guessing why the girl looked so disappointed.

Lizzie took it and sniffed the wrapping. 'Mmm—that's very kind o' thee. I miss not makin' me own. I wish...' She was about to mention Elizabeth but stopped herself in time.

Mary glanced about the kitchen. There were empty bottles on the table, and the smell of raspberry leaves suggested that Lizzie was boiling up a medicine.

'Are you having monthly trouble?'

Lizzie blushed. 'What? Oh, no, no. I just thought I'd make raspberry leaf tea.'

Dottie butted in to get attention. She lifted a basket of dandelions she'd picked.

'We're makin' dandelion tea,' she boasted.

Mary smiled, and knew that Sarah Ezard had always prescribed that particular tea for ailing women. She raised her eyebrows.

'You can tell me, Lizzie. I can help if you're bleeding too heavily.'

Lizzie sat at the table, chewing her bottom lip. 'It's not fo' me,' she confessed.

'It's for Elizabeth, isn't it? I *knew* something was wrong. We never see her these days.'

'Please don't say owt.' Lizzie wrung her hands. 'Please don't. I promised.'

'I won't, but you must tell me about it. She *is* my sister.'

When Mary heard the extent of the bleeding, she was reminded straightaway of Dickon's wife, Isabel. The poor woman had died quite suddenly. Worse was to come. Lizzie informed her that Elizabeth had a lump in her stomach.

'Where exactly?' Mary demanded.

'She said it were low down.' Lizzie lifted her apron to demonstrate. 'About 'ere,' she added, laying a hand between her hipbones.

Mary's eyes pricked with fear. There was no easy cure, if any. Everyone feared a canker. It grew as you weakened, and death, when it came, was slow and very painful.

'I must go to her. I'll help.'

Lizzie began to cry. 'It's really bad, isn't it?'

Mary swallowed, and nodded. She bent down to Dottie. 'Don't worry,' she said, controlling the catch in her voice, 'we'll look after Elizabeth. You help your mother make that dandelion tea. Elizabeth will love it.' She then turned to leave. As soon as she was outside, she burst into tears.

Robert Storey was in good spirits. He no longer worried about Henry Sumpton's interference for, in the middle of May, Henry's wife had given birth to a healthy son. The boy, named after the vicar, was proving to be a great distraction. Robert spent a glorious afternoon inspecting the fields; the crops were growing well and, for the second year in succession, he could predict a plentiful harvest. He smiled with satisfaction as he returned home. Apart from his wife's debility, the future was promising.

As he neared the church, he saw Mary standing there as if waiting for him. When she hailed him, he strode across to join her.

'Robert, can I have a word? It's about Elizabeth. I didn't know she was ill.'

'Oh, she'll be better soon. The summer weather will work wonders. God will provide.'

'Do you mind if I come and see for myself? I could help.'

'As long as you don't bring in any more herbs. The house reeks of mint and all sorts, and I'm having to pick my way through lavender—it's strewn everywhere.'

They found Elizabeth sitting hunched by the fire although the day was warm. She had a blanket round her shoulders, and raised her head in alarm at the sight of Mary.

'I was just passing by,' Mary lied, shocked to see her sister's sunken eyes. 'I'm on my way to Uphall. I haven't seen you properly for a long time. Are you alright?'

'I haven't been well, it's true, but I'm drinking plenty of Lizzie's teas. Robert, could you go out and fetch more kindling, please.'

As soon as he'd gone, Elizabeth asked Mary to sit beside her. 'Robert doesn't know how ill I am. I can't bring myself to tell him. He hates women's ailments.'

'You do look pale. Is it to do with your age? Are you bleeding?'

Elizabeth nodded. 'I make a hot poultice when my stomach aches, and I manage to keep clean—most days anyway. I don't sleep with Robert now—that makes it easier.'

'You will tell me if I can do anything?'

Robert returned and dumped a load of faggots in the corner.

Elizabeth smiled weakly at her sister. 'Lizzie brings me lots of tea, but I would like to see you too.' She shivered and pulled the blanket higher to her neck. 'Dottie doesn't understand why I can't play with her anymore. I hate being like this.'

Mary put a hand on Elizabeth's knee and gave it a rub. 'Don't get too disheartened. I'm sure Dottie will be happy to sit by you and hear stories. You used to sing to the boys when they were little. Dottie would love that.'

That summer, as Elizabeth's bleeding became heavier, Mary visited regularly to clean the bed linen and clothes. She soaked the worst stains in sorrel juice. When she found Elizabeth weak and dizzy, she made her drink sweet sage

226

tea. She recalled Sarah Ezard saying that nettles were good for the blood and so had her sons gather the leaves for a soup. Nothing seemed to help.

One morning in late July, Elizabeth was so weak she couldn't get out of bed. She told Robert he'd have to see to his own breakfast. Until now, she'd suffered the dragging pain in silence, as well as the discomfort and shame. She'd also suffered Robert's ineffectual prayers when she really wanted to scream and demand to know why God was being so cruel. Now, the lump in her stomach had grown and it was making her back ache more. She'd even found blood in her urine. When Robert knelt by her bed to pray, she rested a hand on his head, knowing that, soon, she'd have to tell him the truth.

Chapter 37

'Why didn't you tell me sooner?'Robert rubbed his forehead in frustration. He knew that cankers spread to other parts of the body.

'I don't know.'

'But it could have been cut out.'

'No, I couldn't have borne that. Robert, listen.' She took hold of his hand across the table. 'I don't want a surgeon. People have died horribly at their hands. There's nothing anyone can do.'

'Come on, I'm sure there must be other remedies—like arsenic or mercury. Surely there are ways to destroy it, or burn it out.'

She shook her head. 'If you try such things, it might only make it worse. It might get to know and then get angry, and then I'll suffer more.'

Robert shuddered at the thought of the 'thing' inside her as something alive. He had a vision of a large worm or maggot feeding off the rotten flesh in Elizabeth's body. Surely, her illness must be due to sin as well as weakness. He wondered if it was partly his fault because he'd done nothing about Richard Jordan; he'd failed in his moral duty. He didn't know what to say. It was all such a shock. He needed time to think, time alone and preferably out of doors.

He stood up to leave. 'I have to go to the fields now. Lizzie or your sister will call round no doubt. They'll tend to you.'

Once out of the house, he ambled to the wheat field, still not reconciled to his wife's fate. There he stood alongside the other yeomen as they sampled grains to see if they were ripe for harvest. When he rubbed the ears of corn between his palms to separate the grain from the husk, all he could think of was the evil thing in Elizabeth's stomach. Like the wheat, she could be attacked from within, go black and decay.

Women, he believed, were more prone to disease; it was their wombs that were to blame, wombs that could harbour bad humours. Yes, he decided, that was the problem. Elizabeth had been melancholy, and that humour had settled in one place. A surfeit of black bile had caused the canker, and now the thing grew in her, grew ever larger in a stagnant pool of bile while she grew weaker. Yes, that was it. He could pray and he could fast, but he feared it might be too late. It was God's will.

As he let the wheat fall from his hands, he recalled shelling peas as a boy. When his mother wasn't looking, he'd open a pod and stuff the peas into his mouth. One day he'd been horrified to see the pod full of maggots. That pod was like Elizabeth's womb. At this very moment, a multitude of worms might be gnawing away at her insides.

Mary sent William to the apothecary in Hunmanby. The man suggested a mild purgative and liquids made from nightshade and henbane to relieve Elizabeth's pain.

William returned and placed the bottles and packets of powder on the table.

'He didn't hold out much hope, I'm afraid. He said Elizabeth should keep to a cool diet—nothing too salty or spicy, and no wine.'

'Hmm, she's had that diet all her married life.'

'When I told the apothecary she's not had children, he said that could be the trouble. Childless women are more likely to have such problems.'

Mary was not convinced. 'Robert's told Elizabeth she has too much of one humour. Your mother's heard about it and she agrees. She's given me a recipe for a broth—it's supposed to get rid of the bad humour.' She shrugged. 'I'll get John to gather the plants.'

The next day, Mary gave John his instructions. 'I want you to pick melancholy thistle. You'll find it growing at the bottom of the meadow where it's damp. It has long stems, no prickles. The purple flowers are soft, and the buds look sad the way they tilt to one side. Take Dottie to help

229

you and, while you're doing that, I'll gather borage with Lizzie.'

The two women, united in their fears for Elizabeth, filled a basket with the blue flowers. They also picked a few young green tops to put in a salad. As they passed the well on their way home, they overheard rumours. Elizabeth's mysterious illness was the talk of Reighton.

'I bet she 'as a canker. It'll be like a wolf—wild an' greedy... eatin' 'er away.'

'Nay, it'll be more like a crab. It'll clasp an' cling to 'er innards an' won't let go.'

The conversation hushed at the sight of Mary and Lizzie. One of the bolder women, a strapping milkmaid, stepped forward.

'At last place I worked, me mistress was same age as Elizabeth an' she 'ad same trouble. They got a load o' centipedes, an' squashed 'em an' steeped 'em in ale. After they'd strained it, she drank it morn an' night.'

'And,' queried Mary, 'did it cure her?'

'Don't know. I left soon after. It were supposed to draw out whatever was inside 'er—a thing wi' lots o' legs *I* reckon.'

Lizzie was interested. 'That's right, now I come to think. I' Rudston I 'eard tell o' such a cure. It were made o' powdered worms an' insects.'

Mary pulled on Lizzie's arm. 'Come on, we've the broth to make. I'm sure it'll be more helpful.'

They left the well and walked down the lane, deep in thought. As they reached Mary's house, Lizzie paused.

'I remember thoo can put a warm kitten, or a puppy, on a growth.'

'I suppose the warmth eases the pain, eh?'

Lizzie shook her head in frustration. 'Nay. Whatever's eatin' Elizabeth, it'll be tempted to eat young flesh of a kitten instead.'

Mary was sick of such talk; it really didn't help to think of some ravenous creature lurking inside her sister. She'd have nightmares about flesh-eating worms.

For the rest of the summer, and during the busy harvest time, Mary continued to do Elizabeth's daily washing, and see to her intimate needs. She was even glad when Lizzie visited each day, bringing Dottie to sit with Elizabeth to hear Bible stories.

Robert was relieved to leave the details and encumbrances of his wife's illness to the two women. He could devote his time to the harvest that was exceeding all expectations and keeping him outside from dawn until after sunset.

Any anxieties about Henry Sumpton diminished as he watched the man wielding a scythe. He realised that Henry, though full of talk, did not possess even the basic skills of a yeoman. By contrast, he noted what a fine worker young William had become. The surly boy, with the swaying gait of a mariner, was now a robust young man who could manoeuvre the sheaves and make the stooks faster than anyone; it was a pity his grandfather wasn't here to see the transformation.

Young William compensated for his lopsided walk with brute strength. Every muscle was toned and, apart from one leg seeming shorter than the other, he was perfectly proportioned. Even Mainprize and Jefferson had stopped their snide remarks.

Ann Smith was also aware of the change in William. She and her family attended the wheat harvest. Together, she and her sisters made a garland of cornflowers and poppies to decorate one of their stooks and, while supposedly occupied doing this, Ann kept an eye on William. She saw him tuck his shirt back quickly into his breeches when he caught sight of her looking his way. Cousins could marry, she thought. Her mother wouldn't mind, although her father did want her to wed a gentleman.

As if reading Ann's mind, her mother leant over the girls and whispered a charm that she knew would guard against a childless marriage.

'Do it without bein' seen. Steal three long straws, two fro' wheat an' one from oats. Then plait 'em, an' wear 'em round tha left leg all weekend. If garter stays i' one piece, thoo'll be blessed wi' two boys an' a girl.'

'Did you try this?' Ann asked.

231

'Nay, I never 'ad time. Our wooin' was too quick.'

Ann gazed at William still stacking sheaves together as if he'd never tire. 'I'd better get on then and make this charm.'

The Uphall harvest supper was held in the yard for the barns were too full of corn waiting to be threshed. Trestle tables were set up laden with pies and cheeses, and casks of ale were stacked by the buttery.

Young William shaved in preparation, using the mint soap that Lizzie had given him, and donned his best Sunday shirt and white neckcloth. Tonight, he hoped to dance with Ann and, as this was just a family celebration, he wouldn't have to contend with Stephen Jefferson.

The Smiths arrived late. William had seen them strolling up Speeton Lane, probably taking another look at the new house, the walls finished now and awaiting a roof. He didn't waste any time. As soon as he saw the Smiths sit at a table, he strode over and welcomed them. He offered to bring them mulled ale, and bade them help themselves to the food.

'And there's tobacco over yon, and pipes if you need them.' He meant to smile at Ann, yet he was so happy to see her that he found his mouth stretching to the widest of grins.

She blushed and stared down at her hands.

'Well then,' he said, wiping his damp palms down his breeches, 'I'll go and get the ale.'

The hired lads had been drinking for some time already. They were getting careless, spilling their ale and then singing for more.

> Drink, lads, drink,
> And see tha do not spill,
> For if tha do, thoo must drink two.
> We'll see tha drink tha fill.

They tried to bring William and his brother into their game, but he avoided them, determined to be sober enough to dance properly with Ann. He waited impatiently for the women's circle dances to end. When it grew dusk, lanterns were hung

232

about the yard, making Ann even more alluring than last Christmas in the subdued light.

At last, it was time for the paired dances. Ann's mother and father stood up, leaving her with her younger brothers and sisters.

William approached her table. 'Ann,' he asked politely, 'would you like to dance?'

'Thank you,' she replied with a coy smile, and rose to take his hand.

The couple slipped into perfect step. He knew that, when he danced, he could bend his body and twirl so that his limp went unnoticed. Full of confidence, he spun her round and round the yard, dance after dance until the music slowed. Then, instead of sitting down to rest, they continued to dance. He was only slightly taller, and found that her body nestled so perfectly against his. It was both disturbing and exciting.

Suddenly, she held his hand tighter and gazed into his face.

Her huge dark eyes took his breath away. She looked so serious, almost imploring. Gone was the cheeky smile. Her lips were parted as if in wonder; they were also moist and swollen. He couldn't help himself. He tilted his head and kissed her mouth. It was but a moment, yet he'd never felt anything so right before, never been more sure. They were still clutching each other when the dance ended. In a daze, he escorted her back to the table.

The kiss had been noticed.

Dorothy Jordan narrowed her eyes. She'd thought it before—the youngsters were like two peas in a pod, more like brother and sister than cousins. She folded her arms and waited until she could speak to Mary.

'Woe betide them two think o' courtin' each other,' she hissed into Mary's ear. 'Ann's father will 'ave better suitors i' mind. Thoo'd better warn thy son before it's too late.'

Mary did not warn her son. Instead, she spoke to her husband.

He listened, but he'd been drinking. He leant back against the stable wall, stretching his arms and yawning.

233

'I've had enough of Matthew's fancy ideas,' he grumbled. He was still smarting over the fact that, although he'd paid the £70 to secure his two oxgangs, it was only thanks to an advance from Matthew. He'd been forced to continue as a carrier well into the summer.

'Your brother thinks he owns Reighton. Isn't it time others shared in his good fortune? Think about it... if they *were* to get married, it would bring wealth into our own family.' He belched. 'I for one will be very happy if a son of mine courts Ann Smith.'

Mary didn't agree. She knew Matthew would disapprove of the match, and it would cause such an upset. Luckily, neither he nor his wife had seen the kiss or much of the dancing. They'd been deep in conversation with the carpenter, no doubt discussing more plans for the new house. She'd let matters take their course for now. *After all*, she reflected, *there's many a drop spilt 'tween cup and lip.*

Chapter 38

Elizabeth lay in bed listening to the music and shouts from the Uphall yard. Robert sat by her side, praying. She sighed and rested a hand on his arm. For days, she'd had no appetite and could only stomach watery soup. She feared the canker had spread for the pain was hot—on a good day like pricking needles. She was so weary, and yet the ache in her back prevented sleep.

Robert could see she was restless. 'Shall I get the laudanum?'

'No, I'll wait. Mary will drop in on her way home.'

'You don't want another sleepless night.'

'Nor you. I'm sorry, Robert... I know you're very busy... you need your sleep too.'

He hoped Mary wouldn't be too long. Whenever Elizabeth's pain worsened, he felt so helpless. As soon as he heard the back door open, he went into the kitchen.

'She's refused her laudanum—been waiting for you.'

'Has she drunk her soup, and kept it down?'

'She's had half of it.' He sat at the table and steered the bottle of laudanum and the glass of water towards Mary. He lowered his voice. 'Here, I think she'll need more drops tonight.'

'She watches me though,' Mary whispered. 'She counts how many, says she doesn't want to forget where she is.'

'But I can't bear to see her fight the pain. It's wearing her out.'

Mary lifted the bottle to the firelight to see how much was left. 'Pass me a mug instead. I'm going to put ten drops in now, before I go in. Then she can see me add twenty more. She won't notice the darker colour in the mug. Is that alright?'

He nodded as Mary began to drip in the reddish-brown tincture. When she'd finished, he admitted, 'I don't like us going behind Elizabeth's back.'

'No, me neither.' Mary held Robert's hand for a moment, something she'd never done before or dreamt of doing.

Elizabeth was relieved to see her sister enter the chamber without Robert. She watched Mary uncork the bottle of laudanum and add twenty drops to a mug. Then she let Mary raise her up so she could drink. She noticed immediately that the drink tasted more bitter than usual. Casting a questioning glance at Mary, she emptied the mug anyway.

'Thank you. I'll be able to sleep soon. Sit down next to me and stay a while.' The act of sitting up had tired her and, with a grimace of pain, she sank back against the pillow. 'I don't think I can have Dottie visit tomorrow. I don't want her to see me like this.'

'Don't worry. I'll make up a good excuse. Do you want Lizzie to come though?'

'No, she'll only get upset. And I don't want Matthew to see me like this either. I'd rather it was just you and Robert.'

Mary moved her chair even closer and leant over to stroke her sister's forehead. 'We worked well together, didn't we—getting Francis's cottage ready? I'm sorry I was jealous of you with Lizzie. It wasn't fair.'

Elizabeth gave a half smile. 'It doesn't matter now.'

Mary ground her teeth, trying to stem the tears. She and Elizabeth needed distraction.

'Remember that time you took Francis and our Mary on the sands? I only found their shoes later when you'd gone home—it took me ages to get the salt marks off.'

Elizabeth's face became more animated. There was even a sparkle in her eyes. 'That girl... she ran straight into the sea with all her clothes on... I couldn't catch her. I ended up wading in myself... way past my knees.'

She paused and shut her eyes to better picture that summer's day. They were good times. Suddenly, she opened her eyes.

'I even had to strip off my skirt... I dried it on a boulder.' She smiled again as she recalled an image of young Mary running naked on the beach. 'She used to come to our house

236

smelling of old Ben... you know... that mix of wood smoke and apples...'

'And tar,' Mary interrupted. 'Remember those waterproof hats he made?'

'Yes, and he made his own mead.' Elizabeth began to cough, and held her side.

'I'm sorry, I shouldn't make you talk.'

'No, I'm fine. I was just thinking of Mary getting those names wrong from the Bible.'

'Don't tell me, they were Shadrat, Meshat and...'

'Tobedyougo!' they cried in unison.

Elizabeth held her side again. 'Don't make me laugh. Your Mary was so upset at the time.'

'It was good of Robert to help teach her to read.'

'Yes.' Elizabeth shut her eyes again, thinking how different things might have been for everyone if young Mary had not died.

Mary could see the laudanum was taking effect. 'You get some rest now. I'll stay a little while longer and hold your hand.'

'Thank you,' Elizabeth whispered, still with her eyes closed. Within a minute she was asleep.

The next few days were an ordeal. Mary increased the doses of laudanum, and still Elizabeth had to fight the pain.

'Should we increase the dose even more?' Robert asked early one evening.

Mary bit her lip in thought. 'See how she is in the night. You have the bottle—I'll leave it up to you. Don't worry about the cost. Matthew said he'd see to the apothecary's bill. Let her have a long sleep tonight, and I'll see her tomorrow.'

Robert thanked Mary for her help and returned to Elizabeth's bedside. He lifted her hand and studied it as never before. It was now so thin, the veins raised and blue. Her palm was rough, the result of years of washing, gardening and salting meat, not to mention reaping the corn. He'd not treated her with the love and kindness she deserved. Not once had she stopped him following his own strict path, not once

237

stopped him reading when they could have been spending time together. She'd never even complained at the lack of a child.

He knew it would always be a dilemma, to follow Jesus *and* be a good husband. Unable to do both, he'd chosen the path best suited to his nature. Now, it hit him—he might have chosen the more difficult path that would have been better for his wife. It would have been his greatest test—to have accepted his manhood, not denied it.

He rubbed Elizabeth's hand against his forehead in anguish, and quoted from a psalm. 'I am a worm, and no man; a reproach of men, and despised of the people.' A tear slid down his cheek and onto the bedcover.

Elizabeth turned her head to him as he sniffed back more tears. 'Oh, Robert, don't be so hard on yourself.' The effort of talking made her wince in pain. She peered into his face and braced herself to speak again. 'I know you've done your best.'

He shook his head. 'I didn't do right by you.' He realised he couldn't make amends. It was too late. He was going to lose her. 'I'm sorry, so sorry,' he choked.

'Robert, God will forgive you. God sees into our souls.' She squeezed her eyes shut and grasped his hand as another wave of pain seared through her lower back.

He felt her grip tighten as she fought for breath. When the pain subsided, she relaxed and let go of his hand.

'Take a few deep breaths,' he advised. 'That'll help. I'll get more laudanum.'

'No, we've talked about this before. I don't want to leave this world in a stupor.'

Another bout of agony gave them no option.

She gave in to his pleas and drank a glass laden with over fifty drops. As she seemed to sink deeper into the bed, he held her hand again.

'I love you, Elizabeth. I wish...'

'I know,' she whispered. The laudanum was such a warm, pleasant sensation, flooding outwards from her stomach. Any pain and anxiety melted away. Half asleep, she murmured, 'Robert, don't torment yourself. It's over now. Let it be.'

He knelt by her bed throughout the night. She never regained consciousness, and her breathing stopped just before dawn.

He couldn't take it in. He needed to get out, stretch his legs, walk miles—God knows where. After pulling on his boots, and grabbing his long coat and hat, he left the house. Striding to the cliff top, he headed north where the biting northeast wind struck his cheekbones.

At the ravine, he stopped. The sun was about to rise and a grey light, pale as a pigeon's feathers, hovered over the horizon. The sight gave him no hope. He knew, at the Last Judgement, when the wheat is separated from the chaff, he'd be found wanting.

The overheard words of Dorothy Jordan came to mind. Was he really nothing but the dried husk of a man?

Chapter 39

Elizabeth's funeral was held three days later. Robert stood in the garden waiting for Matthew Smith and the others to arrive. The day was calm, and warm for autumn. He couldn't help but notice the apple tree laden with fruit. Mid-October was a time of ripening, of storing the good produce of the earth, not a time of loss and burial.

He walked alone behind the coffin, paid for by Elizabeth's brother. It was draped in black and carried by Matthew and his two sons with William and his two eldest sons at the other side. The rest of the Smiths followed alongside Mary and her family. Lizzie and Dottie led the rest of the village.

In church, Mary overheard murmurs that Elizabeth's death was Robert's fault because he'd never given her a child. She saw him sitting at the head of the coffin by the altar, his head bowed. Most likely, he was aware of the gossip.

Very few people, apart from the family, attended Robert's house afterwards. He'd been reluctant to have any visitors at all, and had warned Mary and Lizzie not to provide unnecessary food and drink. The two women passed round a diluted fruit punch along with a plate of oatcakes which, despite Robert's wishes, they'd spread with butter. There was nothing resembling the rich arval cake served at Uphall after other funerals.

When Lizzie began to cry, Mary put an arm round her shoulder.

'I'm sorry,' she whispered, 'it's a miserable affair, a poor last goodbye, and I know how much you'll miss Elizabeth.' It hurt to admit it, but she swallowed hard and added, 'Elizabeth loved to spend whole days with you and Dottie... she hadn't been so happy for a long time.'

Francis noticed his wife's tears and was afraid of Robert's disapproval. Surely, Elizabeth would have her rightful place in heaven and, instead of weeping, Lizzie should be grateful.

240

When he whispered words to this effect, it only made her worse. He took her by the arm.

'Come on, you're upsetting Dottie. Perhaps it's for the best if we leave Robert to himself now.'

Dottie waved a sad goodbye to John, her favourite uncle, and then toddled after her parents.

The guests became even more subdued. Mary and William attempted polite conversation with Matthew and his family, but the sight of Robert standing aloof by the window discouraged their efforts. Young William cast yearning glances at Ann; this was not the time to be doing much else. Before long, everyone left the house and left Robert to his grief.

Robert became even more of a recluse. For weeks after Elizabeth's death, his tall, dark figure haunted the many tracks and pathways as he walked miles seeking peace. He tried to convince himself that all was well. He had his role as churchwarden, he had his Bible and he had a friend in Francis. Reighton even had a resident vicar. No, he did not need a woman in his life. When Mary continued to visit, taking him cooked food, he told her to desist.

'I can manage on my own, thank you. Take Elizabeth's clothes—take what you want.'

When she'd gone, he lit a bonfire and burnt the rest. As the smoke rose in the still autumn air, he persuaded himself he was free of women and could devote himself more to God. When he returned to the kitchen, though, he saw the stain on his wife's chair—another reminder of what he'd lost. As he wondered whether to scrub it clean, his treatment of Elizabeth lay heavy on his conscience. He looked back on his married life. What good had his abstinence done?

One evening in December, Robert and Francis were sitting huddled together beside a meagre fire in Robert's kitchen. Ice was forming already on the inside of the window. Robert held his hands towards the hearth as a piece of gorse burst into flame.

241

'I value these visits of yours, Francis. No one else calls round.'

Francis was sorry, knowing Robert didn't encourage visitors.

'How are Lizzie and Dottie?'

'In good health.'

'I don't see them anymore. I think they only wanted to see Elizabeth.'

'That's not true. You were teaching Dottie about the Bible.'

'Dottie liked her treats. She's not interested in reading, not without a crust of bread and honey. I'm thinking we must see to our bodies as well as our minds and souls. It's all very well fasting...'

Francis was confused. He'd been following Robert's teachings since a boy. He watched the gorse collapse softly into a pile of ash. The fire gave out little heat.

'But,' he protested, 'you've always spurned meat and rich foods... and avoided other temptations.'

'Listen, Francis, there are other ways to show your love of God. It's not too late for you. Be kind to your wife. Life is short.'

Francis scratched his head. Robert was grieving, that was it; he'd lost his way for now.

'Thank you, Robert. I'll give it thought.'

He made an excuse to leave early, yet decided to carry on his regular evening visits. After all, he understood Robert better than anyone.

Dorothy Jordan saw Robert as she looked out of her chamber window at dawn. She watched him set off, a lone figure, on his long walk round the fields, or to the hills and the cliff top.

''E's not at peace with 'issen,' she muttered as if to her husband. She imagined his reply. *Was 'e ever?*

As she went downstairs to organise the maids, she heard Samuel in the kitchen grumbling over the price of wheat; apparently it had dropped by over a shilling a bushel, no doubt because of the bumper harvest.

242

'Like tha father,' she said as she walked past, 'thoo's never satisfied. Be grateful our barns are full o' sheaves.' Their storerooms were stacked high with sacks of dried peas and beans, and the loft was full of apples. 'Think on—ev'ryone i' Reighton 'as prospered. We'll manage.'

Since the harvest supper, young William had found no opportunity to meet Ann. A few days before Christmas, though, his uncle Matthew invited the family for drinks at the new house.

'Don't get your hopes up,' his mother warned. 'We won't be there long. The house isn't finished inside, and there's no furniture. Your uncle just wants to lord it over your father.'

'I don't suppose Father's too pleased then.'

'No, he'll go under sufferance.'

They set off in the afternoon before it grew too dark, the frost sparkling already on the road as they made their way up the hill and past the church. When they turned to go along Speeton Lane, the half moon hung directly ahead, casting a cold light. Young William's heart sank as the new house, so imposing, loomed ahead to his left.

Matthew was standing by the grand entrance, waiting to greet them. 'You're our first visitors. Come on in. We've lit a fire in the kitchen, and there's mulled wine ready.'

The kitchen, despite the large fire, was icy. The only furniture was an old table the carpenters had been using, and there was nowhere to sit. Although a lantern had been placed on the table and one in each corner of the room, the scene remained dreary. Matthew's family was standing close to the fire.

Young William stood uneasily next to his mother and father while his younger brothers hovered behind, in awe of the high ceiling. He kept an eye on Ann as she helped to fill the glasses. She was more beautiful than ever in her long red cloak. When she lowered the hood, her hair tumbled about her neck. How he longed to bury his face in those shining, black curls. Given the chance, he'd kiss her neck and then her lips.

She smiled at him, knowing the effect she had, and passed him his drink.

243

'Thank you,' he murmured, unable to hide a wide smile.

When everyone was ready, Matthew raised his glass. 'May this toast be the first of many more to come. May this house be full of light and happiness—and prosperity. Here's to Reighton Hall.'

'To Reighton Hall.'

'Now,' said Matthew, 'I'm going to show William round the house. He's fetched most of the materials—now he can see the results of his labour. You all stay here by the fire and keep warm.'

'Wait,' interrupted Mary, 'I think we should raise a glass to someone who can't be here—our sister.'

'Sorry, yes, of course... here's to Elizabeth... a most kind and caring sister... and a long suffering one. May she rest in peace.'

As soon as the toast was drunk, the two men left the kitchen.

Young William took the chance to walk over to join Ann and her brother Thomas. John followed him, much to his annoyance, while the others stayed by their mothers.

'Will you be playing football again this Christmas?' Thomas asked.

'No.' William glanced at Ann. 'I can think of better ways now to spend my time.'

John was puzzled. 'What are you going to do then?'

Ann butted in. 'He's going to take me to Hunmanby.'

'Am I?' He had no idea what she was talking about.

'I'll be visiting Hunmanby Hall twice a week in the new year. I'm to have dinner there... and meet people, as well as do embroidery... and improve my singing.' She gave him a cheeky smile and winked. 'I'm sure you can find the time.'

As William's face lit up, John's clouded over. 'Won't you be at home anymore when I come to see our sheep?'

'John,' she said kindly, 'you keep on visiting. I won't be in Hunmanby *all* the time.' Suddenly, she had an idea; John, naive and obedient as he was, could be the perfect go-between.

'Yes, John,' she added, and took both of his hands in hers, 'I'd love to see you just as much next year.'

William saw how Ann's eyes glittered when she glanced back at him. He was so happy that he didn't even care when his father returned to the kitchen with a face like thunder.

There was such a chill between the two men that both families prepared to leave. Young William, desperate to kiss Ann's hands, dared to kiss the hands of her sisters first. This unusual farewell went unrebuked, but only because it was Christmas. He ignored the suspicious frown on his uncle's face, and strolled back home full of hope for the future.

Part Five

Secrets

Chapter 40

On Christmas Eve, young William helped to bring in and light the Yule log. Then he settled down at the table to savour the sweet, milky foods that his mother had prepared. Even his father, calm and content, had recovered from whatever had upset him at the Smiths' new house. When his father lit the Yule candle, and it began to burn well, it was another hopeful sign.

Unwittingly, John, of all people, broke the spell. 'Who's going to fire the gun now Grandfather's gone? Are you going to shoot it, Will? You used to be really good with the gun.'

Young William launched a kick under the table. The last thing he wanted was a reminder of his time with that gun.

The table rocked.

'Steady lad,' warned his father, 'you'll be knocking over the candle.'

Everyone watched as the Yule candle stood firm, but the flame flickered in the draught caused by the commotion, and then sputtered out. There was an immediate hush. No one dared speak.

Young William had been too little to remember the candle ever going out. He'd been told, though, that it had happened the Christmas before his sister died. Unlike his parents, he couldn't believe that one of the family would die just because a candle had gone out. He apologised and tried to make light of it, but his parents' faces were grim. Then he realised it was only two months since Aunt Elizabeth had been buried. Illness and death would still be on their minds.

John began to cry. The candle going out seemed to be his fault. He remembered the ash-stick duel when his brother had lost the fight. He'd warned William at the time about the kiss of an ash plant bringing bad luck. He felt for William's hand under the table and clasped it for comfort and reassurance.

249

There was nothing more he could do. Even relighting the candle would not make amends.

The Christmas Day at Uphall was subdued and uneventful. It was Dorothy's first Christmas without her husband. She did her best, though it was never going to be quite the same.

A week later, news arrived that Reighton had avoided a violent storm. People thought themselves lucky for the storm had swept right through Hornsea the night before Christmas Eve. Young William was eager to hear more about it. He'd heard plenty of tales about the Great Storm of almost thirty years ago, about how Dickon had been nearly blown down the hill, yet he could hardly imagine such a strong wind. When his father heard rumours of a safe smuggling store being uncovered, the two of them went to the forge to find out more.

'It's just gossip,' the blacksmith reported. 'It might be folk in 'Ornsea gettin' their own back, but they do say their parish clerk 'ad a seizure when 'urricane blew church roof off.' He dropped his voice. 'Strange, though... it were just as 'e were storin' casks i' crypt.' He rubbed the stubble on his chin. 'Hmm, I wonder what became o' that brandy.'

Young William was more interested in the storm damage. 'What about everyone else's roofs? Did the wind take them *all* off?'

'Nay, not everyone's—only if they was i' wind's path. I 'eard there were a woman an' 'er bairn i' bed together. When their roof blew off, they was blown into street, bed an' all. An' they wasn't even 'urt.'

'What else happened?'

'A windmill were blown over. Aye, an' even its millstone were blown a *long* ways away.'

Such news unsettled young William. He remembered the Yule candle going out and thought of his love for Ann Smith and his hopes for the future. Suddenly, he felt vulnerable.

Robert Storey took the 'hurricane' as proof of God's vengeance against the ungodly. Without Elizabeth's loving nature to temper his stance, he discussed the storm with the

250

vicar and expected John Sumpton to use it as the theme for his next sermon.

'They must see it as a mark of God's displeasure,' he argued. 'It's to chastise folk, get them to repent and return to the path of godliness. They have sinned in Hornsea and they have been punished.'

The vicar, unlike many in the village, took Robert Storey seriously. 'Yes,' he agreed, 'and would you be so kind as to find me relevant passages to read out? That would be a great help.'

Robert was smug as he strode home. It was good to have purpose in his life, and he could ask Francis to share the task. The next sermon would be full of warnings.

Robert and Francis were fully gratified on Sunday. The vicar compared the afflicted in a reading about Babylon.

'Behold the day of the Lord cometh, cruel with wrath and fierce anger, to lay the land desolate; and he shall destroy the sinners thereof out of it.' He then turned to Psalms and read, 'He causeth the vapours to ascend from the ends of the earth; he maketh lightnings for the rain; he bringeth the wind out of his treasures.'

Robert Storey got up and stood before the great Bible to read the passage he'd chosen for himself.

Francis leant forward in rapt anticipation while young William rolled his eyes and winked at Ann Smith across the aisle.

'The Lord trieth the righteous,' Robert read out, and then paused to glare at the congregation. 'But... upon the wicked he shall rain snares, fire and brimstone, and an horrible tempest.'

'Amen,' cried Francis.

The vicar ended by giving thanks; after all, Reighton had been spared. 'Pray God give us grace to be thankful, and never forget His great mercy.'

Afterwards, on the way home, Francis caught up with his brother William. He'd noticed him gazing at Ann throughout the service.

'Have you no respect for the church, for God's house? Do you have to take your lustful eyes everywhere?'

Mary and her family stopped walking as they saw young William's face redden in anger and embarrassment.

'Leave Will alone,' she said quietly. 'It's a day of peace.'

Francis held up both hands in submission, but Mary noted his expression remained one of disgust. She was shocked when, in one move, Will grabbed him by the throat.

'There now,' he snarled, 'what are you going to do now?'

She knew Francis would not fight back and feared for him as Will squeezed his throat harder.

Francis's eyes began to bulge.

Lizzie pulled Dottie away, and John began to cry.

Mary knew for sure that her husband would not intervene. In a panic, she beat on Will's back and shouted at him until he let go.

Young William stood back, breathing heavily and glaring with hatred.

Francis rubbed his neck and coughed, unable to fathom his brother's violent reaction. Then, without saying a word, he turned and joined his wife and daughter.

As Mary walked on ahead with the family, she overheard Lizzie warning Francis he'd better be more careful in future and not provoke his brother. 'Yes,' Francis had replied. 'He's obviously crazy.'

Mary said nothing though they were all shaken by the attack. She wouldn't forget the speed of Will's temper and the wild look in his eyes.

Chapter 41

1733

Once the ploughing began in early January, young William and his brother Francis were too exhausted to goad each other or fight. Besides, William had better things to think about. Ann Smith and her brother would be starting their visits to Hunmanby Hall, and he hoped to see her as she rode out or returned. Each evening, before supper, he questioned John. As the two washed their hands in the garden, he flicked water at his brother.

'You been to see your pet sheep today?'

'No.'

'Are you going tomorrow?'

'I might.'

'Well, if Ann gives you a letter for me, leave it in that hole in the cowshed wall. And don't tell anyone.'

Two days later, John folded up Ann's note and pushed it into the hole as arranged. Now his brother would give up pestering and wouldn't flick water at him.

Young William retrieved the note and, with trembling fingers, read that Ann would return from Hunmanby tomorrow afternoon just before dusk. She'd get rid of Thomas, and there were instructions to wait on the north moor, not far from the shepherd's hut. He thanked God that he'd learnt to read. If only he had the time and opportunity to write back, he would let her know what he hadn't the courage to say.

The next day was fine. By the appointed time, the wind had dropped and the sky was clear. He waited, hiding behind a clump of gorse in full flower. The sheep dotted below him were silent as he listened out for the sound of her arrival. Soon, he heard the familiar snort of her horse and his heart leapt. He hurried from his hiding place and there she was—alone and just for him, her cheeks flushed from the ride.

On seeing him, she let her hood fall. Then she gave him such a wide smile. 'You got my note then.'

He nodded, grinning like a lunatic.

'So... help me down, or do you want to talk up to me?'

He knew she needed no help, but held the horse steady while she dismounted. The moment she was at his side, he kissed her cheek.

She cocked her head to one side and raised one dark eyebrow. 'Is that all I mean to you?'

'No...' He was unsure how to proceed, didn't know what to expect from their first meeting alone. He licked his lips and swallowed.

She laughed at him. 'I'm not going to eat you!' She took his hand and held it to her cheek. 'Come on, hold me close— it's been a cold ride.'

He wrapped both arms round her and held her tight to his chest. Now he could nuzzle into her thick, soft hair that smelled faintly of rose petals. He kissed her head a few times until she pulled away and kissed him full on the mouth. The kiss was brief as he fought for air; his whole body felt immediately more alive and about to burst. If they'd been in a bedchamber or a barn, he wasn't sure he'd have stayed in control. Exposed on a hill in January, though, he could just about hold himself in check.

Unaware of his turmoil, she was intent on more kisses.

'Wait,' he gasped, 'let me look at you.'

As he held her off, her loving face altered. She frowned, pursed her lips and folded her arms as if cross.

'You're so beautiful, Ann, standing here by the gorse. Let my eyes take their fill—I don't often get the chance.'

'And you won't get the chance much longer. I have to go home soon.' She tapped her foot. 'Well?' When he didn't move, she raised her chin and said goodbye.

'No, don't go, not yet.' He stood still, hesitant, until she took hold of the horse's rein. Then he grabbed her hand and apologised. 'Ann, wait a moment longer.' He pulled her towards him and gave her a long, gentle kiss on the lips, full of love and tenderness.

When he let go of her, she stood in amazement. After a pause for reflection, she told him she'd be there the day after tomorrow. 'The same time...so will I see you?'

'As that gorse is ever in flower—yes, I'll be here.'

The next time that young William waited for Ann, the weather had changed. A strong wind blew straight off the sea, so he found a sheltered spot for them both in a grassy hollow. When she arrived, he took off his coat, and laid it down. To avoid temptation, he began to tell her about his ploughing and harrowing.

'And my father wants me to help cut reeds to repair the roof. We're very busy—there's all the fences to mend. How's your new house? Will it be ready soon?'

'We're hoping to move in the spring. The plaster needs to dry so we can't rush.' She glanced warily at the darkening sky, thinking it might rain soon and their time together would be cut short.

'And what did you do in Hunmanby today?'

'Oh, this and that. They invite others to dinner—young gentlemen... you know... possible suitors. But don't worry, I like you best.'

'Do you love me?'

'I love your kisses.'

William needed no more encouragement and controlled himself so long as they sat upright. When she lay on his coat though, he joined her and could not hide his passion. He knew the dangers, yet she seemed oblivious and was hungry for more kisses.

Suddenly, large spots of rain began to fall.

She pushed him away and stood up. 'I'll write a note about next time. I'll give it to John.'

In February, snow and sleet prevented Ann Smith's journeys to Hunmanby. She passed notes to John, but could find no way of meeting William unseen. One impulsive idea led the couple to sneak into the Smiths' new house. She knew her father was busy at home with his accounts and, if she met any workmen, she could say she was checking something for him.

They knocked the snow from their boots and entered the hallway. They'd just begun to climb the staircase when they heard hammering and sawing.

'It's no good, Will, I daren't. I'm sorry, there's nowhere to go.'

'What about the dovecote?'

'But it's freezing out there.'

'It's not much better in here. And,' he added with a wink, '*I* can keep you warm.'

The newly built dovecote was dry at least and, since there were no doves yet, the floor was clean. William was about to take off his coat for them to lie down.

'No, not here,' she warned. 'If anyone finds us, we'll be in such trouble. Quick, move away from the door. We can stand here at the side out of sight. I could always say I was showing you how it was built.'

He wrapped his arms round her and tried to warm her up. 'You know,' he whispered in her ear, 'it was so cold yesterday that my mother had to cut the bread with an axe.'

'I wonder how everyone is in Hunmanby,' she replied, her voice muffled by his coat.

'Do you miss them?'

'I miss the dinners and...'

He pulled back. 'Would you miss me?'

'Of course, silly.'

They began to kiss, gently at first, then with more urgency. It was William who stopped, worried and embarrassed by his lack of control.

'We'd better not stay too long.'

She stamped her foot. 'Oh, this is no good. We must find somewhere else to meet. What about the shepherd's hut?' she cried in desperation. 'I can find out from John when it's safe to go.'

John played his part, and the couple found an opportunity to meet at the hut on the moor. It was not ideal. The place stank

256

of tar and tallow, and there was nowhere clean to lie down. Ann paused by the shepherd's bed.

'I'm not even touching that! I bet it's as flea-ridden as his dog.'

William was hurt by that remark. There was nothing wrong with the dog, though he had to admit the bed looked filthy and the pillow greasy.

They didn't dare rekindle the fire because the smoke would give them away. As in the dovecote, all they could do was stand and hold each other tight, talk and kiss.

Ann sighed. She was getting bored of Reighton and longed for the spring when she could ride to Hunmanby again. She missed the elegant company at the Hall, but would never admit this to William. Instead, she tried to sound cheerful.

'In spring we'll be able to meet again twice a week.'

After much kissing and cuddling and letting him feel her breasts, she released her grip on him and began fastening up her coat.

'It's no good coming here—my hair will smell of tar.' She was afraid to go home reeking of the shepherd's hut, and prayed the walk home through the falling snow would air her clothes. 'I know it's hard,' she added, 'but let's wait until spring. As soon as I can, I'll let John know. Let's have one more kiss... make it the best yet.'

In March, they began their former trysts on the moor. William now took a blanket and a fleece to lay on the ground in their hollow by the gorse. After an initial spell of kissing, he stopped to tell her that the dry weather meant a good year for corn.

'We're putting soot on the wheat field.'

'So that's why your hands are so dark. They must be ingrained with it.'

'Sorry, it won't rub off on you.'

'It better not. I've been learning how to keep a fair complexion and keep my skin soft. In Hunmanby, they mix lemon juice and egg whites, and they get the maids to cook it *really slowly*. It comes out like butter. It's lovely to smooth on your face.'

He decided to shave more often, especially on the days he met her. She'd appreciate his scented shaving soap.

'The Osbaldeston ladies wash their faces with white wine that's had rosemary flowers boiled in it. They let me drink a bit too—it sweetens your breath.'

He'd remember to chew parsley or mint next time they met. 'We'll be finished soon with the spring ploughing, and we've had our first calves. Your father must be busy, what with his herd *and* your new house.'

'Mmm.' She was still thinking of the Osbaldestons. 'In Hunmanby, the women blacken their eyebrows.'

'Yours don't need blacking. They're perfect as they are.'

'They use burnt cork or they burn cloves over a candle and use those.'

He was amazed at the lengths women would go to for their appearance. 'My brother Francis and Robert Storey don't know half of what you women do. They'd be shocked, say it was all vanity.'

'I heard that Robert Storey has been asking questions in Hunmanby—about a couple of mollies who live there.'

The blood rushed to William's face. He wasn't sure how much Ann knew.

She laughed. 'Apparently, they went quiet in winter. It was probably too cold for them. Anyway, now that it's spring, the man—Emsley, I think, or Helmsley—he's moved.'

'Oh? Where's he gone to?'

'*I* don't know. Why are you so interested?'

'I'm not.'

'I think Carnaby was mentioned.'

William covered his blushes with another bout of kissing.

One day in early April, William had an idea. He knew that John would be up all night helping with the lambing. Ann might be interested in getting another orphan lamb and she might like to accompany John and himself one evening. As he'd hoped, she jumped at the chance.

258

John led them to the pen of ewes and pointed out those likely to give birth that night. He and Jack would be busy there for hours.

William had his fleece ready and wandered off with Ann to sit in their hollow by the gorse. They lay on their backs on the fleece for a moment and stared upwards. It was a cold, clear night, the sky full of stars. They held hands and gazed in wonder, neither of them speaking. Beyond the occasional bleat of the ewes and lambs, they could hear the distant shush of waves on the beach.

'My sister loved the stars. When she died, I used to go out sometimes at night with Stina. I'd look up and wonder which star was Mary. Now I wonder if one of those stars is Stina.'

She leant her head against his shoulder. 'Do you think, one day, we'll be just stars in the sky?'

'As long as we're together, I won't mind.'

She paused and snuggled closer. 'Me neither.'

Chapter 42

Ann Smith could not meet William while her family moved into their new house. Instead of going to Hunmanby, she spent each day at Reighton Hall, helping with the furniture and setting up the kitchen. She had no opportunity to write notes because, although more maids were hired, they needed to be watched.

It was the middle of spring. Hawthorn blossomed over the lanes, and birds rustled in the hedge bottoms seeking nest material. Young William wandered back from the fields, oblivious. It was a mere two weeks since he and Ann had gazed at the stars, yet it seemed an age. To make matters worse, he was hearing talk of her next birthday. She'd be twenty-one and, instead of celebrating at the new house, the Osbaldestons had offered to hold a special supper at Hunmanby Hall.

'We won't be invited,' his mother told him when they were alone in the kitchen. 'And even if we were, I don't think we'd fit in. There'll be gentry coming from all over. It'll be a big gathering—a perfect time for Ann to be seen.'

William kicked the table.

'Now, don't look so glum. What did you expect?' When he didn't answer and went out to the garden, she followed him. 'Do something useful—chop that wood for us.'

She returned to the kitchen and listened to him splitting the logs. They'd sharpened the axe recently, and there was a pleasing rhythm to the sound. After a while, though, the rhythm was lost, and she could tell the axe was not hitting the wood properly. Then she heard a yelp of pain and a curse.

She dashed outside to find him hopping about and clutching his leg. There was a slit in his breeches just below the knee, showing a dribble of blood. She got him to sit on the chopping log while she inspected the wound. The cut was horizontal, a gaping but neat slice, about three inches long.

'Oh, William, I wish Sarah Ezard was here. She'd know what to do.'

'Ask grandmother—she'll know.'

'Wait, I'll get a piece of linen.'

She told him to hold it over the wound, and then she rushed up the hill to Uphall.

Dorothy Jordan had an instant answer. 'Clean it, then pack it wi' cobwebs an' bind it.'

'What about stitching it up?' Mary asked. 'The barber-surgeon in Hunmanby could do it.'

'Nay lass, I'll gi' thee an egg an' rosewater mixture to pour over wound—that'll 'elp it get better. It's no good closin' wound up—it needs to drain.'

Mary did as advised, but when the other boys came home with their father, there was trouble.

William was angry. 'Fancy asking my mother! You know she sticks to the old ways. No, I'll take Will to Hunmanby in the morning—get him fixed up properly.'

Next day, the two set off on the cart, young William with his leg stretched out and bound tight.

The barber-surgeon inspected the cut and cleaned it. Then he lifted an old horn from a hook and tipped out a selection of fine, iron needles. He asked how the injury happened as he threaded a sailmaker's curved needle. When asked if it was sharp, he was offended.

'See for yourself. They're all sharp and polished—not a bit of rust on any of them.' He smiled. 'I'm used to stitching up.'

'Will it take long?'

'Not if you let me get on with it.' He told young William to sit very still and grip the chair arm when it hurt. 'I've seen much worse at sea... legs and arms almost cut in two. The sailors never made a fuss.'

William was determined to be brave. With sweating hands, he held on to the chair and fixed his eyes on a fly in the corner of the ceiling. It was near a cobweb, soon became entangled and buzzed to be free. Suddenly, he flinched as he felt the needle. He wanted to cry out but kept quiet, his nails digging into the chair arm.

261

His father looked on, helpless. He knew how much it hurt by the tears in his son's eyes.

Young William endured five stitches.

'That'll be two shillings,' the barber-surgeon reminded them. 'You'll be fine. Just keep it covered and don't bend your knee. It should heal in a couple of weeks. Then you can snip the stitches yourself and pull them out. Or you can leave them in. They're only catgut and they'll rot away. Be more careful with your axe in future.'

When they left, William treated his son to a much-needed tankard of ale at the nearby inn. There was a huddle of men full of talk about the death of a man in Pocklington. It certainly took young William's mind off his sore and throbbing leg. A travelling performer had been killed while attempting to 'fly'; he'd been attached by a rope to the church.

'Aye,' a man continued, slavering with excitement, "e wore wings like a bat. They was tied to 'is arms an' legs. 'Is rope 'ad mebbe gone too slack, though, an' some'ow 'e crashed inti battlements. A sad story, eh? 'E broke 'is skull.'

Young William shook his head, amazed at the daft things people did for a few pennies. He was interested, but wanted to get back to Reighton. Ann would feel sorry for his injury. One thing did worry him, though. It wasn't like him to be clumsy with an axe, or any tools for that matter, and, just lately, he'd dropped and broken a few things. To save face, he'd blamed the hired lads.

Ann did hear about William's leg and gave him a sympathetic smile when she saw him hobble into church. She had plenty of other things on her mind though—the plans for her birthday and the new gown to be made. Soon, she'd be resuming those visits to Hunmanby.

For the next two weeks, while his leg was healing, William avoided work in the fields. Instead, he hung about the house and garden doing jobs for his mother. He was often bored, so when John asked him if he wanted to help clip Lizzie's chickens, he couldn't wait to go.

They found Lizzie already in her back yard with Dottie. She was holding a pair of clippers and a small blanket. Young

William wasn't sure what was expected of him, but John gave Dottie a quick cuddle and then cornered a hen. He grabbed it and held it upside down by the legs.

Lizzie threw the blanket over it and told John to hold it still.

William could see that John was perfect for the task. His brother calmed the chicken with softly spoken rubbish about it being the loveliest hen in Reighton.

'Right, John,' instructed Lizzie, 'keep it under thy arm an' I'll spread out a wing. Look, Dottie, I'm goin' to snip off these long feathers 'ere so it can't fly away.' She took a firm hold of the clippers and began to cut. 'Mind, Dottie, they're sharp an' these feathers are tough.'

As William couldn't help catch the hens, he offered to do the clipping. 'My hands are stronger, Lizzie. You see to Dottie.' He was glad to be of use and smiled when Dottie chose a feather to give him as a present.

'It's for luck.'

'Thank you. I'm sure it'll make my leg better.' He doubted this very much, recalling the 'lucky' rabbit's tail the gypsies had once given him. It hadn't saved his sister, and he'd ended up throwing it on the bonfire.

Dottie then did something that reminded him again of his sister Mary. She imitated his stiff walk.

'You walk funny, like this,' she grinned. 'Can I see your leg?'

'You wouldn't like it. I'll show you when it's mended... and then I'll chase you round the garden.'

By the time William's stitches could be pulled out, Ann and her brother were visiting Hunmanby again. She had the pet sheep moved to Reighton Hall so that John would visit and be able to pass on her secret notes.

William's leg was still very stiff, yet he limped as fast as he could to the north moor to meet her. His efforts were not rewarded; all she talked about were the plans for her birthday.

'It was *my* twenty-first birthday last month,' he retorted, 'but we didn't do anything special. We don't reckon with such

263

things—except when it's February. Then my father goes quiet… and we all know why.'

'I suppose it was when your sister died.'

'Yes—a death day, not a birthday.' He felt his eyes fill up, not because of young Mary but because he always remembered the day he'd shot Stina.

'How's your leg?'

'Alright. It's left a scar.'

'Can I see?'

'You're as bad as Dottie. No, you can't see it, not yet.'

'Then I can't kiss it better.'

'Come here.' He pulled her closer and proved to her what she'd been missing. 'There, I bet you'd like *that* on your birthday.'

The next time they met, she appeared in a new riding habit. She looked so magnificent that he held her horse shyly while she dismounted. He felt like a stable groom before his mistress. Again, she was full of talk about the Osbaldestons.

'Do you like my riding costume? They've been kind enough to lend it. Today I've been inchered.'

'What? That sounds painful.'

She laughed. 'Don't be silly. The tailor's been measuring me up for the hoop and new gown.'

'You're lucky. My mother has to make do with her old skirts. She mends them or alters them so they're a bit different.'

'Well, that wouldn't do for me at all. We've decided on the style and they've ordered the material. It's silk brocade— dark, grass green with a pattern running through it like lace. I'm told it costs more than what the tailor charges. Aren't you impressed?'

He thought it was a waste of money. 'I hope it wears well. Maybe you can hand it down to your sisters.'

She put her hands on her hips. 'William, you can't begrudge me a new gown. Lots of people spend a small fortune on their clothes. Why, I've heard of ladies spending up to a hundred pounds just on their lace.'

'It doesn't mean *you* have to.' This aping of the gentry was annoying and, when she spoke of getting white silk stockings, he laughed in her face. 'No one wears such things round here. You'll look ridiculous.'

She decided not to tell him about the plans to cut her hair and change her coiffure. 'If you're going to be so unkind, I'll go.'

'By all means, go. Don't let *me* keep you.'

She fiddled with the horse's reins. There was no mounting block out there on the moor, and she needed his help.

He folded his arms and stood his ground for a while, enjoying her dilemma.

With great reluctance, she gave in first. 'Well,' she pouted, 'are you going to help me or not?'

He moved forward and, as he held her foot to give a push up, he looked her in the eye. He saw sadness.

'I'm sorry,' she said. 'I'll try not to talk so much next time. Give me a kiss and say I'm forgiven.'

He leapt at the chance. All was forgotten until the next time.

Chapter 43

Young William and Ann met as usual a few days before her birthday supper. He kissed her and then took off his coat and laid it on the ground. She began to prattle on about her family's new clothes before she'd even sat down.

'My father showed us his new waistcoat—it's beautifully embroidered with leaves. Of course, his coat and breeches are dark and plain, nothing fancy about them, but he's bought a new shirt with lace ruffles and a lovely Indian silk handkerchief. Oh, and a new cravat.' She sat down at last.

He replied in a monotone. 'My mother buys muslin and makes our own neckcloths.'

'Yes, but my father must look his best on my special night.' *And*, she thought, *I'll be the centre of attention.* She held his hand, her eyes glittering at the prospect.

He was not impressed. 'What about your mother?'

'Oh, don't let's talk about *her*. She can't get used to her new whalebone hoop, says it's far too big. You know, we make her practise walking round the furniture… but it's hopeless.'

'I wonder how she'll cope with the Osbaldestons.'

'Father's told her to just smile and say very little. Oh, and she hates his new wig. It's a short, white one you tie with a bow at the back—cost seven guineas.'

'Why does she hate it? It must be a good one at that price.'

'It's not the wig; it's the powder she has to puff over it. Father says he'll have to partition off the bedchamber—make a separate little room for powdering. Mother complains the stuff stinks of lavender and it makes her sneeze.'

'I bet she'll be glad when it's all over.' *And*, he thought, *so will I.*

Ann was silent for a moment, deep in thought about the shoes she'd wear. She hoped the embroidered ones would match the gown; the shade of green was crucial.

266

He nudged her from her reverie. 'Ann, you will still meet me after your birthday?'

'Of course. Why not?'

'Well, you're bound to be introduced to lots of young men. That's what this is all about. I trust you've never cared for anyone else in Reighton, not even Stephen Jefferson. You would tell me if there was anyone in particular?'

'Yes, but anyway, Jefferson's always with Mainprize, that huge boar of a man—he's even ginger and whiskery like a fat old pig. John's scared of him, and I'm not surprised. Listen, William, no one will be able to kiss like you. Come on...'

He surrendered happily to her demands, yet at the back of his mind he wondered if that was all she wanted.

At home, young William was clumsy. He bumped into doors, spilt his beer and was 'all of a ditherumdotherum' as his grandmother had said. He could do nothing about it; he just felt strange.

'He'll trip over his own shadow one of these days,' his father announced, as William stumbled into breakfast and crashed against the meal chest.

The whole family was puzzled, and then William began to have nightmares. He'd fidget in bed and, after falling asleep for a while, would get up and sleepwalk about the room, moaning to himself. The broken nights made everyone irritable.

His mother was always the one who got up to see to him. She knew he was half asleep and didn't know what he was doing.

'Get back into bed,' she'd whisper firmly. Then he'd whimper and crouch low before climbing meekly back and curling up into a ball. She didn't know what else to do with him.

On the days following Ann's birthday, there were no notes left for William. He heard the rumour that Ann was staying at Hunmanby until after May Day, a whole week away. He imagined all sorts going on and became so distracted that his grandmother stepped in.

267

'It's 'is body that needs a good clear out,' she told Mary. 'That's what's wrong with 'im. Mix some powdered dead bees i' water, an' get 'im to drink it ev'ry mornin'.'

Mary ignored that remedy, though she did try laxatives in case it was a simple matter of constipation.

Young William suffered the indignity of loose bowels and, after a near accident in the fields, noticed by others, he refused any more 'cures'. He accepted various sleeping draughts instead; these did not help either. When his mother suggested he sleep in the loft, away from the rest of the family, he agreed without complaint.

John helped him rearrange the space in the loft. He moved the apples and other stores, and banged the dust off the old mattress.

'I'm sorry you're up here, but does it mean *I* can have your bed now?'

'I suppose so.' William sighed. 'I don't really care. You need your sleep and I just disturb everyone. I don't know what's wrong with me.'

The nightly disruptions continued. Mary lay beneath the loft, listening to William bumping about in the dark. Often, she got up, climbed the ladder and shouted at him to get back into bed.

In the mornings, young William descended the ladder, dishevelled and with wild, staring eyes. He'd have trouble fastening his buttons and, at breakfast, he had a habit of jiggling his knees up and down beneath the table. There was nothing peaceful about him.

Two days before May Day, the family were finishing breakfast and the day's work was about to be organised. Young William looked pale, with bags under his eyes.

'Listen,' said his father, 'there's the ditches to scour in the lower meadow. If they're not finished by Friday, we'll have to pay a shilling fine for every oxgang. Will—are you up to the job?'

'I'd prefer to work somewhere else, maybe on my own.'

'Why's that then?'

'The others laugh at him,' John explained innocently.

268

Young William was appalled. 'No they don't!'

'What others?'

'Mainprize and Jefferson.'

Young William scowled. It was too late to kick John under the table. Luckily, their father didn't take it too seriously.

'Ignore them. They've always been envious of us. Get that ditching done, and take John with you. Just make sure you scour them the full two feet wide and one and a half deep. There's no Dickon to check on it, so I hope I can trust you.'

When young William and John arrived at the meadow below the hills, they found others already doing the job. One of them was Mainprize, recently the proud father of another son or, as their grandmother had remarked, 'another ginger-'aired piglet.' With him was Stephen Jefferson, still single. William suspected that Jefferson still harboured a longing for Ann Smith, though nothing had come of it. The two men had never been his friends, partly because they were ten years older and they'd always poked fun at his limp. Lately, due to his clumsiness, they'd started to goad him again.

When everyone stopped for a drink, the two brothers sat apart from the rest, hoping to avoid any hurtful banter. This didn't save them.

Mainprize nudged Jefferson before starting on William.

'I 'eard thoo nearly shat thassen t'other day. Ann Smith 'ad better watch out, eh? It's a strange way to be courtin'.'

John blushed. Ann Smith was supposed to be a secret.

On seeing the others grin, Mainprize sniffed the air. 'Hmm, what's that funny smell? It's comin' from over yon. Is it young Will? Thoo 'asn't gone an' done it again?'

John wondered how much William could take before he lost his temper. He sensed the others looking on warily, no longer laughing, yet Mainprize didn't stop.

'I'm goin' to 'ave words with all lasses—tell 'em about tha trouble an'—'

As William leapt up and lunged forwards, the large yeoman was prepared and delivered a hefty punch to his belly. When William doubled up, Mainprize threw a punch under his chin that rocked his head and jarred his teeth.

269

This was followed up by another blow to the side of his face that split his lip. William fell to the ground, semi-conscious.

The much smaller Jefferson took advantage and gave him a kick.

The sight of William curling up to defend himself only incited Mainprize to launch a few kicks as well.

Others stepped forward at last and hauled Mainprize away.

William stayed on the ground, trembling.

John knelt by him and asked if he was alright. Then, blinded by tears, he stared up at Mainprize.

'You're a bully!' he shouted.

The man just laughed. 'Thee an' 'im's not worth first fart o' me arse.' He turned to the others and made a crude joke at John's expense. 'I wonder if it's true… do 'alf-wits 'ave big rods instead o' brains?' When no one laughed, he jeered and gestured with his thumb at William. 'An' look at tha *big* brother—'is back's all skew-whiff an' I bet 'is arse is cowclagged. An' *thoo*,' he glared at John, poking him with his boot, 'thoo'll never come to owt.' He spat on the grass. 'Thoo's as soft as a lass.'

The others felt sorry for the two brothers. They knew that Mainprize and Jefferson had gone too far. If Dickon had been there, he'd have shamed them. Unwilling, though, to face up to Mainprize, they sidled away and returned to their job of clearing out the ditch.

Young William, mortified, walked home as fast as he could. His face and ribs were sore and his lip was cut and bleeding.

John kept pace at his side. 'You'll be alright soon.'

'Hmm. I won't be out on May Day, that's for sure.' He winced as he tried to talk on one side of his mouth. 'I'll stay at home. You can have fun without me.'

His mother helped to clean up his face. She smeared grease on his swollen lip, and knew better than to ask what had happened.

His father reacted differently when he came home. 'Who's trodden on *your* tail then?' he asked as soon as he saw William's face. 'I hope the other fellow's worse off.'

John ignored his brother's icy glance and blurted out the whole story.

Their father seemed pleased. 'That's fine then,' he said, rubbing his hands, 'there's plenty of witnesses. I'll see your uncle Matthew and arrange for a summons. I don't relish calling at the Hall, but it's time someone curbed those two. It'll be good to have the law on *our* side for a change.'

'No, don't,' pleaded William. 'I don't want *everyone* to know about it.' He meant he didn't want Ann to know.

'But from what John says, the attack was uncalled-for.'

William shrugged. 'I'd rather just forget it.'

On May Day, young William refused to go out and join the festivities. He stayed indoors all morning, nursing his wounded pride and wondering what Ann might be doing in Hunmanby. At noon, he sat in the garden close to where Stina was buried. He chewed a piece of cheese carefully so as not to reopen his lip, and thought of Ann and Stina. His eyes filled up as he realised how much he missed them.

The incident with Mainprize was not forgotten. Matthew Smith discussed it with the steward of the Manor, John Grimston. Five days after May Day, a summons was written and delivered. Mainprize was to appear at the next quarter sessions in Beverley—*to answer unto such matters as shall be objected against him by William Jordan the Younger of Reighton.*

Ann heard about it from her father. She'd been so excited by her stay in Hunmanby and the May Day celebrations there that she'd hardly given young William a thought. Now, back in Reighton, she felt guilty and wrote a note.

She met William at their usual place on the moor, and was saddened to see his bruised face and cracked lip. He looked tired, and the skin under his eyes was blue. While she'd been dancing and enjoying all manner of new foods and drinks, he'd been in pain. She stroked his cheek gently.

'I'm sorry. I didn't know until yesterday. Does it hurt much?'

'No, not so much now.' He was more concerned that he couldn't kiss her. 'I suppose you had a good time with the Osbaldestons?'

271

She was silent for a moment, unusual for her, and then she sighed and gazed into the distance towards Filey Brigg. 'I can't begin to tell you... it was all so... beautiful.'

'Oh...' It was as bad as he thought. He tried to take a deep breath but his chest hurt. 'I suppose you'll find Reighton boring now.'

'Maybe, but I'm back now, and I want to know what happened to you.'

He shook his head. 'I don't want to talk about it and I don't want to go to Beverley.' He didn't feel confident enough to stand before strangers in a courtroom, and dreaded to think what Mainprize might divulge.

'Can't you see I'd be humiliated? It's bad enough being beaten without having to admit it in public. Can't you get your father to quash the summons?'

She frowned. 'Do you really want that?'

'Yes.' He took hold of both her hands. 'Please—do this for me.'

'Alright.' She sniffed with a determined expression and then stood perfectly still, eyeing him up. 'You can't kiss me, can you, not with that lip?'

'No, though there's nothing to stop you kissing me.'

Chapter 44

To Ann's dismay, her father preferred to allow justice to take its course and he didn't hold with the idea of meddling with a summons once delivered. However, she worked on her father and, unable to abide her tears, he gave in.

He slammed on his wig, annoyed to have to go out and speak with John Grimston again, maybe even Osbaldeston.

'That young William's always been trouble,' he growled. 'He doesn't get it from *our* side of the family. My sister should never have married a Jordan. I hinted as much to William at Christmas.'

Ann shed more tears as he left the house. The rift between the two families was wider than ever.

To young William's relief, and his father's great disappointment, the summons was cancelled. Both hoped that Mainprize and Jefferson had learnt their lesson, but young William feared the peace wouldn't last. He was still so clumsy. How long before even Ann would mock him? He barged into doorways so often that his elbows were permanently bruised.

He continued, though, to meet Ann in secret whenever he could. She visited Hunmanby as before and always returned at the same time. The trouble was that he was usually busy in the top fields, spreading muck and ploughing the fallow. He couldn't just rush off to see her. Also, he was afraid she'd notice his shaking hands.

After a few missed meetings, Ann began to think he'd lost interest. Maybe he was fond of another girl. She couldn't really believe this and so cornered John when he came to visit the sheep.

'What's the matter with William? He doesn't come to meet me anymore.'

'He's not well. Mother's put him in the loft.'

'Why? Is it something we can catch?'

273

'No, he can't sleep. I hear him banging about. At breakfast he's all of a dither.'

'Tell him to come and see me. Tell him I miss him.'

She left John, fully expecting to be with William again soon and enjoying their secret kisses. Each time he didn't appear, she cried a little. In church, she caught his eye, but he looked away immediately. Something was very wrong.

When haymaking began in July, young William resolved to concentrate harder at work and try to be his confident old self again. Early, on a bright, sunny morning, he ambled down to the meadow with his father and brothers. Matthew, just turned thirteen, was to help sharpen the scythes and bring the beer. They received the usual instructions from their father.

'Keep in a staggered line and don't take too wide a swipe. It's no place to show off. And make sure the grass lies straight.'

Once they'd begun, young William found his legs start to tremble and his hands shake. After another poor night's sleep, he was no longer equal to the other men or even his older brother Francis. When they stopped to sharpen their scythes, he spilt half the sand from his grease horn. To test the blade, he ran his thumb along the edge, but his thumb slipped. He drew it back in pain, blood dripping from a deep cut.

'Spit on it and bind it with something,' his father shouted.

One of the women came forward with a strip of linen.

William wished it had been Ann, although that wouldn't have been a good idea with Mainprize and Jefferson so close. Using his left hand and his teeth, he managed to bind his thumb and tie a knot. Then he took his place again in the line of mowers. Tired as he was, he could still find pleasure in the scent of freshly mown grass, and enjoyed handling the scythe. The tool was heavy yet had such a good curve and it was perfectly balanced. He took hold of the short wooden handles sticking out from the shaft; the todgers were smooth and suited his grip. He smiled at John.

'How are *you* doing? Are your todgers in the right place for you?'

274

Mainprize overheard and couldn't resist a bawdy response. 'Hey, young Will, thoo'll need to watch thy own todger! If thoo 'as an accident an' cuts it off, tha future wife won't be pleased.'

Jefferson and others laughed at the remark, but William ground his teeth, determined not to be provoked. He realised that he was so inept today that he really might cut himself again—or hurt someone else. He ignored further banter and concentrated on mowing.

All morning the men worked, stopping from time to time to re-sharpen the scythes. By midday, they'd mowed half an acre. They rested when the women and children brought the cheese and drink.

Ann Smith arrived with her mother and sisters. When she approached, she noticed William sitting alone by the edge of the meadow with his head between his knees. He was trying to keep in the little shade available and, even from a distance, looked sickly. She felt sorry for him.

'What's the matter?' she asked in a sympathetic voice. 'Are you ill? You never come to meet me.'

'I'm fine.'

She handed him a mug of beer. 'You don't look fine. Maybe you should have water instead.'

'I just need to rest. My head hurts. It's too bright—I can't think straight.' He felt so hot and nauseous. His head throbbed, and the slightest movement made it worse.

'You should go home. You won't be much use here.'

'No, I'll carry on. We've another half an acre to do... got to make on while it's sunny.'

She knew better than to argue. She left him and returned to the women.

Young William finished his drink, and then staggered to his feet to rejoin the others in the glaring sunlight. He clenched his teeth against the stabbing pain in his head, and tried to ignore the reds and browns seeping into his vision, something he associated with his disturbed nights.

When the mowing recommenced, he found it hard to keep his mind on the job. Despite his wide-brimmed hat, the sun

275

seemed to flash in his eyes and blind him. The voices of the men nearby were too loud, and he struggled to mow in rhythm. Just as the heat and the light were getting too much to bear, he faltered and caught the tip of the scythe in his left leg. The sudden, sharp pain made him drop the tool. He clutched at his calf where blood was now oozing through the tear in his stocking.

'You blatherhead,' grumbled Francis as their line of mowers had to stop. He shouted over to the women. 'Someone come and see to Will. He's hurt his leg.'

Ann was about to run and help, but her mother held her back. 'Don't! Thoo's already been seen tendin' to 'im. Don't cause trouble. 'Is mother can see to 'im.'

Mary rushed over and knelt to check the wound. 'It's not so bad. It's a clean nick and I can bind it up.' Then she added quietly, 'Do you want to go home?'

He knew he should stay, yet his head was pounding and he didn't want to be sick in public, not in front of Ann.

'Don't worry,' she whispered. 'I'll see to this.' She stood up and announced with conviction, 'He really can't carry on. I'll help him home and see to the cut.'

Francis and his father exchanged glances, rolled their eyes and recommenced work. Will didn't seem capable of doing much at all these days.

From that day, whenever Ann sent him a note about when to meet, he knew he couldn't face her, not the way he was, not with his problem, whatever it was. He couldn't confide in her and felt isolated. When he walked out alone, he didn't even have a dog to keep him company. John was always kind, but then John was kind to everyone and had about as much understanding as a gnat.

Ann was upset by William's absence. She'd looked forward to showing him her gift from the Osbaldestons—a new paper fan from London. It was painted with scenes of sheep and waterfalls. Also, she'd been bathing her face with strawberry juice. It was to avoid a tanned complexion, and she'd left it on all night as instructed and then had rinsed her face with chervil

276

water. She'd hoped he'd notice her clear, white face, not a freckle in sight. Even her hair was darker thanks to an Osbaldeston recipe. She knew she looked her best, and William was never there to see.

In bed at night, she cried tears of frustration. It wasn't that she wanted to show off, as her father did, she just missed talking to William. She liked to hear what he was doing in the fields and, especially, she missed those long, hot kisses that left her breathless.

Young William's parents decided he should be bled by the apothecary in Hunmanby. He sat patiently while leeches were put on his arms. When this had no effect, he was sent back to Hunmanby for more treatment.

The bloodletting only made him weaker and then delirious in the middle of the night. He paced the loft unable to understand the change in himself. There'd been a time, not so long ago, when he'd been one of the best workers, when he loved Ann and she loved him back. Now, he couldn't work at Uphall or be out in the fields without breaking something or hurting himself. He was no good to anybody.

In the parlour below, his mother lay in bed listening to his ravings. She did not go up the ladder to see him, but felt guilty. Wide awake, she remembered how Dickon had been before he died. She nudged her husband and whispered.

'Our Will reminds me of Dickon; *his* hands used to shake too, *and* he was clumsy.'

William yawned and turned to face her. 'They're not the same. Dickon was an old man. All his joints were seizing up—that's why he was clumsy. Our lad's only twenty-one.'

'I remember when I had to strip off Dickon's clothes and wash him down in the kitchen.'

'Yes, but that was *your* fault. You gave him too much of that... what was it called?'

'Peruvian bark. And it wasn't *my* fault,' she hissed. 'You didn't tell me it was a laxative.'

Both were silent for a while, and then Mary began again.

'Perhaps we should get a physician to see him. He's not right.'

William turned over, away from her. 'I'm not staying awake *any* longer. He's young and he'll soon be back to his old self. Besides,' he grumbled, 'it's only the likes of your brother Matthew call in a physician. Go to sleep.'

One afternoon, when Mary and John were at home together, they saw Will enter the garden carrying a sack. They pulled a face and shrugged.

After a few minutes, John smelled smoke and looked through the window.

'Mother, quick, Will's lit a bonfire.'

They both shot outside to see young William tossing onto a fire his best cravat and waistcoat, bought once to impress Ann. He ignored their questions and attempts to stop him.

Onto the fire went his little knife from the Bridlington Fair along with his favourite old catapult and sling. Then he threw on his collection of moleskins. He no longer felt any connection with his former self, and watched his once prized possessions go up in flames. Finally, he rummaged in his pocket and threw on a wad of papers.

John knew they were the letters from Ann. He could not understand his brother. Tears filled his eyes as everything burnt. He remembered how his brother had behaved when the dog had been killed, how he'd walked the hills, talking to himself and waving his arms about. Perhaps William was bewitched. Perhaps the devil himself had gotten into him and taken advantage. He'd heard their grandmother say as much. He decided to keep an eye on him, follow him when he went out alone, and then he'd tell his mother what he saw.

278

Chapter 45

After a busy day harvesting, John noticed his brother William sneak out the back door. He followed at a careful distance and, on reaching the hills above the sea, he used the clumps of gorse as cover. He watched William stride on purposefully and then pause at the top of Speeton cliff. The sun was setting, and the moon was just beginning to rise above the sea—an enormous pink globe. While his brother gazed at the horizon, John took the chance to creep closer. He could see William take off his hat and sit right on the edge of the cliff, his legs dangling. The sea breeze was blowing the hair away from his face, and John thought his brother seemed at peace.

As he was plucking up the courage to join him, his brother made a sudden movement as if stung, and then leapt up and howled at the moon. William waved his fists as if fighting off a demon. Now, John was sure that his brother was mad or possessed. He left him alone on the cliff and hurried home to tell their mother.

Mary was alarmed by John's latest report. She didn't want to believe that Will had lost his mind or been taken over by an evil spirit, and yet some action must be taken. Even after he'd returned home, eaten his supper and then climbed the ladder to his mattress in the loft, she still hadn't decided what to do.

She talked it over in bed with her husband, explaining in a low voice about Will's antics.

'You see, I'm afraid for him. He's really not himself.'

'I'll take him back to Hunmanby then, get the apothecary to blister him.' He turned over, ready to sleep.

'No,' whispered Mary, 'that man didn't help before. His bloodletting made William weak.'

'At least we got some sleep,' he chuntered into the pillow.

She thumped him in the back. 'Don't you care? I'm not having him blistered.'

William rolled back to face her, annoyed at being disturbed. They were in the middle of harvest and he was so tired.

279

'Listen, Mary, if he carries on like he has been, everyone'll think there's madness in the family. That's the last thing we want. My mother says she'd duck him in salt water. She's hinted more than once about having him put away.'

When Mary gasped, he added quickly, 'I know it *sounds* bad, but she says there's a place in Bridlington that could take him in.'

'Over my dead body! And don't you dare mention that again.'

He gave a big yawn and turned over, certain that either their son would get better or that Mary would come round to his mother's way of thinking.

In early autumn, young William's worst fears were realised when the hired lads at Uphall began to laugh behind his back. Although the ones who'd be staying wouldn't tease him openly, the others didn't care if they were overheard.

One lad barely shielded his mouth as he cried, 'Ey up, 'ere 'e comes—didderin', dodderin', can't do nothin'.'

His grandmother showed little sympathy either. As the lads came in for dinner, she took him aside in the yard and prodded him in the chest.

'What ails thee, lad? What's wi' thy eyes on stalks? Thoo looks wild, as if thoo's' been pulled through an 'edge back'ards.'

When he just shrugged and blushed, she gave him a good shake. 'Thoo needs to frame better.'

He suffered her rough treatment without complaint and murmured an apology.

'Alright then,' she conceded in a gentler tone, 'thoo'd best get on. Go i' kitchen an' eat tha dinner. Everyone else will 'ave started.'

She watched him at the table, saw how skittish he was, jumping at any sudden noise or movement. She scratched her head. 'Why, lad, thoo's like an ill-sittin' 'en.'

The hired hands smirked.

News of young William's worsening state reached Ann Smith and her family. She'd wondered why he'd not left any

280

notes to explain his absences, and thought she deserved better. She'd not met him alone for ages now, and had shed many tears of anger and regret. Lately, she'd been dwelling more on his soft words and ardent kisses. It was almost a year since that wonderful harvest supper and their first kiss.

Her father, thinking of his position in Reighton, soon put paid to any hopes of her meeting young William again.

'From now on,' he told his family, 'you will all ignore your cousin William. Shun him if he happens to approach any of you after church. He's no longer fit to be seen with us.'

Seeing Ann about to cry, he carried on regardless.

'That family are trouble... haven't even inherited Uphall... have to rely on loans to keep their land. I tell you, your cousins will be worthless, all of them.'

This time, Ann's tears had no effect. She was so sorry, and now she was forbidden even to speak to William in public.

In mid-October, the Jordans, including young William, were ploughing in the oat stubble. As so often happened these days, he had a sudden blinding headache. Fearing to be sick in front of the others, he retreated to the side of the field where he retched a few times. It was no secret what he was doing. When he returned to the plough, the lad goading the oxen was sniggering. Hardly a day passed now without one embarrassment or another.

On his way home, young William always had to pass the forge. The two spinster daughters of the blacksmith were standing outside in conversation with Ann and admiring her horse. As he walked by, they stopped talking. Then he heard them giggle. At that moment, his feet tangled together somehow and he fell flat on his face in the dirt and horse muck. When he got up, he looked round. The women were staring at him, their hands stifling their laughter.

His face reddened with shame. He turned away quickly and carried on walking, aware that his lopsided gait would only add to their amusement. Ann being there was like a knife through his heart. He could bear a lot of teasing, but never such humiliation in front of her. How could he ever have thought to have courted her? The way he was these days, he was no good to any woman. Even Ann would see he was pitiful.

As soon as he got home, he cleaned himself up with a bucket of cold water in the garden. Then he told his mother he didn't want any supper.

'I'm tired. I'll go to bed early. Don't let anyone disturb me—not even John. I need to try and sleep.'

She hoped he wasn't sickening for the autumn fever that was going round. A widow had been buried just yesterday.

'Shout down then if you need anything.'

Ann Smith was appalled by what happened at the forge. William would think her cruel. He'd think *she* was laughing at him too. She'd been desperate to run after him and explain, but couldn't admit to her feelings in front of the girls. Besides, she was forbidden to be with him. On her way home, she decided to call at his house. Her father hadn't actually told her to avoid Aunt Mary or the rest of the family, and they wouldn't know she was to keep away from William.

She found her aunt alone in the garden, throwing out scraps for the chickens. 'I can't stay long,' she explained. 'I wondered if I could see Will for a moment.'

Mary didn't answer straight away. It was a strange request. She thought whatever was between Ann and William had ended a while back.

'I'm sorry, you've come too late. He's already gone to bed, and he said he didn't want to be disturbed—not by anyone.'

Ann felt her eyes fill up. 'Alright,' she managed to say as she turned to leave, 'I'll come another time.'

'I'll say you called. Was there a message?'

'Just say that I'm sorry... Oh, and tell him I think it's going to be a clear night tonight. Tell him I'll be looking at the stars... He'll understand.'

The next morning, young William did not come down for breakfast, so his mother took the lantern and climbed the ladder to wake him. She smiled to herself at the thought of passing on Ann's message. That would cheer him up. As she neared the top, she wasn't sure why, but her heart missed a beat. It was so silent in the loft.

She lifted the lantern up through the open trap door to set it down. What she saw made her drop it with a thud. Her legs shook as she gripped the ladder with both hands and then scrambled out on all fours.

He was hanging from the roof beam, his head lolling to one side, held by a leather belt. His cheek had a deathly pale, bluish hue.

As if she'd been punched in the stomach, she doubled up in pain. A large chasm had opened inside her, bottomless yet sharp and jagged at the edges like the teeth of a saw. Gulping hard, she tried to shout down for her husband; nothing but a hoarse whisper came from her throat. When she tried to stand, her legs gave way and she collapsed back onto the floor gasping for breath.

She found herself crawling towards the overturned stool that William had used. Though her legs trembled, she stood up and managed to rest his weight on it. She reached up and fumbled the belt loose.

He fell to the floor with a heavy thump, the noise making her heart stop. Suicide was such a sin, and her family below must have heard. Her son would be an outcast from the church—buried who knows where.

She needed to act at once. They couldn't be allowed to think he'd taken his life. He did not look, though, as if he'd died peacefully. His dark brown eyes were wide open and bloodshot. His face, especially round the eyes, had tiny blood-red freckles, and his mouth was open and distorted with such blue lips.

She then noticed his huge Adam's apple, and the marks on his neck left by the belt. After failing to rub the marks away or even make them fade, she pulled up his nightshirt collar to hide them. Then she dragged him onto the mattress and tucked him in as if he'd died in his sleep. Next, she took down the leather belt and hid it under his clothes.

She knelt over him and, though her hands shook so, she closed his eyes. At last, he'd achieved the peace he'd craved so

283

much. Then, with great tenderness, she kissed his forehead. He was so young and innocent, just a boy. It was only when she smoothed his lips together, that she broke down.

'Ann came yesterday,' she whispered. Then her throat tightened and she couldn't speak. When she'd recovered and blown her nose, she whispered into his ear, 'I'm to tell you she's sorry. She said she'd be looking at the stars.'

Fresh tears poured down her cheeks. Was it her fault? She hadn't paid him enough attention. It was too late for such thoughts and she hadn't the time right now. She turned his head to face away from the ladder and took a last glance round the loft to make sure she'd left no evidence. Then she stood up and held onto a roof beam for support. Her heart beat so wildly, she thought she'd collapse. She took a few deep breaths and was about to call for William when she caught sight of something carved into the beam.

She took the lantern closer to see a heart with the letters W and an A inside. There were deep gouges through the middle as if he'd tried to erase it.

Dazed, she staggered back to the ladder and, in a broken voice, shouted down for help.

'What's up?' William called back.

She held her chest and snatched a breath before replying. She needed to sound calmer.

'It's Will. I can't wake him.... Can you come up and see.'

She waited in agony while he climbed the ladder, thanking God she'd been the only one to see Will hanging from the beam.

William shook his son roughly. 'Come on! Wake up, lazy good-for-nothing.'

When his son's head fell unnaturally towards him, he stepped back in fear. Now he could see the blue lips and the pale face. He touched a cheek. It was cold and damp like their chalk walls. He couldn't believe what had happened.

'Mary,' he struggled to say, 'he's gone... I don't know why... but we've lost him.'

Mary didn't answer. She bit her lip and held a hand over her mouth, afraid to give anything away.

William rubbed his forehead hard as if that would help him think. 'Maybe he had a nightmare. Maybe he was frightened to death. I have heard that happen.'

Mary still didn't answer.

'Or maybe he had the autumn fever and we didn't know.'

Mary began to sob, as much with relief as with grief. William suspected nothing, and she was determined no one would know the truth. He held her in his arms to comfort her, yet she was already planning ahead. She needed to be strong-minded and alert. She alone would wash and prepare the body; people would understand her need to do that. When Will was buried safely in consecrated ground, then she could grieve properly—and not before.

She pulled away from her husband. 'You go down and tell the boys,' she said quietly. 'I'll stay here with Will if you don't mind. You can all see to your own breakfast.'

He used the back of his hands to wipe away his tears. 'I'm going to have to tell my mother… and the vicar.'

'Tell people not to call round until tonight. You can help me carry Will down once the boys have gone out.'

As soon as William descended the ladder, the boys knew something was wrong. Their father's face was strained and his hands were shaking.

'Where's Mother?' asked John, fearing something had happened to her.

'Your mother's fine. It's Will.'

He looked at his sons seated at the table waiting for their breakfast, and hated to tell them. He swallowed with difficulty and his eyes filled with tears again.

'I'm sorry but…' He gripped the edge of the table, making his knuckles white, and managed to find the words he never expected to say.

'Your brother's dead.'

Though he saw the boys were stunned, he turned away from them, and moved towards the fire and the half-made porridge. He felt so weak he could hardly hold the spoon.

'Here, John, can you see to the breakfast? I can't do it.'

285

He grabbed his coat and hat and mumbled, 'I need to go to Uphall and tell folk.'

He added as he opened the door, 'Don't go up to see him. Your mother wants to be alone for a while. Just eat your breakfast, and then go and get on with your jobs. I'll see you all later.'

When the door closed behind him, John saw to the porridge and then dished it up. He said nothing, too upset to speak. For once, there was no banter over breakfast, only the dull scrape of spoons in the wooden bowls.

Chapter 46

Mary listened for the boys leaving. Her first moments of panic had passed, yet she couldn't stop shaking. She knelt beside the mattress and stroked the hair away from Will's forehead. He did look so peaceful.

'Oh, why... why?' she cried. 'Why?'

She knew he was tormented, but he'd given no hint as to his thoughts last night. It was cruel to leave her like this, cruel to his father and John and the rest of the family. She heard the back door close. The boys had gone out. Alone at last, she clenched her fists and fought off the tears. There was work to do.

She went down, heated up water and took a bucket back up to the loft. First, she cleaned Will's face and neck. When she couldn't remove the marks left by the belt, she concealed them again beneath his shirt collar. Then she took her time with the rest of his body.

As she washed his legs, she thought back to the time he'd come home, when very little, his legs red with nettle rash. His sister was always dragging him off somewhere, leading him into trouble. And now it had come to this. He should have been looking forward to life.

Tears fell again as she blamed herself. All those nights she'd shouted at him to get back into bed, and then allowed the bloodletting and the purgatives... She should have been more understanding. This was *her* fault. She laid her head across his chest and cried repeatedly.

'I'm sorry. I'm sorry.'

She stayed in the loft until William returned, bringing a shroud and a white cap. Once they'd lowered young William down the ladder, they laid him on the table for the final preparations. She insisted the nightshirt remain on for now; William must not notice the marks on the neck.

William shaved his son's face and then left Mary to get on with the rest; it was women's work and he didn't trust himself

287

not to start blaming her. She should have let him go to the apothecary again.

Alone once more, Mary removed the nightshirt and spoke softly to her son, apologising as she tied his legs together and fastened his arms to his sides. There was no dignity, she thought, in either birth or death.

It was a struggle to get him into the long shroud without any help as his body was stiffening, but she managed eventually and tied the loose ends into a tuft below his feet. Now, only his face was open to view. She wiped her eyes and gave him a gentle kiss on the cheek before placing the cap on his head, fastening it with a broad chin cloth to keep his jaw closed. She'd just finished and placed a square of flannel over his face when the carpenter came to measure for the coffin.

Bart Huskisson never uttered a word of regret or consolation. Not wasting any time, he took out his length of string and asked Mary to hold one end.

'I expect tha wants pine?'

She nodded.

'I reckon I'll be busy this week—there's plenty ill wi' that fever. I'm i' right trade—folk aren't satisfied anymore wi' usin' village coffin.'

Mary was glad when he left and relieved that he assumed Will had died of illness. The front door had hardly closed before there was a knock on the back door. It was Lizzie; she'd been thoughtful enough to have seen to Mary's cow and brought the fresh milk. She'd also brought Dottie along.

Mary gave the girl a basket. 'Off you go in the garden— see if you can find a few eggs.'

She was desperate to confide in someone, yet dared not tell Lizzie the truth. Lizzie might tell Francis, and then Robert Storey would hear and then... It didn't bear thinking about. Everyone knew that suicide was a sin, a rejection of God's gift of life. She would hate to see her son buried at the crossroads or even at the north side of the church. Outcasts could be treated badly, their bodies cast into the grave face down or with a spade bashed against their skulls.

Mary steeled herself against the need to cry and allowed Lizzie to give her a hug. She noticed over Lizzie's shoulder that the boys hadn't put away their porridge bowls. Using that distraction, she pulled away and went to the pile of bowls left on the floor.

'Just look—they haven't even cleaned them!'

'I'll do it,' Lizzie offered. 'Show me where thoo keeps tha sand an' I'll scrape 'em clean. An' I'll 'elp get dinner ready.'

'Thank you. Take the bowls outside and then you can see to Dottie as well. I'll make a start on the potatoes.' She gestured towards the fire. 'I've stew left over from yesterday. I just need to warm it up.'

When the boys came home for dinner, they stood by the table and peered at their brother's face and the shape under the shroud. John had tears in his eyes. He gulped but said nothing while the other two were full of questions. Why was this? Why was that? Mary was sick to the teeth.

'I don't know!' she cried.

Then William walked in and began. 'When Will came home yesterday, was he unwell? And why did you let him go to bed without supper? My mother thinks you've neglected him.'

It was the last straw. Mary tore off her cap and apron and threw them on the floor.

'You do better then! All of you... you stand there... none of you help!'

She charged out of the back door, slamming it behind her.

The three boys exchanged blank glances, their eyes wide in shock. Their father shrugged.

In the garden, Mary marched up and down, unable to control her anger and grief. Tears sprang from her eyes at the enormity of what Will had done and the fact that she'd kept it to herself. Suddenly, her legs gave way and she collapsed onto her knees. She curled up into a ball, sobbing.

John was the only one to venture outside to his mother. He put his hand on her back and stroked it as he would a hurt or frightened animal.

'Don't cry. Everything will be alright. William will be in heaven, won't he? He'll be with Stina.'

She dried her eyes on her skirt. 'Yes, John, everything will be alright. There now, I shouldn't upset you. You go in and I'll follow you. We don't want the stew boiling over, do we?'

She wiped her eyes again and blew her nose. When she stood up, she felt so shaky that she took a few deep breaths before returning to the kitchen.

No one could sit at the table for young William was laid there. Instead, the boys and their father were sitting by the fire, each with their empty bowl in their lap. They waited in silence while Mary dished out their dinner, not putting anything in her own bowl.

'I'm not hungry.'

Mary had two more days to get through before the funeral. She was afraid there might be rumours circulating about the cause of Will's death. So far, she'd had few callers as William had made it clear she wanted time alone. Even the vicar did not stay long; luckily, John Sumpton had so many in his parish needing his services just now. Mary suffered his condolences, his hurried rendering of 'the Lord gave, and the Lord hath taken away'. His words offered no comfort.

When the carpenter arrived the next day with the coffin, he rested it across two trestles in the kitchen. Mary helped him lift young William into it and then he left straightaway.

'Can't stay. There's a poor lad o' death's door i' Speeton. 'Appen I'll be makin' another coffin before day's out.'

Mary couldn't bear to be in the kitchen. She went into the garden where everything was the same and yet now looked completely different. There was the axe left by the wall after Will's last turn at chopping wood. There was the little homemade cross marking Stina's grave. She wouldn't see her son sitting there anymore. Taking advantage of being alone, she knelt and prayed that God would show mercy and forgive them both.

The prayer, and the tears shed, brought some relief. She stood up and smoothed down her apron. Today there'd be a stream of visitors.

Lizzie and Dottie were the first, knocking politely on the back door as usual.

'You don't need to knock, Lizzie,' Mary explained as she ushered them in. 'You're family, and I appreciate your kindness.' She could see Lizzie had brought fresh milk again and a basket of water mint leaves to mask any unpleasant odours.

Without being asked, Lizzie began to scatter the leaves round the coffin.

'Thank you,' breathed Mary. 'It's very good of you. At least we can sit at the table now. I'll pour Dottie some milk.'

'Shall I 'elp wi' dinner an' 'elp make stuff for after funeral?'

'Yes, please.' Lizzie's thoughtfulness brought tears to her eyes. 'I'm sorry—I am glad you're here. Dottie, would you like to hunt for eggs again when you've had your milk? The basket's there.'

Dottie ignored the basket and, curious, wandered to the coffin. She rested her hands on the side and peered in.

'Uncle William looks asleep.'

'Yes,' Mary answered, 'he's at rest. Come on, have your milk now.'

Dottie sat up to the table. ''E's dead,' she announced flatly as she picked up her beaker. 'Like Aunt Elizabeth.'

Both women nodded and gave weak smiles.

'They're both wi' Jesus now,' Lizzie said. 'They'll probably be walkin' together in 'eaven, i' sunshine an' glory.'

Dottie jumped down from the bench and picked up the basket by the door. She'd had enough milk and was more interested now in searching for eggs.

The two women sighed as she went out. Young children were distracted so quickly.

Mary had a question she was eager to ask. 'How has Francis taken the news? He hasn't been round yet.'

'No, 'e's been prayin' wi' Robert though. 'E'll call tonight.'

Mary dreaded that meeting, especially if Robert came with him. To avoid thinking of it, she talked about preparing dinner.

'You can scrape and chop the carrots. Today we'll have ham in the pot. And I'd better make bread and oatcakes, then sweep and tidy up ready for others coming.'

291

She also gave Lizzie the onions to peel; she'd done enough crying for one morning.

In the afternoon, Mary's brother visited. Unusually for Matthew, he was most apologetic.

'I'm so sorry, Mary. I had no idea he was as ill as that. It explains a lot.'

'Sit down and have a drink, won't you? There's a good ale Martha Wrench sent us. I've added sugar and spice, and there's sops of bread in it as well.'

'Thank you, yes, that sounds perfect.'

As Mary hung the pot to reheat over the fire, he sat at the table and explained that he'd visit again in the evening and bring the family.

'Ann's very upset. She's hardly eaten since we heard. She seems to think it's *her* fault. God knows why.'

Mary kept quiet. The least said the better. She turned her back on him to watch the ale.

'I've been racking my brains,' he continued. 'I've been trying to think back... Do you remember the two of them being especially close? I remember last Christmas I thought your lad had set his heart on Ann... but then nothing came of it... not that I know of...'

Mary had her suspicions, yet it was no good thinking about it; things would not have worked out any differently. She lifted the pot off the fire and, with trembling hands, poured him a full tankard.

'It's all such a shock, Matthew. We can't take it in.'

She poured herself a drink and sat down opposite him. Releasing a great sigh, she remembered that tonight she'd have to face Ann as well as Francis and Robert Storey.

292

Chapter 47

Francis knew he'd never got on with his brother William and felt hypocritical paying his last respects. Now, he waited in trepidation for Robert Storey to call round.

Robert arrived at last, eager to help send another soul to heaven.

'Come along then,' he said to a hesitant Francis. 'Let's not waste time.' He then strode up St Helen's Lane, ignoring Francis lagging behind. Halfway there, he stopped and turned.

'What's the matter? It's not like you to drag your feet.'

Francis caught up with him. 'It's just... you don't know how badly I've treated my brother. I even called him a blatherhead when he cut his leg mowing. I showed no compassion whatsoever. I could have helped him... and instead I made things worse.'

'Don't blame yourself. We all know how clumsy he was.' Robert resumed walking. 'Anyway, Francis, you've told me he attacked you—more than once. He was violent... always had been if you ask me.'

Francis traipsed behind again. He recalled his brother's enjoyment of bull baiting, his obsession with killing birds, and his love of a fight. He remembered how often Will had teased him for knitting and for praying and fasting. No, they'd never got along. Still... young William had loved the dog and had walked all the way to Rudston simply to ask if dogs went to heaven.

Robert reached the house first and knocked loudly on the door.

Mary let them in and cast a worried glance at her husband as the two men knelt immediately beside the coffin. Much to her relief, their prayers were silent. She sat down again at the table with the rest of her family to finish supper, and then waited patiently, wondering what to expect next.

At last, Robert stood up and declined the offer of a drink. Francis followed suit and the two accepted places to sit by the

293

fire. While Robert sat bolt upright and stared at the family with confidence, Francis squirmed in his seat and couldn't look his parents or brothers in the eye.

Suddenly, Robert cleared his throat. 'I heard news from Speeton. Little Thomas Shutling died last night. You know his mother was made a widow only in August. I'm thinking this latest illness must be God's will, but it says in the Psalms, "Fear thou not; for I am with thee... yea, I will help thee; yea, I will uphold thee with the right hand of my righteousness." All will be well.'

When Mary clasped a hand to her mouth and began to cry, he held up his hand.

'Don't weep, for we know that, if the earthly tent we live in is destroyed, we have a building from God, an eternal house in heaven, not built by human hands.'

Seeing his mother was so upset, Francis got up and stood behind her. He leant over, wrapped both arms round her and kissed the top of her head. 'I'm so sorry, Mother.'

She shuddered and tried to collect herself. 'It's alright, Francis. You sit and pray some more with Robert. That's all any of us can do now.'

This set John crying.

Mary despaired. She'd just finished wiping her eyes when the Smiths were at the door.

John leapt up to let them in. As soon as they were all in the kitchen, he rushed towards Ann and held her tight.

No one had the heart to pull him away.

The rest of Ann's family shuffled awkwardly until John let go of Ann at last.

He sniffed back more tears and watched her rearrange her cloak. Her hood had fallen, revealing her dark, shining curls.

'You look lovely,' he choked, and couldn't resist putting his hand out to stroke them. 'William loved your hair.' Suddenly, he pulled back his hand and made a pout. 'He said I mustn't touch girls' hair anymore.'

'I know.' She blinked a few times, trying not to cry.

As there was so little room in the kitchen, Robert and Francis stood up ready to go. There was so much greeting and

294

leave-taking that Ann took the chance to go to the coffin unnoticed. She saw William's face was peaceful. After checking no one was looking, she took off her glove, kissed her fingers and placed them gently on his lips.

'I'm sorry, Will,' she mouthed. 'I did love you, honestly.' She straightened up and joined her family, now being served mulled ale.

'Here's to young William,' Matthew announced. 'He'd been a good worker, strong and dependable.'

'Aye,' his wife intervened. 'An' 'e'd 'ave made a good 'usband to many a lass.'

Matthew coughed. It wasn't like Ellen to butt in.

'She's right,' Mary retorted. 'He *would* have made a good husband.'

The two women exchanged a knowing look before Mary added, 'Yes, he was fine… before he was ill.'

Everyone mumbled in agreement.

Ann did not join in the ensuing conversation about young William's prowess in all kinds of sport. She knew she could have paid more heed to him instead of blathering on about the Osbaldestons. She endured her father's commiserations and wished everyone would disappear so that she could sit alone with Will and keep her own vigil. It became almost unbearable when her mother cast sideward glances in her direction; no doubt, she had her suspicions.

There was a cold reserve between William and Matthew and, as a result, the Smiths did not stay long. Matthew kissed Mary on the cheek as he bade goodbye and then, as he reached the door, he spun round to William.

'You still have four healthy sons, you know. You're fortunate in that.'

William swallowed hard and managed a reluctant, 'Thank you.' He saw Ann and her mother pause to touch the coffin as they went out.

As soon as they were alone again, William and the boys settled down for the all-night vigil. They lit their pipes while Mary served them more mulled ale and the salted beef pasties that, so far, no guests had eaten.

Mary wasn't hungry, and the secret about Will was like a millstone about her neck. She felt so much guilt that it must show on her face; it made her a stranger in her own family. There was no way she could sit all night with them.

'I'm so tired,' she said, making an excuse to leave the kitchen. 'I don't think I can stay up with you, not when I have so much to do tomorrow.'

Apart from her guilt, she didn't trust herself to be all night beside the coffin and not blurt out the truth.

'I'm sorry, truly, but please understand I'll have to face a lot of people tomorrow, and I need some rest before that.'

She saw their disappointed faces. 'You have plenty of tobacco, and the ale will keep warm by the fire. William—you know where the cheese is, and the oatcakes. Perhaps you could read the Bible and say prayers as well as talk.'

From her bed in the parlour, Mary listened to the murmurings from the kitchen. It was John doing most of the talking—a seamless recount of the best times with his brother—when they'd help clip the sheep and see to the ram, when they'd taken the sheep to Hunmanby Fair. There was no mention of his being led through thick snow to poach rabbits. His brother's pranks with the itching powder and the dead moles he'd hung from the apple tree had also been forgotten, as had the number of times Will had teased him and kicked him under the table.

Mary turned over to try to sleep. There was the funeral in the morning and, until it was over, she must be on her guard.

Chapter 48

Young William's funeral on the Saturday was the second one of the week, between a widow's on the Tuesday and the Speeton boy's to be held on Sunday. It was unusual to have three in a week, but they helped Mary's cause—to let people think William had died from the same illness.

Once they'd all washed and dressed, Mary handed out the sprigs of rosemary that Lizzie had left.

'Listen, boys, you're to throw them into the grave... at the end... when the vicar's finished. You're to remember William how he was... last year... at his best.'

John had tears in his eyes as he put the rosemary in his pocket. He stood holding his mother's hand while his father nailed down the coffin lid. As the last nail went in, the church bells began to toll nine times.

William helped his sons slip the bearing bands beneath the coffin, and then they lifted it carefully off the trestles. Carrying it between them at hip height, they left the house and set off up the lane, followed by Mary. Others joined their procession as it made its way slowly up the hill to the church.

It was almost a year to the day since they'd buried Elizabeth. Mary kept thinking of that autumn day last year. The weather had been warm. Today, a mist hung over the village. Smoke drifted down from the cottages, adding to the gloom. Most of the leaves on the sycamore trees had already fallen and were covering the pathways. She shuddered as she thought of her son's last moments. If only he'd left this world as easily as a leaf drops from a tree.

It was cold and damp inside the church. Mary walked mechanically up the aisle to sit at the foot of the coffin while William sat at the head, the enormity of losing a son beginning to sink in. Of all his sons, his namesake, young William, had been most like himself.

The rest of the mourners took their places in the main body of the church.

Mary smiled at Ann's brother Thomas, helping to officiate as a churchwarden. This was some consolation until she saw Robert Storey standing stiffly to attention. She shivered and glanced at her husband, but his head was bowed.

When the vicar began the service, his nasal intonation grated, and Mary thought he spoke too quickly for the occasion.

'I read from Ecclesiastes. "For man also knoweth not his time: as the fishes that are taken in an evil net, and as the birds that are caught in the snare; so are the sons of men snared in an evil time, when it falleth suddenly upon them."'

Mary was appalled. Had Robert chosen that reading? Certainly, the vicar had no idea of young William as a boy. Most of the congregation would remember, though, how he'd spent his time catching birds in various homemade snares. Worse was to follow, as if the vicar could see into her mind.

'I read from Corinthians. "We must all appear before the judgement seat of Christ; that every one may receive the things done in his body, according to that he hath done, whether it be good or bad."'

Mary pressed her hands together tightly. She was praying, not just for her son's soul, but also her own. Now, she could only trust in God's grace. The rest of the Bible readings were lost on her until Thomas Smith moved to stand by the great Bible.

He spoke in a gentle voice that still carried to the rear of the church.

'Lord, teach us to number our days: that we may apply our hearts unto wisdom. Turn thee again, O Lord, at the last and be gracious unto thy servants.'

When it was time for the coffin to be taken outside for the final committal, Mary stumbled behind, holding onto the pews for support. She avoided eye contact with the congregation.

A mere handful went with the family to the graveside. It was warmer outside, and Mary could see the sun trying to pierce through the mist. Young William was about to be buried at last. She trembled as the coffin was lowered into the freshly dug grave. Not long now, she thought, hoping the vicar would be brief. His nasal voice irritated more than ever.

'Man that is born of a woman hath but a short time to live, and is full of misery. He cometh up, and is cut down, like a flower... In the midst of life we are in death... Thou knowest, Lord, the secrets of our hearts; shut not thy merciful ears to our prayers; but spare us.'

Mary didn't know where to look. Did anyone suspect her secret? Did Ann know? The earth was thrown in, followed by the sprigs of rosemary. She felt even more guilty and alone when the vicar uttered his final words.

'From henceforth blessed are the dead which die in the Lord: even so saith the Spirit: for they rest from their labours.'

Mary gulped. It was all over. The deed was done. But would William be blessed? Would his soul be saved?

There was food and drink to be had afterwards at the house. People arrived to pay their respects, drink heavily and feast on the arval bread brought from Uphall. Mary, overcome by the ordeal of the last few days, sat slumped on a chair by the fire. She was given a strong drink, the first of many as she fended off the usual condolences that gave no comfort. Yes, there had been other deaths in the area lately, but she knew William's was so unnecessary. She just wanted to be left alone to grieve in peace.

She had John close to her, often putting his arm round her shoulder. No doubt, he thought he was helping, yet she didn't deserve kindness after what she'd done.

'Leave me, John. You go and talk to Ann. She's upset, look. Tell her... oh, *I* don't know...'

John's eyes lit up. 'I know—she'll see Will in heaven. They'll be together one day.'

She watched him talking with Ann and was relieved to see her smile again. She'd defy anyone to remain unmoved by John.

Dorothy Jordan had been keeping an eye on Mary. She could see the toll the death had taken. Compassionate for once, she encouraged people to leave the house and take food away with them. Then she persuaded Mary to have a lie down.

'Thoo rest a while. Thoo needs to keep tha strength up. Life goes on.'

Mary went into the parlour and lay on the bed with her eyes closed. Despite her worries, she soon fell asleep. When she awoke an hour later with a headache, the guests had gone. She got up and tottered into the kitchen to find William and the boys sitting at the kitchen table, their heads in their hands, staring at the mess left behind. Drinks had been spilt, crumbs of food scattered everywhere, and bits of cake trodden into the reeds on the floor. Despite her thumping head, she began to clear up.

Only John got up to help.

When she saw the tears in his eyes, she broke down, put her arms round him and sobbed. As they tidied up together, she wondered at the others' lack of concern. William, she knew, did not show his feelings readily. Maybe they were all guilty; every one of them could have shown more sympathy for Will. As his mother, though, she felt the most to blame. And William, who'd hardly spoken to her since, was probably thinking the same.

The next day was a Sunday, and the boy from Speeton would be buried. Mary feigned illness and sent her family to church. She stayed at home, yet couldn't bear to stay indoors. Instead, she walked out alone. Wandering rather aimlessly away from the village, she found herself on a pathway that led towards the cliffs. A groaning archway of hawthorn trees swayed above her, the branches grinding and scraping together in the wind. She hurried on as if she might see a sign, something to reassure her about young William and find peace, but she returned as disconsolate as she'd left.

In the days that followed, she took many similar walks, always searching for something and always in vain. Her emptiness could never be filled, and she heard of rumours going round the village. Stories about Will's behaviour were exaggerated. Some were convinced he'd run up gambling debts, others thought he'd gotten a lass with child. She heard one pedlar passing on the idea that William had a disease of the brain that drove him mad. The one constant was that her son had a sudden change of character in his last months and had lost his senses.

At the forge the men discussed how long William had been acting strangely; some said it had happened overnight due to a shock or a witch's curse; others argued he'd been going slowly mad for months.

Robert Storey was interested from a religious point of view. He was concerned for William's soul and had sympathy for a young man driven insane by things beyond his control. He decided to visit Mary.

He found her alone in the garden. She was standing motionless, staring at the apple tree with a glazed expression. When he hailed her, she ignored him. He walked right up to her and touched her elbow.

She turned her head and spoke with unusual calm and determination. 'Leave me in peace.'

'Sorry,' he mumbled, 'I didn't mean to trouble you. God knows you've suffered enough.'

'Suffered enough,' she repeated in a monotone. Suddenly, she lifted her arms up to the sky and then let them fall heavily to her sides again. 'There's no end... no end.'

He touched her arm once more. 'Rather than disturb you, I've come to offer comfort.'

She stared at him strangely as if just recognising him.

'How the hell can *you* help me? No, you can't, can you. You've no children. You wouldn't know.'

She turned away and marched back into the house. Noticing he was following her, she stopped in the middle of the kitchen.

'Look,' she said. 'They're all out. No one wants to linger here in a place tainted by madness and—' She clutched her head in despair. She was so tired and it was more madness to be stuck with Robert Storey of all people. There he stood in the doorway, unsure what to say for once, and he seemed genuinely upset.

301

'Oh, I'm sorry, Robert. For Elizabeth's sake, sit down and have a drink. There's diluted beer, if you like.'

They sat at opposite sides of the kitchen table, the same table where William had been laid out only weeks earlier. Robert sipped his drink thoughtfully and realised the speech he'd planned to give was of little use. She needed time to grieve.

Without any prompting, Mary gazed down at her clasped hands and began to recount the past few months.

'There's some say he was mad. But William wasn't mad.' She raised her eyes and looked Robert straight in the eye. 'I know my son. He was very sick.' She got up stiffly from the table and walked to the tiny window. 'He couldn't help it, poor lad,' she added as she gazed at the garden beyond. 'I should have known how to help him, but I didn't know what to do.'

'He'd been ill for a long time, I hear.'

She walked back to the table and sat down. 'Yes, much longer than need be. We weren't to know what ailed him. We're not physicians.'

'What form did his illness take?'

'Well… think what you'd be like if you couldn't sleep. I'd hear him clattering and banging about… and howling at times, like an animal. I had to shout at him to shut him up. He'd cower as if I was going to hurt him. Nearly every night the same.' Mary stopped to wipe away her tears. 'No one could get any rest.'

'Couldn't you give him sleeping draughts?'

'We tried everything. It wasn't just the lack of sleep though. He got all jumpy, couldn't sit still. He dropped things and barged into doors. He used to be so good with his tools and then he was so clumsy.'

She paused for a moment.

'It was like having a different person in the house. He chucked his things about, tore his best clothes… even set fire to his favourite waistcoat.' She wiped her eyes again and swallowed hard. 'I'm sure he used to see his cousin Ann, but then I think that stopped. I know he was sweet on her, but he never told me anything. Maybe she's at the bottom of it, though I suppose she couldn't understand him either.'

302

She rubbed at a stain on the table. 'Something must have been the last straw.' It was the closest she'd come to admitting William might have ended his own life. Realising she'd said too much, she grasped Robert's hand.

'He couldn't stand it anymore. It's not his fault—I should have stood up for him. I'm to blame.'

'No, you couldn't have done more, I'm sure.'

To her horror, she found herself telling him the truth, heard herself saying William had hung himself from a beam in the loft. She even mentioned the heart carved into the wood.

He pulled his hand away as if he'd been stung.

'No one knows except you,' she added quickly. She couldn't believe that, of all people, she'd succumbed to Robert Storey.

For a second or two he was stunned into silence. 'But the Bible says—'

'Robert—shut up! There's many a thing we can both be sorry for.' She glared at him across the table. 'Don't you forget I was your wife's sister and I loved her. There's been many a time I've held my tongue when I could have shown you up, Robert Storey—many a time!'

He made no immediate answer, and they stared at each other, unsure where the conversation would lead.

Suddenly, he cleared his throat and reached for his hat.

She had no idea what he'd do next. Could she trust him to keep quiet? She tried a final plea. 'Won't a loving God see to the heart of things?'

He didn't reply and stood up to leave. In the doorway, he turned and whispered, 'I'm sorry. I am, truly.'

Instead of going home, Robert walked up the hill towards the crossroads. There at the field boundaries was the place allotted to suicides. There were no flowers in the unsanctified plot and only a few piles of stones to denote the profane burials. He took off his hat and murmured a prayer for the souls of those less fortunate. Young William had obviously been ill to be so tempted by the devil. Did a crazed soul deserve eternal damnation? He shuddered to think of what might have happened if the villagers had known. Would they have taken William's body and dragged it naked through the street face

303

down to bury it up here, away from the church? Would they have driven a stake through his heart to pin him to the earth? Were *all* suicides unworthy of Christian mercy?

Robert prayed fervently that William had asked for forgiveness and salvation the night he died. The prayer brought some peace. A slight breeze blew in from the east, bending the long stalks of dry, dead grass. After inhaling deeply, he spent a few moments gazing at the bleak, open fields. A part of him felt inclined to keep Mary's secret.

'Lord, forgive me,' he murmured. Then he turned and walked slowly back to his empty house.

Chapter 49

After days of worrying about Robert Storey, Mary began to relax. So far, nothing had happened. She sat wearily at the kitchen table and dropped the potato she'd been peeling. Why did she carry on, day after day, doing the same repetitive tasks? After almost thirty years of married life, she'd had enough. The memory of William's face when they were courting all those years ago seemed more like a dream. That first time they'd been alone, a full harvest moon had shone through the window of their new house. His brown eyes had looked so serious in the moonlight. He'd whispered that he never wanted to leave her. That was before the lost babies. Now, no one in the house listened to her; no one noticed when she sat down to rest her back and legs. Some days, she thought, if it wasn't for John, she'd think of hanging herself too.

She finished the potatoes, chopped them, put them in the pot of water and started on the carrots and onions. She had no appetite, but the boys were growing and needed plenty to eat. It was three weeks since the funeral and her skirts felt loose; no one noticed she was thinner.

Tears welled up as her mind drifted. The sudden loss of her son had opened old wounds. She knew she hadn't come to terms yet with her sister's death, and then, of course, there was young Mary. She'd never grieved properly for her only daughter; there'd always been the boys to see to, and then two more were born and she'd had the worry over William's drinking. After wiping her eyes with her apron, she added the other vegetables to the pot. She blew her nose and tried to think of happier times, but past griefs overwhelmed her. She missed old Ben and Dickon, and, of course, Sarah Ezard. It seemed that everyone she'd grown attached to had died—even poor Milcah Gurwood, Francis's first love.

She stretched and rested her hands at the small of her back. Her monthly bleeding had not happened. She put this down to the recent shock. Certainly, she was not with child. She sighed as she stoked up the fire. Now in her fifties, she knew she'd be facing more changes. 'This won't do,' she told herself and took up her knitting. Dottie would be six in the new year, and her birthday vest and stockings wouldn't knit themselves.

William remained distant. He couldn't speak to Mary about his grief, couldn't help thinking she was to blame, and he couldn't see much hope in the future. Just now, everything was wrong; he wasn't getting any younger, the price of wheat was low, and it was unseasonably warm for November.

Each evening, he read the Bible, hoping for guidance, and bade his wife and sons sit at the table and listen. One night, he chose to read from Ecclesiastes. The verses suited his mood.

'All is vanity. What profit hath a man of all his labour which he taketh under the sun? The sun also ariseth, and the sun goeth down... The wind goeth toward the south, and turneth about unto the north; it whirleth about continually... All the rivers run into the sea; yet the sea is not full; unto the place from whence the rivers come, thither they return again. All things are full of labour.'

Mary could have done with a more uplifting passage. The words summed up her feelings exactly and added to her misery.

John, sensitive as ever, reached over the table to touch his father's hand.

'Don't be sad, Father. I like my labour. I like working with the sheep—so does Jack.'

William shrugged him off and read from the next chapter.

'I said of laughter, it is mad: and of mirth, what doeth it?' He read silently the next sentence. *I sought in mine heart to give myself unto wine.* He remembered his drinking bouts after the death of his daughter. Low as he was now, he would not succumb to brandy again. He looked up from the Bible at his three sons. John, though nineteen, remained a simpleton. As for Richard, he'd always been a restless child as his grandmother had predicted. The youngest, Matthew, was just thirteen and, though he was quiet and hardworking for now,

306

only time would tell. They might inherit land, but would they prosper? He turned to the Bible again and read aloud.

'I hated all my labour which I had taken under the sun: because I should leave it unto the man that shall be after me.' He looked up again at his sons. 'And,' he added, quoting from the verse he knew by heart, 'who knoweth whether he shall be a wise man or a fool?'

Though it was late November, Mary stood up and moved to the window to feel the cool draught. She felt sorry for her sons, stuck as they were with two parents who'd lost their way. How long would William keep the boys at the table listening to such dispiriting passages?

She opened the curtain. It was dark outside but, as she'd done often enough lately, she imagined she saw young William out there. She missed seeing him by Stina's grave, missed seeing his lopsided stroll.

The next day, Lizzie visited, hoping to get Mary active again outdoors. She ran up the lane with Dottie and almost fell through the door.

'There's a good wind blowin' so Francis is goin' to 'elp wi' threshin'.' She paused to catch her breath. ''E said thoo should come an' 'elp wi' winnowin'. *We're* goin', aren't we Dottie?'

The little girl was already pulling on Mary's apron. 'Come on.'

Lizzie raised a questioning eyebrow. 'It'll do thoo good—a bit o' work with others.'

Mary hadn't winnowed corn for years, not since she'd been married. Now that her boys were all old enough for work, there was nothing to stop her. She remembered how she'd enjoyed sharing such tasks with Elizabeth.

'Alright, why not. Wait a moment.' She took an old, much longer apron from a hook by the door, and changed her cap for an outdoor bonnet. Then, as she was about to leave, she rummaged in a box for her arm coverings.

She followed the other two out of the house, hoping she was up to the work. It could be strenuous, and she was out of practice. She half hoped that Lizzie really wanted her to mind Dottie instead.

As they reached the Uphall yard, they heard the rhythmical beat of the flails on the barn floor. It reminded her of the songs the women used to invent with the sole purpose of teasing the threshers. The men had always taken the banter in good heart, glad of the attention. Today, though, as she peeped round the large open door of the main barn, there was only Samuel and Francis with two men she didn't know. A strong westerly breeze blew right through the barn from the opposite open doors. It was a perfect day for the work.

Suddenly, Dottie noticed two of her young uncles had come up behind them.

'Where's John?' she asked.

Richard rolled his eyes. 'Aren't *we* good enough for you?'

'We've come to learn,' Matthew explained. 'Your father's going to show us. Are you going to help your mother?'

Dottie frowned and nodded in a serious fashion. She hadn't a clue what she'd be doing.

Mary hailed Samuel to show they'd arrived. Already, she could see the men were sweating. Threshing was usually a good job for a November day, yet the weather today was warm. The men paused in their work to take off their jackets. Then they rolled up their sleeves and undid their top shirt buttons. The two hired threshers pulled their shirts loose. They were huge men, both about six feet tall and with arms like their blacksmith. Francis and Samuel looked puny standing opposite these giants.

Samuel gestured with his thumb towards the back of the barn. 'You two lads fetch more sheaves. Before you toss them here though, pull out any weeds. We don't want any in the straw afterwards—they'll spoil it when we chop it up for fodder. If you watch us thresh this morning, maybe you can have a go after dinner.'

While the boys saw to the sheaves, Mary and Lizzie waited outside until enough grain had been threshed. They sat on stools, sheltered from the wind, but Dottie would keep

308

going inside. She stood amid the cloud of dust, transfixed by the unchanging rhythm of the flails.

Samuel shouted to the boys as he worked. 'You see how we do it, lads? We take our time… one, two, three, four… all in perfect time.'

'Aye,' laughed one of the giants. 'If thoo can't keep up, thoo'll end up clattered over 'ead.'

'Or get our flails taffled up,' warned the other. 'I know, let's change our rhythm.'

Dottie clapped her hands in delight and began a little dance, hopping from one foot to the other, keeping time with the flails.

After half an hour, the men stopped so that Richard and Matthew could get the shakeforks and rake the straw away from the threshing floor. The boys shovelled the remaining grain and chaff onto a large sheet and carried it outside to their mother and Lizzie.

Mary smiled as she remembered how, in the past, the threshers would sometimes pretend to trip and drop the sheet. Her two sons, though, as novices, had serious faces and placed the sheet down carefully.

'Thank you.' She winked. 'You're both doing well.' As she picked up two corners of the sheet, ready for the first toss, she hoped that Lizzie would not be rough and jerk it too quickly. Elizabeth had been the perfect partner.

'Ready, Lizzie? I'll count. One, two, three and hup!'

Lizzie was more exuberant than expected, almost pulling the sheet from Mary's grasp. They carried on tossing the sheet, letting the breeze blow the chaff away and leave the grains behind. Soon, as they grew used to each other, they worked in a rhythm like the threshers. Mary smiled again. She realised how much she'd missed working outdoors with others, especially with women. She laughed as Dottie, despite warnings to stand aside, kept trying to catch bits of chaff as they flew by. Mary wasn't even discouraged when her mother-in-law appeared and stood beside them, hands on hips.

Dorothy Jordan clicked her tongue a few times as if to disparage their efforts. 'Toss grain more,' she ordered.

'Let biggest an' 'eaviest fall into middle o' sheet. Wind'll blow lighter grains to side. I want thoo to store 'em separate. We're keepin' best grain for Up'all.' Then she pointed inside the barn. 'Thoo'll find our corn screen i' there. Use it, an' there's a long basket to go with it—we don't want owt except grain when thoo's finished. Dottie can 'ave a go.'

They put down the sheet and Lizzie brought out the corn screen. 'Come on, Dottie, watch what I do.' She grabbed a handful of grain and threw it against the wires. 'See? Any insects or bits o' muck'll go right through, an' grain'll roll down into this basket.'

Dorothy Jordan stood there for a while to oversee the women. Once satisfied, she added begrudgingly as she left, 'I suppose thoo'd better join us later fo' dinner.'

Mary glanced at Lizzie, raised her eyebrows and pulled a face.

Lizzie began to giggle which set Mary laughing.

'Stop, Lizzie! You're making me ache.' Mary held her side. 'It's the first time I've been asked to dinner as a worker. It's a good job we passed muster.'

'Come on,' urged Lizzie, 'there's another sheet full of grain ready. We'll winnow that load before dinner.'

As Mary bent down to pick up the corners, she put her hand to her side.

'No, don't start laughing again,' Lizzie warned.

Mary wasn't laughing. She'd felt a lump the size of a lemon appear without warning under her apron.

'What's wrong?' Lizzie asked. 'Thoo's gone pale.'

'I'm fine... I was just thinking of... you know... young William. Never mind me, let's get on.' She ignored the lump. It didn't hurt or prevent any movement. She picked up the sheet and they continued winnowing.

When it was time for dinner, Mary excused herself, said she had work to do at home.

Her sons were disappointed. 'But it's us threshing this afternoon. Don't you want to see how we do?'

'I'm sorry, Richard. I'll watch you another day.'

Matthew butted in. 'What about Lizzie? She can't winnow on her own.'

'I'm sure your grandmother can send one of the maids to help.'

Lizzie shrugged, equally dismayed. She thought Mary had enjoyed the morning.

Chapter 50

Mary walked home from the barn much more slowly than she'd set out. She found the house empty; William and the younger boys were at Uphall and John would be with the shepherd all day. She sat at the table, put her hand under her apron and traced the outline of the lump with her fingers, amazed how such a thing could appear with no forewarning. Maybe she'd strained herself. She'd heard of men complain of such things, usually after lifting heavy sacks, and then afterwards they'd wear a belt for support. Perhaps it was all that tossing of the sheet above her head. She wasn't used to it, and then she'd been doubled up laughing. More likely, she realised, she'd been weakened already by the effort of dragging young William back onto his mattress. Would the consequences of that night never end?

She poured out a mug of small beer and eased herself into the chair by the fire. There was little heat from the hearth and she couldn't be bothered to add more fuel. The weather was warm, and the family could make do with a cold supper. After finishing her drink, she fell asleep.

John was the first to come home. He was surprised to find his mother dozing by a cold hearth. He shook her arm gently.

'Are you alright? You've let the fire go out.'

'Oh, John, it's you... oh dear, yes, I fell asleep. Could you see to the fire while I get supper?'

As soon as John went to get the kindling, she held her side, hoping to keep everything in place while she stood up. No one would notice anything wrong and she could trust the apron to hide the lump.

The cold supper went without too much comment for the boys had eaten a full, hot dinner at midday at Uphall.

When Mary retired, she was glad she slept on William's right side. He'd not notice the lump and, besides, he'd never

3 1 2

bothered her in bed since the trouble over young William. Even if he did happen to find out, he'd simply say she was too old for winnowing and should have known better.

A few weeks later, in December, something happened to make Mary's subterfuge even easier. In bed at night, she was too hot. The winter was very mild, never below freezing, and she tossed and turned so much that William couldn't sleep either.

'It's like being next to a hot, wet sow.'

She couldn't argue with that as she laid on top of the covers once more, her body damp with sweat.

One night, he'd had enough. 'That's it. I'm taking John's bed. He can move up to the loft.'

John had only slept in the loft a few nights before he noticed the carving of the heart on one of the beams. He could read capital letters and knew why men carved names inside a heart; his mother had one on her knitting sheath. It was odd, though, to carve a heart where no one would see it.

One morning, Ann Smith happened to look out of her bedroom window and see John in her garden with their pet sheep. She hurried downstairs to meet him.

'How are you, John?'

'I'm alright.' He carried on rubbing the back of the sheep's head.

She began to stroke the sheep's ear. 'I'm sorry not to see you much. I've been busy. I wonder how you're all coping... without William.'

He shrugged. 'Father's got my bed now, says Mother's too hot to let him sleep.'

'So who do *you* share with?'

'No one. I'm in the loft.' He half spoke to the sheep. 'There's a heart carved on the beam.'

'Sorry, what did you say?'

'It has an A and a W inside it.' He didn't notice her turn pale. 'My father carved one on Mother's knitting sheath. He said he gave it to her before they got married. It's daft carving one in the loft... no one can see it.'

313

Ann blinked, trying not to cry. It was no good thinking what might have been.

'Anyway,' he continued, 'it was all crossed out.'

'What do you mean?'

'There were scratches right through it—like this.' He made his hand into a claw and imitated a cat.

She thought back to that last day she'd seen William, when he thought she was laughing at him. She dared to ask, 'Were the scratches fresh, do you think?'

Still stroking the sheep, he mumbled, 'Mmm, I think so.'

'I'm sorry, John.' She couldn't say any more for her throat was tight. She ran back to the house in tears.

Word of Mary's trouble with her nightly sweats reached Uphall. Her two youngest sons often complained to their grandmother at dinnertime.

'She can hardly bear to cook for us,' Richard moaned, hoping for second helpings. 'She keeps having to go in the garden to cool down.'

Much to the boys' surprise, their grandmother didn't take their side. 'Lads know nowt,' she grumbled. 'Think on... who's to look after thee when she's gone?'

The next day, the milkmaid from Uphall appeared at Mary's door with a special headband.

'Me mistress 'as soaked this i' rosewater an' egg white. It's to 'elp thee sleep. An' she says to try soakin' tha feet in an 'ot mustard bath.' As the girl left, she added, 'If thoo 'as 'eadaches, try grated nutmeg i' water.'

Mary thanked her and tried the remedies in good faith. Nothing really helped and, due to the lack of sleep and often feeling flushed, she grew shaky and unsure of herself. Despite drinking sage tea all day to keep calm, she made a botch of even the simplest jobs. It made her realise how young William had felt.

In the evenings, father and sons sat round the hearth with their pipes while Mary knitted well away from the fire. The only sounds were the rapid click of her needles, the occasional knocking of a pipe against the wall and the hiss as someone's

3 1 4

spit hit the backstone. It still amazed Mary how men could take such an inordinate amount of time and pleasure in pulling tobacco from a pouch and tamping it down with their thumbs before finally lighting up. It was quite a ritual. Their clothes stank of the stuff and their fingers and thumbs were stained dark yellow. She sighed as she thought of the imminent Christmas. The lump remained in her side, and she didn't relish standing over a fire to make the usual treats.

Lizzie was upset when Mary declined all offers to go winnowing again. She tried to explain to Francis how his mother had lost weight and must be grieving still. She hoped he'd offer comfort, but was disappointed.

'Don't fret, Lizzie. Robert always used to say, "Misfortune is the school of virtue." We think it's not Christian to grieve so and, thinking of winnowing, it's written in the very first psalm, "The ungodly are like chaff which the wind driveth away... the way of the ungodly shall perish." So, think on. My mother should be thankful and praise God for young William's life.'

Lizzie's eyes pricked with tears. Francis was still so influenced by Robert Storey. It had been better when, straight after Elizabeth's funeral, Francis had kept his distance from Robert. That didn't last long, though, and now Francis was often at Robert's house and seemed to be his only friend. Much to her horror, Francis even invited the man to supper sometimes. She always had to bite her tongue; after all, Robert was Dottie's godfather.

As Christmas approached, John grew excited and visited Dottie more often. In the final week of advent, he danced round her kitchen holding both her hands.

Lizzie smiled weakly. 'Mind Francis doesn't come in an' catch thee.' After looking out of the window to check the road, she added, ''E doesn't believe i' celebratin', especially not wi' dancin'. 'E's fastin' an' just 'as one meal a day.'

'He'll let you enjoy Christmas Eve, won't he?'

Lizzie shook her head. 'We'll be 'avin' a quiet supper... nowt special.'

315

'Not even Yule cakes and frumenty?'

She shook her head again.

The thought of such a poor Christmas wiped the smile from his face. He kissed Dottie goodbye and walked home in misery.

As soon as he entered the kitchen, his mother asked, 'John—has someone upset you?'

'No.'

The rest of the family ignored him. John could change from cloud to sunshine and then back again in a moment. It was a waste of time trying to fathom him. As they began their supper, another cold plate of ham and cheese, John told them about Francis.

'Not even frumenty on Christmas Eve!' he concluded.

Mary decided that tonight was as good a time as any to mention her own thoughts on the subject. 'We won't be having the usual foods either. I can't be standing over a hot fire for hours. I'm sorry, but there it is... I can't do it anymore. And I don't want the Yule candle either.'

The boys shuffled on the bench and looked to their father for help. Surely, he'd have something to say. When he didn't object, Richard broke the ominous silence.

'But what about Christmas Day? Won't there be any hackin pudding for breakfast?'

'Not unless *you* want to keep the fire going and boil the pudding for six hours.'

He turned to the others for support, but his father kept his head down, and his two brothers were too shocked to say anything. Surely, she didn't mean it.

The next morning, John brought Lizzie and Dottie to the house. He stood in the middle of the kitchen and made an announcement.

'Mother, we've come to help.'

'What with? I don't need any help.'

Lizzie intervened, not trusting John to explain adequately. 'Francis won't let us make any Christmas food—not for ourselves anyway... so I thought maybe we could make stuff 'ere.'

316

'I'm sorry—I can't stand the heat from the fire.'

'What if we did all mixin' 'ere, an' then I cook everythin' i' *my* kitchen? An' then I fetch it back?'

John's eyes sparkled. He grabbed Dottie's hand. 'Me and Dottie will help.'

'Oh, John...' She could hardly refuse.

With Mary giving strict instructions and following her own recipe, they made a hackin pudding. Dottie and John stirred the sticky mixture of suet, dried fruit, brandy and spices, and then Mary stuffed it into the sheep's stomach they'd brought.

Lizzie took it home in a cloth to boil for the rest of the day. She'd return it before Francis came home. He'd smell the wonderful richness of the pudding, but she could assure him the food wasn't for them.

The next day was Christmas Eve. John went out with Dottie to collect holly and ivy to decorate the house, while Lizzie and Mary made a gingerbread loaf and a small Yule cake for each of the family. Again, Lizzie took them to her own cottage to bake.

By the time it grew dark in the afternoon, Lizzie and Dottie had returned, and everything was ready in Mary's kitchen apart from the frumenty drink. The wheat had been in soak all day, and Mary thought Dottie could stay to help. Her own daughter used to love the preparations.

'Come on, Dottie, you and John can do the next bit.'

She spooned the sodden wheat into a strong bag and handed it to them. 'John knows what to do. Watch him and then you have a go.' Seeing Dottie raise the bag over her head and wallop it on the floor reminded her of young Mary. 'Steady, lass, or you'll break the bag open. Gently does it.'

When she deemed they'd bashed it enough, she emptied the bag into a bowl of water. 'There you go, Dottie. See how the husks float to the top? How fast can you pull them out? John's good at it.'

Just then, William and the other two boys arrived home. They blinked at the kitchen festooned with greenery and the scene on the floor where John and Dottie were sitting, competing noisily over a bowl. Husks were being flicked everywhere.

Mary smiled at the boys. 'Yes, we're having frumenty tonight. Do you two want to join in?'

Richard shook his head. At sixteen, he felt too old for such games.

Matthew, only thirteen, wanted to have a go yet declined with a sad shake of his head.

Mary shrugged. 'Never mind then. Go with your father and collect the spiced ale from Martha Wrench.'

Before he left, William placed a large bottle on the table. 'My mother's sent this. It's elderberry syrup. I think she feels bad about not having the old feasts at Uphall anymore.' He turned to Lizzie. 'I don't suppose you and Francis will be celebrating much tomorrow either.'

'No, we'll go to church an' celebrate i' prayer. Come on, Dottie, it's time we went. It's dark an' tha father'll be 'ome soon.'

Mary gave Lizzie a hug and kissed her. 'Thank you— you've helped a lot and you've taken my mind off other things.' She sighed as Lizzie and Dottie left the house; it was such a pity they couldn't stay longer.

John saw his mother was sad. He leapt towards her with a sprig of mistletoe and gave her a big, sloppy kiss.

'Happy Christmas!'

Chapter 51

1733-34

Despite Lizzie's efforts, Mary had little appetite for the rich food or for any fun and games on Christmas Day. It was far too soon after young William's death to enjoy celebrations. She knew the boys pretended that all was well, yet they could not lift her or William's spirits. After a quiet day, she sent the boys to bed.

Mary and William retired soon afterwards, to their separate beds and their separate concerns. William feared for the coming year; the weather was still unseasonably mild, hardly ever freezing. He'd face more trouble with weeds and crop diseases.

Mary lay with one hand guarding her side, probing the lump to check if it was bigger. She couldn't tell whether it had grown or she was thinner. It was worrying that her sister had died of a similar complaint. She tried to calm herself and sleep, but she couldn't get Dorothy Jordan's words out of her mind, spoken as everyone had left church. 'A green Christmas makes a fat churchyard.' She prayed that William's mother would not find out about the lump. So far, it had been easy to disguise the weight loss, and a cloak hid everything. She needn't worry until spring.

In the new year, John visited Lizzie and Dottie frequently. Since Elizabeth's death, the little girl had stopped going to Robert's house and she was bored indoors. To cheer her up, John showed her things he'd found—an unusual bit of driftwood in the shape of a snake and a red stone with a hole in the middle.

'It's my birthday soon,' she boasted to him late one afternoon. 'I'll be six.'

'Then you'll soon be old enough to marry me.'

She giggled and jumped up from the floor to sit on his knee.

Her mother frowned. 'Don't go doin' that when tha father's 'ere. 'E won't like it—thoo sittin' in other people's laps.' She never minded John though. While he'd be twenty in the summer, he had the mind of a child and he loved Dottie, would never think to harm her. Francis, though, was full of mistrust, like Robert, always suspecting the worst in people.

John had only been gone a few minutes before Francis arrived home. He was in a good mood and swung Dottie round the kitchen.

'I have news for you, young lady, you're going to have lessons. As soon as you're six, you can join the little group the vicar's getting together. You can learn to read.'

Lizzie knew nothing of this. ''Ow often is this goin' to 'appen?'

'Every day so long as he's not busy. It was Robert's idea since she doesn't go to him anymore.'

The mention of Robert was alarming. She feared his influence on the girl. 'Is Robert goin' to 'elp?'

'I don't think so. He might have suggestions.'

'Hmm. What do *you* think, Dottie? You'd like to learn.'

Dottie wasn't sure. It did sound exciting to go to the vicarage and be with other children. 'What about John?' she asked. 'He'll miss me. He'll have no one to play with.'

Lizzie bit her lip, trying not to smile. Then she had an idea. 'Maybe he could go too… when he's not needed by the shepherd.'

John had seen his mother put her hand to her side and take a deep breath, and he'd noticed she was thinner; he'd even felt her ribs sticking into him when they hugged. When he went to call for Dottie to go to the vicarage, he confided in Lizzie.

'Mother's not too well just now.'

'What's the matter?'

'I don't know. She won't say. She holds her side here.' He pointed to his lower stomach.

Lizzie thought immediately of Elizabeth and feared the worst. 'She'd best see a physician then, an' sooner rather than later.'

John worried about it and, as soon as he returned home, he asked his mother if she was alright.

'Don't fuss. I'm fine... honestly.'

'You hold your side there. Does it hurt?'

'Sometimes, but don't fret. It'll clear up.'

It didn't 'clear up', and the whole family caught her wincing with pain one evening as she carried the heavy pot to the table.

Once the boys had gone to bed, Mary finally told William about the lump, now almost as big as her palm.

His eyes widened in fear. He remembered Elizabeth and dreaded a tumour that could not be treated. Trying to sound calm, he told her he'd see the apothecary.

The next morning, William rode to Hunmanby.

The apothecary listened to William's description of the symptoms and grew more concerned. 'Women are more prone to these things,' he pronounced. 'You say she's in her fifties and can no longer have children?'

William nodded, uncomfortable at describing his wife's ailments. It had been bad enough the other year when he'd had to explain about Elizabeth.

'There are two opinions about such diseases,' the apothecary continued. 'Take a seat while I explain. Some say it's because of internal worms—hundreds of them, all in a lump, and they devour the flesh.'

William shuddered. 'And what's the other opinion?'

'That your wife suffers from a surfeit of the melancholy humour. Judging by her age and habits, her lack of energy and her general lack of interest in life, I think it's black bile—it's built up inside her. It's quite common once women are past childbearing. The bad humour gathers in the unused womb. Tell me, and I'm sorry to have to ask, is she still carrying out her duties as a wife?'

'No, she's not. You see she wasn't sleeping and she gets hot at night so we sleep in separate beds.'

321

'I see.' The apothecary linked his hands together and stretched them out. 'I only ask this because it's possible her vital fluids are being blocked.'

'So what's the cure?' William asked in despair. 'Is there one?'

'It could be cut out, though that's dangerous and costly and, anyway, I wouldn't trust the barber-surgeon here. You'd have to find a proper surgeon in Bridlington.'

'So what do you propose?' William was getting impatient.

'Mild purgatives might be best. We don't want to wage outright war on the thing—that could just provoke it to grow faster. No, I suggest a mild purgative to expel the melancholy. I'll give you one and you can have a bottle of black nightshade water for the pain. She can either drink it or use it in a compress.'

When he handed William the bottles, he added, 'Tell her to avoid salty and rich foods, and not to drink strong wine.'

William remembered the man had said the same about Elizabeth's diet. It was a hopeless situation; at this time of year, they relied on salted meat, and he didn't have much faith in the purgative.

Mary listened to what William had to say and took her medicine. She recalled the horrible things said about Elizabeth's illness, about the disgusting creatures that lived inside her, eating away. As she lay in bed at night with a compress at her side, she couldn't avoid thinking of the lump as a separate being, as a living thing that was growing and taking her nourishment. Even worse, she worried that God was punishing her on account of young William.

By the end of February, Mary was painfully thin and found it hard to do her chores. The boys now took turns to do the heavier jobs. Matthew proved a godsend; he was much more amenable than his older brother, Richard, and didn't mind fetching water every day. He was a familiar face at the well and, with his large eyes, his soft, wavy hair and gentle manner, he soon became popular with the girls.

322

Lizzie often came to help with the cooking and remarked one day on Matthew's way with the women. ''E's lookin' more an' more like 'is namesake, thy brother. 'E 'as same 'igh fore'ead, an' them eyes, blue as cornflowers.' She began scraping the carrots. 'It's no wonder all lasses smile at 'im.'

Mary sighed as she put the last peeled potato in the stew. 'I wish Richard was as easy. He does help, but with such ill grace at times. Of course, John is good, but he spends more time now at the vicarage. Do you know how he's doing? I can't always tell from what he says.'

'Thoo'll laugh when I tell thee—vicar's son 'as joined in— plays word games with 'em when they've 'ad enough o' readin' an' writin'. 'E tries to get John to speak better... thoo knows, speak more like a gentleman. Dottie tells me ev'rythin' when she comes 'ome. Mother, she says, what's wrong wi' sayin' in a muck sweat? John says it when 'is 'ands sweat an' 'e can't 'old 'is quill.'

Mary smiled. 'Did he really say that?'

'Aye.' She began to chop the carrots. 'An' they play a game called sillymies. It sounds silly enough—they 'ave to say what somethin' is rough or as soft as. Your John said a woman's 'and was as soft as a mouse's ear. Vicar's son said, I think rose petals would be better.'

Mary smiled again. Her own daughter's ideas had always amused their old vicar, but she could imagine Henry Sumpton's face.

'Dottie loves to go an' learn wi' John. She sits by fire afterwards an' mutters to 'erself, then comes out wi' such funny stuff. She told Francis 'is chin was as rough as a cat's tongue. Then, bless 'er, she said my cheek was smooth as inside of a seashell. I don't know who 'as most ideas, Dottie or John. Does tha want onions i' pot?'

When Mary nodded, Lizzie took down a string and pulled out one of the largest. As she began to cut off the top, she paused. 'Them Sumptons are full of ideas an' all. They've been talkin' to Samuel an' they're wantin' a winnowin' machine.'

'What on earth's that?' Mary wasn't sure she wanted to know. It implied change was afoot and she wasn't up to it.

323

Lizzie frowned as she peeled off the onion skin. 'I don't really know, but I 'eard Francis call it a windmaker.'

'I don't see how that would work. I'll ask William—see if he knows.'

That evening, Mary questioned William about the machine. He did know about it and seemed more annoyed by his brother Samuel siding with the Sumptons behind his back.

'I can't keep up with them. That Henry Sumpton's always sticking his nose in. He's been talking to Samuel and John Grimston as well as the Osbaldestons and, of course, *your brother*. They're all keen to get the machine. Fancy—there's only me and Robert Storey against the idea.'

'Lizzie said it makes the wind blow.'

'No, not exactly. It's like a set of sails on a drum. They say it takes two men to work it and it's quicker than winnowing grain the old way with a sheet. And you don't have to wait for a windy day.'

'Oh.' She was getting too old for such changes. It would be a different kind of life if men did both the threshing *and* winnowing; they wouldn't need women at the barn anymore.

'So,' she asked, 'if it's so good, why are you against it?'

'Well, it's not been tested round here. It's come from the Dutch and it's expensive. I've heard it takes some getting used to—it's not as simple as they make out.'

'And what about Robert Storey? Why doesn't he want it?'

'Oh, he says it's unnatural. God creates the wind, not man.'

'Hmm, I agree there. I wonder whose side our Francis will take.'

Francis had heard Robert's views on the winnowing machine, yet couldn't help being interested. As soon as Dottie had been put to bed, he lit his pipe and tried to convince Lizzie of the benefits of the new machine.

'Don't you see—there'll be no more waiting for the right weather. And you know how cold you get in winter with both barn doors open. What's good about the winnowing fan is you can use it inside or carry it outside if it's sunny. Just think—two can do the work of six in half the time.'

Lizzie shut her eyes for a moment. It was too much to take in. She sighed and leant back on her chair. It was true she didn't like the dust, and the prickly chaff did give her a rash. On the other hand, she enjoyed winnowing with the sheet.

'It doesn't sound much fun—just two women turnin' a wooden 'andle.'

'No, it's the men would do it. It'll save you the job.'

'Hmm.' She wasn't happy about it. 'Where will it end if we start makin' our own weather?' When he didn't answer, she stared at him. 'Since thoo seems to know all what's goin' on, 'as thoo seen tha mother lately? Does tha know she's not well?'

'No... I didn't know. I'll ask my grandmother tomorrow at Uphall. She'll know what's wrong.'

Chapter 52

Dorothy Jordan had been keeping an eye on Mary, judging her health each Sunday in church. So far, she'd kept her peace, yet when she saw Mary walk so slowly to her pew, holding onto William's arms, she knew the problem was more than grief. Then, one dinnertime, Francis stayed behind to question her about his mother.

'It's probably just women's problems,' she tried to reassure him. 'She'll soon get over it. We all do. We 'ave to.'

When he'd gone back out to work, though, she decided to catch William on his own and get to the bottom of it.

A few days later, she found him alone in the yard.

'Come i' garden a while,' she coaxed. 'Let's see if we need owt doin'. Them new maids don't like gettin' their 'ands mucky.'

The weather was mild with a gentle westerly breeze. It was the first spring-like day of March, hardly the best day to be discussing illness. She didn't waste much time. After they'd sauntered once round the vegetable plot, she began.

'So, William, what's up wi' Mary? Thoo can't pretend all's well.'

'No, it isn't.' Reluctantly, he explained Mary's lump and his visits to the apothecary. He told her what the man had said.

She agreed instantly with the worm diagnosis. 'Why, that's it for sure. 'Er womb 'as gone bad an' worms'll be eatin' away 'er flesh. I've 'eard thoo can eat crabmeat. Instead of eatin' Mary, worms'll eat crabs.'

'But,' he argued, 'there aren't any crabs to be had in March.'

'Nay, thoo's right, so listen.' She began gesturing with her hands as she explained what he should do. 'Get a bit o' pork, tie it to a length o' string, this long, an' shove it up Mary's backside. Then, draw it out nice an' slow, an' worms'll be lured out with it. Simple, eh? Better than medicine.'

William gulped. There was no way he'd try that remedy.

'It'll work,' she cried, full of confidence. 'You mark my words.' She rubbed her hands together almost gleefully and walked back to the house, her mission completed.

At the end of another long day in the fields, William ambled home with his sons to find Mary had already gone to bed and left them a cold supper. There was no doubt—she was getting worse.

Mary listened to the racket they were making in the kitchen and hoped they'd tidy up when they'd finished. She did her household chores as if yoked to them like an ageing ox to the plough. The work never ended and she got no thanks. Despite her tiredness, they still expected their clothes washed and repaired on time, and ate vast amounts of food. She wouldn't have minded so much if they behaved better at the table, but of late, like her health, they were worse. William was no help. Only yesterday, she'd seen Richard and Matthew blow their noses into their hands and wipe their hands down their breeches; William had said nothing.

William was aware that he was growing more and more like his father. Now, for his health each morning, he drank a tablespoon of limewater in his milk as his father had done. He'd also begun a habit of inspecting the fields, grumbling if they were not weeded properly. He heard himself repeating Dickon's well-used argument—one year's seeds is ten year's weeds.

Lately, maybe because he was worried about Mary, he found he had less patience with his sons. He was tempted to cuff them round the head if they were slow or lazy. Richard, in particular, was a worry; he was sixteen, had the physique of a man, and it was springtime. William caught him more than once eyeing the maids at Uphall and, too often, saw him lurking by the dairy.

His mother warned him. 'That lad o' thine, Richard, 'e's a lad no longer. Why, 'is buttocks are 'ard as cheese. Thoo'd better keep 'im off me maids, or else.'

When William had words with his son, Richard just resolved to be more careful. The maid-of-all-work at Uphall

327

was always the first up in the morning and the last one to bed; he had plenty of opportunity to catch her on her own.

Mary struggled on doing the lighter chores. At breakfast, she couldn't be bothered to join in the conversation. The talk was only about work and the weather and was done so briefly as if it cost them a shilling a word. One day was very much like another, and she began to go back to bed soon after William and the boys had left.

Fewer chores were accomplished each day and, if it hadn't been for Lizzie, the garden would never have been planted up or the baking and cooking done. She was too tired to care and, though her lump flattened somewhat when she lay down, she never escaped the dull, dragging pain in her stomach. Remembering her sister's fatal illness, she determined to say no to any useless infusions and purges. She'd also say no to any bloodletting. If, or when, the worst happened, she'd take plenty of laudanum. She would not suffer like her sister.

One day, William grew anxious when he returned home with the boys in the early evening and found Mary already in bed again. A cold supper had been left on the table as usual, yet it was odd to see the fire so low. She must have retired hours ago. As soon as he'd replenished the fire, he let the boys start on their supper. Instead of joining them, he went into the parlour. Finding Mary awake, he sat on the edge of the bed.

'Are you alright?'

'I was just tired. I'll get up soon. Go on—you have your supper. I'll be there in a moment.'

She would have preferred to stay in bed, but forced herself up, winced at the sudden sharp pain in her stomach and wandered slowly into the kitchen. She eased herself onto her chair, forced a smile and began to nibble at a piece of cheese.

The boys hesitated in their eating for she was unusually pale. They saw her sigh heavily and leave her cheese. John passed her the plate of oatcakes, but she shook her head.

William poured her a mug of small beer. 'There, you need to keep your strength up.'

She drank it and felt a little better. 'I'll clear away when you've finished. I don't think I'll sit up knitting and mending, though. I could do with a good night's sleep.'

She stayed a while and listened to the boys chatting about their day's work. Richard and Matthew had been threshing in the main barn and reported there was still no sign of the winnowing machine.

'I'm glad,' said Richard.

'And we all know why,' his father replied. He winked at Mary. 'He'll have one eye on the women.'

Richard didn't even blush. He grinned and punched Matthew on the arm. 'You wait till you're a bit older... When they toss the sheet... you'll see.'

Mary turned to John. 'And what have *you* been doing? You'll be moving the sheep soon, won't you?'

'Not just yet. I'm helping grub up the whins with Father and Francis.'

William smiled at his son. 'That's right. We'll have our share of whins rooted out before Lady Day. *We* won't get fined.'

When Mary saw that they'd finished eating, she began to tidy up.

William and the boys moved to the fire and lit their pipes. They didn't notice when she went to bed.

Mary struggled on for a few more days, before letting Lizzie take over. She was especially glad of the help when she began to bleed. Both women knew it was not the regular monthly occurrence for Mary hadn't bled since October, five months ago. As well as the indignity of having to keep clean, she kept wanting to pass water. It didn't make any difference if she drank only a little; her bladder soon felt full and, before long, she'd be desperate to go again.

One morning, Lizzie arrived to find Mary sitting on the chamber pot.

'It's no good,' Mary complained, having given up any chance of dignity. 'I want to go, but it won't come out, and it hurts.'

Lizzie bit her lip in thought. She knew of a tonic that the Gurwoods had used in Rudston.

329

''As thoo 'eard o' Hungary Water? Gurwoods swore by it whenever any o' them were ill. It 'as brandy in it an' it's flavoured wi' marjoram flowers.'

'Is it expensive?'

'I don't know. Get William to find out. Gurwoods drank it cold twice a week, diluted i' spring water.'

'Alright,' Mary agreed, 'I'll give it a try.'

William bought a bottle in Hunmanby and stocked up with laudanum just in case. When he sat on her bed that evening and handed over her first drink of the tonic, he discovered that she'd been feeling nauseous all day.

'You've not *been* sick though?' He wasn't sure how much she ate these days; Lizzie was never there to ask when he came home.

'No, not actually sick... not yet.'

'I'll ask my mother for something. She has a cupboard full of bottles.'

Mary groaned. 'I've told you—I don't want any strange cures or infusions, but I will have a few drops of laudanum tonight to help me sleep.'

'Is it because of the pain in your stomach?'

'Mmm. It doesn't leave me, and my back aches.'

He knew it sounded so similar to Elizabeth's illness, yet didn't mention it. Instead, he said, 'John wants to come and sit with you. Is that alright?'

'He can come any time. Lizzie is so good and she tells me all the gossip, but there's no one like John to cheer me up.'

John put his head round the parlour door. 'Hello, are you feeling better?'

'Yes, thanks, much better for seeing you.'

William left them alone and rejoined his other sons in the kitchen.

John sat on the bed and chatted while she sipped her tonic. 'Uncle Matthew's had another calf today. He's going to use a different bull this summer—one from Bempton. It's come all the way from Holland. Did you know, Mother, if you feed a calf on porridge, it just makes its belly fat, and then it ends up not growing so well?'

'No, I didn't know.'

'The herdsman says boiled linseed oil and milk is best.' He paused for a moment, thinking hard about what he'd learnt. 'Did you know a cow goes all droopy just before it drops a calf? Like this.'

He stood up, let his arms hang loose and lowered his head as if about to fall asleep.

'And, you know you have to watch some cows—they try to run from the milkmaids. You see they don't want to give up their milk. They want all the milk for their calves.'

'I don't blame them. But you seem to be spending a lot of time with the cattle. Have you given up on Jack and the sheep?'

'No! Never! I love the sheep. There'll be lambs soon.'

'Good. Jack's grown very fond of you.' She put down her mug and relaxed into the pillow. She was so tired.

'Do you want to know about Uncle Matthew's fall out with his herdsman?'

'Save that for another day, John. You go and get your supper. I'll have a little sleep.'

The next day, William spent time at Uphall with his mother as she went through her shelves of remedies. He found her eager to help.

''Ere, what about this?' She passed him a bottle of peppermint water. 'An' look 'ere—this is just what she needs for aches an' pains.' She handed down a tiny bottle. 'Be careful wi' that—it's comfrey oil. It's taken two years to mature. Tell 'er not to mind 'ow it stinks an' to use it on a compress. I'd suggest frogspawn on a cloth, but it's too early i' year.'

As he was going, she added, 'Give 'er a spoonful o' blackcurrant preserve ev'ry mornin' when she wakes up. That'll stop 'er feelin' sick. Aye, that an' a drink of 'ot water.'

He returned home that evening, relieved that the remedies were mild and that Mary would not object. There was no point telling her that his mother thought a violent purge would sort her out. His mother always blamed constipation. He sat on the bed and prised the cork from the bottle of peppermint water.

331

'Here, smell this. I'll dilute a bit in water and then maybe afterwards you'll feel like eating something. I see Lizzie's left a ham pie for us.'

Mary sniffed the bottle. 'It's lovely, thanks. You have your supper and send John in later with a slice of pie—a tiny slice, mind you.'

The peppermint made her belch a lot, but she felt better for it and sat up straight to wait for John.

He tiptoed in, a broad smile on his face. 'Father said you'll like this.' He handed her the plate with its neat slice of pie and a large pickled onion that threatened to roll off onto the bed.

'Thank you, John.' She took a small bite and wiped the pastry crumbs from her chin. 'Mmm, Lizzie's done a good job.'

'You can't beat fresh pastry, eh?'

'You can't!'

As Mary finished the pie, a few crumbs went down the wrong way. She coughed and spluttered so much that blood oozed between her legs, like after childbirth.

John thought she was about to choke to death. 'Shall I fetch Father?'

'No,' she managed to croak between coughs. 'I'll be alright. Pass me my drink.' The peppermint water soothed her and she leant back against the bedhead. 'Now, John, tell me why Matthew fell out with his herdsman, then you can leave me to sleep.'

'Bullock George wants to put cow dung in the calves' mouths. He says it keeps them safe from witches, but Uncle Matthew won't have it, says he won't abide such a thing. He won't let George tie a red thread round their tails either, but George said it keeps evil away. At Uphall Dickon was allowed, wasn't he?'

'Ah, well, we'd had Dickon working there for years, and maybe your grandfather didn't mind him using the old ways.'

'I think Uncle Matthew must like the *new* ways. Does Father like the new ways?'

Mary took a deep breath. 'I'm not sure. I don't think so. Off you go now, John. I'll have a sleep.'

She settled lower into the bed. While the 'new ways' were a worry, she doubted she'd be there to see them.

Chapter 53

When Lizzie arrived with Dottie the next morning, Mary questioned her immediately about any new ways to be used in Reighton.

'William tells me nothing,' she explained as she raised herself higher in bed, 'and I can't trust John to give a proper account.'

''Asn't thoo 'eard? James Cockerill 'as taken over from 'is father as Lord o' Manor, an' Robert Grimston's takin' over from *'is* father as steward.'

The news took Mary's mind off her illness, but it made her feel old. No wonder there was talk of new ways, and no wonder William was so tight-lipped; he'd be thinking the Smiths would be conspiring already with the younger steward.

'That's not all,' Lizzie added. 'There's trouble brewin' over drainage. Francis an' Robert aren't keen on steward's new ideas, an' they've argued wi' vicar's son about it.'

At this point, Dottie became bored and pulled on Mary's arm. 'Granny, can I see if there's any eggs today?'

'Of course, off you go. Be careful.'

As soon as the girl had gone, Mary resumed the conversation. 'I remember—didn't Robert have trouble with Henry Sumpton when he first arrived? From what I gathered, Robert put him in his place. Henry's no farmer.'

'Well, it's diff'rent now. Henry's got together wi' thy brother an' our steward an' now they want to drain our fields better. Even most o' yeomen are for it. Francis says it means a lot of 'ard work fo' no gain.'

'It's strange that William's never mentioned it. Maybe he thinks it'll never happen.'

'Oh but it will. It's all they talk about at Up'all. Francis said 'e saw a load o' wooden poles arrive. Don't ask me what they're for. Francis thinks some sort o' pipes are goin' to be put in.'

333

Mary gasped, about to speak. Instead, she had a coughing fit.

Lizzie grew alarmed. "Ere, thoo'd best 'ave a drink.'

'I think,' Mary spluttered between coughs, 'I think I've still got pastry crumbs stuck in my throat.'

'Thoo looks worn out. Make sure William gets you a bottle o' cough medicine.'

'It's not just the cough. I'm afraid you'll have to rinse out my sheet. I bled again last night.'

'Oh, Mary, thoo must 'ave a physician. 'Ere, let me 'elp thoo get up. Thoo can sit o' chamber pot while I sort out tha bed.'

As Mary was helped up, she repeated her objections. 'I've told William I'm not having a stranger asking questions about my body.'

She eased herself onto the chamber pot and apologised. 'I'm sorry, it's putting a burden on *you*, but you must understand—a physician will only prescribe useless pills and whatnot, and then end up fetching a surgeon. And I couldn't go through that.'

'I'm sure Matthew would pay for any doctorin'.'

'Ha—as if William would accept that. No, I'll manage as I am—with your help of course. I can't thank you enough. Maybe it won't be for long...'

'Don't say that.' Lizzie turned away to change the sheet and hide her tears. It seemed a hopeless situation.

When William came home, Mary could tell he was angry by the way he strode into the parlour. He didn't even enquire how she was. He just paced up and down, paused briefly to look out of the window at the garden and, finally, slumped onto the bed.

'So,' she asked, 'what's chafing you?'

He ground his teeth and heaved a great sigh before answering. 'There's talk of draining the fields better—not yet, thank goodness.' He shook his head. 'It's not right, though. We've chalk under those top fields—it draws the moisture well enough and keeps the soil open. We certainly don't need *pipes* under them.' He rubbed his forehead in frustration.

334

'What's wrong with our furrows, eh? They drain the land *and* we have ditches. We don't need anything else. I blame your brother. He gets his ideas from Osbaldeston and other such *gentry*.'

'Maybe you've misheard. Maybe the pipes are for other fields.'

'Hmm. I admit I walked out—didn't hear all their nonsense.'

'So... what are you going to do?'

'I know what *I'm* going to do. I'm going to get our boys to help me put this drainage under our own garden. Then everyone will see it's a waste of time and effort.'

Mary was horrified. She took a deep breath that started a coughing spasm. When she'd recovered enough to speak, she complained.

'Surely,' she spluttered, 'now's not the best time to mess up the garden! Lizzie won't thank you. She's just finished the planting.'

He stood up to leave. 'She can plant again when we're done.'

Mary stared at the closed door, tears pricking her eyes. She could see there'd be no peace for her with them working close by. They'd wreck the precious garden *and* they'd bring dirt into the house.

Work began the next day. William brought a cartload of narrow, four-foot wooden poles and dumped them in the garden. He handed each of the boys a spade and marked out where to dig the first trench.

Mary lay in bed, alone in the house. She hadn't dared tell Lizzie about the garden and had sent word not to call round today; William would be at home to see to things. She listened to the noise of digging and grumbling going on outside.

'Go deep,' she heard William order the boys. 'Dig a full foot and a half down into the clay, and a foot wide.'

At that moment, the perpetual dull pain in her stomach gave its familiar sharp nudge. Reaching out for her laudanum, she added a few drops to her mug of water and drank it eagerly.

335

Soon, the pain retreated, cowering away like a hungry yet wary wolf. Then she lay still, trying not to imagine the devastation going on in the garden.

William was very particular with his instructions. Once enough of the trench had been dug, he took one of the poles, nailed a chain to its broadest end, and laid it along the bottom.

'Now, boys, pack the clay round the pole. Ram it hard and tight because when we pull the pole out, it'll leave a clay pipe behind. That's the idea anyway.'

He watched them for a while, making sure they were doing a good job.

'No, John, don't cover up the chain—that's what I'll use to pull out the pole.'

Satisfied with their progress, William began to dig and lengthen the trench. When he'd finished, he inspected the boys' work.

'That looks fine to me. Now, I'll just punch holes in the top of the clay. You see, once I pull the pole out, the water can go through those holes into the pipe space. Then the water can drain from the garden—hopefully.'

When he'd done this, he stood back, took off his hat and scratched his head. 'I'm not sure we've done this right. I should have listened more to what Grimston said. Still, this could work down here at the bottom of the village. This garden's always too wet. Anyway, let's stop for a drink before we pull out that pole.' He had to admit the work was not *too* arduous, but then a garden was nothing compared to the size of a field.

He prised off his boots and went into the kitchen for the mugs and a jug of small beer. Before he went out again, he popped his head round the parlour door. He could see Mary was asleep, her head to one side, facing the window. He hoped she hadn't peered out; the garden was a complete mess already.

The day was warm and sunny for March, and the clay turned pale as it dried. After starting another trench, William reckoned they could ease out the first pole. First, he put on Dickon's old hedging mitten and carried a load of gorse from

336

the fuel pile. Then he took his axe and chopped the gorse into little pieces. He called John over.

'Here, wear this mitten and sprinkle bits of gorse over the pipe. It'll stop the soil falling in and clogging up those holes I've made.'

John was happy to pull on the mitten. It still smelled of Dickon. Once he'd finished, he and his brothers stood back to watch the pole being taken out.

William stepped into the trench, knelt down and grabbed hold of the chain attached to the pole. 'This'll be the real test of our work. Let's see if I can pull it out without breaking the clay.' He pulled gently at first. The pole did not budge an inch.

'Should you wiggle it a bit?' Richard suggested.

'I can't, not with a chain.' Then he remembered. 'I know what's wrong—I should have put a long handle on the end as well as a chain. Never mind, we'll manage without one. John, take off your mitten and lie down in the trench. See if you can loosen the pole with your bare hands while I pull.'

Eventually, with Richard and Matthew urging him on, John helped to ease out the pole. He was filthy and grinned through a mask of drying clay.

'Don't let your mother see you like this,' William warned. 'We'd best try and finish the work today so Lizzie can get replanting.' He surveyed his sons in their begrimed clothes. 'Matthew, you're the cleanest, go in and fetch bread and cheese and another jug of beer. We'll eat outside. Oh, and look in on your mother—see if she wants anything.'

Matthew kicked off his boots at the door and padded in stocking-feet to check on his mother. He found her raised on her pillow.

'Can I get you anything?'

'No, thank you, I'm not hungry, but you could fill this jug again with water.'

When he returned, she asked him about the drainage work.

'We'll be done by suppertime.'

'Is everyone as mucky as you?'

'No—they're worse.'

337

She blenched. 'God knows how Lizzie will feel having to wash all your clothes. And what about the garden? What state is *that* in?'

'Well,' he replied, sounding less confident, 'it's not finished yet... but once we've filled in the trenches...' He pulled a face, raised his eyebrows and asked, 'Maybe you'll not see much difference?'

'Hmm.' She found that hard to believe.

'Father thinks the pipes might really work. He says you won't have soggy patches again. He thinks the pipes might last for years.'

When he'd gone to the kitchen, she sighed and drank a mug of water with a large dose of laudanum. Soon, she felt as if she was floating on a raft above a sea of pain that had threatened to pull her down. She lay absolutely still until the garden no longer mattered.

Chapter 54

Mary only left the bed to use the chamber pot. For the rest of the day, she slipped in and out of laudanum-induced sleep. Whenever she awoke, she listened for the birds singing, always a good way to tell the time. She picked out the song of a robin, remembering the bird she'd seen in the apple tree before she gave birth to her first child. How full of hope she'd been then. She closed her eyes to recall more clearly those spring and summer days when she and William were so in love. She could now hear the gentle cooing of doves on the roof. The rhythm was soothing. She remembered how she'd loved his soft chestnut hair, how he used to nuzzle into her neck in bed. With such thoughts, she drifted into another dreamy sleep.

Random moments of her life became so vivid—the Christmas when their Mary took her puppy to bed with her and they had to feed it with a bottle, the day when the Scottish pedlar, Speckledy Golightly, gave her the lucky coin. Faces appeared of those she'd loved; she remembered the smell of old Ben with his love of tar and tobacco, and the lavender and liquorice aroma of Sarah Ezard's kitchen.

When she awoke again, the blackbirds had begun their chinking calls. William and the boys would be coming in soon for supper, and there was nothing prepared for them. They'd have to see to themselves. She heard them outside, trying to wash off the worst of the dirt before they entered the house.

Sighing, she realised it was much easier to cope with her illness without the boys' presence. She had a private world of pain they could not share. They were so vigorous they made her tired just to look at them. She knew they tried to be calm in her presence, but they were so used to being outdoors and working that they couldn't sit still. Richard was the worst; he always fidgeted and twisted her bedcovers and tapped his foot up and down. Every few minutes his eyes would wander to the window, no doubt to check the weather and decide on his next job. Like his Uphall grandfather, it was as if he had soil, not blood, in his veins.

After a while, John walked into the parlour and stood by his mother's bed. There was still dried clay caked on his face and his clothes were filthy. He picked up her hand and stroked it, alarmed to see her in pain.

'Is it your lump hurting?'

'Just a bit. Don't you worry though.'

He was silent for a moment, trying to remember what he'd heard at the forge. There was a remedy would get rid of a lump. Suddenly, he knew what to do.

'I'm going to help you get better. I won't be long. I'll be back soon.' He almost ran from the room.

Half an hour later, he returned having found what he was searching for by the pond—a toad lurking under a boulder. He carried it carefully in his hands and presented it to his mother with a triumphant grin.

'Look!' he cried as he opened his hands.

She shuddered, dreading what he expected of her.

'Mother, listen, if I rub its back until it goes wet, then I can sit it on your lump. They say the wetness works wonders.'

He was so eager and excited that she didn't want to hurt his feelings. 'I'll do it,' she fibbed, 'if you go and wait outside.'

When he'd gone, she gazed at the poor creature sitting in her palm, not moving. It was an ugly, warty thing and, rather than moist, it was warm and dry. It was healthy, though, and it would live to see the summer. It was strange to think of all the creatures, the mice, the spiders, the worms that would still be alive when she wasn't. She looked the toad in the eye, sorry for its capture, and called out for John.

When he came back to her bed, she smiled and passed him the toad. 'Thank you. Now, make sure you put it back where you found it, and don't squeeze it too hard, poor thing.'

That night, she was very restless. Despite the laudanum, she could not get comfortable and was afraid her coughing would keep the others awake. Due to the tightening in her chest, she could not breathe when lying down, yet sitting propped by the pillow, her stomach hurt too much.

In the morning, William said he'd fetch cough medicine from Uphall. He ignored his mother's advice to get Mary to spit on a frog's head, March being just the right month for this cure. Instead, he returned with a jar of dried dill in honey.

'This should ease your throat if nothing else.' He placed it with a spoon by the bed. 'I could go back to the apothecary if you like.'

'No,' she whispered, wishing Sarah Ezard was there with her special syrup of honey and herbs. Forgetting for a moment about William's garden experiment, she said, 'Get Lizzie to dig up some comfrey roots—they'll help my cough.'

When Lizzie heard about the ruttling in Mary's chest, she went out immediately with Dottie to dig up the required roots. She'd heard all about the trenches from John, so dug the roots from her own garden. She grated them in Mary's kitchen and mixed the resulting mush with ale. For good measure, she added a spoonful of the dried dill and honey.

'There, Mary,' she announced as she entered the parlour, 'this'll make thoo breathe easier.'

Suddenly, Mary remembered about the garden. 'Oh no—what's Dottie doing? She's not in the garden is she? It'll be a mess out there.'

'Nay, an' don't fret—I know all about tha garden. I'm keepin' Dottie i' kitchen. I've given 'er a bucket o' water an' John's breeches to scrub.'

'Thank God, and keep her busy there—I don't want her to see me like this.'

In the afternoon, Mary was left alone. She relaxed and appreciated that Lizzie had not made a fuss about the rows of trenches. As usual, she listened to the birdsong and the lowing of the cattle to mark the hours. From time to time, she caressed the lump, convincing herself that it had reduced.

She was more worried about her chest; Elizabeth never had that problem. As she reached for her drink, an excruciating pain made her gasp. Her heart raced and she thought she'd faint. She collapsed back onto her pillow, trying to relax, but could only take shallow breaths. Her chest would not expand and, in her panic, her heart beat even faster. She stared hard at the window, focusing on a cobweb that blew in the slight draught. The distraction began to calm her nerves.

After a few minutes, she grew accustomed to a different way of breathing. If she kept still and didn't panic, she could manage. She longed for William to come home. He would comfort her and give her a drink. Maybe, after another dose of laudanum, she'd breathe more easily and be able to see the boys without frightening them.

William came home in the early evening and went straight into the parlour. All day he'd been haunted by Mary's face. Her eyes last night in the candlelight had been full of fear, and nothing he did could make her comfortable. Today, he'd told the boys not to disturb her and let her sleep. Now, as he sat on the bed and felt her forehead, he had plenty of time to observe her features.

She was nothing like the young woman he married. Her cheeks were now gaunt and her lips thin and pale, so unlike the full and inviting ones of her youth. Yet, when he looked deep into her eyes, he could still recognise the woman he loved.

He propped her up further in bed, but she still fought for breath.

When he mixed her laudanum, he added extra drops. 'Perhaps you'd better not have the boys in to see you tonight. Wait until you feel you can talk.'

She gave a barely perceptible nod and then whispered, 'John.'

'You want John?'

'Mmm.'

'Drink your laudanum first, and then I'll let him in.'

'No.' Her voice was very weak. 'Now—while I'm wide awake.'

'Are you sure? You must be in a lot of pain.'

'Yes.' She knew she'd soon be taking so much laudanum that she'd be insensible. She worried for John's future. He was so credulous. He needed to find a young woman who would love him as he was and take care of him.

When John walked in, she put on a brave smile. 'Tell me what you've been doing. I love to hear it.' She watched him sit gently on the bed and hold her hand. He gazed at her with those soft, brown, sheepdog's eyes.

'I've been at the forge. Phineas lets me feed the horses while he shoes them. He never hurts them. He says hooves are like toenails. He slices off a piece—like a half moon—and throws it to the dog.' He wrinkled his nose. 'I don't like the smell when he puts the hot shoe on. The hair gets singed and the hoof stinks when it burns. It makes my nose tickle.'

'Poor you.'

'No, I like being there. I helped his wife as well. Martha let me grind her malt and mash it in a tub. She said I could feed the leftovers to the pigs. Oh, and she sent me to get nettles for her next brew.'

'You *have* been busy.' She paused to get her breath back. 'It'll soon be lambing time.'

'I know.'

She gripped his hand. 'Promise me you'll stay and work with Jack,' she gasped. 'Don't be tempted by the forge or anywhere else. And stay in Reighton... promise?'

'I promise. Had I better fetch Father now?'

She nodded, 'Thank you, John. I love you—you're a good boy.' Much better than me, she thought, always afraid that God had not forgiven her about young William. 'Pray for me, John.'

As soon as he closed the door, she had a coughing spasm.

William came in, saw her struggling to breathe, and held her in his arms, rubbing her back. 'There now, there now,' he soothed. 'Try to relax.'

When she'd recovered and gone limp, he lowered her against the pillow and handed her the strong dose of laudanum. He waited until she'd drunk the last drop, and then decided to stay until it took effect. He and the boys would find something to eat later.

Mary wished she'd not kept her secret about young William. Now, she was ready to confess, but her mouth was dry. She parted her lips to say sorry and explain, but the laudanum was making her drowsy.

343

William leant closer to try to catch what she said. Her lips were moving, yet there was no sound. He thought she might be praying.

By the time the boys came in to say goodnight, she'd closed her eyes.

In the middle of the night, Mary woke. She felt she was drowning and gurgled a cry for help. Although William sat her up higher, it made little difference.

Richard and Matthew were woken by their father's movements, his bumping into their beds and fumbling with the medicine. They gathered round the bed, hating to see their mother fighting for breath. Only John, up in the loft, remained oblivious.

After a horrifying minute, Mary began to calm down though her breathing was rapid and shallow. She grasped the laudanum drink and gulped it down between breaths, determined not to suffer like Elizabeth.

While the boys went back to bed, William sat by Mary and held her hand. He whispered to her about the first time they'd been properly together, before they were married.

'Remember that harvest time, lying on the straw for the roof of our new house... how the moon shone down and I said I never wanted to leave you? Now, I don't want *you* to leave *me*. Please, Mary, hold on—stay with me.'

He prayed silently for a while and then, despite his best intentions, fell asleep and did not wake until almost dawn. The candle had long gone out and the chamber was dark. At that moment, he heard the first morning songs of the blackbirds. He realised he was still holding her hand, but it was as cold as the room.

Chapter 55

William pulled the sheet over Mary's face. Wiping the tears from his cheeks, he went into the kitchen to liven up the fire ready to make the porridge. Then he went back to the parlour to break the news to Richard and Matthew. It was a relief that the boys, half asleep still, seemed to take it well. No doubt, they'd been expecting it for days. Now, though, he had to tell John.

He stepped slowly up the ladder and into the loft where he found John already up and getting dressed.

'John—it's your mother… I'm sorry, lad, come here.' He held John to his chest, something he'd never done before. 'She's left us,' he whispered, his lips brushing John's wavy hair. 'Your mother's gone to join our Will and your aunt Elizabeth in heaven… and young Mary.' His throat tightened so much he couldn't say any more. What was their life going to be like now?

He felt John shudder in his arms. After a few moments, he let go of him, stood back and waited for John to gain control.

'I never said goodbye,' John sobbed.

'None of us did. She died in her sleep. Think of *her*—that it was best for *her*.'

John wiped his nose on his sleeve. 'I'm going to see Lizzie and Dottie.'

'Yes, you do that. They need to know—and Francis.'

Lizzie was practical. She hid her grief and asked John to stay and mind Dottie. She'd go to Uphall with Francis and bring his mother back to help prepare the body.

As they made their way up the hill in the early morning light, the dew lay heavy on the grass verges and silvery-white cobwebs hung draped across the tops of the hedges. It was going to be a beautiful day once the mist cleared, too beautiful for the sad task ahead.

Dorothy Jordan's face hardened on hearing the news. She fought back a tear as she thought of William and the boys.

'I'm sorry, I'm too old to 'elp now,' she explained. 'Look—I can 'ardly unbend me fingers. Shall I send one o' me maids?'

'No,' Lizzie mumbled. 'It's alright. I'll manage.'

'I can see to food, though, an' send it later. 'Ere,' she added as she chose a small onion from the table, 'put this i' Mary's mouth. It'll stop any bad smells. An' don't forget to plug 'er well. It's goin' to be warm today—too warm fo' bodies.'

Lizzie took the onion, glanced at Francis and shrugged. There was no telling what his grandmother really felt. When she left him at Uphall, she walked back hesitantly, knowing what was ahead. She hoped she'd do Mary justice, yet feared to fall short.

When she arrived, the house was empty apart from William. He'd sent the boys to work straight after breakfast and was now sitting alone by Mary's bed. He raised his head when she entered the parlour.

'It's alright, thoo go an' get some fresh air. I'll do what's necessary. An' Francis is goin' round tellin' folks. 'E'll see to vicar as well.'

She was waiting for the water to boil when Matthew's wife arrived with Ann.

'We've just 'eard an' we'll 'elp all we can,' Ellen offered. 'It's least we can do.'

As the women proceeded to care for Mary's body, Ellen thought to explain Matthew's ideas for the vigil.

''E insists that Mary 'as a better farewell than Elizabeth. She 'ad such a scant feast an' 'e wants to provide best we can give. Matthew says 'e'll pay fo' coffin too.'

Lizzie acknowledged this, but wondered how it would go down with William. Suddenly, she wanted to be alone with Mary. 'Thoo'd best go now. I know thoo'll 'ave plenty to do at 'ome.'

As soon as they'd gone, she leant over and kissed Mary's forehead.

'I'm sorry. We didn't always get on. It was probably my fault—I spent too much time with Elizabeth. I know thoo always meant well.'

She went outside and told William that Mary was ready for the shroud and for measuring the coffin. Then she traipsed home, knowing she'd played her part and that, from now on, everything was out of her hands.

She found John still at home playing with Dottie and her dolls.

'Go outside now, both o' thee—see if there are any flowers out. Don't pick 'em yet, but thoo'll know where to go o' Monday.' The job, she hoped, would distract John on the morning of the funeral.

On the night of the vigil, Matthew's family arrived early, carrying baskets of food and drink. They paid only the briefest respect to Mary in her coffin on the trestle before unpacking their provisions. In one sweep of his arm, Matthew moved Lizzie's oatcakes and sausages to one side.

William and the boys stared in amazement as Ellen lifted out a plate of cold roast beef. She'd also brought half a dozen small roasted birds.

'They're from our dovecote,' Matthew explained.

William gulped. His face darkened on seeing Matthew unload another basket. He watched Matthew pick up the large stoneware bottle of cowslip wine sent from Uphall and move it onto the floor, and then put a bottle of gin and one of brandy on the table instead. Not content with that, Matthew set out three bottles of French claret.

'You'll need to sweeten the wine before serving,' he advised.

William could not believe what was happening. This display of the Smiths' wealth stuck in his throat. He and the boys saw Ann take a set of glasses from her basket and then a colourful box.

'It's gingerbread,' she explained, blushing. 'It's an old Osbaldeston recipe.' She removed the lid for the boys to see, and the aromas of liquorice, aniseed and ginger filled the room.

347

While William wanted to say exactly what he thought of Matthew and his gifts, he could tell the boys were impressed. He bit his lip for Mary's sake.

John, unaware of his father's humiliation, walked up to Ann and kissed her cheek. 'Thank you. Mother loved gingerbread.'

'Yes,' William added with reluctance and a surly frown. 'We thank you, Matthew.'

The vigil evening, now taken over by the Smiths, became a celebratory wake rather than the quiet family affair William had anticipated. Word of the occasion circulated the village and soon the Wrench family arrived and then Bart Huskisson with his wife and daughters. Even the Sumptons paid a visit. At times, the kitchen became so crowded that people overflowed into the passage and out onto the lane. Lizzie didn't stay long because of Dottie, and Francis left soon after with Robert Storey, both men disapproving of overindulgence.

Dorothy Jordan did not stay long either, upset that her homemade wine had been snubbed in favour of French bottles. Before she went, she waved a slice of white bread in front of Matthew. She suspected he'd acquired a taste for it at Hunmanby Hall.

'So what's wrong wi' brown bread, eh? It's good enough fo' me. I'll never know why folk like this soft, white stuff,' she goaded. 'It's got no taste.'

Matthew shrugged. He didn't want a full-blown disagreement with the old woman. 'Let's not quarrel, not tonight of all nights.'

'Aye,' she conceded. 'I suppose thy bread does look cleaner, an' thoo doesn't get bits stuck i' tha teeth.'

Matthew had the last word. He gloated as she left. 'And it won't wear my teeth down either.'

William stood bemused as Ann and John seemed to take the evening in their stride, walking round offering people more food and drink. Unlike them, he couldn't wait for everyone to leave. Normally, he'd have liked to drink brandy and wine, but surrounded by the constant chatter and occasional laughter he felt so lonely. Without Mary, it was as if his body was not working. It was as if he'd had a leg or an arm cut off. John Gurwood's soft lament on the fiddle only served to heighten the loss.

One conversation did lift his spirits a little and, surprisingly, it was one begun by Matthew.

'You'll never guess who I bumped into the other week—an old acquaintance of ours—Mr William Lumley, Inspector of Excise.'

'An inspector now, eh?'

'Yes, quite a promotion. You remember we laughed at him being lean and keen? Well, he has a large paunch on him now. Obviously, his work suits him. He said to be remembered to you.'

William was pleased. The man was probably married by now and had lots of little Lumleys to teach the complexities of excise. He surveyed his own sons. Richard was the most interested in crops although Matthew was coming along nicely and it was early days. As for John, well, his future was the most uncertain. No wonder Mary had worried so much.

At last, when there was no more drink, the guests departed. With John's insistence, the boys cleared up the mess and put the leftover food to one side for after the funeral. The simpler fare had hardly been touched.

The next morning, John took Dottie to pick flowers for the funeral. She scurried ahead to Speeton Ravine, nipping backwards and forwards, lively as a squirrel. While he gathered violets, she put wood anemones in her basket. He saw the white petals were flushed with a delicate pink and held one up to her.

'They're like your face.'

She smiled. 'Will you still marry me then?'

'Yes, of course, when you're twenty-one.'

She smiled again. Neither of them was thinking he'd be a middle-aged man by then.

On their way back, John noted a change in the weather. The wind was now coming from the northeast, bringing a salty chill.

'It's getting cold now, Dottie. We'd best hurry.' He stopped, though, by a hedge overgrown with ivy and used his knife to cut down a few lengths. 'My mother always liked ivy leaves. She used to hang them up at Christmas.'

After leaving the flowers and ivy at the church, he walked Dottie home. Then he made his way up St Helen's Lane with the wind at his back. He found his father and brothers waiting for him. They were to eat their breakfast and then be ready for the funeral procession.

The coffin, containing Mary's wasted body, was made from pine as William had insisted, despite Matthew's preference for oak. The boys carried it easily as their father led the way into the wind and past the bare hedgerows, the hawthorn only just beginning to show green.

He recalled there'd been an east wind with rain when they'd buried young Mary. Then, the slap of icy sleet in his face had been a welcome pain. Thinking back to last October, to his son's funeral, he trembled at the speed at which his life was changing. As he passed the pond, he was reminded of old Ben. Always an avid observer of the weather, Ben had a rhyme for almost every eventuality. Today, the pond smelled rank. William turned to the boys behind.

'When ditch or pond offend me nose, look fo' rain or stormy blows. Old Ben used to say that. Let's hope he's wrong today.'

When they reached the church, the wind whipped round the end walls. They gazed out over the bay to see that the sea and sky had merged into a grey smudge. There was nothing uplifting in the scene.

The vicar greeted William at the door and led the way up the aisle.

William, once more, sat at the head of the coffin, knowing all eyes were on him. His sons sat close by with Francis, Lizzie and Dottie while his mother stayed with Samuel in the Jordan pew. He noted that his brother Richard had come from Carnaby, and acknowledged him with a nod and a half smile.

He could see the Smith family praying in their pew; Ann looked especially affected and held a handkerchief to her nose. People were kind, he thought, but he was a widower now and with three sons still at home. No one would help him for long; people would be too busy with their own families.

350

Thomas Smith, as a churchwarden, opened the service with the words from a psalm.

'The Lord hears the needy and does not despise his captive people.'

Then the vicar took over and read a psalm requested by Robert Storey.

'O Lord, thou has searched me and known me. Thou knowest my downsitting and mine uprising, thou understandest my thoughts afar off... and art acquainted with all my ways.'

For Robert, who had never forgotten the secret about young William, the psalm was an opportunity to ask for mercy.

'Search me, O God,' the vicar intoned, 'and know my heart: try me, and know my thoughts: And see if there be any wicked way in me, and lead me in the way everlasting.'

William listened, his hands clasped tightly to stop them trembling. He'd been puzzled by Robert's choice of reading, yet didn't give it too much thought. More to his liking was John's request for Psalm 23—*The Lord is my shepherd*. He wished John could have read it out himself, but then John had never been a good pupil.

Thomas Smith read the psalm in his gentle voice. He glanced occasionally at John for John knew many of the words by heart and was murmuring them to himself. By the time he'd finished, John was in tears.

As people left for the final committal into the ground, Thomas and Ann Smith stood in the porch and handed out sprigs of rosemary for mourners to throw into the grave. When the two followed on behind, Ann whispered, 'I know Aunt Mary kept herself to herself, but everyone knows she's had a hard life. Uncle William's not been easy, and then there were young William's problems... I hope everyone will remember her with sympathy.'

As the brief outdoor service ended, Ann had no reason to doubt. Mary's coffin was covered in sprigs of rosemary.

351

Chapter 56

That night, William couldn't sleep. He tossed and turned as he wondered once more how they'd cope without a woman in the house. Lizzie had promised to help with the washing and mending. That was kind of her, and it was a blessing that most of their midday dinners were at Uphall. His mother had even said they could have Sunday dinners there too. It would never be the same, though, coming home every evening to an empty house and a cold hearth. Maybe Lizzie would see to the fire and milk the cow, but she couldn't do everything.

He turned over again, restless. He knew he'd taken Mary for granted, had never appreciated the warmth of the fire in the morning and the hot breakfasts. Even while she'd been ill, she'd tried to do her best. What didn't bear thinking about was how he'd never see her again bending over the fire stirring the pot, or sitting quietly of an evening with her knitting. In bed, he'd have no one to confide in, no one to share his worries.

He thought back to those dark days after his daughter had died. It was a wonder how Mary had put up with him. While he'd been drunk and violent, she must have mourned their daughter just the same, yet he'd never given her grief much thought; he'd been too overwrought himself.

He flinched as he heard the wind grow stronger, now tugging at the thatch. It was going to be a long, rough night.

A few hours later, a terrific gale blew straight in off the sea.

Robert Storey lay in his bed, rigid and alert. The funeral had reawakened his anxiety over Mary's confession and now he believed that the current storm, so timely, must be a display of God's wrath. He got up and, by the light of a flickering candle, pored over his Bible. He found suitable but unsettling words in Isaiah.

God shall rebuke them, and they shall flee far off, and shall be chased as the chaff of the mountains before the wind, and like a rolling thing before a whirlwind.

He spent the rest of the night praying for mercy.

As soon as it was light enough, he strode out, leaning into the weather, one hand keeping his coat collar up, the other holding down his hat. He struggled against the gusts to the cliff top. Though the tide was going out, the sea was wild and high. He saw seaweed piled up on the beach below in long, unending swathes, maybe two feet deep. He raised his eyes to the sky, whispered a prayer, and then set off quickly back to the village. Instead of having any breakfast, he went round knocking on people's doors, telling them about the weed on the beach.

An hour after dawn, as the gale abated, every able-bodied man, woman and child were making their way to the shore with carts, barrows and sledges. Once on the sand, the foam, ripped by the wind from the waves, blew towards them, rolling over their feet in great gobbets of white froth. Men yelled instructions above the roar of the distant waves, cupping their hands as the wind, right in their faces, threatened to carry away their voices.

William and his sons welcomed the distraction. They joined Samuel and the Uphall lads, took sledges down to the beach and began to collect the mixture of kelp and other wracks. It amused William to see Robert Storey and Henry Sumpton working happily together for a change. He nudged Samuel.

'Wonders will never cease. Just listen to them two.'

They moved closer to catch the conversation.

Robert was remembering the Great Storm of over thirty years ago. 'You were too young, Henry, but that terrible storm was God's way to chastise us. Now, God has shown us favour instead. This seaweed is a bountiful gift. Praise be the Lord.'

'Yes,' Henry replied, shouting to make himself heard, 'I think you're right.'

Any disagreements they'd had over winnowing machines and drainage were forgotten as Henry listened attentively.

353

'And you say we must leave all this weed in heaps to ferment?' he asked as he forked more of the slimy and heavy lengths of kelp onto a waiting sledge.

'That's right, Henry, and we need about a dozen cartloads per acre. That's why everyone's here. It's the perfect manure.'

William saw Henry wipe his brow. The vicar's son wasn't used to such backbreaking work and would tire soon, much like Matthew Smith and his two sons. With a smug expression, he turned to Samuel.

'I guess spending time with the Osbaldestons doesn't prepare you for a full day's work.' Then he raised his voice in Matthew's direction.

'How's it going, Matthew?' he taunted. 'Your Thomas looks dog-tired already.'

'He'll be fine.' Matthew was envious seeing William's sons, all working in harmony. He then felt ashamed as he thought of Mary. It was such a pity she'd not lived to see this day. She'd have been so proud.

William smiled to see the masterful efforts of his energetic sons. He recalled how, as a single man, many years ago, he'd been on the beach like this with everyone, just like today, except then it was to take shipwrecked timber. Mary had been there, her cheeks flushed and her eyes sparkling.

He stopped loading and stood still, remembering Mary that day years ago. His weight, now in one place and not shifting, caused him to sink deep into the soft, wet sand. When he looked down, there was a puddle of seawater emerging beneath him and flowing over his boots. He chuckled to himself. He'd done exactly the same in front of Mary that day. He'd been so struck by her as she stood nearby in her shawl, holding onto her donkey, and she'd giggled at his wet feet.

Suddenly, an arm crashed onto his shoulder. It was Matthew.

'Wake up! What *are* you doing? You're ruining your boots.'

'I was just thinking...'

'Well, don't think too long. We have to get this loaded up and off the beach before the tide comes in.'

William did not need reminding. 'I know, I know, and my family will do their fair share…and more.' He wanted to add 'not like the Smiths', but kept his peace.

Later in the day, he saw the women and children coming down the cliff bringing food and drink. Even Henry Sumpton's wife was there though he guessed she'd never set foot on the beach before. Matthew's wife Ellen appeared with Ann, followed by Lizzie and Dottie and Martha Wrench. He watched the women help each other step down onto the beach, full of companionable smiles as if it was a holiday. He realised that, but for his pride, he might have retained his easy boyhood friendship with Matthew.

As soon as she was on the beach, Lizzie let Dottie rummage among the washed-up debris. The girl was to collect any live crabs to boil up for supper.

'Don't bother wi' starfish,' Lizzie warned. 'I know they're lovely, all bright orange like flowers, but we can't eat 'em an' they sting. Look—'ere's John comin' to 'elp thee.'

Instead of searching for crabs, John draped Dottie in yards of weed—tangled and filmy ribbons of bottle green, brown and purple.

'There now, you look like a mermaid. I saw one once at the fair. You're *much* prettier. She looked like this.' He gave a good impression of a sad and wilting scarecrow. 'And she was kept in a tank. She wasn't happy, not like you.'

Dottie didn't like the feel of the wet, slippery fronds round her neck, and they hung heavily on her shoulders. John was so pleased, though, that she put up with it, and her mother didn't scold them.

Everyone worked until the sun had long dipped behind the cliff. It became cold and dark on the beach, yet there were still cartloads to haul away and then dump in the corners of the fields.

William and his sons trudged home after the last load. His back, as well as his arms and legs, ached from the day's exhausting work.

He shivered as he prised off his wet boots and stepped into the kitchen. It wasn't the chill of the room that so unnerved

355

him, it was the sight of the unscrubbed table and the empty oatcake rack. He realised that at fifty-three, he was too old to remarry and, besides, he couldn't bear the thought of another woman taking Mary's place. Richard, only sixteen, was far too young to be wed, and John... well, no one would want him. No, they'd have to resign themselves to living in a house without a woman's presence.

He sighed as he removed his damp coat and looked in despair at Richard and Matthew, standing forlorn by the table.

John, though, was already on his knees by the hearth, adding dry sticks and gorse.

'I'll soon have the fire going. And I know how to make oatcakes. Mother showed me.' He stood up and used the back of his hand to wipe the tear from his cheek. Then he turned to his father, his eyes glistening.

'The Lord is my shepherd. I shall not want. We'll be alright.'

The End

Further Reading

For those interested in the farming history of East Yorkshire, the following books make fascinating reading:

The Farming and Memorandum Books of Henry Best of Elmswell 1642 Edited by Donald Woodward (1984)

A General View of the Agriculture of the East Riding of Yorkshire by Henry E. Strickland (1812)

For readers keen to research their Reighton family history:

Reighton Parish Records 1559 to 1669

Reighton Parish Records 1670 to 1800

Both volumes are transcribed and annotated by Lisa Blosfelds and published by the East Yorkshire Family History Society (2008-2009)

www.eyfhs.org.uk

About the Author

Joy Gelsthorpe writes under her maiden name, Stonehouse. Her father came from Filey, and then moved to Hornsea before the Second World War and married Gladys Jordan, a descendant of the Jordans of Reighton. Her interest in family history led to this series of novels set in the East Riding.

She writes and researches local archives in the winter, often spending days at The British Library at Boston Spa and The Treasure House in Beverley. During the summer she visits local museums. Favourite places are The Yorkshire Museum of Farming at Murton, near York, and The Ryedale Folk Museum at Hutton-le-Hole.

Joy lives on the east coast and finds inspiration by walking in the area, especially along the cliffs and beaches. Memorable times include a walk above Speeton as dawn was breaking, and a visit to Reighton church for a carol service on a frosty, starlit evening.

For more information and details of other books by local authors:

www.hornseawriters.com